Letting Go

Book Two Cari Daniel Series

Betty,
Something to read when your life settles into the "new normal"!
Love,
Sherry

Sherry Martin-Legault

Sherry Martin-Legault

Outskirts Press, Inc.
Denver, Colorado

Letting Go
Book Two Cari Daniel Series

v2.0

Outskirts Press, Inc.
http://www.outskirtspress.com

ISBN: 978-1-4327-6057-1

PRINTED IN THE UNITED STATES OF AMERICA

Dedication

This book is dedicated to Dan and Tannis Arychuk. I will ever be grateful for discovering your Bed & Breakfast, Dew Creek Cottage. You've always made us feel more like family than guests, and you've definitely gone above and beyond, especially during my writing retreat. Thanks so much for all you've done. As always, I can't wait to come back.

Acknowledgements

Special thanks to Lena and Patti, two awesome massage therapists who have helped me to stay 'flexible' through the years, even around surgeries and serious injuries.

Stephane, my hubby of 25 years, words are not enough to express all you do for me.

Amanda thanks for the editing assistance.

Josh thanks for the cover photos.

Joe thanks for your prayers and encouragement.

Thanks to all those who read my first novel and have been eagerly waiting for the sequel.

Chapter 1

Cari Daniels, head of the Security Department for *Richards & Richards* Law Firm, met Gilles Rodriquez in the lobby of the *Wyndham Checkers Hotel.* He exclaimed over how well she looked, especially considering what her health had been like when she'd left Mexico City in March. They went to the *Checkers* restaurant to have supper, and lingered over the delicious meal. Cari was surprised at how comfortable she was with Gilles, after not seeing him for several months. She also found that she'd forgotten just how handsome he was.

Gilles was about 5'10"tall, had black hair, a moustache, and dark eyes. He had an average build, was thirty years old, and had a Parisian mother and a Mexican father. He dealt in international art business for his father. He was fluent in English, Spanish and French. And he'd been directly involved with saving her life while they were both at a resort in Puerto Vallarta.

"So, what happened with the stalker that was bothering you?" Gilles asked between bites of his steak.

"He's dead," Cari replied softly, still uncomfortable discussing Jerry's death. "I killed him—in self-defence."

Gilles finished chewing his piece of meat before responding. "I didn't think you would have done so in cold blood, Cari. But, what happened?"

"Well, I finally figured out that the stalker was aiming towards a specific date—related to the death of my employer's son. Anyway, I thought I might be able to 'force his hand' so to speak, if I went somewhere alone, just before that date. It worked. The stalker turned out to be one of the lawyers at the firm I work for. He'd been harboring a grudge against me for a long time. I went to John's cabin in the Sierras, and Jerry Neilson followed me there."

Cari looked down at her plate and moved her food with her fork, but she didn't eat anything. "It was pretty awful. He caught me off guard at first, and took my gun. Then he spent a full day making my life miserable." She took a sip of ice water. "Jerry knew about my heart condition. In particular, the temporary pacemaker that I was using at that time. He had me switch the batteries in it. Then he made me drink a lot of coffee, stand in the cold without a jacket, and chop wood until I collapsed."

"Why?"

"He was hoping that I'd have a heart attack. Then it would have appeared to be an accident, or death by natural causes. He had a gun, but he didn't plan to use it."

"How did he die?" Gilles' gaze was intense, but Cari could tell his curiosity was tempered with compassion.

"He tried to pull the wire from the pacemaker. He got it loose, and I knew I was in serious trouble at that point. So, I fought with him. I got the gun away from him. Then the struggle heated up. I clawed his face, and he dislocated my left shoulder. I finally hit him in the head with the poker for the wood stove." She looked down at her plate again. "And he didn't get up after that."

Gilles reached across the table and held her trembling left hand. "You must have been terrified. How on earth did you make it back here?"

"John had arranged to give me 48 hours at the cabin, and then he was coming up himself. Thank God he came early." She felt Gilles' grip tighten. "He keeps a two-way radio in his cabin, but I was in no shape to get to it, let alone use it. John notified the Rangers as soon as he got there. He had them send in a helicopter, since I wouldn't have lasted through a three hour drive." Cari forced a smile as she looked at him. "I told you God has blessed me with wonderful friends. You and John have *both* saved my life."

"Let's hope that no one else ever needs to," he replied. He gently stroked her fingers. "So, are you and John really just *friends*—or is there more to it than that?"

Cari was taken aback by Gilles' frankness. She also wasn't quite sure how to respond. "John isn't a Christian, Gilles, so that has brought somewhat of a strain to our relationship. We're good friends. We work at the same firm. He's even come to church with me once. And he told me that he prayed on his way to the cabin. Like I said, he saved my life, too. I know that he'd like a more serious relationship, but I've been holding back so far." She shrugged even as she withdrew her hand from Gilles' gentle hold. "I honestly don't know what's going to happen between us."

"And if he were a Christian?"

"Then—then I think our relationship would already be more serious than it is."

"So, you're praying for him, I assume."

"Yes. And so are some of my friends." She watched him resume eating and focused on her plate. "Why did you want to know, Gilles? You barely even met John down in Mexico."

"True. But I suspected even then that he felt more than just friendship towards you." He finished his steak. "And, I wanted to know if I stand a fair chance with you, myself." He met her startled gaze with an intense one of his own. "I've spent the past four months trying to find you, Cari. And sometimes I wondered if you had gotten married already. I'm glad you haven't." He took a bite of his salad before continuing. "My mother warned me that John was very interested in you, and she suspected that the interest was mutual. I see she was correct." He grinned at her. "But you aren't married yet. Or even engaged for that matter. So, my search wasn't entirely in vain, was it?"

"What are you saying, Gilles?" Cari asked, her throat constricted by mounting tension.

"I'm saying that I'm attracted to you, Cari. And I have been since I met you in March. What I'd like to know now is—will you let me pursue that interest? Or would you rather that I didn't try to contact you again?"

Cari put her hands up to her face. Her cheeks were burning with embarrassment, and she tried to regain her composure. *How do I answer a question like that, Lord? He's even bolder than John! But he is* asking *me what I think. He's not just telling me that he's interested. And he is a Christian. And he's so kind. He's the kind of man that women* hope *to meet. And here he sits waiting to know whether or not he should back off. But what can I say?*

"I didn't mean to make you uncomfortable, Cari. But I don't like to play games either."

Cari swallowed a couple of times before she dared to look at Gilles again. Just then, the waiter came back and inquired if they'd care for some dessert. Gilles ordered some cake and coffee for both of them. The waiter nodded and left them alone.

"Gilles, I - I'm not exactly sure how to answer you," began Cari. "I mean, I enjoyed the time that I spent with you down in Mexico." She smiled. "Except maybe the hospital part. And your mother is a dear." Cari felt her cheeks flush once more. "Your father, on the other hand, made his dislike rather obvious. Though, he did take me to the airport, and made sure that I was safely on the plane."

"Cari, I'm 30 years old. I refuse to allow my father to dictate every detail of my life for me any longer. Please don't let his rudeness stand in the way."

"Well, aside from that, I barely know you, Gilles."

"I'd like to change that," he said, his voice silky, his dark eyes shining.

"I can see that," she stammered. She put her trembling hands into her lap and tried to get her thoughts unjumbled. "And how practical is it to have an international relationship? How often could we even see each other?"

"My schedule is rather flexible," he assured her. "I could come here as often as necessary."

Cari let out her breath in an audible sigh. "You seem to have an answer for everything."

"And you have a lot of questions," he remarked, his tone still gentle. "Look, instead of trying to answer me right now, why don't we spend some more time together this week? You could tell me before I go home on Friday. Okay?"

"I don't know if it'll be any easier to give you an answer then, Gilles. Will a few days really make a difference?"

"I'm hoping that it will."

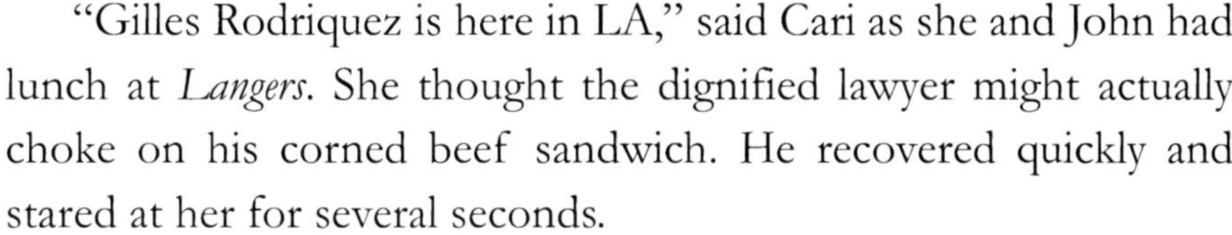

"Gilles Rodriquez is here in LA," said Cari as she and John had lunch at *Langers*. She thought the dignified lawyer might actually choke on his corned beef sandwich. He recovered quickly and stared at her for several seconds.

"Since when?" he asked, obviously not thrilled at the news.

"A few days ago, I think. There was a message on my answering machine Saturday night. We met for supper last night. He'll be here until Friday." Cari thought it would be easiest to just give John the facts, but it wasn't. If she had only *suspected* jealousy in Mexico, now she was certain of it. She plunged ahead anyway. "I'd like if the three of us could get together for lunch in the next couple of days."

John looked at her as though she were crazy. "Whatever for?"

"Why not? You've met him before."

"Yes, I have. And the circumstances left a lot to be desired." He drained his can of *Coke.*

"Well, at present, I'm healthy, no stalkers on the horizon, and things are going well at work. That should make a difference, shouldn't it?"

He didn't return her smile. Rather, his blue eyes looked almost frosty.

"Should it?" He crumpled his napkin as soon as he wiped his mouth. "Look, what would be the point to this little get together, Cari? Trying to make a comparison?"

"What?" She was thankful for the noise all around them when she realized how much she'd raised her voice. "What are you talking about, John?"

He leaned forward and lowered his voice. "I'm talking about your sudden about-face, that's what. Saturday night I got the distinct impression that you enjoyed *my* company. Now you want to make it a cozy little *threesome.* For what purpose? I only met the fellow once. It was pretty plain that his interest in you wasn't solely *humanitarian.* Don't expect me to jump at the chance to have lunch with him."

"This is ridiculous! You're acting like a jealous boyfriend, John."

The plates rattled as he got up from the table. "Maybe because I'd like to *be* one!" Then he turned and left the restaurant, leaving Cari with the bill, and the need to get a taxi back to the office.

Chapter 2

Cari's mood was anything but cheerful when she returned to her office. She'd had an awful time hailing a cab, and she was late for an appointment with Rebecca Richards. Her employer was tactful enough not to question her very much, making it a little easier on Cari.

"I had trouble getting a cab," Cari explained. "And I didn't think walking would be any quicker in my case. Sorry I'm late. I'll try not to let it happen again."

"It's all right, Cari. As I recall, I've been late meeting with you, and even cancelled at least once. Let's just get down to business and not worry about the timing."

Cari got stuck in a colossal traffic jam on the way home. She was very thankful for the tape deck which gave her something to listen to besides honking horns and irate drivers. It took her over an hour to make the normally 20 minute trip, and her right leg was bothering her. She limped to the elevator after parking her car and headed up to her apartment. The light was flashing on her answering machine.

"Oh, forget it! Whoever it is can wait until after I have a shower and something to eat." It was another hour before she listened to the message.

"Hi, Cari. It's John. I just want to apologize for acting like such a fool at lunch today. You didn't deserve that kind of treatment. Rebecca told me that you had trouble getting a cab, too. I'm sorry. Well, if you're still willing to speak with me, you could give me a call at home tonight. If not—well, I'll try to say all this in person tomorrow. Bye."

Cari listened to it a second time, trying to read between the lines, so to speak. *He's sorry, but he doesn't mention Gilles. So, what, exactly, is he apologizing for? For sticking me with the bill, and leaving me stranded?* After several minutes, she dialled his number, and nervously waited for him to answer.

"Hello? John Maxwell speaking."

"Hi, John. It's Cari. I just got your message."

"Oh. So, I can assume that you're still speaking to me?"

"Yes. Did you honestly think I wouldn't?"

He didn't answer immediately. "Well, I did act rather childish, to say the least. I suppose I could have expected the silent treatment. Thankfully, you have more maturity than I do, it seems."

"John, you don't have to be so hard on yourself. Besides, maybe I shouldn't have mentioned Gilles Rodriquez at all. But I didn't want you finding out later, and then wondering why I hadn't said anything. Can you understand that?"

"Yes. I can see your reasoning, Cari." His tone was rather subdued. "However, I still don't relish the thought of sharing a meal with the fellow."

"That's okay." She twisted the phone cord around her fingers, not sure what else to say.

"I *am* jealous," he said. "But," he added with obvious effort, "I have no official claim on you, do I? So, I'll try to keep my mouth shut in the future."

"John . . .nobody has a claim on me—except for God."

"And how am I supposed to compete with *Him*?" John asked. "At least I can see Rodriquez." He sighed again, sounding unusually tired. "Enough of this discussion. Goodnight, Cari."

"Goodnight, John. See you tomorrow."

On Tuesday, after work, Cari picked up Gilles at the hotel and drove to Mike and Julie Patterson's. Mike was her former partner from the LAPD and she still spent a lot of time with his family. And she wanted them to meet Gilles, knowing their opinion would carry a lot of weight with her. *If they can't stand him it'll be much easier to send him home on Friday with a polite 'no thanks'.* Somehow, that didn't seem too likely.

Gilles was charming all through supper. Christa Patterson showed more than a casual interest in him, which surprised Cari. *Then again, she is twenty-one already. I wonder if Gilles would be interested in a 'younger woman'. This is ridiculous. Why am I wasting my time like this? We came for supper, not a course in match-making.*

As Cari had expected, Julie took her aside just after the meal, on the pretence of helping with the dishes. "How do you manage to find such handsome guys, Cari? This makes three in a row now. Rick, John, and Gilles."

"Four, if you count Mark."

"I purposely left him off the list," replied Julie. "I didn't think you'd want him included anymore."

Cari shook her head. No, she tried not to think of Dr. Mark Hamilton too often, even if she had almost married him. After he'd raped her on Thanksgiving Day, 1991, and left her pregnant, she had tried hard to avoid him. That had been possible at first. Then she'd been assaulted while on duty, and nearly beaten to death. She'd lost the baby, spent almost two months in the hospital, and gone through a career change. She'd also acquired a permanent pacemaker in April of 1993. She still limped most of the time too. A year after the rape, Mark had asked for her forgiveness, and offered to turn himself in to the police. He'd also offered her a financial settlement. She'd refused both offers. Mark had donated the money to the Sexual Assault Center instead.

"So, I take it you like Gilles," said Cari, trying to steer the conversation away from Mark.

"Of course. How could I not like someone with such a gorgeous accent? And he's also intelligent, has a fascinating line of work, and he's a Christian. What more do you want?"

"That's what I keep asking myself," Cari replied as she leaned against the kitchen counter. "But I also keep asking: 'What if John were a Christian?' Is one man *better* than the other, Julie? I like them both."

"I can see that." Julie put an arm around Cari's shoulders. "I also noticed that Christa seems to like Gilles too. So, if your heart doesn't lead you in his direction, I don't think she'll lose any sleep over it."

"I noticed the same thing," admitted Cari. "But I'm not sure Gilles noticed *her* so far."

"True."

"Let's get these dishes done, Julie, instead of just standing her speculating."

"So, how many countries have you been in so far, Gilles?" asked Mike just as Cari and Julie rejoined them in the den. They found

Christa sitting in the room, listening intently to the conversation.

"Well, to be honest, I've lost track," replied Gilles. He reached inside his sport jacket. "Here, Christa, why don't you check my passport? Let us know how many countries, please." He handed the book to her and she smiled warmly.

"Sure." Then she started with the first page and began reading stamps, her lips moving as she counted to herself. When she reached the last page, she looked up at her father. "Twenty-three. Europe, Africa, Asia, even Australia." She handed the passport back to Gilles. "And I've hardly ever left LA"

"Maybe that will change once you finish your studies," reasoned Gilles, replacing his passport in his pocket.

"Maybe. Depends on what I end up doing, I guess."

"Actually," said Gilles, sounding apologetic, "This is my second passport. I'm sure there are a few other countries in the first one."

Mike whistled softly. "All that globe-trotting for the sake of art?"

"Art and furniture," replied Gilles. "My mother likes to collect antiques, as well as unique or original pieces. She'll read about something, or see it in a magazine. Then she'll send me to do the negotiating." He grinned. "Other than to visit her family in France, my mother never leaves Mexico. But her home has treasures from every continent."

"I can vouch for that," put in Cari. "The master suite has this most amazing headboard. I've never seen one so tall. And the carving is gorgeous." She turned to Gilles. "Your mother manages to mix a dozen different styles, periods, and woods, and it all looks like it belongs together." She shook her head. "I don't know how she does it."

"With a lot of patience," he replied. He gently patted Cari's hand. Then he turned his attention back to Mike. "So, Cari tells me that you worked together for several years. That must have been interesting. What did you think of having a *female* partner—at the beginning, I mean."

"Well," remarked Mike, seeming to carefully consider his reply. "Seeing as I'd already had a female *marriage* partner for a long time before that, I just figured I could learn to have one in the patrol car too." He winked at Cari as he grinned. "Though I tried to give her a hard time at first."

"I bought *every* cup of coffee for the first six months," said Cari with a laugh. "I can't believe you conned me into that, Mike."

"I was very convincing, I suppose."

After another hour of pleasant conversation, Cari yawned and suggested that she and Gilles head back. "I need to be at the office early tomorrow," she said. "I'm meeting Rebecca Richards for breakfast."

"Of course," said Gilles as he got to his feet and extended his hand to her. "I shouldn't keep you out on my account." He helped her up, but didn't release her hand. "Thank you for a lovely meal, Senora Patterson. Nice to meet you, Mike. And you, Christa. I hope to see you again some time." He cast a glance at Cari. "I'm sure one of my parents will be sending me this way again."

"We're glad you could make it, Gilles," replied Julie. She cuddled against Mike's side as they headed towards the door.

"Buenos noche, Senor Rodriquez," said Christa, blushing slightly.

She received one of Gilles' warm smiles. "And you, Senorita."

Gilles held Cari's hand all the way out to her car. Then he held the door open for her, smiling all the while.

Cari and Pam Martin sat and sipped from their milkshakes as they watched the surf roll in.

"So, you're confused, why?" Pam asked. "A very nice, available, Christian guy is interested in you, but you're confused." She leaned back against the wooden bench and stretched out her legs. "I mean, there aren't even any previous wives or kids to worry about this time, like with Rick Benson. So, what seems to be the problem?"

Cari turned to her friend, and former co worker. "Pam, you know I never seem to have a straightforward answer for these questions. Rick is a good friend, but no spark. John is also a good friend."

"And plenty of sparks."

Cari flicked her bangs out of her eyes. "Yeah, too many sometimes."

"And Gilles?"

"Serious potential in the sparks department."

Pam nodded as she continued to sip. "So, the real problem is that you don't feel like you deserve anybody nice in your life?"

"What? How did we go from sparks to whether or not I deserve somebody?"

"Maybe because ever since what happened with Mark, you've tried to cross every eligible guy off your list if they want to be more than a friend."

"No, I don't. Well, not without a good reason, at least." She rammed her straw in and out of her cup. "Besides, who made you the sudden expert, Miss never-go-out-with-a-cop-or-a-medical-person? When was the last time you even had coffee with somebody interesting?"

Pam shook her head and smiled. "This conversation isn't about me, Cari. You called and said that you needed to talk. But, just to satisfy your curiosity, I went out with someone a couple of days ago. Now, stop trying to change the subject."

"So, you think I should go out with Gilles?"

"I think you should stop selling yourself short."

Cari turned and watched the surf for a few moments. "Okay." She faced her friend once more. "So, who did you go out with?"

Chapter 3

Cari drove Gilles to the LAX on Friday afternoon, and waited with him for over an hour. They sat in a dimly lit lounge and drank some terrible coffee, both hoping that the other would say something. Gilles finally did.

"Well, you've had all week to think about what I said the other night. Do you have an answer, Cari?"

She swallowed hard as she stirred her coffee. "I - I've had a hard time with this, Gilles. I don't like to make quick decisions—unless I have to." She knew that was an evasive answer and she bit her lip as she tried to come up with a better one. "I do know that I've enjoyed spending time with you this week," she added with a smile. He reached for her hand and gently stroked her fingers.

"So have I," he replied. "What is it that makes you hesitate?"

"A lot of things," she answered, Mark flashing through her mind. "There's so much that we don't know about each other."

"Do you and John know everything?" he probed. She shook her head. "My parents have been married over 30 years, Cari, and they still discover new things about each other. Isn't that part of the reason behind relationships? What is it that you're afraid of?"

"That I'll change my mind," she whispered.

"About what?"

"About *us*," she replied. "Look, you already know that I'm

attracted to John." He nodded. "What if you and I try to establish something—and then John becomes a Christian?"

"What if he *doesn't*? Will you hold back for the rest of your life, just *hoping*?"

"And praying." She set her spoon on the table and rubbed at her throbbing temple. "That's what I don't know, Gilles. Would it be fair to you? To eventually change my mind, I mean."

"I'm willing to take the chance," he assured her.

"I see him almost every day," she stated, arguing with herself more than Gilles. "When will I see you?" She felt him squeeze her fingers.

"At least once a month. More, if I can arrange it. And I could call you. And write."

"I just don't know."

"Cari, just for a moment, try to forget about John Maxwell." She stared at him in confusion. "If I'd met you first, would you still be hesitating right now?" She shook her head, realizing it was true. "Are you willing to try?"

"Yes," she whispered. "I'll try."

"Gracias," he replied, caressing her cheek. "I'll call you when I get home, and let you know what my father will have me doing for the next few weeks. We'll arrange some time together. I promise."

Cari looked at her watch. "You need to go catch your flight, Gilles. They should start boarding soon."

"All right. If you insist." He released her hand, got up from the table, and left some money for the bill and a tip. They left the lounge and entered the crowded terminal. "Just a minute, Cari."

She turned around, embarrassed that tears were now on her cheeks.

Gilles placed his right hand behind her head and drew her closer. "I'll call you tonight," he reminded her. Then he kissed her cheek. "And I'll be back as soon as I can," he whispered. He kissed her lips, gently cradling her head. He didn't seem to care that they were in a crowded airport terminal.

Cari felt herself relax as soon as Gilles kissed her. She didn't feel forced or pressured in any way. Neither did she feel guilty, as she had with John. *Maybe I'm making the right choice after all.* She briefly returned his kiss, but then his flight was announced, and they both knew he had to get going. She stepped away from him and smiled. "A dios, Gilles."

"A dios," he replied, his dark eyes glistening. "Tonight," he whispered, just before hurrying off in the direction of his gate.

Cari watched him until he was absorbed by the throng of other travelers. Then she wiped her eyes and made her way slowly from the terminal.

Cari jerked when the phone rang next to the bed. She had waited up for hours, but no call had come. So, she'd gone to bed, wondering if Gilles had been too tired to call her. She reached for the phone after the second ring.

"Hello? Cari Daniels speaking."

"Cari, it's Gilles. Sorry to call you so late. I had forgotten all about my brother's bachelor party tonight. His wedding is tomorrow afternoon, and all his friends from the university had a party for him."

"Which brother?" she asked, trying to remember who was engaged.

"Pierre. And don't worry, there was no drinking allowed. Except for some wine to toast the occasion."

"It's none of my business, Gilles."

"But I'd like it to be. How are you? Did I wake you?"

"Well, almost. I guess I was falling asleep. That's okay. I don't work on Saturdays. At least not usually. How was your flight?"

"I thought about you all the way home."

Cari sat up and leaned against her pillow. "Have you told your parents about seeing me?"

"I told them," he replied, some of the previous excitement gone from his voice.

"What did they say?" she asked, nervously clutching the receiver, while chiding herself for being nervous at all.

"My mother was pleased, and she asked a dozen questions about you. She's glad to know that you've recovered your health."

"What about your father?" she dared to ask.

"He didn't say much," was the evasive reply.

"Okay, Gilles, what *didn't* he say?"

"He still thinks I'm being unreasonable," he admitted with a sigh. "But I'm not a child, Cari. I refuse to be treated like one."

"What is he so set against?"

"You're an American. You're blonde. You have a career in what he considers to be a *masculine* field."

"Oh, brother! So he thinks you should stick to dark-haired Mexican girls who stay home once they get married?"

"Something like that."

"And you still called me tonight?" she wondered aloud.

"Of course," he replied with a laugh. "I already miss you."

"Really?" She was surprised at how glad she was to hear him say that.

"Yes. Now, I really should let you go to sleep, and I'd better do likewise. I'll call again in a few days—and not in the middle of the night, either."

"Okay."

"Wednesday night."

"Goodbye, Gilles."

"Goodbye, Cari."

She hung up the phone, but she sat up in bed for another hour, wondering what it would be like to marry into such a large family. Then she thought of Eduardo Rodriquez and frowned. *And a father-in-law who doesn't like too much about me.* Then she laughed to herself. *I could always dye my hair black. And quit my job.* She frowned again. *But I'd still be an American.* She fluffed her pillow before lying down once more. *Gilles, what on earth are we doing?*

Gilles was a groomsman for Pierre's wedding, and he had fun seeing the sweat on his brother's forehead during the ceremony. And he wondered what it might be like to be the groom. To have his mother weeping during the whole ceremony. To hear his sisters giggling. To place a ring on a slender finger and make promises meant to last a lifetime. Then the thought of his father entered the picture. *He doesn't approve of Cari right now. Maybe he'll change his mind. But if he doesn't, what am I willing to give up for her sake? Is it worth it to go against my own father?*

John sat on the porch of his cabin and thought about Cari. He knew she'd taken Gilles to the airport the day before. He knew they'd seen quite a bit of each other all week. And he didn't like it. But he was no fool either. *He's her age. He can offer her just as much as I can. Maybe more. His mother likes her. Mine hasn't even met her. And then there's the* God *thing. She's just not willing to compromise about that. I'm not sure I'd want her to.* He rubbed the back of his neck, thankful for a slight breeze from the trees not far from him. He got to his feet and looked at the mountains around him.

So, do I just step aside and see what happens? Or do I press my advantage? He shook his head. *Nobody is going to win her unless she wants to be won. But do I just want to have her as a* friend *for the rest of my life?* He sighed as he blinked at the bright sunlight. *I suppose I could do worse than that.*

Chapter 4

Cari sat in her office on Monday morning and tried to concentrate on the files in front of her. She wasn't having much success. Her mind kept wandering back to Gilles, and his father. Specifically, to what their reactions would be if they found out about Mark Hamilton, and the resulting pregnancy and miscarriage. *If Senor Rodriquez thinks me too* liberal *already, what would he think about the baby? And what would Gilles say? Maybe his interest would die just as quickly as it started.* She shook her head. *I have to quit this. I have work to do. Why spend so much time speculating about something that may very well never happen?*

An hour later the files were neatly put away in one of her oak cabinets, and she was on her way to the front desk area to speak with Kelly.

"Anything out of the ordinary today?" asked Cari.

"Not that I've noticed," replied the young woman who watched the bank of security cameras. "Life has been much quieter since Max Gardener and Jerry Neilson don't work here anymore." Her smile faded once she realized what she'd said. "Sorry, Miss Daniels." She shrugged her slim shoulders. "But it really has been quieter. And Pete Willis has been doing a great job training some of the new security staff. I'm sure that's made a difference too."

"True," remarked Cari. "Pete has done a good job. He makes it a lot easier to do mine. And so do you. See you later."

"Sure. Are you going for lunch now?"

"Yes. I should be back in about an hour if anybody is looking for me."

"Okay."

Cari headed for the elevator just as John stepped out of one of them. "Hello, John."

"Good afternoon, Cari. Did you have a good weekend?"

"Yes, thank you. How was yours? You went up to the cabin, didn't you?"

"It was sunny and warm," he replied with a smile. His gaze held hers for a moment. "But somehow, I don't enjoy the solitude as much as I used to." When she looked down at the floor he cleared his throat. "Excuse me." He walked away as she pressed the button for the elevator.

Great! All I need is for John to lay a guilt trip on me as though I dumped him. We weren't even dating. She bit her lip. *Well, not really anyway. Why does life have to be so complicated? Why couldn't I have just met* one *really nice guy, settled down, and gotten married? Why this chain of prospects?* She rubbed her forehead in frustration. *Lord, please help me to make some sense out of all this. I'm not doing too well on my own.*

When Gilles called on Wednesday evening, Cari was sitting up and reading a book. It was somewhat easier to converse while she was wide awake.

"How is your week going?" he asked. "Keeping busy?"

"As a matter of fact, I have been. What about you?"

"My father has been having some problems with a purchase he made recently."

"What kind of problem?"

"Well, it seems that he bought an original painting from the owner in St. Moritz, Switzerland. He had someone else handle the arrangements, and then he channelled the money, using a cashier's cheque. An empty crate arrived on Monday, and my father is furious."

"I would imagine. What do you suppose happened?"

"Well, either the painting was stolen—though it didn't look as though the crate had been tampered with. Or, it was never sent at all. My father has been trying to contact the owner, but he's been getting no response so far. He's threatening to contact *Interpol* or the Swiss authorities. It looks as though this could become quite a mess."

"How much did he pay for the painting?" Cari wondered aloud.

"Over three hundred thousand Swiss Francs."

"What? Just how famous was this painting?"

"It's a work from the 1860s, depicting Central Park in New York City. There are very few works left by this artist, so that's part of the reason it's so valuable. Apparently, it was kept in the same family for generations."

"Then why did the owner sell?"

"Why else? For the money."

"Amazing. So, has your father ever had a problem like this before?"

"Not with anything so valuable. I guess that's why he's so angry about the whole thing."

"Won't it be rather awkward trying to deal with officials in another country?"

"It certainly can be. And the insurance company isn't being too helpful at the moment either."

"What do you mean?"

"Until they have proof that the painting was actually *stolen*, or *lost in shipment* they won't pay a cent. And it's up to my father to find the proof."

"Good grief. I don't envy either of you, Gilles. This sounds like a nightmare."

"I suppose it does. My mother is afraid my father will have a heart attack if he gets anymore upset than he already is."

"Really? That's one thing that I highly recommend avoiding." Having suffered cardiac arrest five times, Cari was more knowledgeable than she cared to be.

"Well, he does have high blood pressure. But mostly, he just has a bad temper. He likes for things to go the way he plans them."

"Don't we all?" she murmured. "How's your mother? Pierre was the first child to get married wasn't he?"

"Yes. Next comes Maxine. Then Henri. Mother took it quite well, though she cried through the whole wedding."

"I think a lot of mothers do that." They were both silent for a moment.

"I miss you, Cari."

"This phone bill is going to cost you a fortune, Gilles," she replied, not answering him directly.

"That doesn't matter," he assured her. "I like to hear your voice."

"Thank you."

"But, I suppose I should get some sleep."

"I have some studying to do, too."

"Really? For what?"

"For a license as a private investigator."

"Oh. You didn't mention that when I saw you last week."

"No. I guess I didn't think of it then. Besides, what would your father think of *that*? If he already dislikes what I do now—somehow I don't think he'd be too impressed."

"Maybe not. But I would be. Isn't that more important?"

"I don't know, Gilles." She bit her lip as she considered what to say. "*Shouldn't* it matter whether or not your father likes me?"

"I'd rather not get into this over the phone. Let's save this topic for a personal conversation."

"Okay. But I should get going now. Goodnight, Gilles. Thank you for calling."

"You're welcome. Goodnight."

Gilles stood on his balcony and stared up at the starry sky. *Why must you worry so much about my father, Cari? Is protocol so important to you? Besides, you could win him over with time. Even if he is a male chauvinist. So you want to be an investigator? Why is that? Because of your law enforcement years? Because of what you do at the law firm? Or because you want to remain independent for the rest of your life? I sincerely hope that isn't the case.*

"John, do you know anything about international art theft?" Cari asked as they met for lunch on Friday.

He stared at her for a moment. "Why do you ask?"

She looked down at her plate. "Gilles' father bought a painting, worth about a quarter million. But it never arrived. It was bought in Switzerland, but only an empty crate made it to Mexico."

"I see," was all he said until he finished his sandwich. Then he continued. "Well, to be honest, it isn't my field of expertise—professionally. But art has always interested me. I take it the painting was from a private owner?"

"Yes. And Senor Rodriquez is having a difficult time tracking him down."

"Where in Switzerland?"

"St. Moritz." Cari suddenly smiled. "Just how well do you know that area, John?"

"Fairly well," he conceded. "But that doesn't mean I've ever met the owner. Usually, I spend a lot of time hiking and horseback riding when I go there. Besides, neither of us has been asked to *help*, have we?"

Cari shook her head. "No. Not yet, at least. But what if we were?" She braced her elbows on the table. "Would you be willing to help track the painting?"

John shrugged. "Possibly. I'll admit, it could be a nice change from investigating accident insurance claims."

"And you're still due for a trip to St. Moritz," she added softly, recalling his remark about hanging around the office now that she was there.

"True." He smiled then. "You don't miss much, do you? You must really enjoy putting all the pieces together in a case."

"Except when I'm the central *piece*," she said, thinking of the weeks of nerve-racking frustration while Jerry Neilson had stalked her. She finished her lunch and reached for the check. John took it from her.

"I think I owe you a lunch after what happened last week," he said.

"But you drove today." Their usual arrangement was that one drove and the other bought lunch.

"Let's break with precedent for a change, shall we?"

"Okay," she agreed. Then she laughed. "But I thought lawyers hate to do that."

Chapter 5

"My father is sending me to St. Moritz to try to find out what happened to that painting," explained Gilles when he called Cari a week later. "And he's leaving it up to me how I handle it. So, Miss Private Investigator, would you like to come with me?"

"What?"

"In an official capacity of course. I'd like to have some *expert* assistance with this. And I'd like to hire you. What kind of arrangement do you have with the law firm?"

"Well, technically, I work for *Richards & Richards*, and keep myself available to the lawyers right here. So, I'm not sure that I could help you, Gilles."

"What if I were to hire one of the lawyers at the firm, too? Like I said, I'd appreciate some help with this. I'm not looking for a figurine worth a few hundred dollars."

"Well, as a matter of fact, I sort of discussed this with John Maxwell last week, Gilles. You see, he usually goes to St. Moritz every August for his vacation. And he might be able to help find the owner."

"What type of law does he specialize in?"

"Usually accident insurance claims. But that doesn't mean he wouldn't be able to assist you. Frankly, I'm not sure what type of specialist you could use. Criminal law, international law? You're still not positive that an actual *crime* was committed are you?"

"No." She could hear him muttering to himself. "All right. Why don't you talk this over with your boss—and with John Maxwell? If they're both willing, will you come with me?"

"Of course." Then she frowned. "Gilles, this could get very expensive."

"I'm aware of that, Cari. So is my father. He's prepared to pay well in order to get the painting."

"Okay. I'll speak with Rebecca Richards. Today, if possible. Do you want me to call you back?"

"No. I'll call you in a couple of days. Then I'll have to start making some arrangements myself."

"Fine. And Gilles?"

"Yes?"

"Thanks for asking me to help."

"Well, what do you think, John? Ready to combine some business with your vacation time?" asked Rebecca Richards as she sat in her office with John and Cari. "It could be both lucrative and interesting."

"I suppose so," he replied.

"Have you even had a chance to work out a table of fees, Cari? You haven't had your license very long."

"As a matter of fact, I was hoping that you might be able to help me with that," said Cari. "I've never worked for anything other than a salary. I've asked around, and fees vary a fair bit." She shrugged. "What kind of expenses would a lawyer get reimbursed for?"

"That depends on the case," answered Rebecca. "And the client.

In this instance, I'd say you could charge for: airfare, lodging, car rental, meals, phone calls, record checks, etc. You can charge an hourly fee, or a per diem rate. I think that would be simpler, since none of us are exactly sure what this case will entail."

"I agree," said John. "In my case, I'll waive the airfare, since I likely would have gone there anyway. I won't charge for the lodging, but I will for the meals, car rental, and an hourly fee, for any actual work that I do."

"Okay. I can see the logic to that. But, I do have another concern."

"What's that?" asked Rebecca.

"Traveling alone with two men," replied Cari, a slight blush creeping into her cheeks. "I realize this is the 1990's, and lots of women wouldn't give it a thought, but—"

"But you do," remarked John. "Well, I suppose you could ask someone to join you. Though, you'd likely have to pay for the added expense. You could hardly expect Mr. Rodriquez to pay the airfare and meals for a glorified *companion*."

"Of course not." Cari clasped her hands together in her lap. "Actually, that shouldn't be too much of a problem." She smiled at her boss. "I get paid so well here, and I haven't changed my lifestyle much since I started, so my bank account is looking pretty healthy these days. Besides, I still receive a pension from the police force. I can pay to have someone come with me."

"Have you got someone in mind?" asked John.

"Yes. And I'm positive that she'd jump at the chance. It's her dad that will be hard to convince."

"You want to take her *where*?" exclaimed Rick Benson. He was

Mike Patterson's partner, and his daughter, Tammy had become a good friend to Cari since she'd had to leave the force. As a matter of fact, Tammy had been rather disappointed that Cari hadn't returned Rick's romantic interest. He'd been a widower for three years, and the teen was anxious to have a woman back in her life, on a full-time basis.

"To St. Moritz, Rick. I know it sounds like a wild idea, but will you at least hear me out, please?"

"Okay," he said, after taking a deep breath. "Go ahead."

"Well, I have some investigative work to do over there. However, I'll be traveling with a male lawyer and a male client. Both are *single* guys. Get the picture?"

"You want Tammy for a *chaperone*?" he laughed. "She just turned 14, Cari. How much *help* would she be?"

"A lot." Cari sighed as she tried to figure out how to explain this to her friend. "Look, John Maxwell and I see a lot of each other, Rick. Sometimes, it was personal rather than business." She felt herself blush. "And Gilles Rodriquez and I are—well, we're—"

"Dating?" he asked, no longer laughing.

"Sort of. It's kind of awkward when we live in different countries. Anyway, the two guys don't have a great deal of *fondness* for each other."

"I guess not. So, you don't want to be caught in the middle, I take it?"

"Right. This whole trip could be a logistical nightmare as it is. It would help me so much if you let Tammy come along. We've bunked together before. And I think it could be a fantastic experience for her." She looked down at the table for a moment. "And I thought we could stopover in New York, so Tammy could see Karen's parents." She looked up to see how he'd handle her mentioning his wife's folks. He only blinked a few times.

"She'd love that," he said in a barely audible voice. He cleared his throat and shifted on his chair. "And I know that they would too. How soon would you need to leave?"

"Next week at the latest. And don't worry; she'd only need a passport, a suitcase full of clothes, and a camera. I'll take care of the rest." She smiled. "Actually, I kind of feel like I owe it to her."

"What do you mean?"

"Well, she never took a cent from me for all those weeks last summer when she did my cleaning, and laundry, and cooked meals. And she helped me again this spring. I'd like to do something special for her."

"She really looks up to you, you know," he said. He laughed again, softening the features of his handsome face. "I wouldn't be at all surprised if she ended up a cop or a PI somewhere done the road."

"Or a nurse," replied Cari. "Her mom made a lasting impact on her, Rick. She won't ever forget that."

"No, I suppose not." He ran his fingers through his dark hair. "Tell you what. I'll figure out Tammy's usual portion of groceries for a month and for her other expenses. And her allowance. Then I'll change it to traveler's cheques. That way she'll have spending money."

"Sure." Cari reached across the table and took hold of his hand. "Thanks, Rick. I really appreciate this. I promise to take good care of her."

"I know. But I want her to call home every three or four days. Just for my own peace of mind."

"No problem."

"And I'll expect regular postcards, too."

"Yes, sir. Anything else?" she asked as she squeezed his fingers.

"Just be careful. You won't be playing on your own turf over there."

"So, you're officially *hired*," said Gilles when he called back. "When can we leave?"

"Well, Tammy and I need to get our passports renewed. And we need to book our flights. That's a bit of a problem, Gilles."

"Why?"

"Well, it's because of my leg. I know I'd never last through an eleven or twelve hour flight. So, what we plan to do is stopover in New York City. Tammy's grandparents live there, and we'll spend the night with them. Then we'll fly to London or Paris. Then on to Zurich by the 31st. I know it would be simpler and cheaper to fly direct, but I just couldn't handle that." The torn ligaments and resulting haemorrhaging in her right thigh had left her with a pronounced limp, or a stiffening of her leg that required the use of her cane.

"No need to apologize. Besides, I always enjoy New York. Plan on stopping in Paris. That's where *my* grandparents are. They'd enjoy a visit, I'm sure. Then to Zurich. By the way, it would be wise for you to bring a cane with you, Cari."

"Why?"

"Well, in case you have any problems with your leg. And it would make it easier for you to get a special parking permit in Switzerland too. That could save you a lot of unnecessary walking."

"That sounds like a plan I could live with. What about accommodations? John said he stays at the same place every year. He has a standing reservation with a lady who operates a small chalet. But he doesn't know if she'd have any available rooms when we first get there. August 1st is Independence Day."

"Well, we'd be in Zurich at that point. I'll see what I can arrange.

Would you have John check about that chalet in St. Moritz? It sounds like a good place for you and Tammy to stay, too."

"What about you?"

"I prefer hotels. And I've learned through the years that there are always rooms available—for a price."

"Now that's a universal thing, isn't it? The same goes for LA"

"So, how much is all this going to cost?" he asked, sounding more curious than professional.

"Quite a bit. You are definitely not hiring the cheapest lawyer or investigator for this job."

"Perhaps not. But you're certainly the most beautiful," he replied. "And I'm sure that counts for something."

Cari laughed. "Try to remember that when you get the bill."

"Of course. So, I'll meet the three of you in Los Angeles next Monday. That'll be the 26th. We could fly to New York on the 27th and to Paris on the 29th. Then to Zurich on the 31st. We could take the train from Zurich to St. Moritz. That will give us plenty of time to go over the accommodations, and ideas. Okay?"

"Sure. It's certainly obvious that you travel a lot, Gilles. I, on the other hand, have been to New York once. To Mexico. And to Kentucky. The rest of my life I've spent right here."

"Well, it looks as though that's about to change, doesn't it?"

"Amen to that."

Chapter 6

"Grandma Jacobs almost squealed into the phone when I called her, Cari," stated Tammy when Cari and Gilles came to pick her up. "I haven't seen them since Mom's—" she swallowed and looked away. "It's been a long time."

Cari put her arm around the girl's shoulders. "I know. I'm looking forward to meeting them myself."

"I still can't believe I'm going to Switzerland! Ricky is still jealous, but Dad reminded him that he'll be going to university next year, so he's got nothing to complain about." She picked up her suitcase and looked at Gilles a little more closely. "Thanks for hiring her, Mr. Rodriquez," she said with a grin. "Otherwise, I'd be stuck at home for the rest of the summer."

"I'm glad you approve," he replied. "Are you ready to go?"

"Almost. I just need to say goodbye to my dad."

"I'm right here, Tammy," said Rick as he came in from the garage. "All set, Sweetheart?"

"Yeah." She dropped her suitcase and scooted over to him, throwing herself into his arms. "Thank you for letting me go, Dad. I promise to behave myself. I love you." She kissed his cheek and squeezed him tight.

"I love you, too," he murmured. "Have a great time."

"I plan to." She stepped out of his embrace and retrieved her suitcase.

Rick came over and extended his hand to Gilles. "I'm Rick, Tammy's father, just in case you hadn't caught that."

Gilles shook his hand and smiled. "I did. Pleased to meet you. And thank you for lending your daughter to us."

"You're welcome." Then he reached for Cari's hand. She hugged him instead.

"Don't worry, Rick. We'll take good care of her. See you in a few weeks. Bye." She stepped back and Gilles placed an arm around her. "And we'll make sure she calls and writes regularly."

"Okay."

"Are we leaving or not, you guys?" asked an obviously exasperated Tammy. "I don't want to miss the plane."

Cari laughed as she moved towards the door. "You won't. We've got plenty of time."

"Is Mr. Maxwell meeting us at the airport?"

"Yes."

John felt a knot develop in his stomach at the sight of Cari and Gilles Rodriquez walking hand in hand. Tammy was right next to her, and could have passed for her daughter. *A nice, happy family. This is going to be a* long *few weeks.* He sighed as he walked towards them. Tammy waved to him and smiled. He waved back, more out of habit than desire.

"Is the luggage all checked?" asked Cari when she was close enough to be heard. He couldn't help but notice that her eyes were brighter than they'd been for days.

"All except for Tammy's," John replied.

"I've just got carry on," stated Tammy. "It's easier that way."

John actually smiled. "I'll bet you twenty dollars you come *back* with more than a carry on."

"No bet!" said Tammy. "I already know that too."

"Well, then I guess we can head over to gate 22 and wait for our flight."

"Yeah, let's go." Tammy reached for John's arm and linked hers through it, catching him off guard. "And trust me, Mr. Maxwell, this will be your most interesting trip ever."

The flight to New York was pretty uneventful, at least in regards to turbulence. The conversation was another story. Tammy talked for the first two hours. She was sitting between John and Cari, and she told them all about her grandparents, and what she could remember about her mother's descriptions of their apartment. She was eager to hear anything that Gilles could tell her about Central Park, or his favorite restaurants and theaters. Half way through the flight they were served supper, and Tammy's flow of words eased off.

"How's your leg?" John asked when the supper trays were taken away.

Cari tried to smile. "Let's put it this way—I can hardly wait to get off this plane." She turned to Gilles. "Speaking of which. Excuse me, Gilles. I need to go to the washroom."

"Certainly." He stood up and stepped into the aisle, allowing her to pass. He frowned when she had to grab hold of the seat back to regain her balance. "Are you all right?"

"I will be," she replied. She carefully made her way up the aisle, her limp aggravated by sitting so long. *What am I going to do on a transatlantic flight?* She smiled to herself. *And I think I'll need a muzzle for Tammy. Good grief, that girl can talk!*

"We should have booked a flight on the Concorde between New York and Paris," said Gilles when Cari returned to her seat. "It cuts the flight time in half."

"Yeah, but it doubles the cost," she replied. He reached for her hand as soon as she fastened her seat belt.

"I wouldn't have minded," he said softly. "For your sake."

"Now you tell me!" she laughed. "I'll survive. I'll be stiff, but I'll survive."

"Grandma!" yelled Tammy as soon as she spotted the woman she'd only seen pictures of for the past three years. "Over here!" She frantically waved her arm. Then she shoved her suitcase into John's hands and rushed to her grandmother. Fortunately, the woman was well braced on the floor, and didn't topple over at the enthusiastic greeting.

"Hi, Sunshine! It's so good to see you." She gave her a fierce hug, and kissed her cheek. She wasn't much taller than Tammy. And she had the same shade of blue eyes. Her blonde hair was streaked with gray, but she was still very pretty. "Now, how about you introduce your friends?"

"Where's Grandpa?" asked Tammy as she released her grandmother. "Didn't he come with you?"

"He stayed home so that there'd be more room in the car. You'll see him soon enough."

"I guess I can wait."

"Your guests?" prodded Marion Jacobs.

"Oh, yeah." To her credit, Tammy did look a trifle guilty for deserting them. She turned around and carried out the introductions. "Grandma, this is Cari Daniels, John Maxwell, and Gilles Rodriquez. Guys, this is my Grandma, Mrs. Marion Jacobs."

"Pleased to meet you, Mrs. Jacobs," said Cari, extending her hand. "I hope this won't inconvenience you too much."

"Nonsense! You brought Tammy for a visit, didn't you? It's the least I can do."

The men introduced themselves and shook hands with Marion.

"All right, we'll get your luggage and head out to the parking area." She looked at Cari and frowned. "It would likely be a good idea for me to bring the car around. I'm parked quite a ways from here."

Cari smiled at her generous offer. "I'll be fine, Mrs. Jacobs. Actually, I'll be glad to work out the kinks."

"If you say so. Just let me know if you change your mind."

"She will," said John, his tone protective. "Shouldn't you be using your cane, though?"

"Yes," agreed Cari. "I likely should. But it's still with the luggage. From now on, I'll keep it with me."

"A good idea," remarked Gilles, placing his arm around her waist. "I'm sure we'd all feel better if you did."

"This was my Mom's room when she was growing up," said Tammy as she sat down on the bed, clad in her mother's nightshirt. "I've always wanted to visit here." The room still contained several pictures of her mother. Her grandparents had seen to that. "Grandma told me in a letter once that Mom cried when they moved to California for a year. And then she met my dad, and never wanted to come back. Even the wedding wasn't here. They got married in Sacramento. I guess that's why so much of her stuff is still here."

"Like this?" asked Cari, picking up an old teddy bear from between the pillows.

"Yeah. My grandpa won that at Coney Island when Mom was just a little girl."

"Would you like to be alone for a bit, Tammy? I could go out in the living room."

Tammy shook her head. "Unh-uh. I know you're awfully tired. And so am I. And Grandma and Grandpa already went to bed, since it's later here, you know." Her lip began to tremble. "I don't think I want to be alone right now." She started to sob as Cari passed her the teddy, and put her arms around her.

"Shhh. It's okay. I understand. Really. I know you miss your mom. And this is the first time you've been away from your dad. And it's just a short visit here. It's okay to cry." She held her for several minutes, but began to yawn repeatedly. "I have to get some sleep, Tammy. Will you be okay?" She nodded. "Good. Try to rest well. We have some sightseeing to do tomorrow."

"Right. Grandpa even took off work while we're here. It'll be fun." She covered her mouth with her hand. "You know, I might even fall asleep before you tonight. I think I just found out what jet lag is. Goodnight."

"Goodnight, Tammy."

Chapter 7

"Should we bill you for this, Gilles?" asked Cari as the four went for a carriage ride in Central Park.

"I doubt it's very relevant to the case," remarked John, smiling at her.

"I don't know. The painting is of Central Park, isn't it?" she countered.

"True," said Gilles. "But I still think this is related to *pleasure* rather than *business*."

"I'll say," agreed Tammy from her spot next to John. "You've been holding her hand the whole time." She clapped her hand over her mouth, but her blushing cheeks were still visible.

Gilles began to laugh. "Guilty as charged." He released Cari's hand and stretched, putting his hands behind his head. "Is this better, Miss Benson?"

"Yes," answered John, without a hint of a smile.

"Well, we packed a lot into one day, didn't we?" asked Marion as they sat down to supper. Tammy looked as though she might fall asleep on her plate. Cari was still alert, but she was covertly rubbing her throbbing right thigh.

"Thank you for showing us around," said John. "And for allowing us to stay with you."

"It's been our pleasure," replied Ben Jacobs. He patted Tammy's hand. "It's been great to see our granddaughter again." He grinned at her. "Though she's certainly not the 'little girl' that we saw last."

"Of course not!" said Tammy, trying to sound indignant.

"Well, tomorrow we'll just sit around and visit," said Marion. "We don't want you all worn out before you get back on the plane."

Cari laughed out loud at the thought. "Well, it might keep Tammy from talking so much." Even John smiled at that. "If not, I think I'll pour some liquid Gravol into her drink when she isn't looking."

"Was I really that bad?" asked Tammy, seeming uncertain.

"Yes!" replied the others in unison.

"I felt right at home," added Gilles with a grin. "But I have more than *one* sister to do all the talking."

Tammy began to giggle and it was several minutes before Ben was able to say grace.

"We'll see you on the way back," said Ben as he saw them off at the airport Thursday evening. "Have a good trip."

"Thank you, Mr. Jacobs," said Cari.

"No problem." He clasped her hand and leaned closer to her, so that he could lower his voice. "Rick told us how much you've helped Tammy in the past year. We appreciate it."

"Thank you."

"Bye, Grandpa." Tammy hugged him with a vengeance and kissed him for good measure. "See you soon." She wiped at the tears on her cheek and tried to smile.

"Sure thing, Sunshine."

Cari leaned on her cane and gritted her teeth. "I hate going through security," she muttered. "This patched up ribcage of mine always sets off all the bells and whistles."

"Yeah, but it makes it kind of interesting when you explain the reason, doesn't it?" remarked Tammy.

"Interesting? Is that what you call it? I call it embarrassing."

"Why?" Tammy reached for Cari's left hand and squeezed it. "I'm just glad you're well enough to be raising such a commotion. Aren't you?"

Cari stopped walking and turned to face the girl. Then she leaned down and kissed her cheek. "Thanks, Kid. I needed that reminder." Her smile returned. "Okay. Let's go raise another ruckus, shall we?"

Cari was so thankful that they'd decided to travel in business class between New York and Paris. They had much more room, and it was easier to stretch her legs. And once Tammy was issued a headset, she alternated between listening to music, and watching the in flight movie, and reading her way through a stack of magazines. And somewhere over the Atlantic, she fell asleep, leaning on John's shoulder.

"I think she's claimed you as a *surrogate father* for this trip, John," said Cari as she carefully removed the headset from Tammy's ears. "I know she's missing Rick, but she's trying not to show it too much."

"I got the same impression," he replied, looking down at the blonde head resting against him. "I guess I could pass her off as my daughter, couldn't I? I'm old enough."

Cari didn't comment about the age difference. Instead, she asked a flight attendant for a blanket for Tammy. And one for herself. She draped one around the girl, but just held the other in her lap. She wasn't really sleepy, just weary. She turned to Gilles.

"So, are your grandparents expecting us?" she asked.

"Yes. I'm sure grand mere will have croissants and café au lait ready and waiting as soon as we arrive. We'll take a taxi from the airport. It's about 45 minutes, depending on the traffic."

"Do they speak English?"

"Enough that you should be all right. If not, just ask me to translate. Actually, Grandpere speaks it quite well, because of his banking business."

"You mean he isn't even retired yet?" That was a surprise. She figured the couple must be in their seventies by now.

"No. He's the type of man who will likely die on the job."

Cari leaned her head back and closed her eyes. "My father was like that. Until he was killed in a car accident at forty-nine. Some things just can't be planned on."

"Like heart attacks," remarked John.

Cari opened her eyes and turned her head. "True. All five of them." She gently tapped the middle of her chest. "Thank God for pacemakers and CPR."

John frowned slightly. "You *did* speak to Dr. Wilson about this trip, didn't you?"

"Of course. I have a mini file of information with me, a Medic-Alert chain around my neck, a bottle of pain medication, with an extra prescription, and the names of noted physicians in Zurich, Bern, Fribourg, Geneva and St. Moritz—just in case we take a few side trips." She rolled her eyes. "Honestly, the man overdoes it with the term *prepared*."

"Good." John crossed his arms, careful not to disturb Tammy, and leaned his head against the headrest. That effectively ended the conversation.

Cari unbuckled her seatbelt and reached for her cane. With the added space between the seats, Gilles didn't need to get up, but he did anyway. "I'll be back in a few minutes." She walked the length of the cabin, casually noting how many passengers had fallen asleep and how many were reading or talking. Then she went to the washroom before returning to her seat. This time she draped the blanket around her shoulders and reclined her seat.

"Ready to get some sleep?" asked Gilles, reaching for her hand.

"Yeah," she said in the midst of a yawn. "Goodnight."

"Goodnight."

The sun was already up when they cleared Customs. Tammy was still groggy, since it was only 2:00 a.m. New York time, but 7:00 in Paris. She wasn't too talkative. John kept a hand at her elbow as they made their way through the Charles de Gaules airport, and went to get a taxi. Cari's cane and pronounced limp made that wait a little shorter. Numerous people stepped aside and allowed them to the front of the line. Cari was both grateful and embarrassed. But she was almost too tired to care about either. Gilles spoke to the driver, gave him some extra francs for taking care of the luggage, and helped Tammy and Cari into the back seat of the cab. John slipped in next to Cari, and Gilles rode beside the driver.

Cari almost fell asleep on the way to Quai D'Orleans, on Ile St. Louis. She opened her eyes wide at the sight of the 300 year old homes along the street. The cab pulled to a stop in front of Numero 23. She was suddenly awake and anxious to see the inside, if it at all matched the grandeur of the outside. Gilles opened the door and they all got out, Tammy mumbling over and over, "I can't believe I'm actually in Paris, France." Gilles paid the driver, retrieved the luggage, and then hastened to knock on the door.

A beautiful woman opened the door and greeted Gilles with a kiss on each cheek. To Cari, it was obvious that this was the mother of Constance Rodriquez. *If I look half that good at her age I'll be happy.* Gilles made the introductions, and Cari didn't miss another resemblance between mother and daughter. Madame Pelletier eyed her from head to toe, and then smiled sweetly, seeming to get the message that her beloved grandson was interested in this woman! Cari smiled back.

Then, to her amazement, John began to rattle off in perfect French. She had no idea what he was saying, but Gilles and his grandmother apparently did. Gilles looked rather startled himself, and John looked smug. And Madame Pelletier gave John a couple of kisses and ushered him into the house as though he were a frequent visitor.

"Well, well, aren't you full of surprises!" said Cari as they handed their jackets to a member of the household staff. "And how long have you spoken French, *Monsieur* Maxwell?"

"Since high school," he replied, still looking a bit cocky. "Didn't you ever notice the French novels in my office?"

Cari's eyebrows furrowed. "Now that you mention it . . . "

"I think it's cool," said Tammy. "All I know is *please* and *thank you, hello* and *goodbye*."

"That'll likely be enough on such a short visit," said Gilles. "Now, would you care for some breakfast? Like I thought, Grand mere has it all ready in the breakfast room." He gestured with his left arm. "Shall we?"

"*Certainement*," replied John.

"I like this stuff," said Tammy, referring to the café au lait. "Dad never lets me drink regular coffee at home. He says I'm too hyper as it is. But I guess this hardly counts, seeing as it's half milk."

"We won't squeal on you," assured John.

After the light breakfast, Cari and Tammy were shown to an enormous guest room. They both looked around, mouths open.

"Is this for real?" Tammy whispered.

"I guess so," replied Cari. "I'm almost afraid to touch anything."

"Me too. But how else are we supposed to sleep tonight?"

"True." Cari eyed the vaulted ceiling, the huge canopied bed, and the plush chairs, and marble fireplace. Then she began to giggle. "Get out the camera, Tammy. Your dad will never believe this."

Chapter 8

Cari woke up to the sound of someone rapping on the eight foot high bedroom doors. She stretched lazily before answering. Tammy was stirring beside her, obviously not fully awake either.

"Cari?" came Gilles' voice from the hallway. "I've made a dinner reservation for in an hour. Can you two be ready by then?"

"Sure," she replied, giving Tammy a gentle shake. "We'll be down in—" She glanced at her watch. "Twenty minutes." Then she thought of something. "How formal should we dress?"

"Just casual. And the restaurant isn't far from here, so you don't have to rush."

"Okay. Thanks." She could hear his footsteps echoing on the hardwood flooring. She sat up and rubbed her eyes. "Wow, it's amazing what a simple nap can do for you." She nudged Tammy again. "Hey, Sleepyhead. We have a dinner date to get ready for. Let's get ourselves organized."

Tammy moaned. "I really don't like this time change thing," she mumbled. She managed to sit up, but her eyes hardly opened. "I'm still tired."

"You'll get used to it. Besides, there won't be another dramatic change until we head back home again. You'll be fine." Cari got off the bed and headed in the direction of her suitcase, which she noticed had been carefully placed on a small table. Tammy's was next to it. She didn't remember putting it there. "Somebody must have put our things here for us. I guess we were too awed by the room to notice earlier."

"Probably," agreed Tammy. "And we took off for some sightseeing. Then we had that amazing lunch that Madame Pelletier had ready for us. I couldn't pronounce the names of most of it, but it sure tasted good." She rubbed her eyes. "No wonder we slept all afternoon."

"Well, we have to get changed for dinner."

"Nothing fancy, right?"

"That's what Gilles just said, so I'll take his word for it."

"How's your leg?" asked Gilles right after greeting Cari with a quick kiss on the cheek. "I thought we'd just walk to the restaurant."

"Much better, thank you," she replied, trying not to blush beneath the bold stares of both Tammy and John. "The walk would be nice, now that I've had a chance to rest."

"Fine, then." He looked down at Tammy, who was still yawning. "Will you make it, *Ma Petite*? You look like you would have slept all evening as well."

"I might have," replied Tammy. "And what did you just call me?"

John answered for her, a warm smile on his face. "The same thing that I was thinking of—*Ma Petite*, or 'my little one'." At her look of uncertainty, he added, "No insult intended."

"I'm *not* just a little kid," insisted the girl. "I'm fourteen already." She put her hands on her hips and frowned, suddenly looking quite awake.

"Of course," put in Gilles, who had started it all. "But you are small, in a delicate sort of way."

Tammy's features immediately softened. "Oh. Like my mom was, you mean. I get it." She daned to smile at both men. "Okay, I can live with the name. Now, let's go have something to eat. I'm starved." She walked over to John and he offered her his arm, which she took. She looked up at him and grinned. "So, what could we call you, Mr. Maxwell?"

"How about *mon ami*? That means 'my friend'."

"Sounds good to me. What about Cari?" She turned back towards her friend as they neared the foyer.

"What's the French term for 'limping'?" asked Cari with a smile. "That would be appropriate."

"Oh, no," Gilles protested. "For you, Cari, let's see—*La femme courageuse*." He looked to John for a response.

John nodded in agreement. "Perfect. It means 'The courageous woman'. That certainly suits you, Cari."

"Okay," replied Cari. "Let's get this straight so far." They stepped outside onto the porch. "John is *mon ami*. Tammy is *ma petite*. I'm *la femme courageuse*. That still leaves you, Gilles. John, what do you think?"

They were down the stairs before John answered her. "How about *l'homme d'art*? 'The art man'."

"Fine with me," said Gilles. "We could even use initials on future correspondence. MP, MA, LFC, and LHA. This could be a very intriguing sort of trip."

"What's the story behind the name, Mr. Rodriquez?" Tammy

asked as she tackled her second course of the sumptuous meal.

"*La Taverne du Sergent Recruteur* refers to the time in history when there weren't enough men for the army. So, various men would be appointed as recruiting sergeants. He would bring them to a place such as this, and then feed them and buy them wine until they were ready to sign *anything*—including an enlistment paper."

"Sneaky!" remarked the girl. "But I doubt that the US had much better tactics over the years either."

"Likely not," agreed John. "But at least the soldiers were fed before signing. Sailors were often just kidnapped and taken aboard a ship."

Cari sighed. "It's so easy to think about history in a setting like this, isn't it? I mean, this tavern is how old? Two hundred years or more? It's fascinating." She'd been gazing at the stone arches, and heavy beams, and leaded windows ever since they'd entered.

"That's nothing compared to some of the places we saw this morning," said Tammy. "I mean, they go *way* back. Centuries even. This is an awesome city."

"Have you ever considered moving here, Gilles?" John asked. "I'm certain that your grandparents would enjoy that."

"I've thought of it a few times. However, when it comes to the climate, I'll take Mexico City over Paris any day. Except for the air pollution, perhaps." He shrugged. "Besides, I travel so much that I'm away as often as I'm at home."

"I suppose so."

Tammy announced that she was 'stuffed' by the time they'd eaten dessert. And they were all looking forward to the walk back to the Pelletier home. Until a patron who'd had too much wine reached out a shaky hand and touched Tammy's pretty hair. He muttered something that the girl didn't understand, but his look required no explanation.

"I want out of here!" whined Tammy as she dug her fingers into John's arm, and leaned towards Cari. "Keep him away from me!" John swiftly ushered her from the restaurant, somewhat baffled by the outburst. He knew she hadn't understood the drunk's remark.

"It's okay, Tammy," he told her in a soothing voice. She seemed not to hear.

"I think I'm going to be sick," she moaned.

Cari put her arms around the girl and tried to ease the tension in her own neck and shoulders. "You're safe, Tammy. Just try to relax. Take some deep breaths. Nobody is going to hurt you. We're just going to walk back to the house now. Okay? You're safe. Do you hear me?"

Tammy was still sobbing, making a mess of Cari's silk blouse.

"Should we call a cab?" asked Gilles, just as confused as John.

"No," replied Cari, her tone stiff and authoritative. "Tammy will be fine walking." She eased the girl away from her, holding her upper arms. "Look at me, Tammy," she ordered. "You're safe. You're not alone. There are three of us with you. Okay?" She used her right hand to wipe away some of Tammy's tears. "When we get back to the house, you and I will have a talk about what happened. For now, I want you to calm down, and walk with John, just like you did on the way here. Got that?"

Tammy simply nodded her head and Cari released her. The girl gratefully accepted the handkerchief that John offered her, and wiped her eyes and cheeks. She mumbled a "Thanks" to him before taking hold of his arm. He gently patted her hand.

Gilles put his arm around Cari as they walked along beside the others. He looked at Cari but all she said was, "Later." He nodded. Then he began to point out some of the sights that he hadn't mentioned on the way to the restaurant. But the walk back seemed much farther to all of them.

"Okay, I have Tammy's permission to fill you guys in," said Cari as she joined John and Gilles in the drawing room. "Mostly because she feels like a total idiot about freaking out earlier." She sighed as she clasped her hands together. Then she looked from one to the other. "At the beginning of February, this year, Tammy was attacked by a couple of guys at her school. They hauled her into a boys washroom, with the lights off, and—and it was a horrible fifteen or twenty minutes for her."

"Was she—" began Gilles, his face suddenly pale.

"No," Cari cut in. "But much too close for comfort. She was hysterical for hours afterwards. And it was a month before she'd go back to school, even knowing that the boys had been arrested. Lately, she's been doing really well. She's not paranoid about the dark anymore. Not so many nightmares either. Until now."

"Good thing she didn't understand what the guy said," put in John, shaking his head. "She would have needed a sedative to calm her down."

"Good thing I didn't know about what happened," said Gilles. "I likely would have beaten the fool for saying it."

"That makes two of us," agreed John, his jaw tense.

Cari sighed again. "You guys aren't getting the whole picture. You see, Tammy didn't need to understand his *words*. She got the message loud and clear by how he *looked* at her, and when he *touched* her hair."

Both men looked somewhat ashamed. Gilles was the first to

speak. "What should we do now?"

"About Tammy? Treat her just the same as you have been. She already trusts the two of you. Besides, she felt utterly humiliated about how she reacted tonight. If you make a fuss about it, she just may lose the ground she's spent almost six months gaining back." She sat in silence for a moment. "And don't breathe a word of this to Rick. Not even in a letter. It's up to Tammy to tell him herself. I told her she has until we reach Zurich. Then she's due to call him anyway."

"Aren't you being a little hard on her?" asked John.

Cari frowned at him. "No, I'm not. I sat up with her all night in February, John. She needed much the same assurance tonight. Safety, companionship, sanity, if you will. She's not a little child who can't think for herself. Had she been *alone* in that restaurant, this would be much different. As it was, she was never in any danger. She *knows* she overreacted. Probably jetlag contributed to that. We talked. She cried. And then she fell asleep as soon as her head hit the pillow. She'll likely have a totally different perspective about this in the morning."

"You're amazing," murmured Gilles as he reached for her hand. "Have you taken courses about this kind of thing?"

Cari cringed at his question. It took her a long time to think of a *safe* answer. "I've done a lot of volunteer work at the same Sexual Assault Center that Tammy was taken to. And I've had some excellent training there." She looked at John, who was looking down at her hands. "Remember Jill Harris? I took her there the same afternoon. I met Rick in the hall and found out about Tammy." He met her gaze for a moment before she focused on Gilles. "But a lot is truly *instinct*, I guess. Knowing when firmness is needed, or when to offer a shoulder to cry on. I've done a lot of both."

« *La femme courageuse,*» whispered Gilles. «It suits you now more than ever.»

Cari smiled. «Thank you.»

John cleared his throat and stood up. «Excuse me. I think I've had about enough activity for one day. Goodnight. I'll see you at breakfast.» He nodded slightly before leaving the room.

Cari got up from the chair, slipping her hand from Gilles'. She went to one of the floor to ceiling windows and looked out, across the Seine, and towards the Notre Dame Cathedral. She sighed just as Gilles joined her, his hands going to her shoulders. «If anyone had told me six months ago that I'd be standing here right now, I would have laughed in their face.»

«If anyone had told me that I'd be standing here *with you*, I wouldn't have dared to hope." He gently turned her around, and gripped her upper arms. "Paris is so very different when I have you to share it with."

Cari smiled and rested her hands lightly on his shoulders. She was still smiling when his lips touched hers. After a moment, her hands met behind his neck. His embrace was warm and comfortable. When he drew back he gently touched her cheek.

"I'm *very* glad that you came with me, Cari," he whispered. "But I'm starting to hate the idea of going home again."

"Then don't dwell on it so much," she replied, stepping away from him. "Goodnight, Gilles."

"Goodnight. Sleep well."

"Of course—*L'homme d'art.*" She saw him smile just before she left the room and headed for the elaborate staircase. *Well, whoever decided that Paris was one of the world's most* romantic *cities certainly has my vote too. Then again, it could just be the company.* And, suddenly, John's comment from the firm's Christmas party came to mind. *"Then again, I much prefer the* companionship *of one, to the* company *of a hundred."* He'd told her that while they stood alone in the courtyard of the Richards' home. He'd kissed her a few moments later.

Cari bit her lip, and paused on the stairs. *Why can't I let him go? Gilles is the kind of guy that I've always wanted to meet. But John is*—she swallowed as her hand clutched the banister. *The kind of man I've always wanted to* marry. She slowly made her way up the rest of the stairs, no longer certain that she'd sleep well.

Chapter 9

"Did you get any sleep last night?" asked Tammy as she sat up in bed. Cari turned and faced her, from her place by the French doors leading to the balcony. "Or have you been sitting there the whole time?"

Cari smiled slightly. "I got *some* sleep, Tammy, though not a lot. And I guess I've been sitting here for a couple of hours. I watched the sunrise."

Tammy got out of bed and walked across the room to join her friend. "What's bothering you? Normally you sleep like a log."

"I have a lot on my mind right now," replied Cari. She got up from the plush chaise lounge and gave Tammy a quick hug. "Thanks for the concern, Kid. I'm sure I'll be fine."

"We still have another flight later. Will you be up to that after not sleeping?" Tammy frowned. "And if you don't want the guys to grill you about it, I think you'd better use some extra makeup this morning."

"Why?"

"Because you have dark shadows under your eyes. That's always a dead giveaway."

"I really look that bad, do I?"

"Yes." Tammy put her hands on her hips. "You didn't tell me what's really bothering you, you know."

"I don't think you need to know," replied Cari, heading towards the closet to get a blouse and a pair of linen slacks.

"It's the guys, isn't it?" observed the girl. "You like *both* of them, though Gilles seems to have most of your attention this trip. Mr. Maxwell is jealous, but trying not to show it—much. Personally, I think he's in love with you. As for Gilles, he's a bit harder to figure out. I think he might be a bit like my dad."

"Gilles Rodriquez is *nothing* like your dad, Tammy," Cari insisted. She chose her clothes and carried them to the bed. "Besides, what makes you think you're such an expert?"

"It's pretty simple, really. My dad was really attracted to you. He still is a little, but he got the message. Anyway, John Maxwell is not just *attracted.* He's always looking for ways to take care of you. Like checking about your cane."

"Gilles does the same thing," countered Cari. "They're both *protective.*"

"True," conceded the girl. "But Gilles is more - more *physical,* I guess. He's always holding your hand, or sitting close or something."

Cari sighed as she got her other things from her suitcase. "He's French and Spanish, Tammy. He's more demonstrative."

"Yeah, I'll say! But you're missing the point, Cari. John shows the same amount of affection—but he can do it just by looking at you. Even from across the room." Tammy crossed her arms over her chest. "You just haven't bothered to notice."

"Yes I have," muttered Cari, under her breath.

"What did you say?" Tammy moved closer.

"I said I've noticed, Tammy." She straightened up, her arms full of clothing. "They're both wonderful guys. Yes, they both like me. But you're forgetting something very important."

"What's that?"

"John isn't a Christian, and Gilles is."

Tammy shrugged. "That could change, couldn't it?"

"I have no way of knowing that. Excuse me; I'm going to go have a bath."

"So, you're going with a sure bet, is that it?" pressed the girl, tailing Cari.

"What are you talking about?" Cari lowered her voice again. "I'm not in the mood for puzzles this morning."

"I can see that," replied Tammy with a smug expression. "What I mean is, you're returning Gilles' interest in you mostly because he's a Christian."

"That's not the only reason," hissed Cari.

Tammy laughed. "Oh, I'm sure you're right. I know he's gorgeous. Christa Patterson couldn't stop talking about him last month. And he makes a fabulous tour guide."

Cari's brown eyes darkened until they were almost black. "Look, this is none of your business, Tammy. Last time I checked *I* was still the adult."

"Right. And that's why *you* need *me* for a chaperone. And trust me; I'll be keeping a closer eye on you for the rest of this trip." She turned and went to select her own clothes for the day.

Cari turned and entered the bathroom, and closed the door none too gently behind her.

Cari picked at her breakfast, but Tammy seemed ravenous. John looked pensive, but Gilles was already talking about their flight to Zurich. Cari found herself looking across the table at John several times. Every time she did, he was looking back at her.

"We should get into the airport about 3:30," said Gilles. "Then we'll stay at the *Zum Storchen* right in the city. It should be a great place to see the fireworks display."

"Fireworks?" asked Tammy.

"Yes. August 1st is Independence Day in Switzerland," replied John. "It's quite something to see."

"Oh yeah, you usually go at this time of year, don't you, Mr. Maxwell?"

He nodded. "Yes, I do. And I always enjoy it very much."

"I'm looking forward to the food," said Tammy a moment later, just before stuffing another bite of croissant into her mouth.

Cari laughed. "That shouldn't pose a problem. You seem to like anything set on the table in front of you." Just then Gilles reached for Cari's hand, but she self-consciously pulled it away. "Excuse me, please. I need to go and pack."

"Of course," murmured Gilles, looking a bit surprised at her sudden departure. "I suppose we should all do that." He smiled at Tammy. "Just as soon as MP has had enough to eat."

John got up from his chair as well. "Excuse me. May I speak with you for a moment, Cari? Alone."

"Certainly." She shrugged and tried not to show her surprise. "Why don't you just walk me up the stairs? That's good for a few minutes."

"Thank you." They left the room together and headed down the hallway. John didn't even wait for the stairs. "You didn't sleep well last night, did you?"

Cari stopped short and looked into his eyes. "How did you know that?"

"Because your eyes aren't sparkling, you barely ate a thing, and you didn't talk much over breakfast. Are you ill?" He gently touched her elbow and held it as they started to mount the stairs.

"No, I'm not ill," she replied, her tone sharper than she intended.

Gilles didn't seem concerned for my health. "I'm just tired."

"Worrying too much?" he asked.

"You're as bad as Tammy," she sputtered, tripping on the carpet runner. John steadied her.

"Pardon?"

"Oh, nothing! I'm just tired. Do you sleep well *every* night, John?!" She stopped and stared at him again.

He slowly shook his head. "No. As a matter of fact, I haven't been sleeping very well since we left L.A." His gaze never wavered. "It's not easy to watch you with someone else all day, especially when I'd gladly change places with him."

Cari thought of the kiss the night before and felt her cheeks flush. "I'm sorry," she whispered.

John withdrew his hand and forced a smile that didn't reach his eyes. "You're sure you'll be all right?"

"I'll be fine. I might fall asleep on the plane. Or during dinner tonight. But I'll be fine. Thank you for asking."

"You're welcome—LFC." This time his eyes reflected the curve of his mouth. "You always manage to come out on top. See you later." He moved past her on the stairs and headed towards his own guest room.

Cari slowly made her way up the remaining stairs, her mind just as active as the night before. *I can't believe Tammy has these two guys figured out so well! She's only fourteen and never even dated. And she manages to peg them exactly. Yes, John shows affection without touching. Gilles seems to have a hard time in that respect. John asked about my health. Gilles assumed I was fine. John is always so honest about his feelings. Gilles speaks mostly of his attraction to me.* She shook her head as she reached the bedroom door. *I have work to do on this trip. I can't waste all my time trying to decide which man is more worthy of my attention. And right now I have a suitcase to pack.*

Chapter 10

Cari didn't even manage to rest on the flight, let alone sleep while it lasted. She was feeling a trifle desperate to find a soft bed by the time they cleared customs. The hand which held her cane was no longer steady, and her limp was worsening. *I'm so tired. I sure hope the hotel isn't far from here.* A sensation of nausea was building; despite the dose of Gravol she'd taken before leaving the Pelletier home. *The last thing I need is to be sick in a foreign airport—or in a taxi.*

"Are you going to be all right?" John asked as he stepped a little closer to her.

"Not if I don't get some fresh air soon," she replied. Her head was pounding and her skin was clammy. She swallowed again. "It's too hot in here."

"No, it isn't," insisted John. "You mustn't be feeling very well." He reached for her left elbow and leaned closer to her ear. "Do you need to see a doctor? This is one of the best countries in the world to find one."

"No, I don't need a doctor," she snapped. "I just need a good sleep. Let go of me!" She jerked her arm from his grasp and hurried ahead of him. That is, as much as her leg would allow. *I need to get out of here!*

Tammy and Gilles were right behind her, but neither of them

even spoke to her. She'd already been rather abrupt with them during the flight, her patience and pain threshold worn thin. Only John had dared to speak with her. And he'd received much the same reception. *What's the matter with me? Why am I so snappy with everybody today? I don't usually get like this even when I'm overtired.* She frowned. *It all started this morning with Tammy's silly questions and comments.*

Cari was the first of the four to step outside. She immediately inhaled the freshness, but her head still pounded, and her stomach still reeled. *I'm definitely going to be sick. I just hope it's not until* after *we're checked into the hotel.* She leaned against the nearest wall and closed her eyes.

"May I be of assistance, Fraulein?" asked someone with a heavy, though pleasant German accent. Cari opened her eyes to find a young man, neatly dressed, standing between her and the closest taxi.

"Yes, thank you. I mean, there are four of us. If you can wait just a moment?" The sunlight felt blinding to her sore eyes. She tried to smile, but squinted instead. *Why did I leave my sunglasses in the suitcase?*

"Certainly," replied the driver. "But would you like to get in the car, Fraulein? You look a little tired." His kind smile penetrated her frosty attitude.

"Thank you, but I'd better wait for my friends. I can't recall the name of the hotel right now." She gritted her teeth as she rubbed her forehead with her left hand. She realized that she was trembling with fatigue. "On second thought—"

"There you are!" exclaimed Tammy just to the left of her. "We lost track of you for a minute." She gently touched Cari's arm. "Boy, you need sleep, Cari. Are you gonna make it okay?" She seemed oblivious to the driver at first. Then she grinned at him. "Would you mind helping my friend to the cab, sir?" she asked sweetly. "I'm afraid she's not feeling very well."

"Of course, Fraulein," replied the young driver. "Just this way. Perhaps you'd like to sit in the front? There would be more room for your legs." A slight flush came into his cheeks and Cari once more tried to smile.

"Thank you. I would appreciate that very much." He escorted her to the cab just as Gilles and John reached the sidewalk, a luggage cart in tow. Tammy waved to them.

"We'd better hustle, guys," she told them in her usual blunt manner. "Cari's sick and getting sicker." She looked to Gilles. "How far to the hotel?"

"Twenty or thirty minutes at the most, I hope."

Tammy frowned and bit her lip. "She may not last that long." Then she shrugged. "But I guess she'll have to. Let's go, guys." She turned and went to the taxi, sliding into the back seat.

Gilles and John helped the driver put the luggage into the trunk and Gilles told him which hotel to go to. The young man nodded and promised to get them there as quickly and safely as possible. Then they all got into the car and headed into the flow of traffic.

Cari rubbed her forehead and temples all the way to the hotel, not saying a word to anyone. *I can't believe this headache! I haven't had one this bad in ages. It must be all the flying and the strange food. I'll have to find my pain pills as soon as we get to our room. I can't stand this much longer.* Just then, the car came to a slightly jerky stop, and the driver came around to open her door.

"Fraulein, perhaps it would be best if your friends went to check in first? You could just wait here for a moment." He gestured to the crowded lobby of the posh establishment. "It's very busy right now. Tomorrow is a holiday, you see."

"I know," she managed to reply. "And thank you, I will wait here. I'd much rather go straight to my room after."

"He's right, Cari," said Gilles. "I'll go sign us all in and get the keys. John, would you mind taking care of the luggage? Tammy, you can wait here with Cari."

"Of course," replied John as he got out of the car.

It still took another ten minutes for Gilles to register, for John to get a bellman to help him with the suitcases, and for Tammy to tear herself away from the fascinating cab driver. Gilles gave the young man a generous tip, and asked him to come by the next morning, so they could have a tour of the city. He readily agreed, though he voiced his concern for Cari. She tried to smile one last time.

"If my roommate will let me sleep until then," she said, her left arm going around Tammy's shoulders, "I should be ready for anything." She grimaced. "For the moment, however . . . "

"Good day, Fraulein. I hope you rest well." He nodded politely before getting back into his car.

Cari barely made it across the threshold to the gorgeous room before surrendering to her fatigue. She set her cane on the nearest chair, kicked off her loafers, and crawled onto the huge bed. She mumbled something unintelligible to Tammy, and fell asleep for the next several hours.

"Is she still sleeping?" asked John when he came to pick up Tammy for supper in the hotel dining room.

Tammy took his offered arm and smiled. "Dead to the world. And I knew she needed sleep more than food, so I didn't wake her. She can always eat later. Besides, I happen to know from experience that she enjoys room service."

"Oh really? I'll have to remember that, MP." He patted her hand. "Have you got a key? I don't want you pounding on the door later."

Tammy took it from the pocket of her skirt. "Good girl. Let's go."

"What about Gilles? Isn't he joining us tonight?"

"Actually, no. He decided to eat about an hour ago. He said he'd make some phone calls to St. Moritz tonight, seeing as we'll be busy tomorrow. It's just you and me. I hope you won't be too bored."

Tammy laughed. "As long as there's food on the table, I won't be bored. And I enjoy your company, *Mon Ami*."

"So, did you call your father yet?" John asked between bites of schnitzel. "I guess Cari didn't have much chance to remind you. Do you know how to place an international call?"

Tammy made a face at him. "Yes, I called my dad. And for your information, I'm not completely clueless. I simply contacted the operator and had her do all the work." She popped some lamb chop into her mouth and smiled, her eyes full of mischief.

"How's your father? Missing you I suppose."

Tammy's cocky expression softened. "Actually, I'm not sure who misses who the most." She shrugged, trying to appear casual. "I told him about freaking out in Paris, but he managed not to book the next plane to Zurich. He's just thankful that I'm with such dependable people." She giggled. "Mind you, I didn't tell him that Cari was crashed out, or that she was crabby on the plane this morning. Why make him worry?"

"Parents are known for that," replied John with a smile. "And so are good friends. You and Cari are very good for each other."

Tammy sighed at that remark. "Yeah. I thought she would have been great mother material too, but she didn't think so. I mean, not that she doesn't like me and my brother. Well, she likes my dad too. She just doesn't like him the way that—"

"I think I get the picture, Tammy." John took a sip of his Perrier before continuing with his food.

"I guess you would." Tammy set aside her fork for a moment

and locked her gaze on his face. "You really like her, don't you?"

"Yes. Very much. Why do you ask?"

"Because I know she likes you too. It's just that—"

"I don't share her faith? I realize that's been a major roadblock up to now."

"And you don't think she's worth the effort?"

"What 'effort' ?"

"Well, getting to know more about God. Asking more questions about what she believes and why. You might find out that God is even more interesting than Cari Daniels." Tammy smiled sweetly and finished her food.

John sat in stunned silence. Eventually, he cleared his throat. "Are you sure you're only fourteen? You seem much older than that, at least a good deal of the time."

"Guilty as charged," she replied. "Fourteen going on forty my dad says." She wiped her mouth with the linen napkin and then nervously toyed with it. "I guess losing my mom has something to do with it. Then moving to a new city. Making new friends." She swallowed as she stared at her empty glass. "And what happened last February," she whispered. She sighed. "Sometimes, I don't really *feel* like I'm only fourteen."

John reached across the table and touched her left hand. "Well, don't try to grow up too fast. Even if you do possess a keener incite than a lot of adults I know."

She looked at him and grinned. "Of course not! That's precisely why I plan to have the most fattening, and utterly useless dessert on the menu. Just because somebody else is going to pay for it."

"Smart girl. Planning to go into law in the future?"

"Possibly," she said airily. "Though, a few other options have caught my eye."

"Like police work? Or nursing? Or being a private investigator?"

She shrugged. "Maybe I'll just have to do all three. Wouldn't that be useful? I could arrest unruly patients, and give first aid to injured officers."

"And do a background check on everybody else," John added with a smile. He signalled the waiter to come over.

"Yes, sir?"

"We'll have dessert now, please. I think sachertorte will do nicely, and some coffee."

The waiter looked from John to Tammy and back again. "And for your daughter, sir?"

John managed not to choke at the mistake, and Tammy said nothing. "The same, thank you."

"Very good, sir." The waiter took away the plates and cutlery and left them alone.

"Well, *Dad*, what is sachertorte?" asked Tammy, trying not to laugh out loud.

"It's probably the richest, most chocolaty cake you've ever tasted. Absolutely loaded with empty calories."

"Sounds great, but what about the coffee? We won't tell my *real* father, will we?"

"Of course not," he assured her. Then he winked. "Furthermore, you will very likely find Cari wide awake when we go back, and *somebody* will have to stay up and keep her company."

Tammy rolled her eyes. "Oh, great! I forgot about that. This could be a long night. Bring on the coffee and chocolate."

Chapter 11

When Tammy returned to the room, she found Cari sitting by the fireplace, her Bible open in her lap. Her hair was still wet from a shower, and she looked well-rested.

"Well, it seems that I missed supper," remarked Cari with a smile. "How was it?"

"The food or the company?" asked Tammy as she sat down on the matching chair opposite Cari.

"Both."

"The food was amazing. You really *must* have the sachertorte for dessert. And John Maxwell was great company. I thoroughly enjoyed myself. So, aren't you just about starving by now? You didn't eat on the plane, and you fell asleep as soon as we got here."

"Yes, I'm quite hungry. I just couldn't make up my mind when I looked at the menu. What did you have?"

"Lamb chops. And Mr. Maxwell had schnitzel. It was a huge serving compared to mine, so take your pick, I guess."

"I think a bowl of soup will do just fine for now." Then she grinned. "And dessert of course."

"I even had coffee with the dessert. I'll probably be up all night, talking with you." She studied Cari for a moment. "You *are* feeling better now, aren't you?"

"Much better." Cari got up from her chair and went to pick up the menu resting next to the telephone. "And I finally got rid of my headache. What a relief." She scanned the pages in front of her, using her index finger for a guide.

"Your limp is almost gone too. You must be okay." Tammy yawned. "I'm not so sure that even strong coffee is going to keep me awake tonight."

Cari laughed as she looked at the girl. "That's okay. I don't mind reading. Don't feel obligated to keep me company if you're tired."

"Thanks. But I should be able to last for a couple of hours yet."

"Fine."

"That was delicious." Cari set aside her empty dessert plate. "Glad you recommended it."

"You should thank Mr. Maxwell, then. I didn't even know what sachertorte was before tonight."

"Definitely worth having again."

"I'll say."

Cari poured more coffee from the carafe and added cream to it. She lingered over it as she sat by the fire. A simple phone call had brought a young man to light if for them, and it was glowing brightly. "Well, this is the life, isn't it, Tammy? Paris for breakfast and Zurich for supper. I think I could get used to this."

"Except for the jetlag part," put in Tammy. "The *luxury* part is just great. Does Gilles always travel like this?"

"I'm not sure about that. It might be for our benefit. Maybe not. His family is *very* wealthy. He could likely travel in this style all the time." It was a rather shocking idea. Cari was still getting used to a large salary, and a company car.

"Mr. Maxwell does okay too, doesn't he? I mean he drives a jag, so he must have money."

"Yes, he does. He also has a beach house in Malibu, spends a month in St. Moritz each summer, dresses in different suits every day of the week, and eats out a lot." Cari laughed. "He also has a twenty year old jeep, and likes to go hiking by his *very* rustic cabin. I hardly recognized him the first time he picked me up wearing casual clothing. I'm so used to his three piece suits."

"He was dressed up tonight for supper, but this is a pretty ritzy place." Tammy grinned as she stared at the flickering flames. "The waiter thought he was my dad, and Mr. Maxwell didn't bother to correct him. I teased him about it for the rest of the meal."

"Well, he is about forty, and he has sandy colored hair, and blue eyes. I guess he could pass as your father quite easily."

"Yeah. And you could *almost* pass as my mother. You're just a bit too young." She sighed again and her smile faded. "I want a mom so bad, Cari. Too bad my dad will have to get married first."

Cari leaned forward and reached for Tammy's right hand. "Maybe he will eventually. He's a great guy, Tammy. And I'm sure some woman will find him to be the man of her dreams."

"Too bad he wasn't yours."

"No, he wasn't. Sorry." She patted her hand. "How be we go down to the lobby of this joint. I can't say that I noticed much when we got here."

"Sure. It's really very pretty." She patted her pocket. "I've still got the key. Ready whenever you are."

"Great."

"Well, good evening, Cari," said John as he met them in the hallway. "Feeling better?"

"Yes, thank you. What are you up to? I know you already ate." She smiled easily and was glad to see him return it.

"Actually, I was just down in the lobby, getting a map and a guidebook for tomorrow. I don't usually see much of Zurich when I come to Switzerland. I normally stay at the airport Hilton, or just catch another flight to St. Moritz. I'm rather looking forward to a tour."

"So, you don't already know every nook and cranny of this city?" asked Cari, a note of amusement in her voice. "I thought you knew almost everything."

"Not quite." He looked down at Tammy. "Still full enough to last until breakfast?"

She rolled her eyes. "I certainly am." She snatched the guidebook from him. "Let's go sit somewhere and look at this."

"By all means, seeing as you're now holding *my* book. Where would you like to go?"

"There's some chairs and stuff in the lobby, isn't there?"

"Yes. But it can be rather noisy down there."

Tammy shrugged. "So? We'll be talking too, won't we? It shouldn't matter."

"I wanted to see it anyway," said Cari. "I kind of missed it earlier."

John offered each of them an elbow and escorted them down to the lobby.

"So, we're taking the train, right?" asked Tammy as she perused the map. "From here," she pointed. "Down to here. All those mountains. It should be gorgeous."

"I'm sure it will be," agreed John, though his gaze was fixed on Cari, not the map. "It's a very beautiful country, full of history and diverse culture. You should find it as educational as it is interesting to look at."

Tammy jerked her head up at his remark. "Speaking of looking at—are there some postcards in the gift shop?"

"I assume so," replied John. "Why?"

"I told Dad I'd write to him tonight. I just remembered."

"I'll go with you, Tammy," offered Cari. "I need to do some walking around anyway. I've been doing enough *resting* since we got here. Fold up the map, Kid, and we'll check out the gift shop." She turned to John. "Care to join us?"

"Why not? Maybe I should pick up a few souvenirs myself."

Cari bought four newspapers. One each of French, German, Italian and English. "It fascinates me that one country has so many *official* languages."

"That's just part of its uniqueness," said John. "But why are you buying papers you can't even read?" he teased.

"Just to prove I've been here," replied Cari with a smug expression. "Besides, you could help me with the French one."

"Gladly," was his soft reply.

Cari looked away for a moment, her cheeks slightly flushed. *Why did I say that? He's going to think I'm flirting with him, when that isn't what I meant at all.* Just then, Tammy waved several postcards in front of her face.

"I found all these. That should give me enough to write every couple of days. Aren't they pretty?"

Cari tried to focus on the collection of cards. "Yes, very. Why don't you show me where you found them? I'd like to get some too. I promised Mike and Julie that I'd write." She turned briefly and looked at John. "Don't you even write to your parents when you're here?"

"Of course," he replied. "But I send letters, not postcards. I think my parents have seen plenty of pictures of Switzerland already. They don't need any more."

"I suppose not." Cari shrugged. "Well, *some of us* aren't as well traveled as you and Gilles. So, we'll keep buying the postcards."

Chapter 12

Despite having slept for several hours, Cari was ready for bed by soon after midnight. Tammy had faded out about an hour earlier, after writing a somewhat hasty message to Rick. Cari closed her Bible but remained in the chair for a few more minutes. *It is so beautiful here. I wonder what St. Moritz is going to be like. I know the altitude is much higher. I hope it doesn't make me sick. If it does, I won't be getting much investigative work done, will I?* She set her Bible on the table next to her and got up. *I wonder where Gilles was all evening. Surely he didn't spend the* whole *time on the phone. Then again, maybe he did.* She frowned. *Why is it that as soon as I decide to pursue a relationship with Gilles, I end up seeing more of John? This doesn't make a lot of sense.*

She readied for bed and shut off the only lamp that was still on. The dying glow from the fireplace filled the room with warm shadows. It reminded her of John's cabin in the Sierras. *His wood stove is so cozy. Actually, the whole cabin is.* She suddenly shuddered. *But I don't know if I could ever really enjoy it again—after what happened with Jerry Neilson.* She rolled onto her left side. *I killed a man, and very nearly died myself. But that could have happened anywhere. It's not the cabin's fault. I'm sure it's just as nice as always. John went there didn't he? I mean, it's not like there's bloodstains on the floor.* She fluffed her pillow. *Why am I thinking about all this right now? I should be going to sleep. I have a city to see in the morning.*

The cab driver, whose name turned out to be Gustaff, came for them at 9:00 a.m. He inquired after Cari's health and seemed relieved to find her looking much better. He offered her the front seat once more, which she gladly accepted. Her leg was not much of the motivator however. She simply didn't want to find herself sitting between John and Gilles the whole morning. She was already confused, and didn't want to make things any worse. Gilles had kissed her cheek at breakfast, and held her hand on the way out of the hotel. But he didn't say a lot, other than to know how she'd slept.

John, on the other hand, had reminded her to bring her cane—just in case. And suggested sunglasses and sunscreen for both Cari and Tammy. He'd commented on her renewed appetite. And he'd even asked her how she liked her room. She simply couldn't help comparing the two men. Each had his merits and faults, and for this morning at least, she didn't want to have to think about what they were.

They saw cathedrals, museums, stately homes, watchmakers, jewelers, book shops. And they strolled along the Banhoffstrausse for nearly an hour. Cari purposely walked next to Tammy, neatly avoiding both men. When they stopped to admire the Zurich See, Cari occupied her hands with her camera. She took dozens of pictures as they went along, including several of John, Gilles and Tammy. By the time lunch rolled around, she was more than ready to return to the hotel and have something to eat, and to rest her leg.

During lunch, Gilles and John spent part of the time conversing in French, effectively cutting out Cari and Tammy. When asked what they were discussing, they both simply said 'business'. Cari rather doubted that, seeing as both men seemed a bit agitated from time to time, but she didn't comment further. She did suggest to Tammy that they buy a French phrase book so that they could eavesdrop in the future. Tammy wholeheartedly agreed.

Gustaff had advised the quartet as to where to go that evening to have the best view of the fireworks, and they listened to him. As they stood and watched the multicolored display bursting above them, they all agreed that it was as much fun as the fourth of July in the States, or Independence Day in Mexico. John showed Tammy how to adjust the filter on his camera, and allowed her to take photos of the event. She relished the attention, as well as the opportunity.

Gilles was glad for Cari's company. She allowed him to hold her hand, or to put his arm around her, but she wasn't especially talkative. That changed as they all headed back to the hotel.

"How about some nice hot cocoa by the fireplace?" suggested Gilles as they strolled through the crowds of people on the streets.

"Sounds like a great way to end the evening," said Tammy. "Especially with loads of whipped cream on top." She licked her lips just before looking up into John's face. "What about you, Mon Ami? Or do you only like your chocolate in your desserts?"

"I like it just fine in a mug, thank you, Ma Petite. As a matter of fact, it's pretty hard to beat when it's made with Swiss chocolate."

Cari made no comment, but Gilles noticed her apparent tension.

"What about you?" he asked.

"I-I think I'd better just get back to the room and get some sleep. We've been busy today and I'm tired."

"But it's still early, and the train won't leave so early tomorrow. Why not?"

"I said I'm tired."

"Please, Cari?" put in Tammy, as she turned around to look at her friend. "I can't exactly hang out with the guys by myself, can I? Besides, I know you like chocolate."

"All right! I'll join you."

Gilles gave her hand a gentle squeeze. "Thank you."

Cari was fine sitting near the fireplace. But as soon as the waitress placed a frothy mug of cocoa in front of her, her hands grew clammy. She closed her eyes for a moment. *It's been a year and a half. Why on earth does the thought of hot cocoa still make me feel sick?* The others kept talking, especially Tammy, for several minutes before they realized that Cari wasn't touching her drink.

"Hey, Cari, you're supposed to drink it," said Tammy. "Not let the whip cream melt all over the table." She used a napkin to try and clean up some of the mess. "Take a sip. It's great stuff."

Cari picked up the mug, but her hands were no longer steady. She got it to her lips, but felt as though she would gag. She hastily set it down, spilling some of the contents again as she did so. A few drops of dark liquid sprinkled her creamy silk blouse. She stared at it for a moment.

"What's wrong?" asked Gilles. "It can't still be too hot. You didn't even touch it at first."

"I need to go upstairs now. I shouldn't have agreed to this." She pushed back her chair and got to her feet. The others looked at her in confusion.

"Do you want me to come with you?" asked Tammy.

Cari shook her head. "No. It's all right." Now embarrassment took over and she felt her cheeks flush with renewed color. "I just need to get to bed. Excuse me." She turned away from the small table, but Gilles reached for her hand.

"Just a minute, Cari. Let me walk up with you."

"You don't need to," she remarked, anxious to get away from the tableful of reminders.

"I want to. Besides, you don't have your cane, and there's a lot of stairs. I'll help you."

She didn't feel like arguing, so she just nodded as he got to his feet. He held her arm as they left the large room. Once at her door, she fumbled with her key, and dropped it on the carpeted floor.

"I'll get it," said Gilles. He picked it up and unlocked the door for her.

"Thank you," she murmured. "Goodnight."

"Hey, wait a second, Cari." He reached for her and pulled her into an embrace, an unwanted one in her present state of mind. Then he kissed her. And this time the affect was altogether different. A surge of anger passed through her, and she slapped his face. He drew back in shock. "What was that for?"

"Don't ever do that again, Gilles," she replied icily. "I don't like that kind of surprise one bit."

"But I—"

"You didn't even ask me, or I would have refused." She noticed the reddening of his left cheek.

"I've kissed you before and you didn't mind."

"That doesn't give you *carte blanche*, does it?"

"No, I suppose not." He straightened up and took a step back. "I apologize."

"Goodnight, Gilles."

He bowed slightly. "Goodnight."

Cari entered the room and closed the door. She moved to the bed and sat down on it with a ragged sigh. *What is the matter with me? I flip out because of hot cocoa. I slap Gilles for kissing me. Am I going crazy?* She got up and moved to the window. *God, please help me to pull myself together before Tammy comes back. I'm hardly a sterling example right now. Maybe I've been so busy helping Tammy and Jill that I haven't taken much time to work through my own hang ups. Please help me, Lord.*

He did just that. By the time that Tammy returned, and Cari answered the door, she was able to smile, apologize for spoiling the fun earlier, and to ask the young girl to help her to decide what to wear on the train the next day.

Gilles stared into the darkness long into the night. *What was the matter with her this evening? She seemed relaxed most of the time. Then she got so off-balance. What is the problem?* He rolled onto his side. *Or am I part of the problem? Maybe I'm crowding her. She hasn't dated for quite a while. She made it plain that she cares about Maxwell. Maybe I need to back off a bit. She may not be ready to be so serious yet.* He punched the feather pillow. *Maybe she just doesn't like the physical aspect. No, that's not entirely it either. She's never slapped me before for kissing her—even in public.* He sighed wearily. *She probably just got too tired today. That must be it. She'll feel better tomorrow, and this whole thing will blow over.* He rubbed his still tender cheek. *But I will never try to surprise her with a kiss again.*

Chapter 13

"Tell me again why we're going to spend all day on the train when we could drive to St. Moritz in about three hours," remarked Cari as the four of them settled themselves on the comfortable seats of first class.

"So we can talk," replied Gilles with a smile. "And to enjoy the scenery along the way. Taking the train is about the best way to see this country."

"Except for hiking," put in John. "But, I'll admit, I haven't seen much between Zurich and St. Moritz myself. I usually just fly."

"I think it's cool," said Tammy with her usual enthusiasm. "Besides, I think it's fun to listen to people talking in other languages. That wouldn't happen if the four of us were in a car driving around." Then she grinned at the two men. "Unless of course, you two started arguing in French again."

"We weren't arguing," said John. "We were just having a lively discussion. Right, Rodriquez?"

"Of course. True gentlemen never argue. They just disagree with one another."

"Oh be quiet!" sighed Cari as she sat down and tried to get comfortable. She had a headache already, and the trip was just beginning. She'd taken medication before leaving the hotel, and was hoping that she'd be able to sleep part of the way. She rubbed her throbbing temples.

"Are you all right?" John asked softly.

Cari met his warm gaze and tried to smile. "Just tired," she replied. "But I say that all the time, don't I?" She closed her eyes and leaned back against the headrest. "Wake me up when we get there, okay?"

"So much for discussing the case," murmured Gilles.

Cari dozed off and on for the next couple of hours. She toyed with her lunch, but ate little of it. Her headache was worsening rather than abating. By the time they changed trains in Chur, she was feeling decidedly ill, but didn't say anything to the others. As the miles wore on, she began to wonder what she was doing in Switzerland at all. She no longer just had a headache. She was battling dizziness and nausea as well. Soon she wasn't able to keep her suffering to herself.

"I'm sick," she moaned as they entered a stretch of tunnel. "I need to lie down." She leaned her head against the window, trying not to lose what little lunch she'd eaten.

"Tammy, switch places with me," said John, his voice edged with concern. Cari soon felt his hand on her shoulder. "There's no place to lie down, but put your head on my lap."

She was too ill to care what he'd suggested. She simply moaned as he rolled up his jacket to pillow her head. Then he eased her to his lap. "Thank you," she mumbled. "What is the matter with me?"

"AMS — acute mountain sickness. It happens to a lot of people when they hit the Alps for the first time."

"Great." Cari swallowed again. "How long does it last?"

"Just a day or two," offered John.

Cari moaned. "This is awful." *Not to mention embarrassing. I'm in a foreign country, and I'm too sick to even sit up.*

"Excuse me," said an unfamiliar male voice. Cari opened her eyes and saw a handsome man, perhaps in his mid thirties. "My name is Dr. Mueller. I couldn't help overhearing your conversation. Is there some way that I could assist you?"

Cari's cheeks flushed with renewed embarrassment. Then she frowned. "Dr. Mueller, you said?"

"Yes."

"Not Karl Mueller?"

"Yes, but how did you know that?"

"You're on my list of doctors."

"I beg your pardon."

"Dr. Kenneth Wilson, from *Cedar Sinai* in Los Angeles, gave me a referral list of doctors. You're one of them."

"Ken Wilson? I haven't seen him in a few years. He's a fine cardiologist."

"I know. He saved my life, more than once." She tried to sit up but found herself beaten back by dizziness. "But he didn't warn me about this. What can I do?"

"I'd suggest taking a dose of Gravol for the nausea. And you need to drink as much water as you can. Dehydration only compounds the problem." He reached for her wrist and studied her pulse. Then he felt her forehead. "The sooner the better, I'd say. Do you have a file with you?"

"From Dr. Wilson? Yes. It's in my bag."

"I'll get it," offered Tammy. "You don't need a guy digging around in here." She got the bag and soon had the manila folder in hand. "Here you go, Doctor." She kept looking. "And here's the

Gravol, Cari. Do you need one or two?"

"I don't know."

"May I see those, please?" asked Dr. Mueller. He took the package and read the label. "Two for now, another two in a few hours." He continued to browse through the file, his eyebrows furrowing at some points. "You're awfully young to have a pacemaker," he remarked.

"It's better than the alternative," mumbled Cari. She managed to swallow the two pills with a sip of water. "If I try to drink any more I'll just throw up. I'd hate to ruin your pants, John." He gently touched her hair.

"They could be washed. Just try to rest. We're still more than an hour from St. Moritz."

Cari later decided that it was one of the longest hours of her life.

"Can you sit up?" asked John when they pulled into the station at St. Moritz.

"I'll try," replied Cari. He helped her up, but she could feel the color draining from her face.

"Just lean against me for a few seconds. We'll wait until everyone else is off the train, and then I'll carry you."

"No."

"Seems to me we've had this discussion before. I don't think you've got much choice."

"I just want to go and sleep somewhere. Anywhere."

"You will, soon."

Dr. Mueller joined them once more. "Where will you be staying? I'd like to come by and check on you in the morning."

"I've got the address right here," said John, reaching into his jacket for his wallet.

"Fine, fine. You've chosen well, I see." He grinned at them as he handed back the paper. "My aunt will take wonderful care of you. And I'm sure that a couple of days in a feather bed will help you immensely. Fraulein Daniels."

"Ready to go?" asked John. Cari tried to nod, but her head hurt too much. "Okay, just lean on me." In a moment, she was in his arms and he was making his way down the aisle.

"I'll bring your stuff, Cari," Tammy said from behind them. "And Gilles can bring yours, Mon Ami."

Cari briefly wondered what Gilles was thinking about the whole situation. He hadn't said much since Chur. And for the moment, she was too sick to care what he was thinking.

Cari didn't even open her eyes in the cab that took them to a small chalet in St. Moritz Bad. She was content to lean against John's sturdy chest. Once there, John left her and Tammy while he went to meet Frau Mueller. She heard bits and pieces of the conversation, and somehow knew that she was going to meet a Swiss equivalent to Julie Patterson.

John carried her inside, up a narrow staircase, and into a sunny room, completely paneled in darkened pine. Then he eased her onto the bed and she sighed. "Can I sleep now?" she wondered aloud.

John laughed. "For as long as you like." She thought he kissed her cheek, but she wasn't certain. The fresh smelling sheets and plump pillows were dazzling her senses.

"Thank you," she mumbled. That was the last she said or heard for several hours.

Gilles checked into the *Walhaus* while the others settled in at the Mueller's. His mood was far from cheery. *First she slaps my face. Then she practically ignores me. Then she lets Maxwell come to the rescue as though he's some kind of hero. She didn't even speak to me. Now they're staying in the same house together. Why did I agree to this? Then again, Cari is too sick at the moment to care where she is or who she's with. Besides, Tammy is there too, sharing the room, I believe. That should help to keep them away from each other.*

He paced his room and rubbed his hands over his face. *I came here because of a painting. Not because of Cari. I'd do well to remember that.* He frowned once more. *And Maxwell had better remember the same thing.*

"How are you feeling?" asked Tammy when Cari awakened after supper.

"How long have I slept?" countered Cari as she rolled onto her back, still fully clothed.

"A few hours. Do you want something to eat or drink?"

Cari frowned. "Just some water, I think. And more Gravol." She moaned as she tried to sit up. "I can't believe I'm so sick. I'm missing half of this trip. It's ridiculous." She took the pills from Tammy with a shaky hand. "Thanks, Kid. I'm sorry to be such a lousy roommate." She managed a few sips of water.

"Do you want some help getting into a nightshirt?" Tammy suggested. "Or are you just going to stay like that?"

Cari looked down at her rumpled clothes. "This is pathetic. Yes, I should get changed." She looked around the room. "By the way, where is the bathroom? Can't say I saw much on the way in."

"It's right next to us, between our room and Mr. Maxwell's. He's worried about you, you know." Cari was too embarrassed to meet her look. "And Gilles was practically seething with envy. Good thing he's staying at a hotel, instead of with us."

"Give it a rest, Tammy. Please. I can't handle a major discussion right now."

"Sure. Want me to get your stuff out for you while you're in the bathroom?"

"I'd appreciate that, provided I can make it to the bathroom." She eased herself to the edge of the bed. She eventually got to her feet and held onto the bedpost.

"You look awful, Cari," Tammy remarked.

"Thanks a lot." She very slowly made her way across the room, and leaned against the door. "Care to show me which way to the bathroom?"

"Sure. But you'll have to move away from the door."

Cari managed to get to the bathroom and back without incident. She even got into a night shirt with a little help from Tammy. Then the dizziness was back with a vengeance. "Goodnight," she muttered, pulling the eiderdown up over her shoulder. Sleep took over before she even heard Tammy's reply.

Chapter 14

"Guten morgen, Fraulein," Frau Mueller said as she brought a tray of food into the bedroom. "Would you like something to eat?"

Cari eased herself to a sitting position with her back against the headboard. She smiled at the woman, though she could feel her cheeks flushing with color. "Thank you, Frau Mueller."

"My nephew is downstairs, Fraulein, and he wishes to see you — but not before you eat something, he said." She set the tray down on the night stand. There was a bowl of muesli, a roll with butter, and a mug of something hot. "It's not really tea or coffee, Fraulein. It's made from grain. No caffeine."

"It smells good," Cari replied. "I'm so sorry for the inconvenience I caused yesterday. I had no idea that I'd get so sick."

"You are only one of many. Not everyone adjusts readily to mountainous areas." Frau Mueller patted Cari's right hand. "I'm just glad that you're feeling better this morning. Your friend, Herr Maxwell, has been quite worried about you."

"Oh." Cari felt extremely self-conscious. "He's rather protective."

"Well, enjoy your breakfast. I'll come back for the tray a little later."

Cari ate a token amount of the food, and drank part of the

hot grain beverage before Dr. Mueller came to check on her. This time he was carrying a black bag with him, reminding her of an old episode of *Marcus Welby, MD*

"How are you feeling this morning, Fraulein?" he asked as he gently took her wrist in his hand.

"Much better, thank you." She remained silent as he checked her blood pressure.

"Good. But I don't want you doing anything much today yet. Perhaps go downstairs with your friends. Read, rest in bed if you like. I'll come see you again tomorrow. By then you should be feeling quite yourself." He took out his stethoscope and listened to her heart and lungs for a full minute. "No problems there. Just rest while you get used to the altitude."

"I don't think I'd be able to do otherwise," Cari remarked. "I'm awfully tired considering I've been sleeping since yesterday."

"That's quite normal." He patted her right hand, much as his aunt had done earlier. "You've gone through quite an ordeal in the past sixteen months. I'm sure that a little altitude sickness shouldn't be much of a problem for you."

Cari laughed. "True. But I would have enjoyed seeing the sights, before seeing a doctor. No offense."

"None taken, Fraulein." He got to his feet and closed his bag. "Have a good day. I'll see you in the morning."

"Thank you, Dr. Mueller."

"You're welcome." He nodded just before leaving the room.

Cari closed her eyes for a moment. *Well, I certainly feel better than I did yesterday. But I didn't need a warning about not exerting myself. I couldn't if I tried. But, I suppose I could get dressed and make an appearance downstairs. I don't even know if there is an Herr Mueller to go with Frau Mueller.* She flicked the bedding off of her legs and got out of bed. To her immense relief, the room didn't sway as it had the day before. *Look out St. Moritz — here I come.*

"Good morning," John said as he got to his feet. He walked to the foot of the stairs and reached for Cari's hand. "Glad to see you looking so much better."

"Thank you. But I guess I'm still under house arrest for today. I'm not sure how exciting that will be for you and Tammy."

"Don't worry about us. We'll take a walk around while you curl up with a good book or Frau Mueller's photo albums." He led her over to a beautiful rocking chair just as Frau Mueller entered the room with Tammy.

"Here you are," Tammy said with a grin. "I was about to go hunting for you. How was breakfast?"

"Just fine, thanks. And I'm glad to report that it all stayed down."
"My nephew wants me to be sure that you drink plenty of water today, Fraulein Daniels," Frau Mueller put in. "Even if you don't feel thirsty, he said."

"I understand." Cari gently tipped back the rocker and immediately frowned. "I think I'd better stick with stationary furniture today yet." She got up and went to a small loveseat by the fireplace. "That's better."

"Still dizzy?" Tammy asked.

"A little. John tells me you two are going to go for a walk. Why don't you pick up some postcards for me?"

"Sure. Then you could write some later today. That shouldn't take a lot of energy, should it?"

"Hopefully not." Cari covered her mouth to stifle a yawn. Then she laughed. "You'd be surprised."

"I think Gilles is planning to come over this afternoon some time," John remarked, his former smile noticeably absent.

"Where is he staying?" Cari asked. "I've forgotten." She rubbed her forehead. "I guess I've been forgetting a few things lately."

"The Waldhaus. It's quite a nice hotel. I'm sure you'll enjoy having dinner there some evening." When she made no reply, he turned towards Tammy. "Well, Ma Petite, shall we go?"

"Yeah, let's. See you later, Cari."

"Bye."

After they left, Frau Mueller sat down on the rocker that Cari had vacated. "He's such a nice man," she remarked. "He's been coming here for years. And he always brings such lovely gifts."

"Gifts! That reminds me," muttered Cari, her cheeks a bright pink. "Up in my suitcase, I have something for you." She started to get up, but Frau Mueller motioned for her to sit down.

"Never mind. I wasn't hinting. I enjoy having guests, but I must say that Herr Maxwell is one of my favorites. He reminds me very much of my son, Rudy."

"He certainly fits in around here, doesn't he? Blonde hair, blue eyes, tall. He loves hiking." She shook her head carefully. "But his grandparents were from England."

"He thinks very highly of you, Fraulein. When he wrote to us about having you and the young girl staying here, he said that you were someone special, and he wanted to be sure that you'd be comfortable during your stay here."

"I-I had no idea he said any such thing. He just told me that he'd taken care of the arrangements."

"Don't you return his interest, Fraulein?" Frau Mueller asked, obviously surprised.

"Well, I-you see we-" She bit her lip. "I work with John back home, and we're good friends. But I've been seeing someone else recently."

"Ah." Frau Mueller nodded. "This Gilles person?"

"Yes. Gilles Rodriquez. He's from Mexico. Actually, John and I are both here because of Gilles. We're working for him."

"Some matter of art, isn't it?"

"Yes. As a matter of fact, you may be able to help us, Frau Mueller. The owner of this missing painting lives here in St. Moritz. Or, at least she used to. Louise St. Denis. Have you heard of her?"

Frau Mueller's face blanched at the question. "Louise St. Denis? Yes, I know her. But I don't understand how she could be connected with this."

"She sold a painting to Gilles' father, but it never arrived," Cari explained.

Frau Mueller shook her head. "Frau St. Denis only had one painting worth selling, and I can assure you, she wouldn't have parted with it."

Cari was more puzzled than ever. "But she did. You say *Frau* St. Denis. She's married then?"

"She was. Her husband was killed in an accident just a few weeks ago. I haven't seen Louise since the funeral."

"A few weeks ago? That's when all this confusion started. No wonder she hasn't been answering the correspondence from Gilles or his father." Cari was suddenly very fatigued and closed her eyes. She opened them a moment later. "How was her husband killed?"

"He was hit by a car while crossing a dark street. There were no witnesses."

"How awful," murmured Cari, even as the hair stood up on the back of her neck. *Something isn't right in all this. Actually, a few things don't add up. A painting that shouldn't have been sold. A husband killed in a hit and run accident. This whole scenario may not be too cut and dried after all.*

John and Tammy returned at lunch time, only to find Cari sound asleep on the loveseat. Frau Mueller ushered them into the kitchen area, assuring them that Cari could have something to eat later.

"How can she still be tired?" Tammy asked. "She slept from seven last night until eight this morning."

"Tammy, you should know as well as I do that Cari doesn't have the same stamina as the rest of us. Frankly, I think she does amazingly well as it is. I'm sure she'll be feeling better by tomorrow. For now, don't give her a hard time about it."

"Of course not."

Cari woke up just as the others were finishing. She was embarrassed to have slept through another meal, but Frau Mueller told her she was glad she was resting so well. Cari had no sooner finished eating than there was a knock at the door. She noticed John tense his shoulders. Frau Mueller ushered Gilles into the living area a moment later. In his right hand was a box of Swiss chocolates, in his left, a bouquet of wildflowers. He gave the flowers to Frau Mueller, and the chocolates to Cari.

"Thank you, Gilles," Cari replied with a blush. "I guess you remembered my weakness for chocolate."

"I did. How are you feeling today?" he asked as he reached for her hand.

"Much better. I've slept most of the time since I got here. I'm under doctor's orders to take it easy for the rest of the day. He'll let me know tomorrow morning if I'm allowed to be out and about. What have you been up to?"

"Not a lot, actually. I've made a few inquiries about Louise St.Denis."

"So have I."

"Without leaving the house?"

"Frau Mueller knows her." She explained what the woman had told her.

Gilles simply nodded. "I've been getting much the same story. Louise St. Denis would never have sold that painting. And then her husband was killed—right about the time it should have been shipped to my father."

"I think we'll have to be very careful with this Gilles."

"What do you mean?"

"Hit and run isn't always what it seems, Gilles. He may have been murdered."

"Why?"

"Because of the painting. I think we'd better see what we can find out about Mr. St. Denis before we try to talk with his wife. I'd hate to ask her the wrong questions."

"I suppose you're right. Have you talked with Maxwell about this yet?"

She shook her head. "I haven't had the chance. Why don't we all sit outside for a little?"

"Are you allowed out?" he asked with a slight frown.

"And why not?"

"Just checking."

Chapter 15

Frau Mueller had invited Gilles to stay for supper, and he'd gladly accepted, sitting next to Cari during the meal. Tammy and John helped to keep the conversation going during the light meal. Cari was flagging by the time the table was cleared. Gilles said that he should be heading back to the hotel, and give his father a call. Cari walked him outside, her hand in his.

"Gilles, I want to apologize for the other night," she said softly. "I can't exactly explain why I was in such a horrible mood, but I'm sorry for treating you like I did."

He gently squeezed her fingers. "That's okay. I realized that I've likely been crowding you. I haven't given you much chance to sort out your feelings."

"I suppose that's been part of the problem for me." She smiled at his understanding. "Thank you for coming over today, and for the chocolates." She laughed. "If I can hide them from Tammy, they should last me for a while."

"You have such a beautiful smile, Cari," he whispered. He reached up and caressed her cheek. This time Cari leaned towards him, rather than pulling away. He flashed her a smile just before kissing her. "Goodnight. Rest well."

Cari surprised them both by kissing him back. "Goodnight, Gilles. I'll see you tomorrow."

She waved to him as he walked to his rental car, a late model *Passat.* Then she stepped back into the house, only to be met by the penetrating gaze of John Maxwell.

"Well, I'd say you're adjusting just fine, Fraulein," said Dr. Mueller the next morning. "Maybe not ready for any serious hiking just yet, but well enough to enjoy getting around."

"Thank you. I'm looking forward to that."

"I'll leave you my card, in case you need to contact me." He set it on the night stand. "Please let me know if you're having *any* problems. Dr. Wilson does not want you taking any chances on this trip."

"I'm aware of that. He's a bit like a protective father," she remarked with a smile. "But I'm grateful, truly. And thank you for your help. I'm sure I'll do just fine with your aunt's wonderful cooking, too."

"Everyone else seems to."

"Dr. Mueller, may I ask you something?"

"Certainly."

"If Frau Mueller is your aunt, how is it that you've never met John Maxwell before? He's been coming here every August for several years."

"That's quite simple, really. I've been practicing in Bern until just this past year." He grinned broadly. "But I just got married at Christmas, and this is my wife's home area. So, I moved my practice to here."

"And you get to take care of all the sick tourists?"

"Something like that."

"What are you going to do about a rental car?" John asked during breakfast. "I know a good place not far from here."

"I hadn't really given it much thought," Cari replied, taking a sip of the hot beverage, realizing that she was growing accustomed to the taste of it. "What did you rent?"

"Same as always, a four wheel drive vehicle. They may not be flashy, but they're ideal for the kind of trekking around I like to do."

"I think you should rent a sports car, Cari," Tammy said between bites of her cheese. "That'd be fun."

Cari shook her head. "Tammy, do you have any idea how much it would cost to rent a sports car? Gilles is paying for this, remember? I have to be reasonable."

Tammy frowned. "Shucks."

Cari turned back to John. "So, where's this dealer I should go to?"

"Not far from here. He's a little more expensive, but always reliable. And he's never minded if I switched vehicles during my stay."

"Could Tammy and I just walk there?"

"I think so. Are you sure you're not too tired?"

"I'm fine, John," she replied with a sigh. "Don't pester me."

Cari stared at the very pregnant receptionist behind the counter. "Trish? Trish Henshaw?"

The young woman lifted her head and looked directly at Cari.

Then she got to her feet, as hastily as her condition would allow. "Cari? What on earth are you doing here? I haven't seen you since my wedding. By the way, my name is Lehman now. It has been for over three years." She noticed Cari's cane in her right hand. "What happened?"

"Well, I see we've both been out of touch for a while," remarked Cari. "I retired in spring of '92."

"Accident?" asked Trish, sounding a bit hopeful.

"I wish. A drug user with misinformation." She suddenly remembered Tammy beside her. "This is Tammy Benson. Her dad is Mike's new partner."

"Pleased to meet you," said Trish as she shook Tammy's hand.

"Tammy, this is a friend of mine. We went to the police academy together. Then Trish came here for a ski vacation, and Hans Lehman swept her off her feet. She came back long enough to get married." She turned back to Trish. "When is the baby due?"

"Three or four weeks," Trish replied with a sigh. "Feels like forever yet. Hans lets me come into the office just so he can keep an eye on me." A door opened and closed behind them. "Speak of the devil. Hans, come and see who's here. Do you remember Cari Daniels? We were on the LAPD together."

Cari suddenly recalled part of the reason that Trish had found it easy to leave the force and move to a new country. Hans Lehman was stunning. And his smile could do in just about any female, she was sure. It was hard to keep from laughing at the open mouthed expression on Tammy's face. Cari held out her hand.

"Nice to see you again, Hans. And congratulations on the coming baby."

"Thank you," he replied, his warm gaze flitting to his wife for a moment. "What brings you here? Vacation? Trying to follow in Trish's pattern?"

Cari blushed, even before Tammy's quick retort. "As if she needs any help. There are already two guys fighting over her." Tammy had the good grace to slap her hand over her mouth, but not before Trish raised an eyebrow.

"This I'd like to hear all about, Cari. What are you doing for lunch?"

"We already have plans. Actually, I'm here on business. And I need to rent a car."

"Business? What are you doing?"

"I'm a private investigator, for a law firm in LA, *Richards & Richards*."

"Not just *any* firm. They handle only the most famous and the richest people in that city, Cari. How on earth did you land a job there?"

"Long story. Seriously, I need to rent a car."

"Sure. How long?"

"The story or the rental?" They both laughed. "I don't know. Three or four weeks, maybe. I should probably pay for a week at a time."

Trish looked from Cari to Hans, then back again. "Still do any rally driving?"

"Not lately. Why?"

"Have I got a car for you!"

"What are you talking about, Trish? I didn't see anything in the lot but sedans and four wheel drives."

"I'm talking about *my* car. You'd love it." She reached for her husband's hand. "What do you say, Hans? Cari is an expert driver. Besides, you haven't let me use it for months now."

"Trish, what are you up to?" Cari asked.

"I suppose we could make an exception—for an old friend," Hans replied. "A special lease, just the insurance cost, and fuel of course."

"Wait a sec you two. I haven't even got a clue what you're talking about, let alone agreed to anything."

"Oh, you'll agree, Cari. And you'll have lunch with me tomorrow too. We have a *lot* of catching up to do by the sounds of things. Just go around back with Hans while I type up the agreement."

"I don't know if I should trust you, Trish. Just what will I be driving?"

"You are *not* going to believe what Cari rented, Mon Ami," exclaimed Tammy as they ate lunch. "Not in a million years."

"Well, suppose you show me after we eat? Maybe take me for a drive?" Cari grinned at Tammy, but said nothing. John paused his fork on the way to his mouth. "Just what are you two hiding?"

"You'll see," Tammy laughed.

"How did you manage this?" was John's incredulous response as he stood next to a bright red Porsche 911 Carrera 4. "And what is it going to cost Rodriquez?"

"Actually, it's costing me less than anything else they had," Cari replied as she leaned against the shiny sports car. "You didn't tell me who the owners were, John. Trish Lehman is a friend of mine."

"So I see. This is her car, isn't it? I mean, I saw her driving it last year, I think."

"That's right. She thought I might have fun with it while I'm here. No rental charge, just insurance coverage. How could I refuse?"

"Rodriquez is going to have a fit, you know," John added.

"Why? I told you, it was cheaper than—"

"Because he still thinks of you as some sort of invalid, doesn't he? I'm sure he doesn't expect to see you driving around in a car like this." John grinned at her. "This could be very interesting." He crossed his arms over his chest. "Very interesting indeed."

"You're driving a *what*?" Gilles exclaimed when Cari met him at the Waldhaus for dinner.

"A Porsche 911 Carrera 4," she replied quietly.

"I heard you the first time!" he snapped.

"Then why did you ask me again?"

"Do you have any idea how powerful those cars are?"

"As a matter of fact I do. Two-hundred forty-seven horse power, capable of 157 miles per hour. Too bad the speed limit only goes to 75 in this country. Maybe we could make a quick trip into Germany or Italy."

"You're crazy!" he remarked, even as he held her chair for her at their table.

"I've been told that before," she replied evenly, trying to remain civil, despite his outburst. Then she began to laugh out loud.

"What is so funny?" he demanded.

"I was just thinking of your father, Gilles. Can you imagine the look on his face if I drove up to your villa in that car? He'd likely have a coronary on the spot."

A smile slowly crept across his face. "Very possible." He began to laugh with her. "And you know what else? My mother would likely ask you for a ride in it."

Chapter 16

"So, Cari," Trish began as they sat together at the kitchen table, "tell me about these two guys who are fighting over you."

"Tammy was exaggerating, Trish. They haven't exactly been *fighting*. Competing maybe, but not fighting."

"Still sounds interesting. Who are they?" Trish watched as color flooded her friend's cheeks. "Out with it, Cari."

"You know at least one of them."

"Really? Somebody from the force?"

Cari shook her head. "No, a lawyer. Apparently he rents a vehicle from you every August. A four wheel drive."

Trish was crazy with curiosity. "Who?"

"John Maxwell."

Trish's eyebrows touched her hairline. "You've got to be kidding! That man has had women after him since I've known him, and before that, according to Hans. He never even has dinner with any of them. How did you manage to catch his eye?"

"I have no idea." Cari shrugged her slim shoulders. "We both work at the same place. I met him my first day there. And, well, it seems that being a bachelor is losing its appeal these days."

"You could do a lot worse, Cari."

Cari rolled her eyes. "I'm aware of that, Trish." She smiled then. "But you also haven't met his competition either. Gilles

Rodriquez. He's from—"

"Mexico."

"How could you possibly know that? I just met him in March myself. And I'd never heard of him before."

"That's because you never paid any attention to professional soccer. Ten years ago, he was a household name in the sport. He was on magazine covers. He was gorgeous."

"Still is," murmured Cari. "Now he's a dealer in international art."

"How did you meet him?"

"While on vacation in Puerto Vallarta."

Trish sat and shook her head. "Only you could pull off something like this. Me—I had to come skiing in St. Moritz to find a husband. You find a guy at work and one while on vacation."

Cari laughed. "There was also Tammy's dad. He's a handsome widower. He was interested, but there was just no spark on my side. He's an ace *Scrabble* opponent though."

"So, what are you investigating?"

"A missing painting. Chances are you know the owner, Louise St. Denis."

"Louise? Sure. She's my massage therapist. I mean she has been, until just recently."

"Until her husband, Pierre, was killed?"

"Yes. How did you find out about that?"

"Frau Mueller. She also said that Louise only had one painting of value, and that she never would have agreed to sell it."

Trish furrowed her brow. "No, Louise wouldn't have been willing. But Pierre would have."

"What do you mean?"

"Pierre St. Denis was in debt to every gaming house around here, very heavily in debt. Rumor has it that he owed some dangerous people a lot of money. I wouldn't be surprised if he sold the painting."

"But how could he? It was registered in Louise's name."

"Cari, surely you've heard of *forgery* haven't you? Pierre could have stooped to that, if he was desperate enough. Chances are, he was more than desperate."

Cari shook her head. "And just who are some of these 'dangerous people' that he owed money to?"

Trish reached across the table and took hold of Cari's hand. "Don't even try to find out. They don't take questioning very kindly."

"Do you think Pierre St. Denis was murdered?"

"Quite possibly, but you'd never be able to prove it. And even if you did, it would be too dangerous to do anything with the proof."

"Why?"

"Cari, these are *powerful* people that I'm talking about. They have connections in very high places. Let the Swiss authorities handle them. Don't try to interfere. Please."

"I've never known you to back away from a challenge before, Trish."

"I've never been so happy before, Cari. I have a wonderful husband, and we're looking forward to this baby. I'd hate to see you meet with an 'accident' while here. Go ahead and ask Louise about the painting, but don't go after these other guys, especially while using *my* car. Promise me that you'll be careful."

"I promise. Besides, this may not be such a big mystery anyway. Maybe Louise did decide to sell the painting, in order to help Pierre pay off his debts. Wives have done that before, haven't they?"

"Some wives, yes, but Louise, no. Ask her about the painting.

You'll find out for yourself why she'd never willingly part with it. Anything else she'd gladly give up, but not that."

"What is so special about this painting?"

"Ask her for yourself. She'll tell you." Trish smiled as she watched Cari unconsciously rubbing her right thigh. "And have her schedule in some massage therapy. She's the best there is."

Cari blushed again and moved her hand.

"Still sore? Last spring you said?"

"Yes. And yes. April 4th, 1992." Cari's facial expression immediately sobered. "A twenty-seven year old guy spaced out on crack." She forced a smile. "Aside from the cane I've got a metallic ribcage, and a pacemaker."

"What did he do to you?"

"Smashed my left side with his steel soled boot. His knee was enough to do in my right thigh. I didn't walk for weeks. Actually, I didn't even *breathe* on my own for a few weeks."

"What happened to the guy?"

"Mike shot him. He was killed instantly."

Trish tightened her hold on Cari's hand. "I'm so sorry. I know how much you enjoyed being a cop."

Cari managed a smile. "Yeah. I even made it as far as sergeant before I had to retire."

"How did you end up at a law firm?"

"I was hired as head of the security department."

Trish nodded. "Then you became an investigator?"

"That's right."

"But how did you end up at *Richards & Richards*?"

"Actually, it was Luke and Rebecca Richards' son who tried to kill me."

Trish shook her head as she leaned forward. "They hired you—after what happened to their son?"

"Yes. You see, they pushed for an inquest, because of the use of 'deadly force'. I was barely even walking by then, but I didn't have a choice. Anyway, I collapsed during cross examination—that was before the permanent pacemaker was in. Well, Rebecca Richards kind of came to her senses, I guess. She almost fired the lawyer who was handling the inquest for her. After a couple of weeks, I got a letter from her, apologizing for ever demanding an inquest in the first place. She asked me to call her, which I did. She met with me and offered me the job. I've been working there since last September."

"You make it sound like it's no big deal, Cari. You almost died. You had to change careers. Your health isn't what it used to be, and you sit here and calmly tell me about it."

"Would you rather have me go into hysterics over things that I had no control over?"

"Of course not. Look, I'm just glad that you're okay. And that you're here for a little while. Just please be careful."

"I will. Especially with your car."

"You seem to attract dangerous people like a magnet," commented John as Cari went over her conversation with Trish. "She's referring to European mobs, isn't she?"

"I assume so."

"Have you warned Rodriquez about this?"

"Yes. He just told me that he'd look up some former bookies from his soccer days. They might be able to shed some light on the subject."

John put his hand on her shoulder and turned her towards him. "Worried about him?"

"Gilles? Not really. Mostly I'm wishing that I hadn't brought Tammy along. This could be far more complicated than any of us thought."

"What would we do without our favorite chaperone around?" he teased, even as he gently cupped her face in his hands. "Make life more 'complicated'?" He kissed her before she even had a chance to reply. He could feel her leaning against him, her hands on his chest. *Why won't she admit to what she's really feeling?* He moved to put his arms around her, but heard the sound of a throat being cleared.

"Well, *excuse me*, but I think I came along at a good time," Tammy said in an authoritative tone.

John released Cari, and she turned away, her back to both of them, likely trying to regain some semblance of composure. Then he turned to face Tammy, feeling unreasonably annoyed with her. "Taking your role just a bit too seriously aren't you?" he snapped.

"Somebody had better." She stood there with her arms crossed over her chest, a defiant expression on her face.

Cari turned around, still wiping tears from her cheeks. She didn't look directly at either of them as she moved towards the house. "Excuse me. I think I'd better go inside now."

"Sounds like a great idea to me," Tammy replied. She waited where she was as Cari moved past her. "Don't push her, Mon Ami. She's been hurt before, and I don't want you or Gilles to put her through that again. She's here to do a job, not to try to settle a score between the two of you. Back off—or you just may make the choice for her. Good night." She didn't wait for him to answer before she made her way to the door.

John stood and stared after her. *She's worse than having a nosy grandmother! And she's far too smart for her own good.* He slowly headed for the entrance. *How can she judge people so accurately? Are Rodriquez and I both pushing Cari? Are we forcing her to choose between us? What if she does? Much as I'd like for her to choose* me *I'd hate to see her get hurt. She doesn't deserve that. She deserves to be happy*. He paused at the door. *Am I willing to back off while she decides for herself?*

Chapter 17

"Are you sorry that I interrupted you and John last night?" Tammy asked as soon as Cari was awake in the morning. She knew that Cari had cried herself to sleep, muffling the sobs in the thick feather pillow.

Cari shook her head as she sat up and leaned against the headboard. "No. I'm just sorry that you even had anything to interrupt in the first place." She rubbed her hands over her face. "I'm afraid that I'm being a terrible example to you on this trip, Tammy. I hate to think what your dad would have to say about it."

"Cari, you're not being a terrible example. But you are confused, aren't you? About John and Gilles, I mean."

"Very," Cari replied with a sigh. "How can I say that I'm actually *dating* Gilles, and then turn around and kiss John?" She rested her head against her bent knees.

"Maybe you shouldn't be dating Gilles at all," offered Tammy. She waited for Cari to look at her. "I mean, if you're so attracted to John, then why are you seeing someone else?"

"Because John isn't—"

"A Christian. I realize that. But is that a good enough reason to be dating Gilles? I mean, before you met Gilles, you were attracted to John, but you were handling it okay, weren't you?"

"Most of the time," Cari remarked with a faint smile. "But not always. What's your point, Kid?"

"Just that Gilles is a convenient excuse not to think about John not being a Christian."

"What? Now you're not making any sense."

"I'm trying to." Tammy chewed on her bottom lip for a minute. "Okay, let me give you another example. You went out with my dad, right?"

"Yes, but—"

"But you just wanted to be friends. There was no real confusion about who you liked, was there?"

"No, but—"

"But my dad is not as persistent as Gilles, is he? When you said you wanted to be friends, he accepted that. Why is Gilles so different? I mean, the guy is a hunk, and he's rich, but do you even have anything in common with him—besides the fact that he's a Christian?"

Cari made no comment. She simply sat and stared at Tammy for what seemed like ages. Then fresh tears formed in her eyes. "Now I really feel like an idiot!"

"Hey, Cari, that's not what I meant to do at all!"

"I know. But you're right, Tammy. I barely know Gilles. I didn't even know the guy used to play pro soccer until Trish told me yesterday! I know what he does for a living, and that he doesn't get along too well with his father, but that's about it. What on earth am I doing dating this guy?"

"I think you're lonely," Tammy replied in a softer tone.

"That's not a very good reason." Cari clutched the eiderdown in her hands. "Yes, I'm lonely. I guess I have been for quite a while. I still want to get married. Have kids." She wiped at the tears in her eyes. "And I'm already past thirty. Time isn't going to stand still just for my benefit."

Tammy got out of her bed and went to sit on Cari's. She reached for her hands and felt them shaking. "Cari, I'd really hate to see you marry the wrong guy, just because you didn't want to wait for God's best." To her surprise, Cari laughed and pulled her into a firm hug.

"What would I do without you, Kid?! You make more sense than a lot of adults I know. And here you are giving *me* the kind of advice that *I* should be giving *you*!" She held her out at arm's length. "I am so thankful that you came with me. But how is it that you know so much about male/female relationships at your age?"

"I'm observant. I don't get sidetracked by being a participant—yet."

"You'd better not! Your dad would have a fit if you came home with a long list of *male* pen pals."

"So, are you gonna be okay now?" Tammy asked, once more chewing her lip.

"I think so. I just have no idea what I'm going to say to Gilles at this point, or to John." Her cheeks flushed. "After what happened last night, what *can* I say?"

"There's always the truth, Cari."

"I suppose there is, even when it hurts."

"We need to talk," John said just as Cari stepped out into the hallway. "I told Frau Mueller that we'd be having breakfast somewhere else this morning."

Cari tried to think of an intelligent reply, but found herself staring instead.

"I thought we could go for a short walk. It's rather cool, but the sun is out."

"All right," she said in little more than a whisper. "Just give me a few minutes to get ready." *Even if that won't be enough!* "I'll meet you downstairs."

"Thank you."

Cari went into the bathroom and tried to calm her nerves. But all she could think about was the smell of John's aftershave, and how good he looked.

"About last night," Cari began.

"I apologize," John interrupted. "You've made it abundantly clear to me that unless we see eye to eye on spiritual matters, then I'm supposed to be content with friendship. I accept the blame for what happened last night."

Cari stopped walking along the path and turned to face him, shocked by what he'd said. "John, you weren't the only one who was kissing last night," she murmured. "I'm just as much to blame."

He sighed as he shoved his hands into the pockets of his canvas pants. "So, what shall we do about it?"

"I wish I knew!" She looked down at her feet for a moment. She fiddled with her cane. "Somehow, simple *friendship* just doesn't seem possible for us, does it?"

"Not really."

"But I can't agree to more than that either."

"It's called an impasse, Cari. We both know what we want. But neither of us will yield."

"I know." She met his warm gaze and found it very difficult to keep speaking, especially with him standing so close to her. "I realize that an impasse usually calls for compromise. But this is one area where I just can't. I'm sorry."

"So am I. But I'd be sorrier had I never met you." He smiled with his usual warmth. "You're a very special lady. Don't ever forget that."

"Thank you."

"So, how can I help you in regards to this missing painting?"

"Gilles, I'm truly sorry for ever giving you the impression that I cared for you more than I really did. I mean, I—I do care about you. I enjoy being with you. But I just can't see a serious relationship in our future. At least I can't see that it would be at all wise, for either of us." She swallowed so hard it almost sounded like she was gulping for air. "Loneliness and physical attraction are not enough to build a relationship on."

"I suppose not," he replied. He sat and looked at her across the table in the restaurant. "You're in love with John Maxwell, aren't you?"

Cari almost gasped as she inhaled. She used her standard answer. "He's not a Christian." Then she looked down at her crumpled napkin, knowing she couldn't face the intensity of his dark eyes.

"That's not what I asked you, Cari." He shifted in his chair. "I've been watching the two of you since we left Los Angeles. I think I knew for certain on the train from Chur to St. Moritz." Cari couldn't help but meet his gaze. "I didn't even know how to help you. I suppose that I'm too much like my father in that regard. Maxwell cared for you like a concerned husband. And you let him."

Cari shook her head. "I was so sick, Gilles. It wasn't really important."

"Yes it was. You see, I needed to be reminded of that kind of thing."

"I don't understand, Gilles. In Mexico, you—"

"In Puerto Vallarta, I knew it was a medical emergency. On the train you were just *sick*, nothing life threatening. Had I cared as much for you as Maxwell, I would have responded very differently." He smiled at her. "You were right. Loneliness and physical attraction are not enough to build a relationship on. Actually, my father told me much the same thing. I should have known better." He leaned back in his chair. "You still haven't answered my question."

Cari shook her head, her cheeks blazing with color. "I won't either."

"All right. Just make sure you invite me to the wedding. You are one bride that I would hate to miss."

"How dare you—?" Then she noticed his smile and let her shoulders relax. "*If* I ever get married—to *anybody*, I'll be sure to let you know."

"Thank you. Now, what shall we have for desert?"

"You survived?" Tammy asked as Cari crawled into bed.

"Yes. Telling the truth still works best."

"Even when it hurts?"

"Yes, even when it hurts."

Chapter 18

"So, what have you been able to find out from your connections Gilles?" Cari asked during lunch at the Waldhaus.

"That Pierre St. Denis owed a lot of people a lot of money," he replied. He put another slice of gruyere into his mouth.

"Any idea how much?"

"Close to half a million dollars, US. I can see why he might have resorted to forgery in order to sell his wife's painting."

"How do people even manage to accumulate that kind of debt? They must bet on nearly anything. And lose most of the time."

"Actually, they often win, which makes them willing to keep taking foolish risks. But you're right about what they'll bet on. Once addiction takes hold of a gambler, they will bet on almost anything."

"Like soccer matches?"

"Precisely, or races, or games, or even the weather conditions. If someone will lay odds on it, they'll place a bet." He shook his head. "When I used to play soccer, I had friends on the team who lost everything to gambling, even their families. One committed suicide because he couldn't see a way out of his trouble."

Cari took a sip of her Evian. "So, do you think that Pierre might have stepped in front of that car on purpose?"

He shrugged. "Possibly, since that would look like an accident.

Then, if he had any life insurance, his wife would be able to collect it. People will do almost anything when they're desperate enough. However, if that were true, the driver probably would have stayed at the scene."

"I suppose I should stop speculating and actually contact his wife. Your father must be getting impatient about this." She toyed with her napkin.

"He just wants it taken care of. Let me worry about how long it takes." He smiled. "Are you finally enjoying the scenery?"

"Very much," she replied, returning his smile. "I've always wondered what it would be like to visit a place like this." She laughed. "And what better way to see it than from behind the wheel of a Porche?"

He frowned. "Please be careful with that car, will you? And not just because it belongs to your friend."

"I'm a very sensible driver, Gilles. Don't worry."

"Fair enough." He signalled the waiter to come over. "Bill, please." Then he turned his attention back on Cari. "Tammy seems to be enjoying herself. What's she doing today?"

"John took her for a hike. I'm sure she'll have lots to talk about when they get back later."

"She really likes him, doesn't she?"

"Yes. She misses Rick more than she lets on. Frankly, I think she's good company for John, too. She's interested in a lot of the same things."

"Has she had any problems since that night in Paris?"

Cari shook her head. "No. She's been just fine. Like I said, she was embarrassed when she realized how much she'd over reacted. And talking it over with her dad helped, too."

Gilles smiled again. "Just keep her away from some of those Italian tourists. She's a very pretty girl."

"I know. And sometimes beauty is more of a problem than a help."

"Why do you say that?"

"Past experience," she murmured. "I think I should head back to the house now. I want to get some work done before John and Tammy get back." She looked up when he placed his hand on hers.

"Did I say something to offend you?" She shook her head. "Then why are you trying to rush off? You haven't even finished your coffee."

"Sorry, I guess I got distracted." She forced a smile, trying to shove aside unwelcome thoughts of Mark Hamilton. She rubbed her forehead with her free hand. "I'm still kind of tired, Gilles. I'm not very good company."

"And you're not a good liar either," he said with a smile. He patted her hand and sat back in the plush chair. "But I won't persist."

Cari felt her cheeks flush. "Thank you."

"Have you been walking too much again, Cari?" Tammy asked at supper. "You've been limping more since we got back."

"Do you miss anything? You're back only half an hour and you manage to assess my physical well being."

Tammy shrugged. "No, I don't miss much." She grinned then. "Dad even admits I'd likely make a good cop. Anyway, you didn't answer my question."

"Eat your supper, Tammy," Cari replied, her irritation reflected in her voice. Truth to tell, her leg was driving her crazy. She didn't know if it was from too much sitting, or driving, or walking, or stairs, but she knew it hurt. And, apparently, it was obvious to others as well.

"Yes, Ma'am," Tammy remarked, not quite able to keep the tinge of hurt from her voice.

The conversation seemed a bit stilted after that, with Tammy saying little, and Cari even less.

"Actually, your leg could provide a good way to meet with Madame St. Denis," John said to Cari as they sat near the fire after supper. "Didn't your friend say she's a massage therapist?"

"Yes, she did. But what difference does that make? We're here about a missing painting—not my leg." She clasped her hands together in her lap, realizing that her tone had been much sharper than she'd intended. "I'm sorry. I guess I've been kind of snapping at everybody today."

"Pain will do that, won't it?"

"Yes, but—" she sighed. "Oh, never mind." She watched as the flames danced in the hearth, wishing she were alone.

"Seriously, Cari, it would be better to meet Louise St. Denis as a client, especially if she hasn't been answering any correspondence from the Rodriquez family. This isn't the States. You don't just pick up the phone and announce who you are and what you want."

"I'm not that stupid, John! What kind of investigator do you think I am?"

"A good one," he replied evenly. "But you sometimes take too many chances. Besides, the whole protocol is different here. If you don't want to go through your friend, why not ask Dr. Mueller to arrange it if he can?"

Cari leaned back and crossed her arms over her chest. "And how am I supposed to work the painting into the conversation?"

"You don't. Let Rodriquez and me handle it. She'll find out soon enough who you are, and why you're here. In the meantime, she might be able to help you." He kept his gaze riveted to hers. "You're not fooling any of us, Cari. Maybe it's the stairs. In any case, your limp is worse, and your jaw is tense almost all the time. Frankly, you were pretty rude to Tammy earlier, and she doesn't have much choice about sharing the room with you."

Cari looked away again, too embarrassed to withstand further scrutiny. "All right, I'll see if Trish or Dr. Mueller can arrange anything for me. Satisfied?"

"For now, yes."

By the time Cari went upstairs, it was getting late. She hesitated at the door when she heard someone crying. She knew it had to be Tammy, but she didn't know whether to go in, or to leave the poor girl alone, so she could cry in private. *Well, I need to get ready for bed regardless. I guess I'll have to go in.* She opened the door as quietly as she could, and found Tammy curled up on her bed, sobbing into her pillow. *Now what?* She was still fishing for an answer when she closed the door.

"Do you want me to go back home, Cari?" Tammy asked, her tone as miserable as the expression on her face. "I mean I-I got in the way about John and Gilles. And now you're mad at me about what I said at supper. And I—"

Cari made her way to the bed and sat down, putting her arms around Tammy. "Whatever made you think I'd send you home? I'm glad you're here. It's not your fault that I've either been sick, or grumpy, or mixed up about guys for most of this trip. I'm sorry I've been so hard on you."

Tammy put her arms around Cari. "I thought maybe I was just being a pest. You looked so angry at supper tonight. I thought you might just tell me to call my dad and say that I was on my way back."

"Tammy, even if I was *furious* with you—which I'm not—I would certainly never send you all that way by yourself. Your dad would kill me. For that matter, so would John." She held her at arm's length, noticing the tears in her own eyes. "Now, I think we've both got jet lag, and we aren't used to the time change, or the climate, or altitude." She paused to smile. "And, if I don't miss my guess, a little bit of PMS as well?"

"Yeah," Tammy admitted, wiping at the tears on her flushed cheeks. "All of the above. Poor John, he gets stuck in the same house with a couple of grumpy females. Next thing we know, *he'll* be the one heading back to LA by himself."

"Either that, or he'll take a backpack and head off into the mountains to hide," replied Cari with a smile. "So, how be we both get ready for bed? And maybe by tomorrow we'll be in a better frame of mind."

"Deal." Tammy suddenly grinned. "Yeah. Remind me to tell you about Frau Mueller's nephew, Peter. She showed me some pictures, and he's real cute. And she said that he enjoys having pen pals. She's going to have him come over in a few days."

Cari rolled her eyes. "Great! You pry me loose from John and Gilles, and now I have to chaperone you."

"Nah! John already said that he'll be keeping an eye on me. You know, he sounded so much like Dad when he said it, too."

"Is that so? Well, this could be rather interesting."

"Could be."

Chapter 19

Cari had trouble getting out of bed the next morning, her right leg stiff and painful. When she moaned, Tammy looked over at her.

"You okay?" Tammy inquired, a frown on her face.

"No. I think John was probably right about needing massage therapy while I'm here." She forced a smile. "But don't you dare tell him that I said that. Just let him think it was all my idea." She tried to get up and grabbed hold of the bedpost, her knuckles whitening. "Um, could you please hand me my cane, Tammy?" She tried to sound casual, despite the pain radiating through her thigh and hip. She waited, jaw clenched, while Tammy got the cane for her. "Thanks, Kid."

"Do you want me to get your pills for you, Cari? You're really pale."

"I'll get them, but thanks for the offer." She tried to steady herself, but she faltered on the first step.

Tammy grabbed her arm. "This doesn't look good, Cari. Maybe you should call Dr. Mueller. If you can't walk on a level floor how do you plan to take the stairs?"

"Very carefully," Cari replied. She took another step and bit her lip against the pain. Then she sat back down on the bed, beads of perspiration on her forehead. "Okay," she breathed, "please ask

Frau Mueller to call her nephew. If my leg hurts this bad, I'll likely need stronger medicine than I've got here with me."

"Sure. Do you want me to bring you anything?"

Cari shook her head. "No thanks. I'll just try to rest again before I go to the washroom." She clasped Tammy's hand. "Please don't tell John about this. He already worries too much."

"If you say so. I'll be back in a few minutes." Tammy knotted the robe at her waist and left the room.

Cari took a deep breath and once more got to her feet. *What is the matter with me this morning? My leg hasn't been this bad for months. Not since I went to John's cabin.* She half walked, half stumbled to the door and opened it, just as John was passing in the hallway.

"Good morning," he said with a smile, though his gaze took in her cane.

"Good morning, John. Did you sleep well?" *I hope he heads straight to breakfast before Tammy gets back upstairs.*

"Yes, thank you. How about you?"

"Just fine." That much was true. It was after the sleep that problems started.

"Well, I'll see you later then. I'm supposed to meet Rodriquez for breakfast."

"Oh. Well, have a—a nice, I mean—I'll see you later, John." *Nice breakfast? Those two don't even like sharing the same room. Why are they meeting alone?*

"See you at lunch." He nodded slightly and then went down the stairs.

Cari made it to the bathroom and back to her bed just before Tammy came through the door.

"Dr. Mueller said he'll be over right after breakfast. And Frau Mueller insisted on making a tray for you. She'll be up in a couple of minutes."

"Thanks, Kid." Cari leaned back against the pillows and rubbed at her right thigh. "Does the Doctor know what the problem is?"

"Not really. His aunt just asked him to come over, because you weren't feeling well." Tammy sat down on the edge of the bed. "It's pretty bad isn't it? I mean, you hate to ask for help, never mind a doctor."

"Yeah, it's pretty bad. I'm not sure what the problem is, but it's bad." She let her breath out slowly. "I'm sorry to be such a lousy roommate, Tammy. Switzerland would probably be a lot more fun with someone else." She closed her eyes as a muscle spasm wrenched her thigh.

"I doubt it. I'm having a great time with you and John and Gilles. I'm glad you asked me to come." She touched Cari's hand gently. "Isn't there anything else I can do for you?"

Cari shook her head. "I'll just wait for Dr. Mueller's opinion. Then I'll probably pay a visit to a masseuse as soon as I can. You should go and eat your breakfast."

"I asked Frau Mueller if I could just eat up here with you."

"Thanks, Kid." Cari looked at the girl. "Thought I needed company, did you?"

"Of course not! I just wanted to tell you about Peter."

Cari was still laughing when Frau Mueller entered with the breakfast tray.

"Well, Fraulein I'd say that a visit to Louise St. Denis would be very wise. I can give you pain medication, but your muscles will just keep cramping. Louise should be able to help you. She's very good. And she's familiar with extensive injuries such as yours. She often tends to people who've had car accidents, or sports injuries. Would you like me to call her for you?"

"I'd appreciate that very much. I mean, I'd feel rather awkward to do it myself. 'Hi, I'm visiting from the States. I heard you're good.'" She shrugged. "I think a referral from you would be much better."

"Certainly. For the moment, I'll give you an injection for the pain. It'll relax more than your leg though, so please don't try to drive before this afternoon."

"Of course." She watched him load a syringe from a small labelled bottle. "Will this put me to sleep?"

"It might." He swabbed her thigh with alcohol. "Make a fist now." Cari was familiar with that diversionary tactic. The many nurses in the hospital had used it too. She still flinched as the needle went in. She let her breath out slowly, relaxing her hand as she did so. "There, that should help for a while. I'll go give Louise a call, and see when she could fit you in."

"Thank you, Doctor." Cari smiled. "I can see why Dr. Wilson had you on my list of physicians."

"You're quite welcome." He gathered his things and snapped his black bag shut. "I'll be back in a few moments." When he returned, he was smiling. "Louise said she's just starting to take clients again this week. She'll see you this afternoon, at three o'clock. My aunt has her address. That will give you plenty of time to rest."

"Wonderful," Cari replied. "What did you give me, Dr. Mueller? It seems to be *relaxing* everything."

"Nothing you haven't had before. I checked your records first. It's likely just because you haven't had an injection for a few months. You'll feel more of an effect." Just to be sure, he checked her pulse and blood pressure once more. "Just fine." He patted her hand. "Have a good rest. Call me again if you're having any more problems."

"I will." She closed her eyes as she slid down beneath the bedding. She fell asleep almost as soon as he shut the door.

Cari woke up just in time to get dressed and go downstairs for lunch. Tammy insisted on walking beside her. Her leg felt much better, but she knew that a massage would be helpful too. She mentioned the appointment to John, but didn't tell him that Dr. Mueller had given her anything for pain earlier. Neither did Tammy.

"How was your meeting with Gilles?" Cari asked.

"Fine," John replied, helping himself to another serving of meat and potatoes before Frau Mueller could insist upon it. "He seems to be making some headway on his side. And he filled me in about some of the legalities of dealing in international art. That should help me to plan a strategy, especially if we run into any discrepancies."

"Well, it sounds as though the two of you are keeping busy." Cari tried not to feel left out. *Well, at least I'll soon meet the lady in question. Then maybe I'll feel justified in coming all this way.* "Um, do you have plans for this afternoon, John?"

"Not in particular. Why?"

"I was just wondering if you could keep Tammy occupied while I'm gone. She hung around here all morning. I'm sure she'd like to go out."

"Actually, I'd love to find my dad a couple of gifts," piped in the girl. "I was thinking of a Swiss Army knife, and maybe a good watch." She shrugged. "A cop can always use stuff like that."

John smiled. "I know some good shops we could go to." He turned to face Cari and grinned. "I know you love to drive that Porche, but why don't Tammy and I drop you off for your appointment, and pick you up after?"

Cari frowned. "Well, I honestly don't know how long I'll be. It's likely easier if I just drive." She looked to Tammy. "Besides, I know from personal experience how much this kid likes to shop. She'll probably be dragging you around all afternoon."

"Good thing shops close here earlier than back home," John replied, trying to sound relieved. He laughed when Tammy made a face at him.

"Watch it, Mon Ami. I just may not get anything for you on this trip."

"Is that so? Well, I'll try to be on my best behavior then."

"You'd better be," Tammy replied.

Cari parked in front of a small chalet and frowned at the staircase. Then she got out of the car, cane in hand, and made her way to the front door. Since there was no doorbell, she knocked. A moment later the door was opened by a woman she assumed to be Louise St. Denis.

"Fraulein Daniels?" the woman asked.

"Yes. Are you Louise St. Denis?" Somehow this petite woman didn't match up to Cari's conception of a massage therapist. She had dark hair, and violet eyes. She was very pretty.

"Yes I am. Please come in." She stepped aside as Cari entered the small foyer. "My office is right this way. Please follow me." Louise led the way to what was likely meant to be a bedroom, just off the living area. Cari recognized the massage table, heating pads, etc. "If you'd like to sit down, I'll take a brief history before we begin."

"Didn't Dr. Mueller tell you anything?" Cari asked, somewhat surprised. She sat down on a vacant chair while Louise picked up a clipboard and a pen.

"Very little. Besides, since you're visiting from America, it would be better to get the information from you personally." She sat down opposite Cari. Then she began to ask a series of questions. Age, occupation, type of injury, how it occurred, type of treatment since the injury. Cari answered each question.

"So, it's been quite some time since you've had therapy?" Louise asked.

"I suppose I thought a year was long enough," Cari replied. "It seems that I was wrong."

"After such a traumatic injury, Fraulein, therapy may be necessary for several years, perhaps not on a regular basis, but for an extended period. For the moment, I think it would be wise to come here two or three times per week, for as long as you're in the area. I'm sure I'll be able to offer you some relief."

"I certainly hope so," Cari sighed. "I could barely walk this morning."

"It's not much better now, is it?" Louise countered, obviously well versed in leg injuries like Cari's.

"No, it isn't."

"Then let's get to work, shall we?" Louise asked, no hint of a smile in her tone or on her face.

Great—I get a super conscientious therapist this time. No joking around to get my mind off the pain. All business. Cari unfastened her jeans once Louise had left the room. *I'm looking forward to this about as much as a new filling.* She shifted on the table and winced. *Probably even less.*

Chapter 20

"I wonder how Cari's doing," Tammy said as she and John stepped out of a watch shop. "I think she really needed a massage."

"She didn't fool me this morning, you know," John replied.

"What are you talking about?" Tammy stopped on the sidewalk and stared up into his face.

"It was obvious how much pain she was in this morning, when I met her in the hallway. It always shows in her eyes—even when she tries to laugh it off. I've seen her do it several times." He shook his head. "I suppose I should be thankful that she's at least following my advice, and getting some help." He put his hand on Tammy's shoulder. "Don't worry; I won't make an issue of it. She always hates that."

"Yeah, she does. But you're still worried about her, aren't you?"

"Of course," he admitted. "She's driving around a strange city in a borrowed sports car, working on a potentially dangerous case, and her health isn't holding up too well." He sighed as he met her gaze. "Why wouldn't I worry?"

Tammy smiled and patted the hand on her shoulder. "She's a whole lot tougher than she looks, Mon Ami."

"Aren't we all?" he replied with a laugh. His smile faded when

Tammy remained sober.

"No. Some people aren't nearly as tough as they want others to believe. Like my dad—or you." She stepped away from his gentle touch. "Cari will be fine. Will you?"

Cari moaned and gritted her teeth while Louise worked the resistant muscles in her right thigh. She stared at the ceiling and tried to focus on the soft classical music that was playing. Nothing worked. Her brain was fully aware of the intense pain in her leg.

"Take some deep breaths, Fraulein," suggested Louise.

"It doesn't help," Cari replied, feeling like such a wimp. *I've had surgery, and blood transfusions, gone through months of therapy. Surely I can last through a massage.* Cari jerked when Louise worked towards her hip.

"Please try to relax," Louise ordered, sounding almost annoyed with Cari's behavior.

"Easy for you to say!" Cari shot back, tears stinging her eyes. "What are you doing to me? I don't remember a massage ever hurting this much before." Their gazes locked for a moment, Louise's warm hands still.

"You've waited too long," Louise replied, her voice calm, though not exactly gentle. "Two or three weeks might not have mattered, but a few months certainly have. Why haven't you been taking better care of yourself?"

"Look, I don't need to lie here and have you criticize me! I thought you could help me."

"I can. But this first time will hurt the most. A lot of scar tissue has accumulated. It's not easy to break it down."

Cari took a ragged breath and rubbed her hands over her face. "Okay. I'll try to relax, and to shut up." She bit her bottom lip. "I'm sorry for losing my temper."

Louise almost smiled for the first time. "That's all right. You should hear the men complain in similar circumstances. It shouldn't hurt like this after today."

"I'll try to take comfort in that thought," Cari sighed. She clasped her hands together at her waist. "Okay, go to it."

"How are you feeling now?" Louise asked after the two hour massage was finished.

"Like a rag doll," Cari mumbled. She was face down on the table, her back and shoulders utterly relaxed. "Thanks for making me stick it out. You're every bit as good as I was led to believe. Now, I just have to get myself up from here before I fall asleep."

"Just open the door when you're ready. Then we'll discuss some sort of schedule for you."

"Right." It took a few minutes, but Cari managed to get up, and dressed. She marvelled at the renewed mobility in her right leg. Oh, it still hurt, but she could walk better. She opened the door and Louise rejoined her, a bottle of Evian in her hand.

"Here, have a drink while we talk."

Cari took the bottle and moved towards a chair. "Thanks." She took a sip. "Wow, this is cold."

"Isn't that the best way to have water?" Louise asked, again a slight smile touched her lips. She sat down at her small desk and made some notations on Cari's chart. "Try soaking in a warm bath tonight, before going to bed. And some pain medication might be a good idea too. I don't want you to stiffen up right away."

"Likewise, I'm sure. Okay, when should I come again?"

"In a couple of days." She looked at Cari while she tapped her pen on the sheet of paper. "You are very lucky to be alive, Fraulein. Injuries like yours usually come from car accidents. You've done amazingly well, considering."

"*Considering* two men have tried very hard to kill me." She forced a smile. "Well, I may set off metal detectors everywhere I go, but at least I'm still alive to complain about it."

"Is that how you normally cope—by joking about it?"

"Not always." Cari frowned as she moved her cane from one hand to the other. "I guess I wasn't in much of a joking mood today, was I?" Louise shook her head. "Seriously, I've survived on prayer, and the help of friends. Don't get me wrong, I've had wonderful medical attention from the start, and I'm very thankful for that. But I still know that I wouldn't be alive, maybe *shouldn't* be alive, if it weren't for the grace of God. He's always been there—whether I've been joking, or screaming."

"It's been a very long time since I've met anyone with that kind of faith," murmured Louise, her expression as wistful as her voice. "Not since my grandmother." She tightened her hold on the pen.

"Well, I hardly hold the monopoly on faith. It's available to anyone who asks for it."

Louise shook her head again, her features hardening once more. "I might have believed that once, Fraulein. Not anymore." She cleared her throat. "Shall I schedule you for the same time for the next appointment?"

Back to business, eh? Safer ground. "That would be fine, I guess. And I'll try not to complain quite so much next time."

"I'm not too concerned with the complaints. Just as long as I see improvement." She set aside the pen, after writing on a business card. "I'll see you in two days, then." She handed the card to Cari. "I'll see you to the door."

Cari arrived back at the Mueller's' just as John and Tammy pulled up. She waved to them and got out of the car. She noticed Tammy give her a thumbs up sign when she reached the front door.

"Must have worked," Tammy called from the 4x4. "You're not limping so much now."

"It worked," Cari replied with a smile. "But at one point I thought I might kill her with *my* bare hands." She shook her head.

"That bad, was it?" John asked, his gaze warm and unnerving, like usual.

"That bad," she admitted. Then she shrugged. "But I agreed to go back. Am I a sucker for punishment, or what?"

John mounted the steps with Tammy. "You may be many things, Cari, but a 'sucker' is definitely not one of them."

"Thanks—I think." She felt embarrassed by his statement. It made her wonder what he'd meant by 'many things'. "Well, guys, let's go find out what Frau Mueller is whipping up for supper tonight, shall we?"

"How's Rick?" Cari asked when Tammy came to bed. "Getting used to your being away yet?"

"I doubt it, but he tries to sound brave." Tammy rolled her eyes as she flopped down on the bed. "He must have asked me six times if I'm okay. Isn't that ridiculous?"

"Not for a loving dad," Cari replied. "What's Ricky up to?"

"He got a part-time job at a sports store. You know, selling soccer balls and stuff. He's trying to earn a few bucks before school starts up in September."

"Sounds like a good plan."

"Yeah, I guess so." She reached for her nightshirt beneath the pillow. "So, how's your leg now? Better than this morning, I guess."

"That is a major understatement," Cari replied with a laugh. "I *limped* out the door this afternoon, and *walked* back in. I'd say that's a pretty good deal."

"But you said it hurt like crazy—at least that's what I thought you were saying." She got changed while she talked.

"You understood me perfectly, Kid. Oh, she's very good at what she does. But I had no idea a massage could hurt like that." She ruffled her bangs as she exhaled slowly. "She also bawled me out for not taking care of myself." Cari crossed her arms over her chest. "I mean it's bad enough when friends get on my case, but when a complete stranger tells me off, I don't take it too well."

Tammy giggled. "I can imagine. You have this really fiery look when you get mad, Cari. How did she react to it?"

Cari raised an eyebrow. " 'Fiery look' ? Well, let's just say she's not easily intimidated." She thought back to the end of her time with Louise. "But, somehow, I think she's got an Achilles' heel when it comes to spiritual things. She sounded like she might have believed in God once, but now there's nothing but bitterness left. I'm not sure. Maybe God has more than one reason for me to be here right now."

"Could be," Tammy agreed. She got off the bed and picked up her toothpaste and brush. "So, what does she look like? The way you describe her she must be six feet tall, and weigh 180."

Cari snorted. "Not hardly. Louise St. Denis is incredibly beautiful. Maybe 5'5", dark hair, and these incredible violet eyes. You know, like Liz Taylor. And she might weigh 135 soaking wet." She shook her head. "She may be as tough as a drill sergeant, but you wouldn't know it just by looking at her."

"Really? Sounds interesting. Maybe I'll have to meet this mystery woman myself."

"Maybe. But why the interest?"

"She's a recent widow, isn't she? Maybe she could use some company."

Cari's brows furrowed. "Just what are you implying, Kid?"

"Oh, nothing. Not yet, anyway. It's just that Gilles and John are both at loose ends right now." She shrugged just before opening the bedroom door.

"Tammy Benson, you are just as bad as Julie Patterson when it comes to matchmaking! Do you ever let up?"

"Not too often." She slipped out of the room before Cari could make further comment.

Good grief! We're here to investigate a missing painting, and Tammy is trying to pair up all the stray adults. Her frown deepened. *Mind you, she may have a point about Louise. How long will such a beautiful woman remain alone?* Cari sighed. "That kid is contagious. I'd better go to sleep before she gets any more wild ideas."

Chapter21

"So, Cari, did Louise St. Denis give you the impression that she might lie about the painting?" Gilles asked during supper. This time John and Tammy were with them.

"Not in the least, Gilles. She struck me as exceedingly *honest*—to the point of telling me that I've been neglecting my health—and we just met yesterday." She shook her head. "No, I don't think she'd lie about anything."

"Not even to protect her husband?" John wondered aloud.

"I can't be sure on that one, John. He didn't come up in conversation." She smirked as she sipped her coffee. "I was too busy moaning and groaning to ask many questions, let alone be subtle about it."

"I still think that I should meet her," Tammy stated, with all her usual frankness. All three adults stared at her. "Well, why not? Time is of the essence, isn't it? Why not let me ask some of the questions that you *professionals* seem to be avoiding? She shouldn't feel too threatened by a fourteen year old kid, should she?"

"Tammy, this could get dangerous," John said. "Depending on where that painting is, or who has it." He shook his head. "We need to be careful."

She sighed loudly. "Oh, for Pete's sake! I live in LA, don't I? That's hardly a quiet neighborhood, is it?" She crumpled her linen napkin and frowned. "Not even my *school* was safe," she whispered. "I want to help you guys, not just sit around playing tourist."

"No way," Cari said. "Your dad would kill us, Tammy. He wasn't even keen on letting you *come*. He definitely would not want you *helping* with this case."

"So who said he has to find out?"

Gilles laughed and reached for Tammy's hand. "We seem to underestimate you, Ma Petite. However, I must agree with John and Cari on this issue." He frowned when Tammy jerked her hand from his.

"Look," she said, sounding just a tad furious, "I'm not stupid. I happen to have done some research of my own about this *infamous* painting. And I know who painted it, and when, and who commissioned it. It was kept in the same family for generations, in the same *house* as a matter of fact. Then, when Louise St. Denis moved here, she brought it with her. Now, it's missing." She held up her right hand to keep them from interrupting her.

"However, I think there's a whole other story behind that painting," she remarked. "I mean why cart it all the way here from Boston? Especially when you're only nineteen and you've just eloped."

"What the—how on earth did you find all this out?" Cari asked, spilling some of her coffee as she hastily set her cup in the saucer.

Tammy leaned forward and rested her forearms on the table. "Because I'm curious, that's how. I ask questions. And because I'm just a kid, people will answer them for me. For instance, Frau Mueller knows all kinds of things about Louise St. Denis. As a matter of fact, Louise and Pierre even spent a few days in her home when they first moved here. And you know what stood out in her mind? That Louise carried *one* suitcase—and a carefully rolled canvas. Rather odd for a newlywed, wouldn't you say?"

Cari's brows furrowed. "Tammy Benson, you are a conniving little brat! We have been sharing a room for days, and you didn't breathe a word of this."

"You never *asked*, Cari. None of you have."

"All right, Tammy," John put in, "why don't you enlighten us with whatever else you've unearthed so far? It seems as though you've been very busy since we left LA."

"I have," she replied, her blue eyes glinting with obvious enthusiasm. "While you three have been flirting with each other."

"Tammy!" Cari scolded. "Watch it!" The girl's remarks were getting just a bit too personal for Cari's comfort. And likely for John or Gilles too.

"Sorry," Tammy murmured, immediately contrite. She leaned back and put her hands in her lap.

"Spill it, Kid," Cari said, though her tone wasn't as harsh as the moment before. "You have our complete attention."

"Okay," Tammy replied. "I'll start with the painting."

Two hours later, Tammy was on her way to bed, and Cari and John were sitting on the balcony.

"I can't believe she knew all that stuff and deliberately withheld it," Cari said with a sigh.

"You make her sound like a police informant, Cari. This is hardly the same thing."

"How do we know that, John? Judging from what she told us, it looks more and more as though Pierre St. Denis sold that painting, without any consent from his wife. Especially since she allegedly contacted Eduardo Rodriquez about it, and not the other way around. She wouldn't suddenly sell a painting that she'd gone to such lengths to keep all these years. It just doesn't make sense."

"You go to see her again tomorrow, don't you?"

"Yes, at three. Why?"

"Maybe you *should* take Tammy with you this time."

Cari laughed, though without a hint of humor. "I should lock her in the bedroom is more like it! I can't even trust her right now."

"Now you sound like an angry parent. Are you really *angry*, or just *worried*? Sometimes it's hard to tell the two apart."

Cari let her breath out with a sigh. "I know," she whispered. "I guess a little of both."

"She's a smart girl, Cari. And at this point, maybe we'd *better* keep her in our sights, so to speak." He reached for her hand and held it. "That way, she might share any pertinent information with us when she gets it, rather than later on." He gently squeezed her fingers. "What do you think?"

"I think I'm tired and I want to go inside," she replied. She tried to get up but he didn't release her hand. "John . . ."

"Just a minute. Are you concerned for Tammy's safety, or are you embarrassed that a young girl was able to come up with so much information, before you did?"

"You think I'm *jealous*?" She again tried to pull her hand from his, but he held fast.

"I'm only asking if you are," he replied in a warm and quiet voice. "I'm not assuming anything."

"Well, I don't think that question deserves an answer." She had a difficult time keeping her voice steady, especially while he got to his feet, all the while looking down into her face.

"There's another one that does." He drew her to her feet, still holding her hand.

"What?" She was annoyed to sound so breathless.

"Do you love me, Cari?"

Cari half choked, half swallowed, but she couldn't speak. Surely if he was *asking* such a thing, he must already have decided how *he* felt. She'd wondered for weeks now. *Maybe months.* She was still trying to think of something to say when he kissed her, drawing her into a warm embrace. Despite her brain telling her not to respond, her arms went around his waist, effectively drawing him even closer. *I can't love him! He's not a Christian. It wouldn't be right. But I think I already do.*

Cari's hands slid up John's back to his muscular shoulders. *It's too late—I already love you, John, even though I know I shouldn't. Tammy could see it, even Gilles. Why have I been lying to myself?* Cari allowed herself to touch John's hair, something she'd often wanted to do, but had never dared. It was softer than she expected. *Just like he is. He looks so tough and rugged, but he's so gentle.*

Just then, John lifted his lips from hers. "Was that your answer?"

"I-I don't think I can give you one, John." She bit her bottom lip, and immediately recalled how much she'd just been enjoying his kisses. She quickly withdrew her arms and put her hands up to her flaming cheeks. "I shouldn't have let you do that."

His smiling lips didn't quite hide the hurt in his eyes. "I thought it was pretty mutual."

"It was," she admitted. "But I—I'm sorry, John. It seems like our whole relationship is stop and go like this." She shook her head. "You make it too easy to forget everything I keep telling you about just being friends."

"If it's so easy to forget, Cari, then doesn't that indicate something?"

"Such as?" she asked, dreading what he might say next.

"That you're no more content with *friendship* than I am." His warm hands were still on her shoulders. "That the *attraction* we feel for each other is stronger than that." He clasped his hands behind her neck, cradling her head.

Cari reached out and put her hands on his arms, tears in her eyes. "Attraction isn't enough, John. It never will be." *Didn't Gilles and I come to the same conclusion? But what I may have felt for Gilles was nothing like this.*

"I know that," he replied. "But I'm not just talking about how beautiful you are, though that does play a part. I'm attracted to you for many reasons. You must know that by now."

"Yes, I do."

"We have a lot in common. And there are certainly other things that we could learn about together." His thumbs gently stroked her cheeks. "I told you once before that I'd never met a woman like you. That's even truer now. I—"

They both turned around as the balcony door opened. Tammy was standing there, looking distressed. She was clutching her robe around her, and tears glistened on her cheeks. "Cari, I-I need your help," she sobbed. "Please."

Cari stepped away from John and moved towards Tammy. "What is it? What's wrong?" She placed an arm around the girl's trembling shoulders. "How can I help?" She patted Tammy's cheek and her shoulders stiffened. "You're burning with fever, Tammy." She turned to look at John, and found that he'd moved closer. "Please call Dr. Mueller. Ask him if we should take her to the hospital. I'll get her back to our room."

"Sure." He slipped past them and into the house.

"Come on, Tammy; let's get you back to bed. Then try to tell me what the problem is." She helped the girl to their room, and got her to lie down, but Tammy immediately drew her knees up and continued to weep. Cari stroked her hair, frantically trying to think of what might be wrong. "Is it your period, Tammy? Have you ever had cramps like this before?"

"No," Tammy sobbed. "Not until—not before February. It's

been getting worse each month since then, but never this bad." She tried to take a deep breath, but it sounded more like a gasp. "I was okay until tonight. I just took some Tylenol, like usual. But after we got back, I started to feel so sick. I've already thrown up three times. And I'm sweating and freezing at the same time. And the pain is so bad, I can't stand it." She closed her eyes and moaned.

There was a soft rapping on the door. "Cari? May I come in?"

"Yes, John." Once he was in the room, she didn't waste time. "Did you get a hold of Dr. Mueller?"

"No. But his wife told me he's at the hospital right now, and that it might be best to just go there, if Tammy can't wait until tomorrow morning."

"She can't wait," Cari answered. She looked down at Tammy. "Where, exactly is the pain?"

"My lower back, my pelvis, and down my left thigh."

Cari bit her lip. "She's going to the hospital, John. Will you please drive? I'll get her purse and some extra clothes."

"Sure. How be I carry her down right now?"

"I want my dad!" Tammy moaned. "This shouldn't be happening! I'm scared." She continued to sob as John eased her into his strong arms.

"Switzerland is a great place to get sick," he said, obviously trying to keep his tone light. "Just ask Cari." He shifted her against his chest. "Try not to worry."

I'm worrying enough for all of us, thought Cari as she grabbed Tammy's purse, making certain that her wallet and passport were in it. Then she stuffed a jogging suit into her own overnight bag. *God, please let her be okay. I'm just as scared as Tammy is. And John looked a bit worried himself. Please let her be okay.*

Chapter 22

Tammy vomited twice on the way to the hospital, only adding to her anxiety. She kept alternating between apologies and pleas for her dad. John parked in front of the Emergency entrance and ran inside. He returned with an orderly and a stretcher. He helped to get Tammy onto it, while Cari held her shaking hand. She had to let go when they increased their pace.

"I'll go fill out all the forms," she said. "I have everything with me."

"Go ahead," John replied. "I'll stay with Tammy."

Cari made her way to the reception area and tried to find out where Dr. Mueller might be. The woman behind the desk had him paged while Cari began to read over several sheets of paper. Technically, she was responsible for Tammy while they were traveling. She didn't know at what point she'd have to call Rick. For the time being, she decided to handle the situation herself. She was immensely relieved when Karl Mueller walked over to her.

"What seems to be the problem, Fraulein?" he asked, as courteous as always. "Is your leg giving you more trouble?"

Cari shook her head. "No. It's not me. It's the young girl who's traveling with us, Tammy Benson. She seemed fine during supper. Then she became violently ill. And she's in terrible pain. And she has a high fever." Cari swallowed and tried not to blush. "She has her period, and I was afraid it might be Toxic Shock Syndrome."

Dr. Mueller took in the information with a slight nod of his head. "Where is she now?"

The receptionist answered, "She was taken into room number three. A nurse should have taken her vital signs by now, Doctor."

"Very well. Would you like to come with me, Fraulein? I'm sure she won't want to be alone in a strange place."

"John is with her right now, but yes, I would like to come with you."

"Right this way please." She followed him down the wide, brightly lit corridor, again having trouble matching his pace. She was thankful to reach the treatment room. Until she saw Tammy.

Tammy's cheeks were flushed with the fever, and she was literally writhing on the table. Perspiration had soaked her nightshirt, and her hair appeared damp. She still clung to John's hand, though it looked as though her grip was weakening. She cried out when she spotted Cari. "I want my Dad, Cari! Please."

Cari stepped close enough to reach for Tammy's flailing hand. "Shhh. I'll call him, Tammy. Just as soon as we have some idea of what's going on. You've got to let Dr. Mueller check you over. They'll need to do some tests. They'll take care of you, Kid. Please don't worry." She gave her hand a gentle squeeze and leaned down. "We've both been scared before. We'll get through this too."

John cleared his throat. "I better go move the truck before it gets towed away. I'll wait for you in the hallway." He leaned down and lightly kissed Tammy on the forehead. "You're in good hands, Ma Petite." Then he released her hand and exited from the chaotic room.

"Fraulein Daniels, we must start treatment immediately. If you wish, you may stay right here, but please try not to get in the way." Dr. Mueller's voice seemed to speak calm and order into not just the room, but the situation.

"Of course, Doctor. And thank you."

An hour later Cari stepped into the relatively quiet hallway with Dr. Mueller. "I have a few more questions for you, Fraulein. And I thought it best not to ask Tammy. She's already quite upset."

"All right. What else do you need to know?"

"Is Fraulein Benson sexually active?"

Cari stared at him for several seconds, the color draining from her face. "She's only fourteen, Doctor. Why do you even ask?"

"Because she may have a serious pelvic infection, which often occur in relation to sexual activity."

"Well, Tammy is not, and never has been 'active'. However, she was sexually assaulted a few months ago, at the beginning of February." She passed a trembling hand over her face. "There was no intercourse, but—" She swallowed a couple of times. "But there were some—some *internal* injuries at the time. I don't know if Tammy was given any antibiotics back then." *It's probably just as well that Rick isn't here trying to talk about this kind of stuff.* "But she told me tonight that she never had much cramping with her periods until the assault. And that they've gotten worse each month."

"That's what I feared, Fraulein. She may very well have been infected months ago, and now the problem has manifested itself this way. I'll do an ultrasound first, but I may need to do a laparoscopy to be certain."

"Why? Can't you just give her medication for the infection?" *How can I authorize surgery for someone else's child?*

"Not if there is an ovarian cyst, or a pelvic abscess. I'll know more after the ultrasound. In any case, she'll be here for a few days, on IV antibiotics. I suggest that you call her father as soon as I have the results from the tests. Tammy seems to want him here. For the moment, perhaps you can go back in and talk with her while we get ready. We've given her something for the pain, so she should be resting a little easier now."

Cari went back into the room and took up her vigil beside Tammy once more. The girl was much quieter now, but Cari could still feel the racing pulse as she held her hand. "How are you doin' Kid?"

"They gave me a shot," Tammy mumbled. "That helped." She turned her head. "It's bad, isn't it, Cari? That's why he took you in the hall." She squeezed Cari's fingers. "Please don't lie to me. I want to know what's going on."

"They think you've got a pelvic infection of some kind, Tammy. So, they want to be sure of what it is before they start giving you any medication for it."

"Tests, right?"

"Yeah, at least one or two." *Nothing very pleasant either.* "Once they know exactly what the scoop is, they'll be able to pump you with IV antibiotics." Cari forced a smile. "Just think of all the attention you'll be getting around here. You should be able to line up a bunch of new pen pals."

Tammy yawned and closed her eyes. A moment later, fresh tears were slipping from them. "This is all because of what happened at the school, isn't it?

"It could be. They don't know for sure, Tammy."

"This is the pits, Cari," Tammy mumbled. Her grip loosened. "Thank God for Demerol," she whispered.

"I've said the same thing many times myself." She covered Tammy's limp hand with the sheet. "Try to rest now. I'll be back after I talk with John." No response. *Good ole opiates. Nothing like a drug induced sleep.* She straightened up and rubbed her forehead. *Sleep? I'd settle for any kind right about now.*

"We'll have to do the surgery, Fraulein. The ultrasound indicates the problem area, but not the extent of it. There is definitely a cyst, possibly more than one. You should get her father's consent right away, if possible. I don't want to wait much longer." Cari reeled under the impact of Dr. Mueller's words. She was thankful for John's presence on the chair next to her. "It's not a lengthy procedure. She should be back in the recovery area in about two hours."

"Have you told Tammy anything yet? She already figured out that something serious is going on."

"She slept through most of the ultrasound, but she was coherent enough to listen to me afterwards. She told me that she just wants us to make the pain stop." He smiled. "She has a lot of courage for one so young."

"She's gone through a lot for one so young," Cari replied. "What, exactly, do you need Rick to consent to? He's a police officer; he'll want the 'facts'."

"We may have to remove her left ovary, and part of her fallopian tube. The right side would remain intact." When Cari groaned, he continued. "That would be the worst case scenario, Fraulein. It may only be necessary to clear out the infection, remove the cyst, and any scar tissue. But, I still need his consent to do whatever may arise."

Cari put her head in her hands. *Oh Lord, why? She's too young to be facing the loss of an ovary. Or any of this, for that matter. Please help me to know what to say to Rick. Please let your peace overshadow him at home. Watch over Tammy. Guide the medical staff while they take care of her. Help me not to collapse under the stress myself. And thank you for John. I'd hate to be facing this alone.*

"Cari? Do you want me to call Rick?" John had his hand on her shoulder.

"No. I have to do it. It'd be worse coming from somebody he's only met once or twice." She sat up straight. "I'll go call him, Dr. Mueller. I just pray that he'll be okay. Tammy's a special part of his life." She struggled to her feet, with some assistance from John. "I'll be back in a few minutes—if the operator can place the call right away. Excuse me."

"I'll be there as soon as I can," Rick stated. "Maybe by tomorrow night, your time. Take good care of her for me, please." He paused for a moment, and cleared his throat. "And make sure that John Maxwell is taking care of you."

"Okay. I'll call back after the surgery, Rick. Try not to worry too much."

"Yeah, right! My daughter is hours away, in a foreign country, having surgery, and you want me to stay calm."

"Worrying won't help any of us. Why don't you call Mike and Julie? And Pastor Hiller? Lots of prayer is just what we need right now, both here and in LA."

"You're right. Okay, I'll make some calls—right after I book a flight over there."

"Do that. We'll be waiting for you."

"I'm counting on that."

"I'll ask John to meet you at the airport, when you have the information for us."

"Sure. Thanks for being there, Cari. I mean that."

"You're welcome. I have to get back now. I'll call you later."

"Right. Bye."

"Bye."

"Are you going to make it, Cari?" John asked after checking his watch. It was 2:00 a.m. already, and Cari was trying to stay awake.

"I always have before," she murmured. She turned to look at him. "And you?"

"I can't face the thought of one more cup of coffee," he admitted. He continued to look at her. "You know, the only other time I sat in a hospital and waited for someone to come out of surgery was this past April, when you were getting your pacemaker." He smiled. "It sure would be nice if you and Tammy could lead more *sedate* lifestyles."

"I agree. But, I assure you, John, neither of us has had much choice in the matter."

Just then Dr. Mueller walked towards them, his surgical mask around his neck, and a smile on his face. Cari sighed heavily and remained seated. John got to his feet.

"How is she?" he asked.

"She's doing fine. And she still has both ovaries. We caught the infection in time."

"I need to go call Rick," Cari remarked, trying to get up. She couldn't do it.

"Why don't you let me?" John offered. "You check on Tammy, and then we'll go and get some sleep ourselves."

"That's a fine idea, Herr Maxwell. I'll sit here a moment myself, before I go home." Dr. Mueller took the chair next to Cari. "I'll make sure that Fraulein Daniels gets to see Tammy in a few minutes."

"Do you have Rick's number?" Cari asked.

"Yes. Tammy gave it to me a few days ago. I'll call him and then wait for you back here, okay?"

"All right."

As soon as John left, Dr. Mueller took hold of Cari's left hand. "She'll need to be here for close to a week, Fraulein. And she'll need a lot of follow up once she gets back home. Will you make certain that her father understands that once he arrives?"

"Yes, but, why are you telling me? Why not Rick?"

"Sometimes medical information is less threatening when it comes from a friend."

"So, she'll be okay?"

"I certainly hope so. Of course, we may not know for years just how much damage has already been done, Fraulein. Even a slight amount of scarring can cause infertility."

"Or sterility," Cari added. She bit her lip when he nodded. "But for now, you can treat the infection?"

"Yes. We've already started the medication. Her fever should go down within 24 to 48 hours."

"By then, her dad should be with her."

"Good." He patted her shoulder. "Now, I'll take you to her, but just for a moment. Then you must go and get some rest." He got to his feet and extended his hand to help her up.

"Thank you. For everything."

"You're welcome, Fraulein," he said with a smile. "But I think that God deserves far more of the credit than I."

"I would never argue with that, Dr. Mueller. Never."

Chapter 23

Cari fell asleep on the way back to the Mueller's', so John gently shook her shoulder when he parked the truck. "Cari, we're here. Let's go in and go to bed. Cari?" He shook a bit harder. "Cari?"

"What?" She didn't open her eyes. "What?"

"Cari, wake up. At least until you get to your room." He waited but her only response was to shake her head. "Come on, I'll help you." He got out on his side and went around to open her door. The rush of cool mountain air had the desired effect. John smiled as she looked at him, vacantly, but her eyes were open. "Let's go inside." He slipped his left arm around her and she leaned against his shoulder.

"I'm tired. I just want to sleep."

"Fine, but not here in the truck, please." He unbuckled her seatbelt and then lifted her out of the vehicle. "I'll come back for your purse in a minute." He slammed the door shut with his elbow before heading for the stairs. The door of the chalet opened before he got to the top. "Good morning, Frau Mueller. I apologize for waking you, or keeping you up, whichever the case may be." He passed through the doorway and looked into Cari's face. She was sound asleep again, limp against his body.

"She must be exhausted, John," their hostess remarked with motherly concern.

"She is. I'll take her upstairs, but would you mind getting her tucked in?"

"Not at all."

Once in the bedroom, with Cari's head cradled on the plump pillow, John turned to answer Frau Mueller's unspoken questions. "Tammy had a severe infection, and she needed some minor surgery. They'll be keeping her for a few days, and giving her medication. Her father will be flying in tomorrow evening." John rubbed his face and realized that his eyes felt gritty from lack of sleep. "Since Tammy won't be here, I thought, perhaps, that Rick Benson and I could move into this room, and Cari could take mine, just for the few days that he's here. Would you mind, terribly?"

"No." She patted his arm. "You know that I enjoy company, and helping others. For now, though, you need sleep too, not just Fraulein Daniels. Go to bed. I'll take care of her."

"Thank you. I just need to go to the truck for a moment." He clasped her hand with both of his. "Thank you very much, Frau Mueller. I'm afraid none of us knew how many difficulties we'd have on this trip."

"We never know those things. Don't worry. Now, off with you. Get to bed. I'll make a good meal for you both, whenever you get up."

"I knew you would." He smiled. Then he yawned. "Thank you again."

Cari stretched and blinked against the bright sunlight in the room. She rubbed her eyes and tried to read the hands on her wristwatch. "Eleven o'clock? Why did I sleep so late?" Then she remembered. "Tammy. The hospital." She gradually sat up, noticing that she'd slept in her clothes. She frowned. "How did I get here last night?" *John drove back here, I think. But how did I get to bed?* "Well,

I suppose I should get up, before the rest of the day is shot, and Tammy wonders what happened to me."

It didn't take Cari long to get washed up and dressed. Then she could smell fresh coffee, *and pastries, if I don't miss my guess.* She opened her door and made her way down to the kitchen. She found Frau Mueller at the stove, and John sitting at the table.

"Good morning," she said. "It smells wonderful down here." *Including whatever aftershave John is wearing.* She went to the table and pulled out a chair. "Did I fall asleep on the way here last night?" John simply nodded. "Oh." Her eyebrows furrowed. "Then how did I get in the house?"

"I carried you," John replied. "I tried to wake you up, but you were too far gone." A warm smile softened his features. "You look as though you slept well."

"I did. I really don't recall a thing after the hospital." She smiled when a steaming mug of coffee was set before her. "Has Dr. Mueller called?"

"Just a few minutes ago," Frau Mueller stated, bringing a plate of rosti and sliced meat to the table. "He said that Tammy had a good night, and not to worry."

"Well, that's good to know." She eyed the thick slices of homemade bread with avid interest. She looked at the empty plate in front of John. "Have you eaten yet?"

"No. I was waiting for you. Hungry?"

"Very. Good thing we had such a big supper last night or I'd be even worse."

"Well, help yourself, Fraulein," their hostess insisted. "It's meant to be eaten hot."

"Thank you." Cari reached for the platter while John took two slices of bread. "What time is Rick's plane coming in? I'm sure you told me last night, but I'm drawing a blank."

"At seven tonight. I'll pick him up and bring him to the hospital." He smiled again, sliding more potatoes onto his plate. "I'm sure that a worried father won't bother to stop for jetlag."

"Rick Benson? He doesn't let anything get in his way." She drank some coffee and then sighed. "I still have to work in my appointment with Louise this afternoon. So, I guess I'll visit Tammy and go from there."

"Sounds like a good idea."

"I'll send some sandwiches with you, Fraulein. You must remember to eat, even with the coming and going."

"Of course, Frau Mueller." She turned to her hostess. "I normally take very good care of myself, especially when it comes to meals. And your wonderful cooking is too good to miss anyway. Thank you for being so kind."

Tammy tried to smile when Cari walked into the ward. "Nice day isn't it?" she said in a raspy voice.

"Yes, it is." Cari dragged a chair next to the bed. "How are you feeling?"

"Like a pin cushion," Tammy muttered. An IV tube led to her left hand. Both fluids and antibiotics hung at the top of the pole, gradually feeding into her system. "I mean, I'm thankful for whatever they give me, but does it have to be from a needle? My hips are killing me."

Cari smiled. "As you well know, Kid, I've had far more needles than I care to remember. You'll live to tell about it."

"I suppose." Tammy shifted position and gritted her teeth. "Man, can I tell that somebody was messing around inside last night." She felt Cari reach for her hand. "Dr. Mueller said they got the cyst just after it ruptured. Glad I slept through *that*." She slowly moved her left hand across her abdomen. "It could have been a lot worse, Cari.

I know that. But I'm still really sore. And I'm scared. This could happen again, he said. After one infection, it's common to get more of them." Tammy bit her lip. "I could still end up not being able to have kids."

Cari used both hands to hold Tammy's. "There's always that chance, Tammy, for any of us. We're not God. He's the one who ultimately decides, not doctors. For now, let's be thankful that they caught the infection before it got worse."

"When is Dad coming?" She tried not to whine, but she sure missed him, especially since she'd landed in the hospital.

"Tonight. John will bring him over as soon as he gets in. Is there anything I can get for you? Books or magazines, maybe?"

Tammy shook her head. "No thanks. All these drugs are leaving me kind of fuzzy. I don't think I could read too well." She closed her eyes. "Some music would be nice though. A cassette player or something, so I don't disturb anybody else."

"Sure. I'll try to get one after my appointment with Louise today." Then she paused. "No, I better not wait that long, seeing as shops don't stay open very late. I guess I'll leave here by 2:00 so I have time to stop on the way."

"How are you doing, Cari? You must be tired after last night." She looked at her friend's face. "Are you okay?"

"I'm fine," she replied with a smile. "I fell asleep on the way to the Mueller's', and slept until almost noon."

"Good. I don't want you getting sick just to keep me company."

"I'm not planning on it. Besides, once Rick gets here, he'll be hogging all your time, anyway. Just concentrate on getting well, Kid."

"Of course. What else would I do with a week in the hospital?"

"Oh, I don't know. Maybe flirt with the orderlies or doctors."

Tammy almost laughed, until she thought about how much it

might hurt. "Do you think the 'poor, pitiful me' routine would work? It could make the days more interesting."

"You could always give it a try."

Tammy sobered once more. "Cari, why is that just when I think I can forget about what happened in February, something else flares up and brings it all back?"

"What do you mean?"

"Well, like at the restaurant in Paris. Then when we were having supper last night, and talked about danger. Now this. Dr. Mueller told me that the infection was likely linked to what happened." Her right hand tightened on Cari's. "There is a chance that I may never have kids, later on, because of a few minutes in a school washroom! I still have to have regular blood tests, to make sure I don't have HIV or AIDS. Will I ever be able to forget?"

Cari was silent for a long time. Then she began to stroke Tammy's hair. "I can't really answer that, Tammy. But I can tell you that it doesn't have to hurt as much, as time passes. That's what I've been telling Jill Harris too. And it's what I've had to live through myself. You see, when I was raped I-I tried so hard to forget. I threw out the clothes. I didn't tell anyone. I tried to focus on my job. That almost worked. Then I found out I was pregnant. I had a constant *reminder* of what had happened."

"I didn't know," Tammy whispered. "But you never--"

Cari shook her head. "I had a miscarriage after the beating. I was so sick, though, that it was a while before I found out." Tears glistened in her eyes, but they didn't fall. "I should be able to have other children someday. But, if I ever get pregnant again, I'll probably always think about the first time. You see, I was already half way through the pregnancy. I'd felt the baby move. I'd made plans for keeping it. Just when I was getting used to the idea of being a single mom, I lost it. I could have had a one year old boy by now."

"I'm sorry, Cari. That must have been awful for you. All of it."

"It was." Cari smiled. "But in the middle of all that, I met this really neat cop with a son and daughter. So, you see, God manages to bring healing in the middle of the worst situations. Trust Him for that, Kid." Cari straightened up. "You're special. Don't ever forget that. There are lots of people who love you. And no matter what happens in the next few years, physically or otherwise, God will still be with you. Let Him handle the memories as they come. You'll make it."

"Thanks." Tammy tried to move and felt the color drain from her face. "I think it must be time for another shot by now. At least I hope so." Her skin felt clammy.

Sure enough, a nurse came in soon after that, needle in hand. Cari helped Tammy to roll towards her. "Ouch!" she muttered as the drug was injected into the back of her hip. She let her breath out in a rush and tried to fight the mounting nausea. She sighed when the sheet was pulled over her once more. Then she eased onto her back. "Man, that one hurt." She closed her eyes while the nurse checked her vital signs.

"Try to relax, Fraulein. Later on you'll be given something to eat."

"Oh." The nausea worsened and she furrowed her brows. "I feel really sick right now."

"Try to rest, Tammy," Cari urged. "The nausea is worse when you tense up." She again stroked Tammy's forehead. "Take some deep breaths if you can." Tammy tried. "Great. A few more like that and you might be able to sleep."

Tammy took her advice and kept breathing deeply. She got as far as ten before she stopped counting anymore. Blessed numbness took over. And a sweet break from the pain.

Chapter 24

"Do you ever work on patients in the hospital?" Cari asked Louise during her massage.

"Sometimes. Why do you ask?"

"Well, I have a teenage friend with me on this trip. She developed a very serious pelvic infection, and we had to take her in last night. She had some surgery done, and she'll be on IV medication all week. She was complaining about how sore she was, from needles mostly. I remembered how nice it felt to have a back rub when I was in the hospital. I thought it might help her to relax. All the tension was making her feel sick." *And you're so good at relieving tension, I may fall asleep right here.*

"She's getting injections of Demerol?"

"Yes, I believe so. And I haven't forgotten how much those hurt either, especially if you're unlucky enough to get a nurse with lousy aim."

"How old is your friend? Just a teenager you said?"

"Yes. She's only fourteen."

"Where are her parents?"

"Her father is flying in tonight. Her mother died a few years ago."

"I suppose I could go over and see if there's anything I could do to help. Will you be going back tonight?"

"Yes. I thought I might just eat at the hospital cafeteria after I'm done here."

"That wouldn't be necessary, Fraulein. I don't have any other appointments today. You could stay here if you wish."

Cari was stunned by the suggestion. *Maybe it's just because she doesn't know why I'm really here yet. Maybe she's just very lonely.* "I'd like that. Thank you."

"Why are you traveling with a teenager, Fraulein? Are you dating her father?"

Again Cari was caught off guard. *Why all the questions? Who's doing the 'investigating' around here?* "No, I'm not dating her father, but we are very good friends. And his daughter has been very helpful during my recovery times. I wanted to do something to repay her for her kindness."

"She must be an interesting girl."

Cari laughed. "Oh, that she is! She's wise beyond her years. She has a knack for offering great advice too. I'm sure you'll like her."

"Are you implying that I could use 'advice' Fraulein?" Louise asked, a hint of humor in her tone.

"Not necessarily. However, that's never kept Tammy from speaking her mind before."

"You definitely make her sound worth meeting."

"Thank you very much," Cari remarked as she folded her napkin. "That was a lovely supper."

"I've enjoyed your company," Louise replied. "It's been several weeks since—since I've felt at all like entertaining." She looked away as she stood up and began to clear the table.

"I'm so sorry about your husband. It must have been a horrible shock." For a few seconds she thought of Rick Benson, watching his wife slip away from him in an ambulance. *These two could really relate to each other. Good grief, I'm getting as bad as Tammy.*

"Yes, it was. You know, you say goodbye just like any other time, and then—" She shook her head and turned to face the sink. "It didn't help that we'd argued before he left," she whispered. "I think that's made it so much harder." Her shoulders tensed as she gripped the counter. "If I'd known, I—"

Now she sounds like Rick. Maybe these two should get together. "I know I asked a lot of questions when my parents were killed. We'd been making plans for Christmas, and then I was getting a phone call from another police department, telling me they'd both died in a car accident. There's never a way to prepare for something like that. Never. I was a police officer myself. I knew lots of stats on drunk driving, but that couldn't prepare me for someone broad siding *my* parents."

"At least you didn't have any regrets," Louise murmured.

"Maybe not. Except that I'd gotten out of the habit of telling them that I loved them. They were young and healthy. I thought we'd have plenty of time for that. But, we didn't."

Louise turned and faced her, brushing away falling tears. "I don't know why I'm telling you this."

"I don't mind, really." She got up and walked over to Louise. "I'd like to help if I can. If that means listening, fine. If there's any other way, please tell me."

Louise managed a slight smile. "You could help me with the dishes."

"Hey, Kid, how are you feeling?" Cari asked when she and Louise entered the ward just before 7:00. "I brought someone along to meet you."

Tammy tried to sit up a bit more, but only managed a couple of inches before she slumped against the pillow. "Hi," she murmured.

"Louise, right? Cari told me you had beautiful eyes." Tammy bit her lip and exhaled slowly.

"Are you okay?" Cari asked. "Do you need something?"

"No. I mean, the nurse just gave me something for pain. I didn't want to be looking too pathetic when Dad gets here." She tried to smile, but the attempt fell short. "But now I'll probably fall asleep instead." She frowned as she rubbed her left hip. "She had lousy aim. My leg feels kind of weird. Not like the other shots either. I can't get comfortable."

"Well, actually, that's why I brought Louise along, Tammy. She might be able to help you relax." Cari grinned as she patted Tammy's hand. "Works for me. By the way, you didn't allow a proper introduction yet. Tammy Benson, this is Louise St. Denis."

"Nice to meet you, Tammy. Do you mind if I check your hip?"

"Why not? It's driving me crazy right now."

Louise moved around to the other side of the bed and carefully lifted the sheet away. "Can you show me exactly where the needle went in?" Tammy rubbed the spot. "Okay, I see why it hurts. She must have gotten too close to the sciatic nerve this time. If you can roll onto your right side, I'll try to work the muscles for a few minutes."

"I'll help you," Cari offered. "Just hold my wrist, Tammy." They soon had her on her right side, and Louise was kneading the back of her thigh.

"Oh, that's nice," Tammy sighed. She closed her eyes and slowed her breathing. "You're hired. You're worth every cent—whatever you charge. I'll gladly pay you, since I can't go shopping from here anyway."

"We'll work something out later, Tammy," Louise stated. "For now, just relax your leg." She worked up the hip. "Let me know if I use too much pressure."

"It's just fine so far."

Louise was just finishing when Rick and John walked into the room. Cari turned and gave Rick a hug. "Good to see you, Rick."

Rick returned the hug before approaching the bed. It was obvious that he was struggling with tears. "Hi, Sweetheart. How are you doing?" He leaned down and kissed Tammy's cheek.

Tammy smiled, and managed to open her eyes for just a few seconds. "I'll be okay, Dad. Thanks for coming." She reached for his hand. "You must be tired."

"I'll be fine," he replied. Then he looked at Louise, who was pulling the sheet back into place. He gazed at her for a moment. "Are you a nurse?"

"No, Herr Benson. I'm a massage therapist. Fraulein Daniels asked me if I could come and see your daughter."

"Oh." He swallowed and looked away. But just for a moment. He seemed drawn by her lovely eyes.

"She's great, Dad," Tammy put in. "And beautiful too."

Louise blushed and turned to pick up her purse from the foot of the bed. "I should be going now." She gently touched Tammy's shoulder. "I could come back tomorrow and work on your back and neck. They stiffen up when you have to rest in bed too much."

"That's for sure," Cari muttered. "Too bad you weren't in LA during the past year and a half, Louise. I would have given you a lot of business."

"I'd like that," Tammy said, her voice sounding as drowsy as she looked.

"All right. I can't remember my schedule at the moment, but I'll fit you in. If your leg starts to act up again, ask a nurse for an ice pack. That'll relieve the inflammation."

"Thanks."

Louise stepped around the bed, but Cari reached for her arm. "Would you like to join me for a coffee? I'm sure Rick and Tammy would like to be alone for a while anyway."

"Well, I-I guess I'm in no hurry tonight." Louise seemed to notice John for the first time, and again her cheeks flushed. "But I don't wish to intrude."

"You won't be," Cari assured her. "John, would you like to come too?"

"If you don't mind," he replied. He smiled then. "Just as long as it's not here in the cafeteria. They have terrible coffee."

"Fine by me," Cari answered. Then she turned and touched Rick on the shoulder. "We'll come back in an hour or so, Rick. Then we'll head over to the Mueller's', okay?"

"Sure. I guess I'll have to sleep sometime."

"Of course you will, Dad." Tammy tugged on his cuff. "Did you bring the *Scrabble* board with you? I'll need something to do this week."

"Actually," Rick replied with a tired smile, "I brought your favorite puzzle with me."

"You're so smart sometimes," she replied. Then she yawned. "But I don't think I'm up to it tonight." She looked at the others. "I'll see you tomorrow, guys. Goodnight."

Once out in the hallway, Louise spoke again. "She's a beautiful girl. Does she always try to take care of everyone else like that?"

"Yes," Cari and John replied in unison. Then they laughed.

"She's very *concerned* for everybody's welfare," John added. "She's a real gem."

"I can see that," Louise mused. "I know she was in terrible pain, but she didn't even complain. I've had adults who wouldn't have stayed so quiet." She shook her head. "It'll be a pleasure working with her."

"I'm sure she'd say the same about you," Cari replied. "She looked so much better when you were finished. And, by the way, Tammy *never* gives a compliment that she doesn't mean. She likes you. And she trusts you. You've just won a friend for life."

"I'd like to think so." She straightened her shoulders and looked at John. "We haven't been introduced yet, Sir. I'm Louise St. Denis." She held out her hand.

"I'm John Maxwell. Pleased to meet you." He shook her hand. "Now, shall we go and have that coffee?"

Back at the Mueller's', John and Cari introduced Rick, and sorted out the sleeping arrangements. They were all tired, especially Rick, but he seemed relieved that Tammy's condition was improving. The three of them stood in the hallway, outside the bathroom door.

"Thanks for taking care of her for me," Rick said. He clasped Cari's right hand in both of his. "I really appreciate it." He didn't release her hand, but he looked to John. "And thanks for picking me up, and arranging things with Mrs. Mueller. I wouldn't have known where to start." He shook his head. "I almost never travel, let alone fly part way around the world." He squeezed Cari's fingers and then let go. "Thank God I took out special travel insurance before you all left. I hate to think what all these medical costs would be."

"Rick, if there's anything that isn't covered," John said, "please let me know. I'm sure that *Richards & Richards* would pick up the tab."

More likely you would, Cari thought. "Don't worry about that right now. As for Louise, I'm taking care of that. As Tammy said earlier, she's 'worth every cent'."

"Isn't she the owner of that missing painting?" Rick asked, just before stifling a yawn.

"Yes," Cari replied. "She's also the woman whose husband

was killed in a hit and run accident at that same time. We haven't discussed the painting yet."

"She's very beautiful," Rick acknowledged. "I've never seen eyes like hers." He shook his head. "It's too bad about her husband. She seems awfully young to be widowed."

Cari put an arm around his shoulders. "She's 33, Rick. Just like somebody else who was widowed 'awfully young'."

He looked into her eyes. "Does she have any kids?"

"No. Not in fourteen years of marriage."

"I wonder why not. She doesn't strike me as the kind of woman who would choose a career over children." He shrugged. "Then again, I saw her for what, two or three minutes?"

"Well, I've spent several hours with her, Rick," Cari replied, "and I get the same impression. Anyhow, why don't we get to bed, instead of speculating about Louise St. Denis? And sleep as late as you like. Frau Mueller *always* has food ready when we get up."

"I noticed. I barely got in the door before she offered me something." He grinned. "Despite the circumstances, I may even enjoy some aspects of this visit. Goodnight, Cari." He kissed her cheek and hugged her. "I'll see you in the morning." He opened the bedroom door and went in.

John remained in the hallway, staring after him. When the door was closed, he moved next to Cari. "I wonder if Louise noticed Rick as much as he noticed her."

Cari laughed softly. "I've wondered the same thing. Actually, I started wondering before they even *met.* They seem suited to each other, don't they?"

"I suppose so." He lowered his voice. "Though I can think of a couple of others who are well suited too." He gave her a quick kiss. "Goodnight, Cari."

"Goodnight."

Chapter 25

"I realize that Tammy is in the hospital, Cari, and I'm concerned about her too," Gilles said as he spoke to her over the phone. "But my father is waiting for us to find out *something* about the painting. I can't stall him forever."

Cari sighed in frustration. "Did you tell him that Pierre St. Denis has died?"

"Of course."

"And that doesn't make any difference to him? He's just concerned about his painting and his money?"

"Cari, you're being a bit harsh, aren't you?"

"Am I? I don't think so." She combed her fingers through her still damp hair. "Okay, I'll try to ask Louise some more questions. Actually, Tammy might beat me to it."

"What do you mean?"

"Well, Louise has agreed to visit Tammy again today, to do more massage. And we both know that the girl has a way of asking questions when she wants to know something."

"True." He laughed. "All right, I'll try to stall my father for another day or so."

"Thank you, Gilles." She twisted the phone cord in her hand. "Are you going to visit Tammy? I'm sure she'd like to see you."

"Sure. But I want to get her a present first. I just haven't decided what yet. Any suggestions?"

"Not really. Oh, wait a sec. I got her a cassette player yesterday. Why don't you try to find her some tapes? Not just music. I got her a couple of those, and so did John. How about some language ones? You know, we both kidded around about learning some French or German while we're here. It might ease the boredom, and it would be something to help her remember the trip."

"Great idea. I'll see what I can find."

"I have to go dry my hair. Could we meet for lunch?"

"Of course. Where and when?" He sounded pleased at the invitation.

"Well, I don't know. Um, how about 1:00? I can come to the hotel, and we can go somewhere."

"Fine. I'll meet you in the lobby at 1:00."

"Bye. See you later." Cari hung up just as John entered the kitchen.

"Good morning. Did you sleep well?"

"Yes, thank you. Though it felt kind of strange to be in a different room." She felt her cheeks flush. "You left a couple of things in there. Maybe you could get them after breakfast."

"Sure," he said. Then he frowned. "But what did I forget?"

"Well, um, I-I think it's probably what you've been sleeping in." She looked down at the floor. "They were under the pillows. I-uh, I put them on the chair."

"Oh," he replied, obviously catching on to what she meant. "I'll go move them now." He headed for the stairs just as Rick came down them.

"Hi, Rick. Having any trouble with jet lag?" Cari asked.

"I sure am. My body doesn't know if it's morning or night. I guess I'll just have to take my watch's word for it." He rubbed his hands over his freshly shaven face. "Do I smell coffee?"

"Yes, you do. And the rest of breakfast. Come on. Go and eat. I just need to finish with my hair. I'll be down in a minute."

"You must feel better now that you've slept, Herr Benson," Frau Mueller remarked as she refilled his mug. "You looked so tired last night."

"I'll be fine, thank you." He poured some fresh cream into the mug. "And thank you for breakfast. You make wonderful bread."

"And everything else," Cari added. "Wait 'til you have a full meal, Rick. You'll never feel the same about pizza or burgers again."

"Maybe not." He sipped his coffee. "So, how do I get to the hospital from here? Take a taxi?"

"Oh, that's not necessary. I can give you a ride over. I want to see Tammy anyway," Cari replied.

"Thanks." He reached over and patted her hand.

"You're welcome. Now, I'll just go get ready while you finish your coffee."

After Cari left the room, Rick leaned back in his chair and looked at John. "How's Cari been feeling this trip? She looks tired."

John circled his mug with both hands. "She's been pretty sick a couple of times. She had trouble with the change in altitude. Then her leg acted up. But she's doing better." He smiled then. "But I wouldn't ask too many questions if I were you. She doesn't appreciate it."

Rick laughed. "I already know that, from past experience." He took another swallow of coffee. "But you've been keeping an eye on her, haven't you?"

"I've tried. When she'll let me."

"What about Gilles Rodriquez? I thought they were seeing each other."

John frowned. "I think she cooled things with him, but I haven't asked. It's none of my business."

"Isn't it? Looks to me as if you and Cari suit each other very well."

"Perhaps. Except for a couple of things."

"You're not a Christian," Rick stated simply, holding John's gaze. John nodded. "Don't expect her to back down, John."

"I don't." John looked down at his empty mug.

"What's holding you back? From becoming a Christian, I mean."

"I don't see a need to. I never have." He met Rick's gaze once more. "And Cari made it clear that doing so, just for her sake, wouldn't be right either."

Rick shook his head. "No, it wouldn't. It's something between you and God. But, John, it's the most important choice you'll ever make."

"Hi, Kid," Cari said as she and Rick entered the ward. "How was your night?" She got closer to the bed. "You look tired. Is the pain worse?" She set the cassette player and tapes on the bed tray and reached for Tammy's hand. "What's wrong?"

"I had nightmares," Tammy replied. Then she looked up at Rick. "About all kinds of things. I guess I was screaming so much that they gave me a sedative. I don't remember dreaming after that."

Rick leaned down and gave her a kiss on the cheek. "Do you want to talk about it, Sweetheart?"

Tammy shook her head. "Not right now." She tried to smile. "I'm just glad that you're here." She reached up and patted his cheek.

Cari felt awkward. She suspected that Tammy wanted to discuss her dreams, but not with Rick. *Maybe later.* "So, I brought you something to keep you busy." She gestured to the gift. "Take your pick."

"Thanks, Cari. I appreciate this. Really. I'm just tired after such a lousy night." She shifted on the bed and bit her lip. "My temperature went down, though. Dr. Mueller said that was good." She frowned. "I sure wish I could wash my hair. The nurse told me that I'm supposed to start walking around today. Maybe they'll let me take a shower."

"Likely," Cari replied. "That should feel good." She gently stroked Tammy's forehead. "Have you heard from Louise since last night?"

"Not yet. But I'll sure be glad to see her again. She's very good."

"That's for sure," Cari replied with a smile.

"So, do you want me to pump her for information?" Tammy asked, sounding serious.

"What?" Rick asked. "What are you talking about?"

"Well, somebody needs to ask her about the painting. I've already found out a few things."

"Several things," Cari corrected.

"Okay, several things. So, I figure now that I've met her, I can talk with Louise about it."

"Tammy," Rick began, sounding every inch the cop that he was, and a bit like a concerned father as well. "Just what have you been up to?"

"Just asking questions, Dad. And I have a knack for getting answers too."

"I still don't want you involved in this."

"I already am."

Rick was still with Tammy when Louise arrived, just before 1:00.

"I hope I'm not intruding," Louise said, somewhat embarrassed to find Rick in the room. "I could come back later."

"Now is fine," Rick replied, getting up from the chair next to the bed. "Tammy didn't have a great night, so I'm sure she's glad you're here."

Actually, Tammy looked as though she was almost asleep. She opened her eyes when she heard them talking. "Hi, Louise. Thanks for coming again." She glanced up at Rick. "Dad, will you please help me to roll onto my side?"

"Tammy, would it be possible for you to go on your stomach? I'd be able to do a much better job on your back that way." Louise still felt uncomfortable with Mr. Benson there.

"I guess so," Tammy replied. "I think I did in my sleep anyway. I'll just need help with this stupid IV thing. It gets wrapped around my arm sometimes."

"I'll help you, Sweetheart." Rick held the tubing while Tammy carefully rolled over. She paused on her side, clenching her jaw. Then she shifted again.

"Okay," she muttered. "I'm all yours." Her head was facing left.

"Why don't we move this pole to the other side for now?" Louise suggested. "Then the tubing won't be in the way."

"Sure," Tammy replied.

It only took a moment to complete the task. Then Rick stepped back from the bed. Louise unzipped a small case and withdrew a bottle of scented oil.

"That smells nice," Tammy commented. "Lavender, right?"

"Yes, it is," Louise replied. "It has soothing qualities. I thought it would be best in your situation." She hesitantly looked over at Rick. "Why don't you sit down, Herr Benson? This will take a while."

"Oh. Sure." He pulled the chair out of her way, and sat down.

Louise untied Tammy's gown straps and saw the girl tense. "Is something wrong?"

"N-not really," Tammy replied. "I just—I'm kind of shy, I guess."

Louise was puzzled. She'd just massaged Tammy's hip and thigh the day before, without any trouble. She once more looked to Rick, and found that his face had gone pale. Tammy spoke again before she could formulate a question.

"I-I had a bad night. I guess I'm kind of edgy. I'll be okay."

"Are you sure?" Louise asked, still baffled by the tension.

"Yes. Go ahead."

Louise undid the ties, moved the gown out of the way, and applied oil to her hands. Then she began to massage Tammy's back. As she had expected, the girl's muscles were tense and rigid. "Try to breathe deeply."

"Actually, could I ask you some stuff?" Tammy queried.

"Fine. As long as you relax." Louise kept working, applying more oil as needed.

"How long have you been doing massage?"

"Oh, let's see, about ten years."

"No wonder you're so good at it." Tammy sighed when Louise worked on her right shoulder. "What made you choose this kind of career?"

"Well, I wanted to help people, I guess."

"Your husband must have liked that. I mean, what guy wouldn't like to have a free massage?"

Louise's hands trembled for a moment, and she cast a furtive glance in Rick's direction. To her amazement, and discomfort, he was looking right at her. "Actually, my husband never really enjoyed them."

"Really? That's weird. I mean, I can remember my mom; she was a nurse, working on my dad's shoulders for ages sometimes. I know *he* always liked it."

"Tammy," Rick interrupted. "You didn't need to bring me into this." He sounded cross with her, or hurt. Louise couldn't quite tell.

"Well, it's true, Dad," Tammy replied, her tone defensive. "Besides, I can remember Mom rubbing my back when I was sick. It always felt nice."

Louise moved to the left shoulder, her own back getting tired from the awkward angle imposed by the hospital bed. "How are you doing so far?"

"Fine." Tammy yawned. "Getting sleepy. I guess that means I'm relaxing."

"Usually," Louise answered with a smile.

"You're from the States, aren't you? I mean, originally."

"Yes, from Boston. Why?"

"Just wondering why you came all this way. I mean, Cari's got a friend who married a guy from here, so I can see why she'd move. But you got married in the States, didn't you?"

Louise froze for a few seconds, and she could feel the heat building in her cheeks. "Y-yes. How did you know that?"

"Oh, Frau Mueller told me," Tammy replied, keeping her tone casual. "She told me you and your husband stayed there for a few days, back when you came to St. Moritz. She said you had eloped." Tammy sighed. "That sounds so *romantic*, just like in books."

"Life isn't like books, Tammy," Louise answered stiffly. "Eloping was not the smartest thing that I ever did." *Why on earth am I telling her this? Just to destroy her silly dreams?* She took a deep breath. "It would have been much wiser to stay in college, especially since I had a 4.0 GPA."

"Sounds like my mom. She was a real brain. Right, Dad?"

"True," Rick answered. "Always got top marks."

"So," Tammy began again. "It wasn't romantic to move here. Then why did you stay all these years?"

Louise felt as though Tammy had slapped her. Her question brought back far too many memories, both recent and from long ago. All the letters, returned unopened. All the arguments, the tears, and the painting. *A blessing and a curse.* "It's too hard to explain," Louise managed to reply. "But I loved my husband—and my father didn't."

"Oh, that must have hurt."

Louise didn't answer. She simply continued with the massage, working on Tammy's neck. Tammy turned her head, burying her face in the thin pillow. Louise frowned as she kept on. "Tammy, have you injured your neck before? Perhaps an accident on your bicycle, or maybe in gym class? There seems to be some scar tissue here. Nothing related to the surgery you just had." Tammy immediately tensed, her pulse increasing.

"She, uh—" Rick stammered. "She was—" He looked almost frantic as his gaze shifted from Louise to Tammy, and back again.

"I was attacked," Tammy blurted out. "Six months ago. One of the guys hurt my neck. I-I was too scared at the time to really notice. But it bugs me sometimes." Her shoulders were trembling. "I-I think that's enough, Louise. I need to roll over again."

"All right. I'm sorry. Let me help you." She wiped her hands on the towel she'd brought with her. Then she tied the back of the gown. "Easy now. Herr Benson, will you please hold the IV? I don't want it to pull out by mistake."

"Of course." Rick got up and moved the IV fluids from one side of the bed to the other, while Louise helped Tammy to roll over. "How are you doing, Sweetheart?"

"Much better, just awfully tired." She smiled at Louise and reached out her right hand. "Thanks a lot. Sorry I got—well, *distracted* like that."

"No problem." Louise held the girl's hand for a moment. "It happens to all of us, Tammy."

Chapter 26

"I think I've found at least part of what we're looking for," Gilles said during lunch.

"Really? What, exactly?"

"Well, some of my contacts informed me that Pierre paid off a large portion of his debts—just days before he died. Probably about a quarter million dollars worth of debts. Nobody seemed to know where he got the money though."

"From the painting?" Cari wondered aloud. Then she frowned.

"What is that scowl for?" Gilles teased.

"Oh. Just that I thought of something Louise said. She told me that she and Pierre had argued just before he left, the night he was killed. I wonder if they argued about the painting. My friend Trish told me that it used to hang in Louise's office. The wall is conspicuously empty now."

"I wonder when she found it missing—assuming that Pierre took it without her knowledge."

Cari chewed her piece of schnitzel while she considered. "Probably right about that same time. Maybe she was at a conference or something. We should be able to check on that."

"You mean a conference for massage therapists?"

"Sure. Why not? Lots of them must work all over Switzerland.

Surely they get together sometimes."

"I suppose so. It's worth finding out. However, even if he sold it behind her back, it was still purchased by my father. So, what happened to it?"

"I don't know," Cari murmured. Then she thought of something else. "Didn't you tell me that Pierre owed close to half a million?"

"Yes. Why?"

"Well, what if he tried to sell it twice?"

Gilles cocked an eyebrow. "And how would he get away with that?"

"Well, an empty crate arrived in Mexico City. So, the painting is still around somewhere. Obviously, he couldn't try to sell it again in legitimate circles. But not all art collectors are."

"Not at all. Some of the most famous art objects circulate on the black market. You may be on to something, Cari. I'll ask around some more. I still haven't been able to find out who all Pierre St. Denis owed money to. That could be very important in this puzzle."

"True. But please be careful."

"Of course. Besides, I'm not the one driving a sports car in the Alps."

"Tammy hit a few raw nerves this afternoon," Rick commented as he and Cari and John sat near the fire that evening. "Especially when she asked about the elopement. Actually, any question about Louise's husband seemed to provoke tension. I'd say she's hiding quite a bit. I don't know about the painting, but I'd guess her marriage wasn't totally *pleasant.* And I got the distinct impression that she and her father quarrelled before the wedding ever took place."

"Not bad for someone who's only concerned with his daughter's welfare," Cari remarked with a grin.

Rick blushed slightly before gazing at the flickering flames. "She looks very troubled. Vulnerable. Something." He shrugged. "I guess I wish that I could help."

"Well, you could always invite her out for supper, Rick. The worst that could happen is that she'd say 'no'."

He shook his head. "Actually, it might be worse if she said 'yes'. I don't want to start a Trans Atlantic relationship. Besides, I can only stay until I know that Tammy is leaving the hospital. I really have to get back to LA."

Cari sighed. "Well, I like her. But she's got this wall built around her most of the time. It's hard to get through." Then she laughed. "Unless you're Tammy."

Tammy was alone when Louise visited the next time. She smiled and handed the girl a small bottle of herbal shower gel. "This one is meant to wake you up in the morning. I hope you like it."

"Thank you. You really didn't need to bring me a gift, Louise." Tammy twisted the lid and sniffed the contents. "Oooo, I like this. What's in it?"

"Bergamot. That's what gives it a citrusy scent. It's one of my favorites."

"You have a collection?"

Louise blushed. "It's almost like an obsession. I must have thirty little bottles by now. They fill one whole drawer in my bathroom. Plus, I have dozens of oils that I use for massage."

"Sounds nice." Tammy shifted on the bed, finally able to be half sitting. "Um, I don't know if I need a massage today, but I'd like if we could just talk. Do you mind?"

"Well, not really." Louise sat down on the vacant chair. "What would you like to talk about?"

"You, mostly."

"Why?" Louise tried not to sound as flustered as she felt.

"I find you fascinating. You see, for one thing, you're about the same age my dad was when my mom was killed. So, I wonder how different it is for a woman, with no kids, to put her life back together. My dad has me and my brother, Ricky." She shrugged. "Sometimes I wonder if we're more of a help or a hindrance. I mean, maybe it would have been easier for him to remarry, if he hadn't had kids to worry about."

Louise reached for Tammy's right hand and held it in both of hers. "Don't ever think of yourself as a 'hindrance' Tammy. I would love to have a couple of children to occupy my time, and my thoughts right now. And it's so plain to see how much your father loves you. You're a blessing, trust me."

"Why did you never have kids?" Tammy asked, her tone gentle. "You just said—"

"I wanted to have children, Tammy. Very much. But my husband—Pierre couldn't."

"I'm sorry," Tammy replied with a blush. "I shouldn't have asked. It's just that—well I-I don't know if *I'll* be able to have kids later on. The doctors can't be sure about that. And, well, I needed to ask somebody what it's like—not to have kids."

"Very lonely," Louise sighed. She looked down at the hand she was holding. "I'm sure that most of my acquaintances simply thought that I didn't want to interfere with my schooling and career." She shook her head. "That wasn't it at all."

"Do you have any brothers or sisters?"

"I have a younger sister. She was eleven when I left Boston. She'd be twenty-five by now." She didn't mention her name, or the fact that she'd had no contact with her in the intervening years.

"Oh. Is she married?"

"I have no idea."

"Really? You mean—"

Louise patted Tammy's hand and looked into her face. "I mean I really have no idea."

"Okay." Tammy suddenly smiled. "You'd like my brother. He looks just like my dad, but younger, of course. He just finished high school, and got a basketball scholarship to UCLA. Cool, eh?"

"Your father must be proud of him."

"Oh, he is, but he's not the bragging type. He's really kind of quiet."

"I noticed that yesterday." *He's also very handsome.*

"Ricky is gonna stay at home for the first year, until he gets used to school. Then, next fall, he might move into a dorm. I'd really miss him. He's a great guy—for a brother."

"Do you feel up to going for a walk?" Louise asked. "You must be tired of this room by now."

"I am," Tammy said with a sigh. "But I went for a walk earlier, and it made me feel really sick. I think it's all the medication they're giving me. I feel kind of nauseated all the time." She furrowed her brows. "And it's screwing up my sleep too. I had nightmares again last night—which doesn't exactly endear me to the other patients in this room." She closed her eyes for a moment. "I'll be glad to get out of here. I was sleeping just great at Frau Mueller's. She's so sweet."

"Yes, she is." Curiosity got the better of her. "Which room were you in? The one that faces the hillside?"

"Yes. I just love looking out the window. All those flowers are so pretty." She levelled her gaze with Louise's. "Is that the room that you and Pierre stayed in?"

"Yes, it is. She's changed things quite a bit since then, but the view is still just as pretty."

"What did you love most about Pierre? What made you want to elope with him?"

Louise swallowed before answering. "He was so full of life. He made my home seem so boring in comparison, I guess. He was handsome. He had a wonderful sense of humor. He told me so many wonderful stories about growing up in St. Moritz." She looked away for a moment. "He made all kinds of promises to me. And I believed every one of them."

"You mean he lied to you?" Tammy asked, obviously surprised. "But why?"

"Maybe because he knew that if he'd told me the whole truth, I never would have married him, or moved here." Louise was shocked by how easy it was to share things with Tammy that she'd never told anyone else.

"I'm sorry, Louise. I didn't mean to make you uncomfortable."

"It's all right. I suppose it just hurts to admit that I was sadly mistaken back then."

"But it wasn't all broken promises, was it?" She sounded ever-hopeful. "I mean, you stayed together for all this time."

"Tammy, I loved my husband, and, in his own wild and foolish way, I suppose that he loved me too. Yes, we had some good times. Many of them. It's just that I've had a very long time to look back on my mistakes."

"Like marrying him?"

"I'm not sure about that. As I said, I loved him. But I never should have eloped. Certainly not without knowing Pierre a lot better than I did."

"You said that your father didn't love him. What did you mean?"

Louise sighed. *Oh, why not? I'm telling her everything else.* "I grew up in a very wealthy family. Money and status were everything to my father. Pierre had neither. My father told me plainly that if I married him, that I would no longer be welcome there. And I knew he meant every word that he said. So, I took only what was rightfully mine. A suitcase full of clothes that *I* had purchased, and a painting that I'd inherited from my grandmother. I underestimated him though. Once I left, he didn't allow *any* contact at all. I tried writing to my mother and sister, but all the letters came back.

"So, you see, despite any problems I may have had with Pierre, I had no family to go back to. I burned all my bridges when I walked out the door. At first I thought my father would relent. He didn't. After five years of returned letters, I stopped trying. Pierre and my work were all that I had left. I guess that's why that painting meant so much to me."

"Really? Why? Because it was from your grandmother?"

"Partly. Mostly, though, because it tied me to my home, to the States, and to my family. The painting had been in the family for generations. I was so proud to have it. But it also reminded me of all that I'd walked away from."

"What kind of painting is it?"

"It was of Central Park, when it was first developed. Back before muggings and murders in it. Back when people took strolls and rode horses, and carriages." Louise smiled. "It was a beautiful piece of history."

"You keep saying 'was'. Don't you have it anymore?"

"No. It's gone now." Louise released Tammy's hand and stood up, feeling a need to pace.

"But, why?"

"Because Pierre sold it." She clenched her jaw as she spoke. "He knew it was worth a lot of money, so he'd been after me for years to sell it. I always refused. So, he waited until I went away for a few days. When I came home, the painting was gone. And I was furious. We got into a huge argument over it. He walked out angry, and that was the last time that I saw him alive."

"I'm so sorry," Tammy whispered. "You must have felt betrayed."

"Yes. And terribly guilty too. I knew why he wanted the money. I could understand that. But for him to sell it behind my back, knowing how much it meant to me—"

Just then, Cari and Gilles entered the room. Cari looked pale. She reached for Louise's arm. "We didn't mean to eavesdrop on you two. I'm sorry. But there's something you really need to know, Louise. Pierre sold that painting to Gilles' father, all of the documents signed with your name. But the painting never arrived, only an empty crate. I've been hired to help find it. Or at least to find out what happened to it."

Chapter 27

Tammy looked from one distraught face to the other. Cari was pale, and Louise had flushed cheeks. Gilles mostly looked uncomfortable.

"How dare you?" Louise cried, keeping her voice down. "This is the reason for all the questions, just because you're trying to find the painting? Well, I have no idea where it is. As I just said, Pierre sold it while I was away from home. It could be anywhere by now. That was weeks ago." Her fists were clenched at her sides. "Do you have any idea how *used* I feel right now?"

"Louise," Cari broke in, "please let us try to explain."

"Why? What is left to 'explain'? You wanted something from me, and instead of just asking me directly, you used me. Hired me, paid me for my time." She shook her head and Tammy noticed that her shoulders were trembling. "Find yourself another therapist, Fraulein. I have *honest* clients that I'd much rather work with." She turned to pick up her supply bag.

"Louise, please don't leave angry," Tammy begged. "I'm sorry. We didn't mean to hurt you like this." She leaned forward, but Louise pulled away from her. "I'm sorry."

"I've heard more than my share of 'I'm sorry' since I married Pierre. 'I'm sorry I gambled last night.' 'I'm sorry I lost my paycheque.' 'I'm sorry I lost my job.' 'I'm sorry I sold the painting.'" She shook her head again as she slung the bag over her shoulder. "I am sick to death of 'I'm sorry'." She moved away from the bed.

Tammy flicked back the sheet and blanket, heedless of her bare legs beneath the hospital gown. "Louise, please stay for a little bit. It's just not like you're making it out to be."

Louise turned around for a minute, her intense gaze causing Tammy to flinch. "Oh, you are very good at getting information from people, aren't you?" She sounded so disgusted. "Such a sweet and innocent girl; such a willing listener. You make me sick." She took another step away from the bed and glared at Cari. "Get out of my way, and don't you dare bother me again—for *any* reason."

"Louise," Cari tried again, "it's possible that Pierre's death wasn't an accident."

Rather than pausing, Louise quickened her step. "Don't you think I'm smart enough to figure that out for myself? He owed money to all the wrong people. But, no matter what you may be able to prove about his death—he'd still be *dead*, wouldn't he?" She brushed past Cari, and Gilles stepped aside.

Tammy shifted on the bed and put her legs over the side. She felt dizzy, but she didn't care. "Louise, just give us another chance." She got up on her feet, and had to grab the side of the bed frame with her right hand. They were all looking at Louise's back. Tammy took a step forward, remembering too late about the IV in her left hand. "Ahh!" she gasped and slumped against the bed. She looked down and saw that she'd torn her skin, but the needle was still half in, half out. Blood was trickling across her fingers. She clamped her right hand over her left.

Gilles was the first to turn around. "Tammy! What did you do?" He steadied her with one hand, and buzzed for the nurse with the other.

"What's going on?" Cari asked, turning around.

"My hand," Tammy cried. "The IV. I forgot."

"Get back on the bed, Tammy," Gilles urged.

Louise ducked into the washroom and carried a hand towel over to the bed. "Move your hand, Tammy," she ordered. Tammy complied, despite the flow of blood that dripped all over the blanket. Louise quickly pressed the towel on top of the torn skin, making Tammy moan. "What's taking the nurse so long? Go to the desk, Cari. Tell them it's an emergency." She looked into Tammy's face. "Lie back down and take deep breaths." She increased the pressure on the injured hand, holding it between both of hers. "Don't pass out just because you're holding your breath."

"It hurts," Tammy asserted, but she followed Louise's instructions.

Just then a nurse came in, Cari right behind her. "What's the problem?" she asked, quickly approaching the bed.

Louise replied, "She was trying to get out of bed, and pulled the IV loose. It's still partially embedded, but she tore through the vein, and the skin is ripped too." She lifted the towel long enough for the nurse to have a quick look.

"I'll get an orderly in here. We'll have to take her to have that fixed." She moved to shut off the IV solutions, which were now uselessly dripping. "Keep the pressure on that." She scooted from the room as Tammy stared at the ceiling.

"I just forgot," she whimpered. "I've never had one in before and I forgot."

"Shh," Cari soothed. "Try to relax. They'll take care of it."

"Louise," Tammy whispered. "Thanks for staying." She blinked as tears pushed past her eyelids.

"We'll discuss that later," mumbled Louise. "Just know that

I'm not really as heartless as I may have sounded."

"I already knew that."

Louise looked down at the blood all over her hands. *Tammy's blood, and at least partly my fault.* She was just about to go and wash her hands when Rick Benson entered the waiting area.

"What's going on?" he demanded. "I come to see my daughter and find out she's down here, getting stitches or something." He focused on Louise. "What happened to you?" His tone had altered completely. No more rage, just compassionate interest.

"I-uh, I tried to stop the bleeding," she stammered. She glanced at Cari and Gilles, but they didn't say anything.

"What bleeding? What happened?"

"She forgot about the IV, and pulled it loose, tore it, actually. It made a mess." She saw him clench his jaw, and instinctively moved back against the wall. She'd seen Pierre do that far too many times. Usually right before he slapped her face. "She's getting stitches, and they have to start a new IV in her other arm now."

Rick raised his right hand and Louise inhaled sharply. His hand paused in mid air, and his gaze locked with hers. "How is she?" he asked.

"She was in pain at first, but I'm sure they gave her something for that. And they'd use freezing before doing any stitching. Don't worry."

Rick sighed, running his fingers through his hair. "Famous last words," he muttered.

Louise felt profoundly uncomfortable with Rick standing so close. "Excuse me, please. I need to go clean up."

"Oh, sure. Sorry." He stepped back and allowed her to pass.

Once in the washroom, Louise vigorously scrubbed her hands. Then she realized that some of the blood had soaked into the cuffs of her sweater. She was still drying her hands when Cari entered the room.

"Thank you for everything, Louise," Cari said, her eyes misting with tears. "You seemed to know exactly what to do earlier. I'm grateful." She came near the row of sinks. "And I want to apologize for what's been happening. Honestly, we never meant to use you. You're right; maybe we should have just come straight to the point. But I don't regret meeting you on a professional level. You're very good, and I've appreciated your help. I know that Tammy has too. I'd really hate to try to find someone else while we're here, or worse, to wait until I get back home. Would you reconsider?"

With Tammy once more settled back in her room, a new IV in her right hand, and a thick gauze pad on her left, Rick felt as though he might be able to relax. Unless, of course, he thought about Louise St. Denis. *What is it about that woman that makes me want to do something to protect her? I don't even know her.* Still, he'd asked her to please wait in the hall until he was sure that Tammy was asleep. She'd agreed, though she looked as if leaving would have been her first thought.

Rick leaned over and kissed Tammy's forehead. To his surprise, she wasn't quite asleep yet.

"You promised, Dad," she whispered. "Don't forget."

"I won't, Sweetheart. Now try to sleep. I'll come back later. Okay?"

"Mmm-hmm." She turned her head to the side and let out a slow breath.

Out in the hallway, Louise stood leaning against the wall. She straightened as soon as Rick exited the room. "How is she?"

"Going to sleep. I told her that I'd come back later." He shoved his hands into his pockets and tried to think of a tactful way to phrase his next question. He didn't come up with one. "Um, Tammy made me promise to do something. That's why I asked you to stay." He met her gaze and saw a mix of confusion and curiosity.

"I don't understand, Herr Benson." She fingered the strap of the bag on her shoulder.

"Well, you see, she—well, she wanted to be sure that I took you out for lunch."

"But that isn't—I mean you—it's not necessary."

Rick took some comfort in knowing that she seemed to be as nervous as he was. "I know it's not, but Tammy can be very insistent sometimes." He smiled then. "Often, I should say. She told me that she'd do it herself, if she could. I guess she figures that I'm the next best option. So," he plunged in, "are you busy for lunch?"

"Right now?" she asked, her cheeks crimson. "Or another time?"

"Well," he hesitated, "either. But I'm only here for a few more days. So, I guess that today would be best."

"I-uh, I'm not busy right now. I don't have any more appointments until later this afternoon."

"Is that a 'yes'?" he asked with a smile. *She reminds me of a teenager being asked to the prom.*

"Well," she replied, her lips curving upward slightly, "I suppose it is." She flipped some hair from her forehead. "Though, I assure you it really isn't necessary."

"Maybe not," he answered. "But I won't complain if you don't."

"I-I should go home and change," she said, gesturing to the blood on her cuffs. "Could we meet somewhere?"

"Well, actually, I don't have a vehicle. John Maxwell dropped me off. And, frankly, I don't know my way around at all." He shrugged. "I'm open to suggestions."

"In that case, why don't we take my car? I could get changed, and then I'll take you to one of my favorite places." She seemed to be warming to the idea.

"Sounds good to me." He looked down at his casual clothing. "Am I dressed okay?"

"You look just fine, Herr Benson."

Chapter 28

Rick waited in Louise's car while she went inside to get changed. When she came back out, he caught his breath. She was wearing linen slacks, a silk blouse, and a matching linen jacket. The pants and jacket were a pale mauve, and the blouse was a deep violet, just like her eyes. *She looks gorgeous. Tammy, what have you gotten me into?*

"Ready for lunch?" Louise asked as she buckled her seatbelt.

"Well, I'm hungry," Rick replied, trying to ignore the sudden dryness of his throat, and moisture of his hands.

"Good. Then I know just the place. The cooking is almost as good as Frau Mueller's," she said with a smile. Then she started the car and drove off.

"You were right," Rick stated as he finished the last of his food. "This is fantastic. Do you come here very often?"

The warm smile which had graced her face through much of the meal suddenly faded. "I-uh, I used to. I haven't been here since my husband died."

"Oh." Rick took a sip of water from his glass. "It's hard, isn't it? We get so used to having them around all the time. Then, suddenly, they're gone." He shook his head. "I still forget sometimes, and I'll start to comment on some book that I've been reading." He inhaled slowly. "We got married right after high school. We used to discuss almost everything. That's one of the things that I miss most, I guess."

"At least you have your children to keep you company," she replied. She looked down at her crumpled napkin. "Sometimes I just can't bare the emptiness of the house. I guess that's why I started seeing my clients again." She shrugged. "It eases the loneliness."

"Don't you have friends? You've lived here a long time."

Louise lifted her eyes and met his gaze. "Herr Benson, my husband was a gambler, and a poor one at that. He made a lot of enemies. I never made any friends."

"Could you please call me Rick? This 'Herr Benson' stuff makes me nervous." He was rewarded with another smile.

"All right."

The waiter came and took their plates. "Would you like dessert?" he asked.

Rick had already scanned the menu, and he grinned. "My daughter informed me that I mustn't leave Switzerland without trying the sachertorte. And I'd like some coffee please. Louise?"

"I'll have the same, please."

"How did you meet your husband?" Rick asked while they tackled their dessert.

"In a coffee shop. He just boldly marched over to where I was sitting, and started talking to me."

"I'd bet it had something to do with your eyes," Rick commented, his voice soft.

"So he said." She looked at him, as though memorizing his face. "Tammy has such pretty blue eyes. Did your wife?"

"Yes, she did. And pretty much the same build too."

"She told me that your son looks just like you."

"He does." Rick drank some of his coffee before looking up

again. "It's hard to believe he's old enough for university already. Makes me feel old."

"But you married young," she countered. "You can't be very old."

"I'm thirty-seven," he admitted. "And you?" he asked, though he already knew.

"Thirty-three." She toyed with her piece of cake for a moment. Then she set her fork down. "I guess I'm full. Would you like the rest?"

"No, thanks. I've already eaten too much myself. You could take it with you, couldn't you? Or don't people do things like that here?"

"Sometimes. Actually, why don't you take it back to the hospital for Tammy? Especially since she likes it so much."

"Good idea."

Louise looked at her watch and frowned. "I should really get you back now, Rick. I'll need to return in time to meet my client."

"Oh, sure. Just let me take care of this, and I'll be ready to go." He took out his wallet and withdrew a credit card. "Thanks for joining me, Louise."

"Thank you for asking."

"So, how was lunch?" Tammy asked as soon as Rick sat down.

"Just great," he replied. "I even brought you some leftovers. Louise couldn't eat all of her dessert, so she wanted me to bring it for you." He placed a small pastry box on her bedside tray. "It's sachertorte. You were right, the stuff should be illegal." He grinned at her. "How are you feeling?"

"Better. But my hand hurts quite a bit." She made a face. "The freezing wore off a while ago."

"Oh. Well, please be extra careful with the new IV. You've only got two hands, you know."

"You like her, don't you, Dad?" Tammy asked in her usual manner.

"Uh, yes, I like her. Why?"

"Well, she just seems so lonely. And, I think maybe her marriage wasn't too great. She's said a few things to that effect."

"Probably. She told me at lunch that she doesn't really even have friends. That surprised me."

"Why? Because she's so beautiful?"

"Partly." He shrugged before leaning back in the chair. "She's bright, and interesting. But I think she's terribly shy. I can't help but wonder if she was always like that—or just after she got married."

"You could always ask."

"I don't think so. We're all lucky she's even speaking to us after what happened this morning. I know that Cari felt terrible about it."

"Me too. She was so hurt, Dad. And she made a big deal out of hearing 'I'm sorry'. She said Pierre used to say that all the time."

Rick thought back to earlier in the day. She'd actually cowered against the wall, as though she thought he'd harm her. *I have a hunch that marriage to Pierre was not all bliss by any stretch—and not just because of the gambling.* "Well, just try to be kind to her, Sweetheart."

"Do you wish that you could stick around longer?"

"Why? Will you miss me?" he teased.

"Of course. But I think Louise just might miss you too."

"It all blew up in our faces, John," Cari said after the waiter took their order. "She was so upset. We went about this all wrong."

"So it seems. However, all is not lost, is it? She did agree to talk with you again. Let's wait and see how that turns out."

"I suppose," Cari said with a sigh. "So, how was your day?"

"Interesting. Investigating forgery is a new field for me. I've been trying to find out some of the laws governing that. Also, if Pierre St. Denis was the forger, does that nullify the purchase made by Senor Rodriquez? He bought the painting 'in good faith'. It could all be a colossal mess in court. Especially since the guilty party is dead. Even so, we still don't know where the painting actually ended up. Any ideas?"

"A couple. Gilles is using his *connections* to get some names of black market art dealers. Maybe, just maybe, Pierre owed one of them money, and tried to make a trade."

"But, if that's the case, then why would he end up dead? Surely they'd want the painting first."

"Maybe they were tired of waiting for him to deliver." She shrugged. "I'm still working at finding pieces, never mind fitting them all together."

"Did you know that Rick had lunch with Louise today?"

"Yes, I did. Courtesy of Tammy's conniving mind, no doubt."

"I don't know about that. Rick seemed to be a willing participant."

Cari smiled. "They deserve each other. Sweet and vulnerable she may be, but she has a temper too."

"Really?" John asked with a laugh. "Reminds me of someone else I know."

Cari cocked an eyebrow. "Is that so, Mr. Maxwell? And who might that be?"

"I refuse to answer on the grounds that I may get myself into trouble. Besides, we came here for supper, not an argument."

"So who wants to argue?"

"You've been asking too many questions, Rodriquez," said one of the men wearing a ski mask. "Some people don't like it." He nodded and a punch caught Gilles in the ribs. "If you'd like to fly home in a seat, and not in a box, then take this little warning seriously." Another nod followed by several more punches. Then Gilles was released and he crumpled to the floor. "You wouldn't want your pretty friend to have an *accident*, would you?" The man grabbed Gilles' hair and jerked his head back. "I assure you, we could be quite *creative* in that regard." He shoved his face into the thick carpeting. "So stop asking questions."

Gilles lay on the carpet, his breathing a series of pants and gasps. "Cari. Have to warn Cari." He tried to get up, but didn't make it past his knees. He crawled to the phone and picked up the receiver. "No, she's out with Maxwell." He groaned and dropped the receiver. He felt as though he'd been kicked around like a soccer ball. He made his way to the bathroom, and waited for the inevitable. Shortly thereafter, his breakfast, lunch and supper all came up, mingled with a bit of blood.

Chapter 29

Cari checked her watch for the fifth time and frowned. "Gilles is never late, John. I don't understand why he's not down here yet." They'd already finished a cup of coffee while waiting in the dining room of the Waldhaus.

"Well then, perhaps we should check with the desk and see if he's left a message for us," John suggested.

"All right." She pushed her chair back before John was even on his feet. But she did linger a second before heading in the direction of the reception area.

"Excuse me, Sir," John said to the man behind the desk. "Is Mr. Gilles Rodriquez still in his room? He was supposed to be joining us for breakfast almost twenty minutes ago. He's in room 225, I believe."

"Why, yes, Mein Herr. He just had breakfast ordered up to his room, not thirty minutes ago. It would seem that he forgot about your meeting."

"Thank you," John replied. Then he reached for Cari's elbow. "Let's go see what he's up to. Something doesn't make sense." They headed in the direction of the elevator, both of them knowing that Cari didn't need the added strain of a lengthy flight of stairs.

Cari knocked as soon as they got to the door.

"Just a minute," called a voice from the other side.

Cari frowned again. "That doesn't sound like Gilles," she whispered.

A moment later they could hear approaching footsteps. "Who is it?" It was definitely Gilles speaking.

"It's Cari and John. You were supposed to meet us downstairs, Gilles."

They listened as the door was unlocked. Gilles stepped back as he opened it. "Come on in," he said, still sounding unusually tired. Or tense, perhaps. He closed the door as soon as they entered, locking it behind them.

"All right, Gilles," Cari said, "what's going on? You don't *forget* appointments." Her brows furrowed as she glanced around the room. She noticed the room service cart, with his half eaten breakfast on it. Then she glared at him. "Trying to avoid us for some reason?"

"No," Gilles asserted, shaking his head. "Will you please sit down?" He slowly moved towards the sofa and eased himself down onto it. That was a dead giveaway to Cari.

"You're hurt, aren't you?" she asked. "What happened?"

Gilles sighed as he looked from Cari to John and back again. "Two men in ski masks *happened*."

"What?" Cari leaned forward on the chair she'd chosen. "What are you talking about?"

"Last night. I answered the door without checking to see who it was," explained Gilles. "Something I almost never do when I'm traveling. Anyway, once they were in, I was hardly in a position to tell them to leave."

"What did they want?" John asked, his expression somewhat guarded.

"They informed me, none too gently I might add, that I've

been asking too many questions. Apparently, *some people* don't like it." He leaned back and couldn't quite hide the clenching of his jaw.

"What did they do to you, Gilles?" Cari wanted to know. "Have you seen a doctor?"

"A few punches," he replied. "Just some cracked ribs, I think. I've had worse injuries playing soccer. One of the reasons I quit that line of work."

"Just some cracked ribs?" she exclaimed. "That's nothing to kid about! I happen to know that from personal experience. You still need medical attention for that."

"No," Gilles replied, his tone offering no room to argue. "The fewer questions the better." He levelled his gaze with hers. "And watch your step, Cari. They threatened an *accident*, if we didn't back off. I've no doubt they'd follow through on it."

"They mentioned me?" Cari asked. "By name?"

"Well, no, not by name. They referred to you as 'your pretty little friend'. Who else could they mean?"

"Tammy," John answered. He rubbed his chin, looking thoughtful. "Fortunately, Rick is with her most of the time. And I'm not sure they'd try much in a hospital."

Gilles shook his head again. "No, I'm sure they meant Cari." He swallowed and looked down at the floor. "They mentioned having 'creative' means." The color drained from Cari's face and she gripped the arms of the chair. "Either way, we've stepped on the wrong toes in this whole thing."

"And going to the police could just make it worse," John reasoned. "That leaves Louise St. Denis."

"Louise," Cari asked, "do you know who all Pierre owed money to?" They had just finished the massage therapy, and were sitting in the office.

"No. I told Pierre I didn't want to find out. But there are plenty of rumors, aren't there?"

"Yes. Gilles Rodriquez just got beaten up last night, for checking into some of those 'rumors'."

"Really?" Louise fiddled with the pen in her hand. "Is he all right?"

"Not likely, but he won't admit it." Cari flicked her bangs out of her face. "You said yesterday, at the hospital, that Pierre owed money to 'all the wrong people'. What did you mean?"

"Surely you didn't miss my meaning, Cari." Louise looked right into her eyes. "Organized crime. Men connected with gambling, drugs and prostitution."

That statement led into Cari's next question. "Was Pierre involved with those as well?"

Louise shook her head. "Wasn't gambling enough?" She bit her lip and stared down at her hands. "It destroyed everything," she whispered.

"Did he gamble when you first met him?"

"Yes. But it seemed like such an innocent thing at the time. Card games, betting on trivial things, flipping a coin to make a decision on where to eat. Things like that." She let out her breath in a sigh. "My father saw it for what it was. At least for what it would become. He warned me that a man with Pierre's personality, and love of beautiful things, and loathing of work, would keep turning to the easy way out. I didn't believe him. That was the biggest *gamble* of my life. And I lost it." She fingered her wedding band. "We weren't here six months before Pierre was frequenting casinos. Oh, he won just often enough to keep hoping that he'd score big eventually. He never did."

"I don't understand addictions of any kind, I guess," Cari

admitted. "Though drugs were responsible for the death of my parents, and for what happened to me." She paused as she thought of her conversations with Tammy. "And the murder of Rick Benson's wife." She considered her eleven years as a police officer. "And I've seen lives destroyed because of alcohol, or smokers who died of lung cancer." She let her breath out slowly. "No, I don't suppose I'll ever *understand* it, no matter how many times I may *see* it."

"I lived with it for fourteen years," Louise countered. "And I never understood it either." Cari noticed the tears in her eyes. "There were so many things that I never understood. Like the lying, the excuses, the apologies, the promises, over and over and over." She wiped at the now falling tears. "After a while, I guess I just didn't care anymore. I was so tired of it all."

"But not tired enough to leave your husband?" Cari asked.

"No. I could never bring myself to do that. Oh, I thought about it, many times. But he was still my husband."

"And you loved him," Cari added.

"Yes, in spite of everything." She kept a hand against her left cheek. "He even used to hit me sometimes, and I always forgave him for it." She looked at Cari once more. "Is that *love* or *stupidity*?"

Cari didn't answer, but she couldn't help but think of Mark Hamilton. Why hadn't she reported him when he raped her? Fear or shame? Why had she allowed him to catch her off guard at all? Why had she blamed herself for so long afterwards? None of it made any sense. *Feelings and emotions seldom do.*

Louise straightened her shoulders and stood up. "Now," she said, using a handkerchief to dry her face, "you said that my painting never arrived—just an empty crate, right?"

"Yes. So, either Pierre managed to sell it to someone else, or he stored it somewhere. Do you have any idea where he might have done that?"

Louise rubbed her forehead for a moment. "I'm getting very tired, Cari. Why don't we go and have a cup of tea?"

"Sure." Cari was relieved that Louise seemed to want to help, but she still felt badly for her. "I'm not in a rush."

"Louise, would you have a copy of the police report on Pierre's death? Or, did you at least get to see it at the time?" Cari added more cream to her tea and stirred while she talked.

"No. They simply came and told me that my husband had been hit by a car, and died. And I had to go and identify his body. They gave me an envelope with his 'personal effects' in it."

"So they considered it an accident?"

"Yes. They didn't seem at all suspicious." Louise was staring, as though her thoughts were back in time.

"What about you? Did you wonder if they were right?"

"Not at first. You see I was so upset that I wasn't thinking clearly. And I was ridden with guilt because of the argument we had just before he left that night."

"Do you have any idea where he went that night?"

"No. I only know where he was killed. Not far from the train station. I have no idea why he would go there. Pierre seldom took the train anywhere. I could only suppose that he was as angry as I was, and that he wandered around for a couple of hours."

"Louise," Cari asked softly, "do you still have that envelope, or at least the contents from it."

"Yes." Louise set her cup down on the table and stared at it for a moment. "I never even bothered to open it." Her head suddenly jerked up. "You don't really think that the police would have overlooked something important, do you?"

"I honestly don't know, Louise. If they only thought it was a simple hit and run accident, they may not have gone through his things very carefully. It's worth checking."

"Is it, Cari? Or will looking in that envelope just make everything worse?"

"We won't know that if we don't look."

Chapter 30

Cari looked down at the contents of the envelope as Louise slid them onto her kitchen table. A wallet and a wedding band. Some loose change. Half a pack of cigarettes, and a small ticket or stub of some kind. Cari pointed to it.

"What's this for?" she asked.

Louise picked up the stub and read it carefully. "It's a claim ticket. From the train station, I believe."

"A claim ticket? Do you mean for picking up something that's in storage? Like at some of the bus stations back home?"

"Yes, exactly. But I don't remember Pierre ever doing that before." Louise slowly shook her head as she sat down. "I just don't understand. And why wouldn't the police have checked to see what it was?"

"Probably because they considered his death an accident," Cari replied. "If they knew nothing about the painting, why would they have been suspicious?"

Louise levelled her gaze with Cari's. "You mean that you think the painting is what Pierre has in storage?"

"Possibly. It's worth checking, isn't it?"

"Of course. I-I suppose it could be almost *anything*. Maybe it's time to find out."

"Do you mind if I check in his wallet?"

"No. Go ahead." Louise still fingered the stub in her right hand, no longer looking up.

Cari withdrew all the contents of the wallet, and carefully laid them out on the table. She hesitated at the last item, holding it in her hand and staring for several seconds.

"What's wrong?" Louise asked.

"It's a picture, Louise. Do you know who this is?" Cari turned the photo and showed it to her. It was of a beautiful young woman, with long blonde hair and blue eyes. And she had her arms around a handsome man that Cari assumed to be Pierre St. Denis. There was writing on the back, but it wasn't in English.

Louise furrowed her brows as she took the picture from Cari. Her eyes filled with tears as she stared at it. Then she turned it over and read the brief message. The photo slipped from her fingers and rested on the table. Louise put her head in her hands.

"What's wrong?" Cari asked, her hand on Louise's trembling shoulder. "Who is it?"

"I don't know. I've never met her," Louise stammered. The tears began to trickle down her face. "But obviously Pierre knew her—very well. She wrote that she'd always remember the 'wonderful weekend' that they spent together. The photo is dated by the camera. Pierre was in Bern that weekend, supposedly looking for work. Oh, I knew it was an excuse to just gamble somewhere else. But I never once thought of another woman."

"Are you sure that's what the message means, Louise?" Cari dared to ask.

"Yes! Apparently his 'skill' as a lover was higher than as a gambler." She snatched up the photo and read the back to Cari, translating as she did so.

'Dear Pierre,

I thought you'd like to have a reminder of the wonderful weekend we spent together.

I've never met a man like you before. You're an amazing lover. Let me know if you ever decide to leave your wife. I'll welcome you with open arms.

Love,

Justina'

"Oh, Louise, I'm so sorry," Cari whispered.

Louise tore the photo into several pieces, her hands shaking. "He never made love to me after that weekend. It was shortly before he was killed. For all I know, he was planning to use the money from *my* painting to leave me and join *her*!" She got up from the chair and began to pace the small room. "Now I really have no idea what he may have left in storage."

"Louise, I realize that you're upset, and you have every reason to be. But, did you notice if any of Pierre's clothes or other belongings are missing? Maybe he stored something at the station, and then was going to leave by train."

Louise turned to face her, her shoulders taut. "Are you really so heartless that all you can think of is what is in that locker? I find out that my husband slept with another woman, and you are still intent on the *case*! Don't you have any feelings for others? Or would that just get in the way of your job?"

"Louise, I—" Cari tried to reply.

"I don't want any more apologies! Or polite theology either. I want you out of my house. Oh, you can take your prized bit of *evidence*. Frankly, I'd rather not know what Pierre put in storage. I've had enough surprises for one lifetime." She stalked to the sink and turned on the water, splashing some into her face.

Cari stood frozen for a moment. Then she stepped closer to Louise. "I won't apologize again. And I won't tell you that I understand how you feel. That would be a lie. But one thing that I do understand is betrayal. I do know what it's like to love a man enough to plan to marry him, and then to have him turn on me. To destroy any sense of trust. To wish I'd never *met* him, let alone fallen in love with him."

Louise shut off the water, but didn't turn around.

"I don't know how to help you, Louise, but I'd like to try. I tried to bury my shame at first. But eventually I realized just how much I needed my friends. I never would have gotten through it without them."

Louise turned around and stared at Cari, anger still dominant in her facial expression. "Your fiancé cheated on you?" she asked.

Cari swallowed before answering. "No. He raped me." She went on to explain about the pregnancy and miscarriage. "I tried to keep it to myself. Once I couldn't, I realized that I'd been missing out on support that could have been there immediately." She took another step towards Louise. "I'd like to be there for you, Louise. Will you let me?"

A slight nod was Louise's only response, but it was enough. Cari put her arms around the woman and held her. "I won't shove religion or theology at you, Louise, but I will pray for you."

"All right. I probably need it now more than ever."

"You're deep in thought tonight," Rick said to Cari as they once more sat near the fire. "Is something wrong?"

Cari looked over at him and smiled. "Not for me, personally," she replied. "I'm just worried about Louise. It seems the more I find out about her husband, the less I like him."

"That's an odd answer," John remarked from the chair opposite her. "What do you mean?"

Cari sighed, and tried to sort out just what to say. "He lied to her about so many things." *Like not telling her he was sterile until they'd been married a couple of years.* "And he used to hit her sometimes."

"I thought so," Rick murmured.

"Why?" Cari asked.

"Because of how she reacted the other day. When I put my hand out, she moved away, like she was afraid of me." He smiled for a second. "I don't *usually* have that affect on women."

"True," Cari replied. "She found out today that he'd been with another woman, recently. She has no way of knowing about the previous fourteen years."

Both men looked exceedingly uncomfortable. John was the first to speak. "How did she find out?"

"A picture in his wallet, complete with a love note on the back."

"In his wallet?" Rick asked. "Hadn't she checked that already?"

"No. She hadn't gone through his personal items since she'd identified his body for the police. Not until today." *Maybe I shouldn't have pressed her to do it. Then again, she likely would have found it sometime, and then she might have been alone.* "She's hurting so much. It's like her world is falling apart."

"She needs friends," Rick asserted. "She's carrying everything on her shoulders."

"That's probably what she's always done," John said.

"John," put in Cari, "she doesn't even have family to turn to. She's had no contact with them ever since she left home. And she's never made any close friends here. But that wasn't the case when she was younger. She told me that she could always tell her mother everything. She was even pretty close to her dad. And she knew some girls from school. All those ties were severed when she left Boston. Yes, she's a very lonely woman. But, that doesn't mean that's how she wants it to stay."

They sat in silence for several moments, each with their own thoughts. Then Cari spoke up again.

"I may have a very important lead for us," she said. "There was a stub for storage at the train station, in with Pierre's things. Louise let me keep it. Shall we go check it out tomorrow, John?"

"Certainly," he replied. "Have you called Rodriquez about this?"

"Not yet." She smiled. "I figured we could all use some rest before checking into anything else. It's already been a long day."

"And what about me?" Rick asked, sounding insulted.

"Rick," Cari replied, "you're not on this case, remember? You're here to keep tabs on Tammy. Let the rest of us handle this, okay?"

"Yes, Ma'am," he replied. "I'll leave the *investigating* to the pros."

"Thank you," Cari said with a smile. "Besides, we need you to keep Tammy from asking too many more probing questions. She's already found out more than enough."

"Try to tell *her* that," Rick said with a laugh. "She'd like to know Louise's life story." He frowned. "Some things are best left unknown."

"She's never just *curious* though," John remarked. "She's always sincere, albeit rather *direct* at times." He glanced over at Cari and she felt her cheeks flush. "She's actually proven to be a wonderful chaperone on this trip."

Cari cleared her throat. "Excuse me," she said as she got to her feet. "I think I'll head to bed. It's been kind of a draining day." *And I don't intend to sit here and let Rick ask me about what John is referring to.*

"Goodnight."

"Goodnight, Cari," John answered. "Maybe we could meet Rodriquez for breakfast tomorrow, before checking at the train station."

"Good idea."

Rick got to his feet and stood in front of her. Then he grinned. "You really don't have to run off, Cari," he said. "Tammy has already told me *everything* about her duties as chaperone. Seems she's taken her role very seriously."

Cari put her hands up to her cheeks, certain of their flaming shade of red. "Goodnight," she whispered. Then she stepped past him and hastened towards the stairs, but not before she heard Rick and John laughing in the other room.

Chapter 31

"How are you this morning, Tammy?" Louise asked as she moved next to the bed.

"I'm really tired," was the mumbled reply. Tammy rolled over onto her back, and moved some hair out of her face. "It's the stupid antibiotic side effects, nightmares and nausea. I've had plenty of both."

Louise sat down on the chair next to the bed. "I'm sorry to hear that. Do you think that a massage would help? I brought my things with me."

Tammy let out her breath slowly, and Louise noticed just how pale she was. "Maybe. I guess being stiff and sore doesn't make it any easier to sleep." She rubbed her eyes with her bandaged hand and frowned. "I'm sorry to be such a grouch today. I'll be so glad when I'm done taking all this medication. But Dr. Mueller told me I have another two days of IV, and then ten days of pills. By that time, we might be flying home again."

Louise reached between the rails and patted Tammy's hand. "That's okay. Have you had breakfast yet? I came pretty early."

"No. I was feeling so sick when they brought it, I just couldn't eat any of it." Tammy tried to smile. "One of the nurses told me it'll be good practice for when I have kids. Morning sickness can't be much worse than this."

"Tell you what; I'll use some Chamomile oil this time. It's known for it's soothing properties. And maybe later I could bring you some chamomile tea. It's good for nausea too."

"I'd appreciate that, Louise. Thanks."

"I feel so much better now," Tammy murmured against the pillow. "You were right about that oil."

"Am I interrupting?" Rick asked as he parted the curtains around the bed.

"No, Dad. I think Louise is just about finished. But, I'm ready to go to sleep, so I won't be much company this morning." She yawned, as though to emphasize her point.

"So I see," Rick replied, a warm smile on his face. Then he looked to Louise. "You're here early today."

"Yes. I have other appointments later this morning, and during the afternoon." She wiped her hands on her towel, and fastened the back of Tammy's gown. "Do you want to turn over, Tammy or just stay like that?"

"I'm fine," Tammy sighed, her eyes already closed.

Louise drew the sheet up around Tammy's shoulders. "Have a good rest. I'll try to stop in this evening, with the tea."

"Sure." That was the last comment from Tammy, and Rick and Louise stood there watching her for a moment.

"She had a rough night again," Louise said. "The medication, she says."

"I know. She almost never takes *anything*, let alone potent drugs like what they're using right now. She's not tolerating them too well." He met her gaze then. "I'm sure she appreciates your help. Thanks for coming."

"You're welcome." Louise put her things into her bag, and zipped it shut. "I suppose I should get going."

"Are you in a hurry? Or could you come and have a coffee with me?" He glanced down at Tammy's sleeping form. "I'm not needed here at the moment."

"Well, I—" Louise looked at her watch. "I have time, I guess. And there is something I'd like to ask you."

Rick cocked an eyebrow. "All right. Is the cafeteria okay? I know it's lousy coffee, but it's close by."

"That will be fine." She brought her bag to her shoulder and moved past him. "I'm used to lousy coffee."

"You said you wanted to ask me something," Rick reminded her. "What was that?"

"Well, I realize that I've just met you, and Tammy, so this may seem rather a strange request." She nervously ran her index finger around the rim of her coffee mug several times. "I was wondering if you would allow Tammy to come and stay with me for a few days, after she leaves the hospital. I have a spare room, and she wouldn't have to worry about taking so many stairs. All my rooms are on one floor."

"I guess I don't really understand, Louise. Your interest, I mean. Like you said, you just met us."

"I know." She looked at him then, her beautiful violet eyes reflecting apparent uncertainty. "But I would enjoy her company. And I'd like to help take care of her. Cari and the others may be busy for the next few days, trying to find the painting." Her cheeks flushed and she looked down at the table. "Your daughter reminds me very much of my younger sister, Leanne. She was almost eleven when I left home. And she had so much energy." Louise smiled. "She drove me crazy half the time, but I loved her anyway. And she was forever asking questions, just like Tammy." She bit her lip. "I really miss her sometimes."

Rick leaned back in the stiff chair. "Well, why don't we see what Tammy has to say to the idea? I know this trip didn't turn out the way she planned it." He shook his head. "The way *any* of us planned it. Her original reason for being along was to provide Cari with some feminine company. But I guess she's not doing that from the hospital anyway."

"Do you think that Cari would mind?"

"I don't know without asking her. But, like you said, she and the guys may be kind of busy for the next few days. I'll mention it to Tammy when she wakes up." He grinned then. "You should know by now that she'll have an immediate answer. She makes up her mind a lot quicker than I do."

"Was your wife like that?" Louise asked, her voice softer than before.

Rick was taken aback by her question. "Actually, she was. I guess that helped her to be a good nurse. She could read information, and remember it right away. I always had to study it all several times. Tammy is a top student, just like my wife was. My son is more of an athlete, though he's far from stupid."

"Has it been hard, raising them by yourself?"

"Sometimes, yes." He finished his coffee. "Especially with Tammy. I mean, every girl needs a mother, doesn't she? Tammy has even told me that to my face. Cari has been a big help. They do a lot of 'girl stuff' together. And my partner's wife, she's great with her, too." He crossed his arms over his chest and smiled. "Tammy can cook up a storm, clean the house, tackle the laundry. Sometimes it's hard to remember that she's just a fourteen year old. And I'm not very comfortable with the thought of leaving her alone once Ricky goes to school next month. She's really too old to have a baby-sitter, but—"

"But you still think of her as your little girl?"

"Yeah, I guess so. Sometimes, at least."

"You could always get a housekeeper, couldn't you? Someone to be there when you're at work."

Rick raised his eyebrows. "Tammy would have a fit. She can do all the jobs a housekeeper would." He shook his head. "No, my daughter is hoping that I'll remarry, not hire somebody."

"Is that what *you're* hoping to do?" Her facial expression showed genuine curiosity.

"Yes. I think I'm ready to consider it. It's been almost four years since my wife died. But, actually, I was already thinking about remarriage a year ago."

"Cari?"

"How did you know?"

"Tammy talks a lot." She smiled as she picked up her mug. "She said you just ended up as good friends, though. Were you disappointed?"

"A little," he admitted. "Cari certainly doesn't lack for male admirers though."

"So I see. Tammy has told me a great deal about Gilles Rodriquez and John Maxwell, though I haven't met Gilles."

"He's very nice too, though I still think that John is the favorite. I wouldn't be at all surprised if those two end up getting married."

Louise looked at her watch. "Oh, I'd better get going. I don't want to make my client wait on my front steps." She got up from her chair. "Thank you for the coffee."

"You're welcome. And I'll talk with Tammy later. But I'm pretty sure I already know what her answer will be. You said you'd come back later this evening?"

"Yes. I told Tammy I'd bring some chamomile tea. She's been so sick, I thought it might help."

"Well, I'll probably see you then. Have a good day."

"Thank you." She turned to leave, and Rick couldn't help but notice the graceful way she carried herself.

She is incredibly beautiful, Lord. So, why can't she be a Christian? I think I'm starting to understand how Cari feels about John Maxwell. He shook his head and got to his feet. Then he carried the empty mugs over to the bin near the counter. *Well, Tammy, maybe a few days with you will change things. I can always hope so.*

Chapter 32

"What do you mean, it isn't here?" Cari asked the young man behind the counter at the train station. "Then where is it?" He had just told her, and John and Gilles, that the ticket no longer meant much, since whatever had been in storage was no longer at the station.

"As I told you Fraulein, we open the lockers daily. Any unclaimed items then get sent on to the station in Chur. They are kept there for thirty days, then sent to—"

"All right, so it should still be in Chur?" She handed him the stub once more.

"Yes, Fraulein, but just until tomorrow. It's already been there for twenty-nine days."

Cari grabbed the stub. "But how can we claim it? This stub was for the locker at *this* station."

The young man looked as though he were getting annoyed with all her questions. "Anything which is removed from the storage lockers, unclaimed, is tagged with the matching number. It will simply be a matter of looking for the same number when you get there."

"When does the next train leave?" John asked.

"In forty minutes. But it's already fully booked, I'm afraid."

"How long does it take to drive there?" Cari wanted to know.

The young man scrutinized her, taking special note of her cane. "Only about one and a half hours, Fraulein, if a driver knows the roads well. But the passes can be difficult for—"

"A *tourist*?" she asked. "Or a *woman*?"

The young man had the good grace to flush slightly.

"Where can I purchase a good road map?"

"Just over there, Fraulein, in the gift shop."

"Thank you. You've been such a big help." Cari didn't even try to hide the sarcasm in her voice. She turned to face John and Gilles. "So, let's go get ourselves a map."

"Are you sure you want to ride all the way to Chur?" John asked. "What about the change in altitude?"

"I've been fine since we got here," she retorted. "Besides, I don't plan to *ride*. I intend to *drive*."

"Cari—" Gilles protested.

She ignored him and went to purchase a map. Unlike the young man, the girl in the gift shop was very polite, and helped her to select an appropriate map. Cari paid for it immediately and then handed it to John. "You can navigate. I figure if you can find your way around the Sierras, you should do okay in the Alps. Let's go."

"Cari—" Gilles tried again.

She stopped short and looked into his face. "What?"

"Why don't you let one of us drive? What about your leg?"

"My leg is just fine for driving, Gilles. And you can either shut up and come along, or you can go back to your swanky hotel. But I'm driving."

Nothing more was said as they walked to the parking area. Cari unlocked the driver's door of the Porsche. Then she moved the seat so that Gilles could get in the back. "Are you coming?" she asked, a note of challenge in her voice.

"I'm coming." He got in and buckled his seat belt, looking none too happy about the arrangement.

Cari got in and unlocked the passenger door for John. He had the map folded and was tracing the route with his finger. "What's the speed limit from here to there?"

"Seventy-five miles per hour, most of the way." He glanced at her for a moment. "That's faster than back in LA."

Cari smiled. "I know. I can hardly wait."

Cari had no trouble maintaining the speed limit through the curves of the mountain passes. She expertly manoeuvred the Porsche in and around other vehicles. She shifted gears only when necessary, keeping steady hands on the steering wheel, and her foot on the accelerator. The change in altitude didn't bother her either. In fact, she was more relaxed than she'd been the whole trip.

"You've done this before, haven't you?" Gilles finally asked.

"Done what?" Cari replied.

"This kind of driving."

"Plenty of it, though never with a car as nice as this one." She grinned. "My poor old Camaro served me well for several years."

"You don't drive like this on LA freeways," John commented.

"No. But you do in rallies."

"You've competed?" Gilles asked, obviously surprised.

"Yes. I even have a bunch of trophies collecting dust to prove it. Why do you sound so shocked?" She already suspected a reason for that.

"Well, I-I guess because I've only known you since you were injured. Maybe I just assumed—"

"Maybe you assumed that since I need a cane part of the time, and because I was too clumsy to walk on a beach, and because I got violently sick on the way here, that I couldn't *possibly* have any skills that require physical prowess or coordination?" She shifted and pulled out around the car in front of her. "Well, I didn't know you used to play soccer, so I guess that makes us even."

"How many trophies do you have?" John asked.

"Oh, enough to clutter my bookshelf," she replied. "More than a dozen, I think."

"What else are you an expert at?" he wanted to know.

"Well, let me see." She looked in the rear view mirror and noticed that Gilles had a tight grip in the edge of the seat. "I used to be a sharp shooter. I even considered applying for the SWAT team."

"Used to be?"

"Yes. I'm no longer allowed to tote a rifle. The kickback could mess up my pacemaker."

"Oh. What about with a pistol? Do you still practice?"

"Of course. My accuracy hasn't dropped any since I was hurt. What about you? I know you go hunting, but do you ever do target shooting?"

"Once in a while." Then he laughed. "I do much better with a large rifle, and a powerful scope. I'm not as adept with a handgun."

"What about you, Gilles?" Cari asked. "Do you ever hunt?"

"No, unless artwork counts. My mother has always hated guns. She was born at the end of the war, but she lost plenty of family to it. She's never allowed one in the house that I know of. But my father insists on armed guards for outside."

"Yes, I know," Cari remarked. "I'd say your home is well protected."

"How much is your father's art collection worth?" John asked. "Or is that classified information?"

Gilles laughed. "No. But I honestly can't give you an exact figure.

I'd say in the neighborhood of a hundred million dollars."

John let out a very undignified whistle. "Good heavens! And he's going to all this expense for one painting?"

"Yes," Gilles replied. "My father is very conscious of what *belongs* to him. He paid for it, so he expects to receive it, or at least to get his money back for it. He hates deceit."

"Don't we all?" John said. He looked at the map once more. "Another half hour, I'd say, considering who is at the wheel."

"What time is it?" Cari wanted to know.

"It'll be time for lunch when we get there," Gilles said. "So I don't know if we'd be able to find out anything right away. We may as well eat something first."

"Have you ever been there before?"

"No, I don't think so. Why?"

"So how will we know where to eat?"

"That shouldn't be a problem," John answered. "We'll just have to go to the *Stern*. It's an inn that's over three hundred years old, and they serve regional food."

"How do you know that?" Cari demanded.

"Because I've been reading all about this region since we left Zurich. Guidebooks are always full of useful information."

"Fine. Let's just hope there's room for us when we get there."

"If I eat even one more bite of these dumplings, I'm going to explode," Cari stated as she positioned her knife and fork on the plate. "But they sure are delicious, even if I can't pronounce the name of them."

Gilles and John had both opted for the breaded liver in red wine sauce, and were finishing every last morsel on their plates. There were still a few pieces of anise bread left for them, but even they were reaching their limits.

"This is really a beautiful place," Cari said. "I just love the look of arvenholtz." She looked across at John. "You could always try that at your cabin. It's certainly rustic enough to match, isn't it?"

"I don't think I'd be allowed to ship it home, Cari," he replied. "This pine is native to Switzerland. But I might be able to find something similar back home." He shrugged. "Funny you should suggest that. I've been coming here for years and I've never once thought of using any of the things I've purchased at the cabin. I've just taken everything to my beach house, or given it to my parents, or to the Richards. You might have a good plan."

"Thanks. However, my next plan is to get over to the train station and see if we can find out what Pierre put into storage last month."

"Patience," Gilles admonished. "Enjoy your coffee. I, for one, intend to have dessert." Before she could protest, he added, "And since I hired you, and I'm paying for this meal, you'll humor me. Won't you?"

"Oh, I suppose," she replied with an exasperated sigh. "But how can you possibly have room for dessert?"

"Lots of practice," he said with a laugh. "You've eaten at my home, and at my grandparents'. I'm used to meals like this, whether it's lunch or dinner. I think I'll have a pastry."

Cari shuddered. Until the pastry was brought to the table. Then she pestered for a taste.

They arrived at the station at 2:00 p.m. and explained to a clerk why they were there. He looked at the stub, then at the calendar, then at his watch. A deep frown creased his forehead.

"You only have an hour to look for it, I'm afraid. Then all the unclaimed items will be put onto a train for Zurich. Will you recognize your belongings?"

Cari groaned. *Recognize what? We don't even know what Pierre put in that locker.* "We're actually doing this for a friend," she answered, opting to go with the truth. "Her husband was killed the same day that he put something in storage. She's asked us to get it for her. Unfortunately, we don't know exactly *what* we're looking for. The clerk back in St. Moritz told us that all the unclaimed items would have been tagged, and that we should be able to match this stub with the tag."

The man was still frowning. "Fraulein, do you have any idea how many unclaimed items pass through here?"

"No, I don't. But you said we've got an hour. Can you please show us where to look?"

"Yes, I can do that. But you must realize Fraulein that this would be what you Americans call a 'wild goose chase'." He gave her the stub. "Please follow me." He stepped out from behind his desk and led the way to another section of the station. Then he removed a set of keys from his pocket and unlocked a door. He stepped inside and held it open for them. "I really don't think that one hour will be sufficient for you, Fraulein."

Cari looked around her. Metal shelving was covered with rows of bags, boxes, backpacks. Hundreds of them, possibly thousands. *How can people leave so much stuff behind?* She bit her lip. "Okay. How much of this will be sent out today?"

"All of it," the man replied.

Chapter 33

"Do you have a photocopier?" John asked the clerk. "So that we can make copies of this ticket? Then the three of us can split up to look."

"Certainly. Right this way."

John took the stub from Cari and followed the man.

"Not exactly what you expected is it?" Gilles asked once he was alone with Cari. "Are you sure you want to search through all of this?"

"Do we have a choice?" she countered.

"Well, perhaps the insurance company will reimburse my father, now that we know that the painting was sold fraudulently."

Cari shook her head. "I already asked John about that. He doesn't seem to think so. Our best bet is to go through these things, and try to find whatever Pierre left at the other station."

"If you say so."

John returned with two copies of the stub, and handed the original to Cari. "Well, let's get started, shall we?"

An hour later, Cari read one more tag number. "Got it!" she yelled. She pulled a garment bag from a shelf above her, and carried it over to an empty table. Just then, the clerk returned to the room. Cari grinned at him. "We found it," she said. "Just in the nick of time, too."

"I congratulate you Fraulein. I really didn't expect you to be successful."

"I was a little worried myself. I would have hated to drive all the way back to Zurich for this." She patted the garment bag. She looked to John and Gilles. "Okay guys; let's head back to St. Moritz, shall we?"

Once out in the car, Cari unzipped the bag. "A suit, a couple of shirts, dress shoes. Why would Pierre bother to store these? Wait a sec." She felt along each of the sleeves of the suit jacket. "Bingo." She pushed the sleeve up and discovered a rolled up canvas. "This must be it." She carefully withdrew it from the sleeve and began to unroll it. "You'll recognize it, won't you, Gilles?"

"Yes. I've seen photos of it. But you don't really have enough room to look at it here, Cari. Besides, I'm not sure it's wise to be viewing this painting in public. We should take it back to Louise's, or to the Mueller's."

"I think he's right, Cari," John said. "Let's go back first. Then we can be more thorough."

"I suppose you're both right. I guess I just wanted to see what a painting worth a quarter of a million looks like." She carefully replaced the sleeve and zipped the bag. "Here, Gilles, you keep it back there with you."

"What if Louise isn't home?" Cari asked as they entered St.Moritz.

"Then we'll go to the Mueller's," John replied. "But I think it's best to check with the original owner first."

"All right. It must be supper time by now. Hopefully she's done with her clients for the day." She kept driving until she pulled up in front of Louise's home. "Looks like she's here, unless she went somewhere on foot." She parked the car and shut off the engine. "I'll go check first." She got out of the car and made sure to take her cane with her. A few moments later she was knocking on Louise's door. She soon heard footsteps.

"Cari. Hello. What can I do for you?" Louise was smiling.

"Well, we lucked out today, Louise. Do you mind if we come in? We're almost certain that we have the painting."

Louise's face paled as she clutched the heavy wooden door. "You found it?" she whispered.

"I think so, but John and Gilles didn't want to sit around a train station to check it out. We thought it would be best to bring it back here."

"Of course. Come in, please. I'm finished for the day. I just need to go and get changed. Why don't you wait for me in the kitchen? I won't be long."

"Sure. I'll just have the guys come in." She waited for Louise to leave the entrance. Then she turned and waved for John and Gilles to join her. When they reached the porch, she asked, "Did you lock the car?"

"Yes, I did," John replied.

"Okay, Louise said to just wait for her in the kitchen. Come on in."

This time Cari removed the painting from its hiding place, and unrolled it on the kitchen table. "It's beautiful, isn't it?" she remarked. "A piece of American history."

"Yes," said John. "Central Park in its glory days." He turned to Gilles. "I can see why your father wanted this for his collection."

"And why I always refused to sell it," Louise added as she entered the kitchen. She approached the table and studied the canvas. "The woman in the picture is my great-great grandmother. The baby is my great grandmother. It's not just American history. It's family history." She reached out and gently touched it. "I never tired of looking at this. How did he hide it?"

"In the sleeve of this suit," Cari replied. She moved the painting aside to allow Louise to see what was in the garment bag. "Do you recognize it?"

"Yes. It was his favorite." Louise lifted it out of the bag and ran her hands over the fine material. A crinkling sound caught the attention of all of them. She reached into one of the pockets and withdrew an envelope. Her hand began to shake. "It's addressed to me. He must have been planning to mail it." She shook her head. "But that doesn't make sense."

"It does if he was planning to leave," John replied. "Maybe it'll explain a few things."

Louise licked her lips. "I guess I won't know if I don't open it." She looked at each of them. "But I think I'd rather do that in private. Please excuse me." She set the suit on the table, and left the room, clutching the envelope.

"I don't like this whole scenario," Cari muttered. "Stolen painting, cheating husband, mysterious letter." She shook her head. "What good comes out of a mess like this?"

"I don't know," Gilles answered. "But at least some of the pieces are starting to come together."

In the bedroom, Louise was staring at the single sheet of stationary that she'd pulled from the envelope. Her tears had already dotted the page, smearing some of the ink.

"Dear Louise,

I've just taken the biggest gamble of my life, but it seems to be working. By the time you receive this, I will have paid off my debts, and left the country. No, I won't ever be coming back. Your father was right about me.

I was never good for you. I don't know why you stayed with me all these years. You deserve better.

I've met someone else. Chances are, you already suspected that. Actually, she reminds me of you in some ways. She's young, and rich, and trusting. But she doesn't mind my gambling. So, I'll have the best of everything. And you'll finally have your freedom. Find yourself someone who can make you happy. Don't waste the rest of your life caring about a fool like me.

I really am sorry about your painting. If I could have done this any other way, I would have. It was the simplest way to come up with enough money. I've made a lot of enemies through the years. You know that. Some of them would like me dead almost as much as they'd like their money back. I ran out of time.

Take care of yourself, Louise.

Pierre"

Louise crumpled the paper and the envelope. She threw them onto the floor. Then she hugged herself and began to sob. She was still sitting there when she heard a gentle rapping on her door.

"Louise? It's Cari. Are you okay? Can I come in?"

Louise made no reply, but Cari turned the handle and pushed the door open. It didn't take her long to assess the situation. She made her way to the bed and sat down next to Louise.

"How can I help?" Cari asked.

"You can't," Louise sobbed. "He was leaving me! And he was too much of a coward to tell me to my face." She covered her face with her hands and leaned forward. "He thought he was so smart. He was so sure he could have it all. Instead, he wound up dead!" She dropped her hands to her lap and looked at Cari. "You can't help me, Cari. Nobody can."

Cari put an arm around Louise and pulled her against her shoulder. She didn't even say anything. She just held her and let her cry. She waited until Louise was able to regain her composure. Then she reached for her hand.

"Maybe *I* can't do anything to help you, Louise. But I still believe that God can. I won't stop praying either." She smiled. "For the moment, I think we need to go back to the kitchen and try to sort out what to do about the painting. I'm afraid it could be a bit of a legal mess."

"That I can live with," Louise replied. "It's the emotions that I can't seem to handle right now." She glanced at her watch. "I told Tammy I'd come by later this evening. So, let's go see if we can straighten out at least part of this mess."

Chapter 34

"Gilles, your father paid for this painting, and obviously Pierre received the money for it." Louise was seated at her table, trying to make sense of the circumstances. "However, I had absolutely nothing to do with the sale. It was fraud. Can't he understand that?"

"Not likely," Gilles replied, his expression grim. "You see, to my father, everything in life is black or white. He had no way of knowing that your husband was handling everything—without your approval. He made the purchase on good faith. And since the painting has been recovered, the insurance company has no reason to pay. So, my father has paid a lot of money for a painting which is now back in your possession."

"Legally speaking," John put in, "I'm afraid Gilles' father could make a much better case. And he has the money to pay for it. Are you willing to risk that?"

"No," Louise said with a sigh. "I make enough to live on, but there's certainly no extra. Besides, I'm not prepared to make an international incident out of this." She almost laughed. "My father would dearly love to know that he was right about Pierre all along. I won't give him the satisfaction." She shook her head. "It looks as though your father wins, Gilles. I'm simply too tired to fight." She got up from the table. "Now, please excuse me. Tammy is expecting me at the hospital this evening."

"Are you sure about this, Louise?" Cari asked. "Maybe we can negotiate with Gilles' father."

Louise once more shook her head. "No. It would be a waste of everyone's time."

"All right. We'll go. But I'll be back tomorrow." She smiled. "I'll be glad to see you again after all the driving I did today."

"Fine. I have you scheduled for 3:00 again."

"I'm truly sorry, Louise," Gilles said. "You don't deserve to have so much taken from you, especially all at once."

"No one ever does."

"You look tired," Tammy said as soon as Louise entered her room.

"Well, it's been a busy day." Louise held up a thermos. "I brought some tea. Would you like to try it?"

"Sure." Tammy eased herself to a sitting position, propping the pillows behind her. "Dad just went to the washroom, I think. He should be back in a bit." She grinned at Louise. "I think he was hoping to bump into you again tonight."

Louise didn't comment, but Tammy noticed the rising color in her cheeks. Louise tried to busy herself pouring tea into the lid of the thermos. "Here you go." She handed the cup to Tammy with a slightly shaky hand. "Did you have a good rest this morning?"

"I sure did. They had to wake me up for lunch. I didn't mind, but Dad was so bored. I think he even listened to some of my cassettes, just for something to do. Poor guy. Our taste in music is hardly the same."

Louise sat down at the foot of the bed. "I'm glad you were

able to sleep. You're not so pale anymore."

"You are though," Tammy countered. "Are you really just tired?"

"No," Louise admitted. "But I'd rather not talk about it."

"Sure. Hi, Dad. Look who's here." Tammy grinned at the way Louise jerked her head up to look at Rick.

"Hello," Rick said. "Did Tammy tell you just how *relaxed* you left her this morning?"

"Yes, she did." Louise twisted her hands in her lap.

"Did she also tell you that she'd be glad to come and visit you for a few days?"

"No. We hadn't gotten around to that yet," Tammy replied. Then she frowned as she looked at Louise. "Maybe it's not such a great idea after all. Louise is looking pretty tired."

"I'm fine," Louise insisted. "Just preoccupied." She smiled then. "I'd enjoy having you, Tammy."

"Great. Dr. Mueller said I can leave the day after tomorrow."

"All right. I'll be sure to pick you up. What about your things?"

"Oh, I'm sure Cari could pack them up for me. Don't worry about it."

"I'll be flying out on Friday evening," Rick said, sounding a tad disappointed. "I'll be glad to know that Tammy's in good hands."

"Both figuratively, and literally," Tammy added. She sipped from the cup. "This stuff isn't too bad, Louise. Thanks."

"How's your hand?" Louise asked. "Is it healing well?"

"If it doesn't, it won't be from lack of antibiotics. I know it's itchy now. That's usually a good sign, isn't it?" Tammy frowned at the bandage. "But I think I will have one colossal bruise for a week or two."

Rick laughed. "Then you'll look a bit like your brother. He took a major hit during a soccer match just after you left. His ribcage is a mess."

"Ricky actually got hit?" Tammy asked in surprise. "I thought he was too fast to get caught."

"Apparently not. Besides, it was Jeremy Hastings that got him. It was just a scrimmage."

"Jeremy?" Tammy giggled, bracing her abdomen with her free hand. "Ricky's best friend? What a laugh." She looked to Louise. "Jeremy is as much of a jock as my brother, but he's a really sweet guy. He goes to the same church we do. And he and Ricky do a lot of stuff together, besides sports. They'll both be going to UCLA too."

"Do you have any friends like that?" Louise asked.

Tammy shook her head. "No. I have a harder time than Ricky. And none of the girls at church go to the same school I do. I guess I have some friends at school, but nobody really close." Tammy clutched at the sheet. "Besides, this year got kind of messed up. I missed a month of school." She quickly changed the topic. "I'd say Cari is about the best friend I have in LA. But I still keep in touch with some girls from Sacramento."

"Is that where you lived before?"

"All my life."

"Changes can be hard sometimes." Louise gently patted her foot. "I'm sure you'll make more friends. Give it time."

Tammy finished the tea and passed the empty lid to Louise. "Thanks. That is pretty good for nausea." Then she laughed. "Have you got a good supply at your place? I may need it."

"I have plenty."

Tammy looked at her father and saw that he was watching Louise. "Uh, Dad, how are you getting home tonight?"

"I thought I'd call John or Cari later. Why?"

"Well, since Louise is here anyway, I thought maybe she wouldn't mind—"

"Tammy, don't be rude," Rick warned.

"It's all right," Louise broke in. "I wouldn't mind. Besides, I think that Cari and John went to the hotel with Gilles. They just left my house before I came here."

"Oh. Well, if you're sure it's no bother."

"It's not." She smiled first, and then Rick returned it.

A half hour later, Tammy was shooing both of them from the room. "The tea made me sleepy. Why don't you two shove off?" She covered her mouth as she yawned.

Rick leaned down to give her a kiss. "Okay. See you tomorrow, Sweetheart. Have a good sleep."

"I'll try, Dad." Then she whispered in his ear, "Have fun, Dad."

Rick straightened up and grinned. "I'll try."

"So, they found the painting," murmured Rick as he and Louise rode to the Mueller's. "Now what happens?"

"I suppose that Gilles will personally take it home to his father."

"But you didn't sell it."

"I know. We all know that. But legally, I don't have too many options. Besides, my husband owed money to some very dangerous people. It's much better if I just leave this whole situation alone. I don't want to draw attention to myself."

"You mean you could be in danger?"

"Meaning, Cari and I already suspect that Pierre's death wasn't an *accident*. But I'd like everyone else to think it was. I'd also like them to think that I believe that."

"I suppose that makes sense."

"Here we are." She parked in front of the Mueller's chalet.

"Would you mind shutting off the car?"

"Why?"

"I'd just like to talk. Do you mind?"

She shut off the ignition and turned to look at him. "What is it?"

Rick suddenly felt very self-conscious. "Well, I—I'd just like you to know that I care about what happens to you. And I don't just mean about losing your painting."

She held his gaze in the waning light. "Then what do you mean?"

"I know what it's like to suddenly lose your spouse. I know that it hurts more than anything else. And I also know how important it is to have the support of family and friends. And God. From what I've been able to gather, you don't have any of those."

Tears gathered in her eyes. "No, I don't. You and Cari, and even Tammy, are all trying to help me. I appreciate it. But you couldn't possibly understand, Rick. You see, I would have lost my husband anyway. He was planning to leave me after selling the painting. I've even seen a picture of them together. That's just not the same, is it? At least you know that your wife loved you. I can't be certain of much anymore." She turned and gripped the steering wheel with both hands, leaning her forehead against it.

"No, I can't imagine any man being that foolish, Louise," Rick said softly. "Why would he bother to look elsewhere—when he already had the best?" He reached over and touched her shoulder. "Please don't let *his* choices destroy you. Make some wise ones of your own. Ask God to help you through this."

"I don't even remember how to pray," she cried. "It's been too long."

"But it's not too late, Louise."

"Will you help me?" She raised her head and blinked as she tried to look at him.

"Yes. I'd be glad to." He closed his eyes and bowed his head. "Dear God, thank You for loving us enough to send Your son to die for us. Thank You for taking care of us. Right now I pray that You'll watch over Louise. She knows that she needs Your help. Please help her to reach out and trust You. Help her to believe that *You* will never leave her or forsake her. You're always faithful, Father. Always."

He paused as Louise choked on her tears. Then he listened while she stammered her own prayer.

"I'm sorry, God! I guess I tried to leave You behind when I left home. Please help me. I know I don't deserve it, but I'm asking anyway. I don't know how to get through this, God. Too much has been happening. I need You, God. I know I always did, I was just too stubborn to admit it, or too ashamed. Please help me. Please forgive me." Her words faded as her sobs increased.

Rick slipped his arm around her, much as Cari had done earlier in the evening. "You'll be okay. Maybe not right away, but it'll happen. I promise you that." He gently stroked her hair as she turned against his shoulder. "You're not alone anymore, and you never will be again."

"Thank you." She wiped at the tears in her eyes, and on her face. She tried to smile. When Rick touched her cheek, she held his hand. "I'm glad I gave you a ride tonight."

"So am I," Rick whispered. Then he lowered his head and kissed her. When she didn't pull away, he held her closer. He finally drew back, his face flushed, but she was still holding his hand. "I—"

"Please don't apologize," she said. "I'm not sorry." She gave his fingers a slight squeeze. "Except that you'll be leaving soon." She kissed the palm of his hand. "I'll miss you."

Rick sighed heavily. "Then my interest hasn't been one-sided?"

"No. But I don't know what we can do about it."

"I can't exactly afford to come back for a visit," Rick said with a frown.

"And I can't really afford to leave here either."

"So, I guess that leaves letters and phone calls." He laughed. "I almost forget how to go about this kind of thing."

"Me too. But," she added as she entwined her fingers with his, "you haven't forgotten how to kiss."

"I guess not." He kissed her again, this time knowing he was welcome to do so. He pulled away reluctantly. "I should go in," he murmured. "I'm starting to remember a few too many things." He released her and straightened up. "Goodnight, Louise."

"Will I see you tomorrow?"

"I certainly hope so. I'm easy enough to find. I'll be at the hospital with Tammy."

"Could we have supper together?"

"I'd like that." He opened the passenger door. "And don't forget, some of us are praying for you."

"I know. Thank you. And Rick?"

"Umm?"

"Will you please tell Cari, about tonight?"

Rick grinned. "Just about the praying part or the kissing too?"

Louise's cheeks flamed. "Well, I'm not sure she'll be surprised about either, but I meant the praying part."

"I'll be sure to tell her. Good night." He stepped out of the vehicle and shut the door. He took the stairs two at a time to the front door, feeling better than he had in ages.

Chapter 35

"You just don't understand, Father," Gilles protested over the phone. "Her husband committed fraud when he sold the painting, and when he took the payment for it. And now he's dead. There's no way for Louise St. Denis to return the money for it. Why must you be so unreasonable?" Gilles paced as far as the phone cord would allow.

"What is so unreasonable about this, Gilles? I already paid for the painting. You say that you've managed to find it. What is so difficult about that?"

"It's *difficult* because this is a family treasure to this woman. It's not her fault that her husband was so dishonest."

"Now you sound like a lovesick fool! Keep your mind on business instead of pretty women."

"Is *business* all that you can think of? You leave it up to Mother to think about the family, or anyone's feelings. All right, since business and money are so important to you, *I'll* pay for the painting. That way Louise can keep it, and you won't lose a cent. Is that good enough for you?" Gilles tightened his hold on the receiver. "Or do you need me to pay for the expenses involved in finding it for you?"

"What is the matter with you? Ever since you met that Daniels woman you've been far too defiant for my liking."

"That's because you never like anyone to disagree with you."

"Change your tone of voice, Gilles!"

"Fine. I'll do even better than that. I'll have John Maxwell draw up some papers for me. You can have the business back, Father. I don't want to work for someone who has become so obsessed with *owning* and *getting.* I don't even care what percentage was mine. I'll just take whatever was in the bank when I left Mexico. I have plenty of experience with art. I'm sure I'll be able to find another position somewhere."

"What nonsense is this? This is a family business, Gilles. You're the only one who understands it, besides me. You can't be serious about this."

"Yes, I am, Father. It's been coming for a long time. I enjoy looking for art, and buying it, but it has never mattered to me about *possessing* it. You hold onto everything so tightly, including your own children, that you end up crushing it, or us. But you've never been able to see that."

There was silence for a moment. Then a deep sigh from Eduardo. "All right. I won't waste more time trying to reason with you. You always have been the most wilful of the children. But what am I to tell your mother?"

Gilles hesitated for a moment. "Tell her the truth, Father. You and I no longer agree—about many things. It will be better for all of us this way."

"Your mother will not think so."

"I'll try to explain when I get back."

"Very well. When will that be?"

"By the end of the month. The young girl who travelled with us has been very ill. She'll be out of the hospital soon, but she won't be ready to travel yet." *And neither will I with these cracked ribs.* "I'll call you again when I have the details arranged."

"A dios, Gilles."

"A dios, Father." Gilles hung up the phone and ran his fingers through his dark hair. *I hope that I'm doing the right thing. I'd better start looking for another job. And how will I do this without Louise finding out? I'm pretty sure she won't allow me to buy the painting back for her—if she knows in advance. I'm not sure Cari would either. I think I'll need Maxwell's help for this.* He smiled ruefully. *I never thought I'd say that.*

"Isn't this a bit drastic, Rodriquez?" John asked while the two men met over breakfast. "Paying your father for the painting, and then leaving the family business? Why?"

Gilles smiled as he set down his cup of coffee. "Well, there are some things that you do because you wish to gain favor. Others, to boost your pride or your ego. Others out of a sense of duty or compassion, pity even. Some you do for love. And others, simply because you sense that it's the *right* thing to do. What would you do, given my options?"

John shook his head. "I honestly don't know. I guess, as a lawyer, I'd side with your father."

"But, as a man?"

"I'd want to do something for Louise. She seems to me like a pawn in this whole fiasco." His brows furrowed. "Frankly, I'm not even certain it's wise for her to stay here in Switzerland, at least in St. Moritz. What if someone finds out that Pierre hid the painting?"

"I've thought of that. So has Cari. For that matter, so has Louise. We can all offer assistance, Maxwell, but we can't make any decisions for her."

"No, I suppose not." John drank some of his coffee and

finished his toast. "So, what, exactly, do you want me to do for you?"

"I'd like you to draw up a purchase agreement for me. I'll buy the painting from my father, but I want Louise to be reinstated as the owner of it. I also plan to reimburse my father for the expenses of this investigation." He smiled. "That being the case, I think we should take the Concorde on the way back. I'm sure that Cari and Tammy would both appreciate that."

John laughed. "Very likely." He sobered and cleared his throat. "What else?"

"I'm going to relinquish my partnership with my father. I already told him that I'll only keep what was in my account when I left. I'm not going to worry about getting a *percentage* from him, though, knowing his sense of honor, he may insist upon it."

"All right. How much was in that account when you left?"

"Close to five million dollars, US."

John almost choked on his coffee. Then his professional nature kicked in once more. "Well, I suppose you don't *need* a percentage from your father, do you? You'll have plenty of funds to get yourself re-established elsewhere." *That's a major understatement.*

"Does that surprise you?" Gilles asked, seeming to be genuinely curious.

"Perhaps it shouldn't," John conceded. "I often deal with wealthy clients. For that matter, my employers have accumulated a great deal of money through the years. I guess it just surprises me that someone so much younger than myself would have that much set aside."

"Some of the money I inherited from my grandparents," Gilles explained. "Some is from my days of professional soccer. The rest is from commissions earned from the art business." He smiled. "And compound interest, of course."

"So, where will you look for a new position? I'm sure with your experience, and your gift for languages, you shouldn't have much difficulty. There must be private collectors or stores here in Europe who would be glad to have you."

"There are plenty in the States as well."

The hair on the back of John's neck bristled. "LA in particular?"

"Possibly. There are a couple of art museums there."

"And so is Cari."

"True. Granted, that may have some bearing on my final decision, but it certainly wouldn't be the only factor." Gilles folded his napkin and set it on the table. "This isn't a competition, Maxwell. Cari made it clear to both of us how she felt. She's not some prize to be won. And she has a mind of her own. I won't do anything to force her to choose between us. Besides, I think her choice is already made." He paused as he clasped his hands together. "And it isn't *me*."

John looked down at his coffee for a moment. "I'd like to believe that, Rodriquez, but I'm not so sure." He raised his head. "It's not a simple *choice* at all."

"Oh, I think it is. I also think that you're afraid to make it."

"What? I'm not afraid of anything."

"Aren't you? Then why do you resist God so strongly? Are you afraid to admit that you aren't capable of handling every circumstance? Or that maybe you might need *help* at some point in your life? By *not* making a conscious decision, John, you *are* choosing. You're choosing to reject the very God who would like to give direction to the rest of your life."

John tensed his shoulders. "Look, I've had similar discussions with Cari, and even with Tammy. And I've been to church. I'm willing to keep an open mind, but—"

"But your *heart* is closed, isn't it? There's a very big difference between the two."

John refused to answer. *It's none of his business. I won't rush into something that doesn't make good sense to me. Not now, and not later.*

Chapter 36

Cari kept the conversation flowing while Louise worked on her right thigh. "I have a proposition for you, Louise. Please hear me out before you give an answer, okay?"

"All right," Louise replied, though she looked pretty suspicious.

"Well, you see, I have an extra bedroom in my apartment back in LA. I've always used it for an office or storage area. Anyway, I've been wondering for the past couple of days if you'd consider moving back to the States with me. I realize that would mean leaving the country where you've lived for the past fourteen years, and a well-established practise, but, frankly, I thought you might like a chance to start over."

Louise's hands stopped moving, and her mouth dropped open as she stared at Cari.

"I'd be more than happy to lend you the money for airfare, and I wouldn't charge anything for rent."

"Why are you even suggesting this?"

"Well, for a few reasons, I guess. For one, I don't really know how else I could help you. Secondly, I enjoy your company. Thirdly, you're a great masseuse. Is that enough?"

"How long have you lived on your own, Cari?"

"For about twelve years, why?"

"Are you sure you'd want to have a roommate after all this time?"

"I'm actually not home that much. And I'm sure that you'd be busy too." She grinned at her. "Especially if Rick and Tammy have anything to say about it."

"What about work?"

"Well, you're still an American citizen, aren't you? And you could apply for certification in California. Besides, I'm a resident. I could sponsor you, if need be."

"Have you been planning all this instead of sleeping?" Louise asked with a hint of a smile.

"Partly."

"I'll think about it."

"Okay. Thanks for listening. I realize that I was rambling."

"So, any more reasons why I should move to LA, when I'm surrounded by some of the nicest scenery in the world?"

"Well, given time, I'm sure I'll think of some."

"You probably will."

Rick got to his feet as soon as Louise entered Tammy's room. She was obviously dressed for supper. She was wearing an off-white skirt and blazer, with an emerald green blouse. Her hair was pulled back from her face with a couple of matching combs. She looked gorgeous. And her smile was enough to send his pulse racing.

"Hi!" he managed to say. "How are you?"

"I'm fine, thank you." She looked to Tammy. "And how's the patient? Anxious to get out of here tomorrow?"

"I sure am. But I'm going to miss my dad when he goes home."

Louise glanced at Rick and smiled again. "I'll try to keep you entertained."

"So, you two are going out for supper?" Tammy asked, a satisfied expression on her face.

"Yes, we are," Louise replied. "Do you mind?" She held Tammy's hand in both of hers for a moment.

"Not at all. Actually, I think I'd mind a lot more if you weren't. Where are you going?"

"I don't know. Some place with good dessert likely. We'll try to bring you some leftovers."

"Hey, why not just take something back to your place? I'll be there tomorrow anyway."

"Good point." Louise straightened up. "You think of everything, don't you?"

"If it involves chocolate, you bet."

"Fine, chocolate it is. How about whipped cream?"

"Oh, I could live with that."

"Well, it sounds like we'd better get moving if we have to hunt down a special dessert for you, Sweetheart," Rick said. He leaned down and kissed her cheek. "I'll be back in the morning. Have a good evening."

"Don't worry about me, Dad. I think Cari and John are coming over a bit later. I'll be fine."

"Shall we go?" Rick asked, focusing his gaze on Louise. *Boy, she sure knows how to dress.*

"All right. I'll see you tomorrow, Tammy. Make sure you try to rest up."

"I will. Goodnight."

"Cari invited me to come and live with her in LA," Louise said between bites of food. "I told her I'd think about it."

Rick took a sip of his water before replying. "And?"

"Would I be welcome?" she asked. "Would I be able to fit in back there? Or is it just a crazy idea?"

"I think that you could fit in anywhere, Louise. And, to be honest, I've been wondering all day how I could come up with an idea as good as Cari's." He felt the color creep up his neck and into his cheeks. "It would make it a lot easier to go back tomorrow, knowing that you'd be coming later on."

"Would it?" Louise toyed with her wedding band for a few seconds. "Then last night wasn't just a moment of weakness?"

"No. Not at all. Though, I'll admit, I do feel a bit *weak* whenever you walk into a room." He reached across the table and held her hand. "Besides, I'd save a fortune on phone calls this way."

Louise laughed, making her amethyst eyes sparkle like the real gems. "I suppose that's a good incentive." She covered his hand with her free one. "Cari referred to the move as 'starting over'. She may be right. But I'd like to know that I'm doing it for the right reasons. Coming here was a terrible decision."

"You can't change the past," he reasoned. "None of us can. But I'd still like if you made the move to LA."

When Louise took Rick back to the Mueller's she shut off the car, unbuckled her seatbelt, and turned to face him. "Thank you for a lovely evening."

"Thank *you*." He slipped his arm around her shoulders and drew her closer. With his right hand he cupped her cheek. "I'm *really* hoping that you'll move to LA." Then he kissed her long enough to fog the windshield before pulling away.

"Well, I'd say you're doing your best to help me decide," she remarked. She gently traced his moustache with the fingers of her left hand. Then she cradled the back of his head and drew him back to her. "I think I'll start packing."

This time *she* kissed *him*, stirring desires that he thought he'd buried with Karen. He held her for a long time, but drew back when he realized he was in danger of fanning flames that were just starting to come to life. "I'd better go in," he sighed. "Will you see me off at the airport tomorrow?"

"Shouldn't I stay with Tammy?"

"Yeah, I guess so. I'm sure that John or Cari will give me a ride there."

"Rick, it's probably better if we don't spend much more time alone, like this." She put her hands up to her cheeks. "Being with you in a parked car could be dangerous."

"Yeah, I know." He reached for the door handle. "Well, we'll have Tammy to keep an eye on us tomorrow." He laughed. "According to John and Cari, she's a very efficient chaperone. Goodnight."

"Goodnight."

Rick stood and watched while Louise pulled away and drove down the street. *Hit like a ton of bricks. It's been a long time, Lord. Please help me not to mess this up.*

Louise stood in front of her dresser and removed her wedding band. Then she held it for a moment in her right hand. *I haven't had it off in fourteen years. Now there's no reason to wear it.* She set it down and moved over to the bed. *And there's really no reason to stay here anymore. But am I truly ready to start over? To go back to the States? I fell in love with Pierre and followed him here. Am I only leaving because of Rick?*

She got up and removed her blazer. *No, he's not the only reason.* She smiled. *Though he's certainly one of them. I don't want to spend the rest of my life alone. This past month has been bad enough. I could have friends for a change. I could go to church.* She bit her lip. *And maybe I could finally have children.* She shivered. *What if Rick doesn't want any more? Maybe he already*—She shook her head. *No, I'm not going to think about that now. It may never even come up. And he already has a son and daughter. I'm sure that Tammy would be willing to consider me as her mother. That's enough. That's more than I've had so far.*

She got ready for bed and turned out the lamp. *God, please don't let me make a mistake. If You really want me to do this, please, somehow, make it clear to me. I don't want to do the wrong thing. I want to do what's right, for the rest of my life.*

Chapter 37

John parked in front of the Mueller's and walked around to open the door for Cari. He stood in front of her though, preventing her from heading towards the house. "Did Rodriquez tell you what he's going to do about the painting?" he asked.

"Yes," she replied. "He told me during lunch." She looked up into his face. "He also told me what else the two of you talked about. Please consider what he said, John."

"I will." He gripped her shoulders. "I really don't want to lose you, Cari."

"You won't. But I won't bend either. You know that. All I can do is keep praying."

"Do you really think that God will answer?"

"I'm certainly hoping that He will."

He kissed her cheek and let her go. "Maybe I am too."

"All right! I finally get to leave this place," exclaimed Tammy. "It's about time." She sat in a wheelchair, with Rick standing behind her. "Let's go, Dad."

"Yes, Ma'am," he replied with a salute. "I'm sure the nurses will be glad to get rid of such an ornery patient."

Tammy stuck out her chin. "I'll have you know, Dad, that almost every one of them told me that they'd miss me."

Once at Louise's, Rick carried Tammy up the stairs, to the door, noticing how much weight she'd lost. "You need to put on a few pounds, Sweetheart."

Tammy groaned. "Tell that to my stomach, Dad. It's been arguing with me all week. I'm hoping it won't be so bad now that it's just pills to take. My jeans hardly stay up now."

Louise unlocked the door and ushered them inside. "Well, why don't I make some chamomile tea? That seemed to help the last time."

"I'm game," Tammy said. She followed Louise to the kitchen and sat down on the nearest chair. "Man, I think I'm starting to understand why Cari complained so much last fall. I can't believe I'm so tired, especially since I've done precious little for the past week."

"Oh, not much," Rick chided. "Just had a bunch of tests, and some surgery, and stitches in your hand. You haven't been at all busy."

"Would you like some tea, Rick?" Louise asked while reaching for some mugs.

"Uh, I'd prefer coffee, if it's not too much trouble. I'm not a big fan of tea."

"No trouble," she replied. "I'll just heat up what I made before I left."

Tammy lasted through the cup of tea before asking Louise where the spare room was. "I think that was enough *exertion* for the moment."

"Sure, it's right next to the bathroom, just down the hall." She led the way. "Here you are. I hope you'll be comfortable.

Tammy looked around the room. It was small, compared to the one she had at home, but it certainly looked comfortable enough. All the furniture seemed to have come from an *IKEA* catalogue. Pine, she guessed. The bed had a colorful quilt on it, which made her smile. "It kind of reminds me of the inn that Cari and I stayed at last January. It's pretty." She stifled a yawn before looking at her watch. "Will you please wake me up in an hour? I'll have to pop another pill by then."

"Sure. Just let me know if you need anything."

Tammy sat down on the bed. Then she stretched out on it. "I think I've got everything I need right here, Louise. Thanks." Then she closed her eyes and promptly fell asleep.

Back in the kitchen, Rick was rinsing his mug. "Crashed out again?" he asked.

"I think so." Louise frowned. "She definitely needs more rest before flying home."

"I know. And she's lost a lot of weight. Are you sure you want to play 'nursemaid'?"

"I'm sure." She looked at the kitchen clock. "I have a client coming in a few minutes. Make yourself at home. When I'm done, I'll fix some lunch."

Rick grinned as he looked at her. "Started packing yet?"

Louise shook her head. "No. But I've started *un*packing." She held up her left hand, with its naked finger.

"So I see. Well, I guess I'll let you get to work. I noticed you've got quite a selection of magazines in the living room. I should be able to keep myself busy."

"Good. Oh, in case I forget, Tammy needs someone to wake her up in an hour."

"Sure. Between the two of us, hopefully at least one will remember."

Tammy grudgingly took the next dose of medication. Then she made an attempt at eating some lunch, but she became so nauseated that she had to leave the table. "Excuse me!" She remained in the bathroom for several minutes. Eventually, she heard someone knocking on the door.

"I'll be out in a minute," she answered. Then she rinsed her mouth and washed her face. She frowned at her reflection in the mirror. Then she unlocked the door and stepped into the hallway.

"Are you okay, Sweetheart?" Rick asked as he placed his hands on her shoulders.

Tammy tried to smile. "Sure, Dad. I'll be fine. I just can't seem to eat right now."

"Yeah, I can see that." He slipped his arm around her and led her back to the kitchen. "It kind of reminds me of when your mom was pregnant. All she could eat during the first three months, both times, was dry cereal, crackers, and milkshakes. And I think she drank a lot of club soda too. She lost about ten pounds both times."

"Well, I suppose the consolation is that I'm *not* pregnant," Tammy remarked as she once more sat down at the table. She rubbed her forehead. "I'm really sorry, Louise. I'm sure it's a wonderful lunch. I just can't—"

"That's okay," Louise assured her. "Besides, I think your father will finish off the leftovers anyway." She reached for Tammy's hand. "But is there *anything* that you might be hungry for?"

Tammy shook her head. "Not at the moment. If that changes, I'll let you know. Thanks for asking." She smiled. "Actually, it's kind of ironic. You see, on the way here, especially in Paris, I ate all the time. Pastries, cheeses, anything. And Frau Mueller is such a great cook too. It's a wonder I didn't *gain* ten pounds since leaving LA."

"Are you kidding?" Rick teased. "You just burn it all off by talking."

Rick and Tammy spent the afternoon together while Louise worked on her clients. At 5:00 she came to the living room. "Well, I'm finally finished. Are you ready for some supper?"

"I am," Rick replied. "I'm not sure about Tammy." His daughter was curled up on the sofa, her head on his lap.

"What are we having?" Tammy asked.

"How about some soup? And some toast?"

"I think I could maybe handle that." Rick eased her to a sitting position. "At least a little of it."

"Good," Louise replied. "It won't take me long to get it ready. I just need to warm it up."

"Hey, one whole dipperful of soup and a slice of toast," Tammy exclaimed. "I'm making progress."

Rick was still worried, but Dr. Mueller had insisted that Flagyl and Vibramycin were the drugs of choice for Tammy. He forced a smile. "Well, I'll be sure to have some pizza on hand when you get back home."

Tammy made a face. "Ooo, don't mention anything rich or heavy, Dad." She reached for her water glass and sipped from it. "I may just stick with homemade soup for a few days."

Rick looked at his watch. "John and Cari should be here soon. I'd better get myself together." Sure enough, just after he finished up in the bathroom, the others arrived.

"These are for you, Tammy," Cari said as she handed her a bunch of wildflowers. "Frau Mueller picked them for you. And these are for you, Rick." She handed him a small pastry box. "To eat on the flight home."

"Thanks," father and daughter said in unison.

"Ready to go?" Cari asked. Rick nodded. "How was your day, Kid?"

"Not too bad," Tammy responded. "I think I kept down almost as much as I lost."

Cari gave her a thumbs up sign. "Well, you're heading in the right direction."

Rick turned to Tammy and gave her a tight hug. "You take good care of yourself. I want you to come home rested. Got that?"

"Yes, Sir." She squeezed him hard. "I love you, Dad. Have a good trip, and don't forget to phone when you get home."

"I won't." He kissed her cheek. "I love you too." Then he headed for the door, where Louise was standing. He reached for her hands. "Thanks for taking care of her for me."

"We'll wait at the car," Cari said, obviously sensing that some privacy might be wanted. She and John stepped outside.

Louise stood on tiptoe and put her arms around Rick's neck. "I'll miss you," she whispered.

"And I'll be miserable," he replied. Then they kissed for several seconds. "I'd better go." He caressed her cheek. "I'll call tomorrow, when I get home."

"Okay. Bye."

"Goodbye." He picked up his lone suitcase and headed out the door, feeling a mixture of elation and heaviness. *Please take care of them, Lord. And please give them a safe trip too.*

At the airport, Cari gave Rick a quick hug. "So, you fell hard, didn't you?" she asked quietly.

"Yeah, you could say that," he admitted.

"I'm glad for both of you. Take care. We'll see you again by the end of the month."

"I'll be counting the days."

Cari laughed. "I'm sure you will."

Chapter 38

The day after Rick left, Cari got a phone call from Trish Lehman. "It's a girl! Come over and see for yourself. We're at the hospital." She gave her the room number, and told her when visiting hours would be.

"Okay, I'll be over, Trish, but not until this evening. I'm all booked up for the day. I'll see you about 7:00. And, congratulations."

Cari managed to meet with Gilles and John for lunch, visit Tammy in the afternoon, and buy a gift for the new baby after that. By supper she was getting tired, but she was determined to go see her friend. She took the gift, and her cane, and headed for the hospital, a place she was getting all too familiar with.

Cari exclaimed over the beautiful baby, and spoke with the very pleased parents. "She's gorgeous, Trish. Did you have a hard time?"

"No. It was a breeze. Must be all those years of staying in shape. Granted, I'm kind of sore, but nothing that a good massage wouldn't take care of."

"Well, if you want to see Louise St. Denis for that massage, you'll have to hurry. I've talked her into returning to the States with us."

"You what? Whatever for?"

"Don't get so ticked off, Trish. Let me tell you about one of the reasons. Remember that good-looking widower that I told you about?"

"Mike's new partner?"

"Yes. Well, he was just here for a week, his daughter landed in the hospital for several days. Anyhow, he and Louise met, had a couple of meals together, and a few cups of coffee. That seems to have been enough for serious sparks to fly."

Trish cocked an eyebrow, reminding Cari of Vivien Leigh. "Well, that sounds promising. A widower, eh? With two kids, wasn't it? And he's handsome too?"

"Quite."

"All right, I'll forgive you for swiping my masseuse. So, how have you liked using the Porsche?"

"Silly question," Cari scoffed. "I love it. It handled like a dream when we went to Chur and back. I'd love to own one myself, but I guess I'll try to be content with my BMW." Then she laughed and told them about the reactions of Gilles and John when they found out what a capable driver she was.

"Served them right," Trish insisted. Then she winked at her husband. "Just like Hans being so sure that a poor Californian couldn't *possibly* know the first thing about skiing. I beat him down the slope three times before he realized I didn't need any *help*."

"But I redeemed myself," he said, "by having the nicest collection of rental cars in the city."

"True," Trish conceded. Her gaze shifted back to Cari. "So, how goes *your* love life these days?"

Cari blushed. "Well, I decided not to date *either* of the guys for the time being. It's less complicated that way. And, believe it or not, the guys are getting along just fine with each other now. At the moment, they're both working on some business deals. Go figure." She laughed. "Don't worry; I'll be sure to let you know if anything major develops in the future."

"You'd better." Trish repositioned her daughter on her lap. "Would you like to hold her?"

"Sure." Cari took the baby and smiled down at the blanket wrapped bundle. Then her eyes suddenly misted with tears. *I could've had a baby boy by now. But I would have been a single parent. Trish, you have no idea how fortunate you are.* She kissed the baby's delicate cheek before giving her back. "I should get going. It's been a long day. I'll stop in to see you at home before I head back to LA. And I'll bring Tammy and Louise with me."

"Deal. Thanks for coming." She reached up and clasped Cari's hand, no longer smiling. "You'll get your turn, Cari." Cari simply nodded. The lump in her throat was getting too big to speak around. "See you later."

Cari wiped her eyes as she left the room. But all the crying infants still haunted her as she reached the parking area. She was thankful that it was dusk, and that the area was almost deserted. *The last thing I need is for somebody to ask me why I'm crying. I just need to go and get some sleep.* As she neared the Porsche, she noticed that a black Mercedes, with tinted windows, was parked beside it. *Well, I suppose lots of people in this city can afford nice cars.* She thought no more about it as she got out her keys and stood next to the driver's door.

Both passenger doors of the Mercedes opened at once, and Cari instinctively turned around, dropping her cane and the keys. Not quickly enough. She found herself pinned against the car with a gloved hand covering her mouth and the barrel of a 357 Magnum held to her left temple. Two men wearing ski masks had her undivided attention. The one with the gun did all the talking.

"We warned your friend, Fraulein. Did he fail to pass along our message? He was asking too many questions. You seem to have that same annoying trait. It would have been very wise for you to leave this place, Fraulein. Better yet, leave this country, while you were still able." He gave a quick jerk of his head just before Cari felt a boot connect with her right shin. She closed her eyes against the radiating pain.

"Oh, you dropped your cane, didn't you?" the man continued. "Canes can be such useful tools, can't they?"

Cari gagged as the wood pressed against her neck. She reached up with both hands to push it away. Her upper body was pinned down against the roof of the car, hampering her leverage. She kicked out with her left foot, heartened when she felt it connect with soft flesh. She managed a second kick before the cane began to cut off more air. Her nostrils flared.

"I admire your spirit, Fraulein," the man with the gun told her. "But your curious nature could prove to be your downfall." The cane was pulled away. "You don't seem to know when to quit." She heard the cane being snapped in two, presumably over the other man's knee. "So, it is up to us to satisfy that curiosity."

Cari locked her gaze with his steely blue eyes. He pressed the barrel more firmly against her temple. The other man grabbed both of her wrists and shoved her arms beneath her. Then his hands roamed over her body. She blinked several times, but she didn't try to scream. When he felt beneath her jacket, she swallowed. When he rested his gloved hand over her pacemaker, she grew rigid.

"Such a shame, Fraulein. You really should have just enjoyed the scenery and gone home." He tightened his grip around her mouth. "Too bad you got *careless* about your health." He moved his hand and covered her nose, cutting off any oxygen.

Cari renewed her struggle, but met with immediate resistance. The other man pinned her with his body, gripping her upper arms with bruising force. The lack of oxygen was clouding her vision, and increasing her pulse. She stopped moving, trying to conserve what little energy she had left. *I'll only pass out. They just want to scare me. This wouldn't look enough like an 'accident'.* She began to feel numb, except for the burning sensation in her lungs. *It can't last much longer.* Her knees buckled, but she couldn't fall. Her head hurt. *Not much . . .*

Cari woke up on the pavement next to the Porsche. She slowly rolled onto her back and waited for her vision to clear. The Mercedes was gone, just as she'd expected. Judging from the encroaching darkness, and the nearly empty parking area, she'd been unconscious for a while. She tried to sit up but discovered just how dizzy she still was. *I can't just stay here on the ground. I need to get up and get out of here. I need to go find Gilles and John.* She tried again and managed to lean against the door of the car, breathing hard. Then she noticed the blood.

Just below her right knee her pant leg was stuck to her shin by congealed blood. She bit her lip and tried to move her foot. Pain ricocheted from her knee to her ankle. *Pain or not, I still have to drive this car.* She reached for the two segments of her cane. *Great. Now how do I get around?* She fumbled for the keys which had drifted beneath the car. Her hand came back wet. Holding it up to her face, she could smell fuel. That's when she heard another vehicle approaching.

It was the same black Mercedes, and a gloved hand was holding a lit cigarette out of the passenger window. Cari put the ingredients together quick enough to act. She dove for the ground and rolled several times, until she came to rest against another vehicle. Just in time to see the glow of the tossed cigarette hit the ground beneath the Porsche. Seconds later, the car burst into flames and the ground was rocked by an explosion.

Cari kept her arms over her head until she heard squealing tires and running footsteps. Then she pushed up onto her forearms. She began to tremble while she watched the flames licking at the red paint of the sports car. *If I hadn't woken up . . .If I hadn't noticed the gas . . .If I hadn't gotten out of the way . . .*

"Cari! Cari, where are you?" Hans Lehman was yelling above the roar of the flames. "Cari!"

"Hans!" she called in a choked voice. "I'm over here." She tried to get up but the trembling had worsened. "Over here!"

"Cari?" Hans came running, several others with him. "Are you hurt? What happened?" He squatted down next to her.

"I don't know," she replied. "I-I mean I don't know if I'm hurt. I know what happened, at least partly." She lowered her head down onto her forearms, suddenly queasy.

"Cari? Let me take you inside. You've got some cuts and scrapes. Let a doctor look at you. Come on, I'll help you." He touched her hair.

Cari began to sob, giving in to the mounting terror of what had happened, and of what *could have* happened. *I'm okay. I'll be fine. I just want to go home. I want to sleep. I'm going to be sick.*

"Come on, Cari. Let me help you." Hans grasped her shoulders and she winced. "Sorry. Maybe you should roll over first. Then it'll be easier to get up."

"I'll try." With Hans' help, Cari did as he suggested. She was soon in a sitting position. "My leg hurts. And I don't have my cane."

He deftly lifted her into his arms and cradled her against his muscular chest. "Let's get you inside."

"I'm sorry about the car. I couldn't help it." Her head was pounding. "I'm sorry."

"Cari, forget about the car!" He was almost to the entrance area. "The car can be replaced. I'm just thankful that you weren't *in* it."

But I was supposed to be! Or at least right beside it. I was supposed to die.

Chapter 39

Cari was given a shot of Demerol before a doctor tended to her cuts and scrapes. Several stitches were needed to close up the gash in her right shin. Her jacket was torn from rolling on the pavement. Her right pant leg was cut, to tend to the gash. Her left shoe was missing. The nurse had used antiseptic soap to remove the smell of gas from her hands. When the medical staff had done what they deemed essential, the police were allowed to speak with Cari.

Hans acted as an interpreter for Cari, in order to make sure that the police understood everything that she tried to tell them. They seemed somewhat sceptical, until speaking with the doctor. He assured them that her injuries substantiated her statement. When she told them that she had been a police officer for eleven years herself, they showed a little more respect.

"So, you have no idea who the men were?" asked the senior investigator.

"No. They were wearing ski masks. I've given you a description of height, weight and eye color. That's all I know for sure."

"You said that one of them spoke to you. Would you recognize his voice?"

"I don't know." She rubbed her throbbing temples. "I'd much rather never hear it again."

"And these same men also threatened one of your friends?"

"Yes."

"Why didn't he report it?"

"He thought it would be better to just finish our work and go home."

"That seems to have been a very *unwise* decision, Fraulein."

Cari made no reply. The nausea from the medication and the shock was mounting. She swallowed once more as she gripped the edge of the examining table with trembling fingers.

"When are you planning to leave, Fraulein?"

"Next week. We're just waiting for the young girl with us to recover from surgery."

The investigator furrowed his brows. "This has been an eventful trip."

"Yes."

"Perhaps you should have just stayed at home."

His sarcastic tone irritated Cari. She raised her head and met his gaze. "I came here to do a job. I got it done. And I plan to go home as soon as we're able to. For the moment, I'm a tourist—just like the other million people who come to Switzerland each year. I'll be more than happy to leave you to attend to your own crime syndicates. We have enough of those in America."

The younger officer chuckled softly. "What was your rank, Fraulein?"

"Sergeant. Why?"

"It shows. You are used to *giving* orders, not *taking* them."

Cari managed a weak smile. "True. I also head a security department now. I don't tolerate *rudeness* from my staff." Her bravado quickly deserted her as a wave of dizziness assaulted her.

The younger officer caught her by the shoulders just as she was pitching forward. "Just a moment, Fraulein. Put your head down on your knees." He held her steady for several moments. "Better?"

"I think so," Cari murmured. "Thank you." She straightened up and looked at the other officer. "May I go now?"

"Yes, Fraulein. If we need to speak with you again, we have the address and phone number of where you're staying."

The younger man looked at his watch and then said something in German. The older man looked annoyed, but he only shrugged in response. "I'll give you a ride home, Fraulein."

"But I don't—" Cari protested.

"You no longer have a car to drive, Fraulein."

Cari frowned. Then she turned to Hans. She shook her head. "You need to get back to Trish. She'll already be asking you questions all night." She rubbed the back of her neck. "Okay. I guess I'm in no shape to drive, even if I *had* a car. I just want to go and sleep." She bit her lip. "But I don't have my cane." *And there's no way I'm going to let a total stranger carry me into Frau Mueller's chalet!*

"I'm sure we could get you one from the hospital here. I'll go and ask. Just wait here."

"As if I have a choice."

The officers left the room, but Hans remained. He stood there smiling at her.

"What's so funny?" Cari asked. "The Porsche is a piece of junk. I could have been killed. The chief investigator needs a lesson in manners. What could you *possibly* find funny?"

"You."

"What is that supposed to mean?"

"Trish told me that you've always been like a magnet for men. I see that it must be true. That young officer informed the other one that his shift was over, and that he was going to take you home." He uncrossed his arms and gently patted her shoulder. "And don't you already have an art dealer and a lawyer after you?"

"Oh, stop it!"

"Sorry. But I thought it might take your mind off of some of this."

"Thanks for trying."

The door opened again, and the officer walked in, cane in hand, and a smile on his face. "Just return it before you go home, Fraulein." He passed it to her.

"Thank you," she replied. "Now, let's see if I can stumble out of here."

"Let me help you down," said the officer. He eased her to the floor with a steadying arm around her waist. "Are you dizzy again?"

"A little," Cari admitted as she clutched to the handle of the cane. She was having trouble balancing on her left foot. She clenched her jaw. "Okay. Let's go, please."

"Give us a call tomorrow, Cari," Hans reminded her.

"Sure, unless I'm sleeping." She waited while Hans held the door open for her. "Right now, I just want to make it out of here."

She did. With the help of Officer Rolf Schumacher she made it out of the hospital, and into his Jetta. She allowed herself to close her eyes then. Unfortunately, that did little to ease the nausea or fatigue. When the car lurched forward, she rested her head against the cool glass of the window and bit her lip. She was thankful for the classical music playing on his stereo: it helped to cover up some of her involuntary moans.

When Rolf pulled up in front of the Mueller's home, Cari almost sighed with relief, until he shut off the engine and turned to speak to her.

"I just thought you should know why Herr Kauffman seemed so stiff and formal with you, Fraulein."

"He doesn't like women?" she asked.

Rolf laughed. "I assure you, nothing is farther from the truth. No, he has lost several friends to one or more of the 'crime syndicates' that you mentioned. He is sometimes obsessed with arresting at least *some* of them. I suppose that's why he was angry that your friend didn't report anything."

"My friend was afraid to, and with good reason. How many officers are more interested in *helping* the criminals, instead of *arresting* them?"

"Some. You have the same problem in America."

"Yes, we do. Goodness knows you can make a lot more from drug money than a police salary."

"But an officer with your integrity was never even *tempted*?"

"No. I hate drugs with everything that's in me. I've lost family and friends because of them. A drug addict ended my police career. Maybe you can tell *that* to Herr Kaufman for me. I'm on his side, truly. I'm also realistic. I want to go home in one piece—alive. I've told you what I know. I can't help you more than that can I?"

"I suppose not." He smiled at her, leaned across her, and opened her door. Then he got out of the car and walked around it. He helped her to her feet, steadying her for a moment. "I'll see you to the door, Fraulein."

"Thank you." *Why does it seem like there's twice as many stairs as before?* The freezing had worn off in her shin, and the pain was almost unbearable. She was grateful to have a cane in her right hand, and Rolf's elbow in her left. Halfway up she paused and leaned against the railing. She took a few deep breaths before tackling the rest. When they reached the top, she pressed her forehead against the door.

"Are you ill, Fraulein?" Rolf's arm was supporting her waist once more.

"Mostly, I'm very tired. Would you please knock? I don't have a key."

"Of course, but I suggest you stop leaning on it first." He knocked as soon as she straightened up.

A startled Frau Mueller answered the door. "Fraulein Daniels! What happened?" Before Cari could answer she was adding, "Come in! Come in!"

Rolf helped Cari inside, and tried to explain the situation, once again in German. Frau Mueller didn't like the news in that language any better than she would have in English.

"Herr Maxwell isn't here, Fraulein. How will you get upstairs?"

"He's not back yet?" Cari asked, terribly disappointed. She tried to get her thoughts together. "I-I could wait on the sofa, by the fire." *If I can make it that far.*

"Your room is upstairs, Fraulein?" Rolf asked.

"Yes, but—"

"I don't mind helping you."

Cari swayed slightly, but Rolf kept her on her feet. "Okay. I really think I—" The room spun, and there was a roaring in her ears. *I think I'm going to faint.* She tried to swallow and then say something. Instead, she crumpled against Rolf. *I* am *fainting.*

Rolf eased her to the floor and Frau Mueller brought a cool cloth. Cari shuddered when the cloth touched her face. Rolf rubbed her hands until she opened her eyes. He smiled down at her.

"I fainted, right?" Cari asked.

"Yes, you did," Rolf replied. "I think you'd better get some sleep before it happens again."

"Gladly." She closed her eyes, turned her head, and went limp.

Rolf turned to Frau Mueller and said in German, "I guess she just took my advice. Now, can you show me which room she's in?"

Chapter 40

"What are you doing in here?" Cari asked in a very groggy voice.

John sat up straighter in the chair and rubbed his eyes. They felt gritty. "Well, you see it's like this. I got back here at 11:00 p.m. last night, and found a police officer down in the kitchen with Frau Mueller. Then they informed me about a certain *toasted* Porsche, and a slightly injured, and very tired woman."

Cari furrowed her brows as she looked at him. "Have you been in here all night?" She licked her lips. "And what time is it, anyway?"

"Yes. And it's about 7:00 a.m. How are you feeling?"

"Don't ask," she muttered, trying to pull herself up against the pillows.

"Too late, I already did."

"I feel like I was dragged by a horse." She looked down at her slightly torn and dusty clothing. "That's about how I *look* too." She shifted her legs and her face paled. "Man, I'd forgotten what a kick to the shin can feel like."

John frowned but didn't comment on the bruises on her face and neck. "Judging from what Officer Schumacher told me, it sounds like we should head back to the relative *safety* of LA as soon as you and Tammy are able to handle the flight."

"Yeah, that sounds about right." She looked down at her hands. Her knuckles were chaffed and bruised. "And I'm glad that Louise is coming too. These guys don't seem to care who all they use as *targets*."

"Are you feeling up to some breakfast?"

Cari shook her head. "No thanks. I'm still trying to get past the effects of the Demerol." She smiled slightly. "I suppose they told you I fainted last night."

John nodded, his expression grim. "They did. And the officer seemed much too pleased to have been the one to assist you up the stairs."

"Would you have preferred to have me sleeping on the floor downstairs?" she countered.

"Of course not."

"So, you're just a little jealous?"

"Only slightly."

Cari moved the quilt from her legs. Then she bit her lip and looked around the room. "Do you know where the cane is? I have one very sore leg today."

"It's right under the bed. I'll get it for you." He leaned forward and reached for the cane. Then he handed it to her. "Do you need any help getting up?"

"I don't know yet," she admitted. "Let me find out." She gripped the cane in her right hand, and braced it on the floor. Then she eased her legs over the side of the bed, perspiration breaking out on her forehead. "So far, so good." She made it to her feet, though she didn't look very steady. "Okay, I've mastered standing. Now let's see how I fair with walking."

John stood and moved the chair out of her way. He watched as she took a couple of faltering steps. "Looks like I'll be doing the driving today."

"Who said I'll even be going anywhere?" She clutched the doorframe with her left hand. "The thought of doing absolutely nothing is far more appealing."

John waited in the room until she returned from the bathroom. She looked worse than before, but he didn't rush to *rescue* her, knowing that she might resent his efforts. She made it back to the bed and sat down, sighing heavily.

"Okay, *nurse*. I think your shift is over. Why don't you go and have some breakfast? Or go sleep? I'll be fine." She leaned the cane against the nightstand and reclined on the pillows once more. She closed her eyes and let out her breath.

"Cari?"

"Umm?"

"You had a lot of nightmares last night."

Her eyes immediately opened. "When?"

"All night. That's part of the reason I stayed in here. You were very restless, and you were calling out in your sleep."

"Wh-what was I saying?" she asked, looking very uneasy.

"Things like: 'I'm sorry.' 'Don't hurt me.' 'Please don't.' I assumed you were dreaming about what happened last night."

Cari rubbed her hands over her face, and winced when she touched the bruises. "I'm not sure what I was dreaming about. I can't really remember. It was probably the drugs they gave me." She looked at him then. "Poor Tammy, she's been going through nights like this for the past week. I wonder how she made out last night at Louise's."

"I'll call later to find out. What do you want me to tell them?"

"About last night? Tell them to both be very careful. And you can ask Louise to call Hans and Trish Lehman, and let them know that I'm all right. For that matter, you might be able to go and see Hans at the dealership. I don't know if he'll be at work or not." She touched her neck and flinched again. "Do I really look as bad as I feel?"

"Probably." John neared the bed, leaned down, and kissed her on the cheek. "But you're still beautiful. Try to get some rest." He smiled as he straightened up. "And don't be surprised if Frau Mueller comes upstairs with a tray of food. You know how she feels about skipped meals."

Cari managed a slight smile. "Yes, I do. Just try to hold her off until I have a chance to change clothes."

"Sure. I'll come back after I make a few phone calls." He paused in the doorway. "Getting homesick?"

"Now that the Porsche is scrap, yes, I am. You?"

"I'm just glad that you're still in one piece."

"Hello?" Louise answered as she picked up the phone.

"Louise? It's Rick Benson. Just calling to let you and Tammy know that I got home okay. How are you doing?"

"Fine. Actually, I think Tammy finally had a decent sleep last night. She's not up yet. Do you want me to go and get her?"

"Not if she's resting. I'll be home all day. She can call me later. How are you doing, Louise?"

"I'm fine." She twisted the cord with her fingers. "How was your flight?"

"It was okay. But I was bored. I couldn't sleep after eating those pastries that Cari sent along." He laughed. "Too much chocolate. But I spent a lot of time thinking about you."

"Is that what made you bored?" she asked, half teasing, half serious.

"Not hardly! That's part of what kept me awake. I really miss you."

"Oh. Well, I was thinking about you quite a bit after you left, too."

"Good or bad?"

"Good." She smiled to herself. "I'm looking forward to seeing you again, Rick."

"I told my son about you. He already likes you."

"How did you manage that? He hasn't even met me yet."

"Well, mostly he figures that any woman who leaves me smiling and whistling can't be too bad."

"Is that how you're acting?" She found it somewhat hard to picture.

"Sure." There was a lengthy pause. "Well, I'd better not drag this out too long. This is an overseas call. But it was good to hear your voice."

"Yours too. Good bye, Rick. I'll have Tammy call you later on."

"Bye."

Louise replaced the receiver and stood in the kitchen for several minutes, thinking about Rick. *Am I really doing the right thing by moving so far away? Maybe I should wait a while.* She thought of how he'd kissed her goodbye, and she smiled again. *No, I think the airfare will be cheaper than the number of phone calls we'd end up making. I think it's time to let go of the past, and reach out for something new. And, if that happens to include someone else, why not?*

John shook hands with Hans Lehman across the counter. "Congratulations, Hans. I hear your daughter is a beauty."

Hans smiled briefly. "How's Cari?"

"Pretty sore, but she's been through a lot worse, more than once, for that matter. She's tougher than she looks. But she did admit that she'll be glad to leave as soon as possible."

"The forensics experts are still checking on the car," Hans said. "But they're pretty sure that the gas tank was punctured, enough for some fuel to leak for a while. Just like Cari had suspected." He shook his head. "She is very lucky to be alive." He crossed his arms over his chest. "And she was worried about the car. She apologized more than once about it."

John thought back to when he'd found her at his cabin. Her left shoulder dislocated, a slight concussion, and serious heart trouble. And she'd still tried to say something funny to him. "She's like that."

"Don't you worry about her?" Hans asked.

John sighed. "Often, but she doesn't always appreciate it. Like I said, she's tougher than she looks. She'll probably be up and bossing everybody around by tomorrow."

"Sounds like Trish. She's coming home later this morning, but she would have come last night. She just kept telling me: 'I *only* had a baby, Hans. I'm fine. Don't fuss so much." He rolled his eyes. "Maybe it's because they always had to prove themselves as police officers. Trish doesn't talk about it a lot, but I know she found it hard."

"Cari loved her job, but she's admitted that it wasn't an easy one."

Hans grinned. "I think I'll stick with cars and skiing."

"Right. And I'll just keep being a high-priced lawyer."

"*Some* of us have to do the boring things."

Chapter 41

Cari managed to change clothes, and get back into bed, just before Frau Mueller came in, bearing a tray of food. Cari smiled at her, even though the bruises on her face made it painful.

"Are you feeling better, Fraulein?" the woman asked as she set the tray next to Cari. "I was so worried last night."

"Yes, I'm feeling better. I'm sorry for being such a terrible guest. I really have given you a lot of extra work and worry, haven't I?"

Frau Mueller smiled and patted Cari's hand. "I worry about all of my guests. Would you like something to eat?"

Cari licked her lips. "Well, now that I see those rolls sitting there . . ." She looked up at her. "You spoil us, you know."

"I enjoy it. Would you like some coffee?"

Cari shook her head. "No, thank you. I'll just have some juice."

"Fine. I'll come back for the tray a little later." She quietly left the room, humming to herself.

Cari was still eating one of the rolls when John knocked on the open door. "It's amazing what a difference fresh clothing can make," he said with a grin. "If it weren't for the scrapes and bruises, I'd hardly know where you were last night."

"Thanks, I think." She finished the juice and wiped her mouth with the napkin. "So, how is everybody?"

"Well, Louise said that Tammy was sleeping in, but that Rick had called. He's fine. Hans told me that Trish and the baby will be home later this morning. And Gilles is planning to come over for lunch."

"Oh. Well, I guess that covers everybody, doesn't it?" She closed her eyes and leaned back, resting her hands in her lap. "Sorry you came?"

"Not exactly. I'll admit, I'm used to much *simpler* vacations, but this one has had its good moments, too. What about you?"

Cari puckered her brows before answering. "I'm not sure. I mean, it certainly has been full of surprises, hasn't it? Some good, some bad. But, all in all, I suppose I won't have *too many* regrets about coming here. Though, I never did see a lot of the area, except for the trip to Chur. I'd say that was a highlight."

"Remind me to let you test drive the Jag sometime. I don't think I'd have any worries with you behind the wheel."

"Thanks." She smiled and opened her eyes. "I do manage to be proficient in some areas, at least."

John came closer and sat down on the chair. "So, are you sure you'll like having a roommate after all these years?"

Cari laughed. "Other than Tammy's visits, I've *never* had one. I'm sure it'll be a challenge, but I'm still looking forward to it."

"Good morning," Louise said as Tammy entered the kitchen. It was actually close to lunch time, but she was glad to see her look so much better.

"Hi! I guess I kind of slept in, didn't I?" She looked at the clock and her eyes grew huge. "Oh, brother!" She sat down at the table and rubbed her eyes. "Man, I never sleep this late." Then she frowned. "Shoot! I missed a dose of pills—not that *I mind*, but Dr. Mueller might."

"Well, just take them now, instead. I'm sure that you needed the rest, Tammy. Don't worry about it." She got up and poured her a glass of milk. "Which would you like, breakfast or lunch?"

"Either, I guess. I'm actually hungry for a change."

"Good. I'll warm up some soup and slice some cheese while you get your pills."

Tammy was back in short order. "I will be *so glad* when I take the last of these." She downed them with some milk before sitting down again.

"Oh, I almost forgot," Louise said, giving the soup another turn with the wooden spoon. "Your dad called earlier this morning, but he said not to wake you up. You can call him later."

"He got home okay?"

"Yes. He sounded fine." Louise turned down the heat and went to the fridge to get the cheese.

"You really like each other, don't you?"

Louise got out a paring knife before answering. "Yes, we do. Does that bother you?"

"No. I think it's great. I think both of you deserve another shot at being happy."

"Maybe you're right," Louise replied with a smile. "Apparently, your dad has already told your brother about me."

"Cool. You know, I actually miss Ricky. I guess I'm used to his teasing and stuff."

"Well, you won't have to wait much longer. Just another few days." Then she remembered John's phone call. "Actually, we'll be leaving as soon as you and Cari are both well enough to travel."

"Cari? What's wrong with her?"

"There was an—well, not an *accident*, really. Last night."

"What happened? Is she hurt?"

"Someone knocked her out, and set the car on fire—"

"What?" Tammy's face had completely drained of color.

"Tammy, calm down, Cari's going to be fine. She wasn't close to the car. She has a few stitches in her leg, I think. And some bruises. But she's going to be all right. She's taking it easy today, but I'm sure she'll be over tomorrow. Or we'll go and see her."

"But why would anyone do that to her? I mean, it wasn't a mugging, was it? Why would they wreck the car?"

"I'm not sure. But, I think it somehow has to do with the painting, and the people that my husband owed money to." She set the knife aside and reached for Tammy's now clammy hands. "John wants us to be careful, but not to panic. The police are investigating. Please don't worry."

Tammy took a few deep breaths. "Okay. I'll try not to go crazy. But this is sure turning into a really lousy trip." Then she looked into Louise's eyes. "Except for getting to know you."

Gilles entered Cari's room, a bouquet of flowers in his hand, and a worried look on his face. John was still sitting in the chair. "You sure like to scare us, don't you?" he teased. "In Mexico, or LA, or in the normally *tranquil* Swiss Alps." He handed her the flowers. "Are all private investigators like you?"

Cari laughed. "Not hardly! I'm one of a kind, Gilles. How are your ribs?"

"That," he huffed as he sat on the bed, "is precisely what the police wanted to know. Namely, who cracked them for me." He shrugged. "I couldn't give them any more to go on than you did."

"But it must have been the same guys," Cari insisted.

Gilles nodded. "I believe so." He rubbed his face. "The inspector was not at all happy with me for keeping my unfortunate incident to myself." Then he grinned at her. "The younger fellow— Schumacher isn't it—he was more sympathetic. He thought that you were unusually brave, for a woman, of course."

Cari rolled her eyes. "Bravery had little to do with it. I was angry." She shifted on the bed and winced. "Speaking of angry, have you heard from your father?"

Gilles sighed. "Yes. He wants me to reconsider leaving the business. I told him my mind was made up."

"What about the painting?" John asked. "Are you still paying him for it?"

"Yes. He's no longer arguing about that."

"What about your mother?" Cari asked. "Have you spoken with her?"

"Not yet. That is a conversation that I wish to have in person." He smiled. "As you know for yourself, my parents are very different. My mother is always willing to listen."

"I know," Cari replied. "Though your father isn't *all* bad, Gilles."

"No, he isn't. But this is one time that we simply cannot reach a compromise. It's best if we separate, before hurting each other more than we already have."

"Well, financially speaking, you should do just fine on your own," John said. "You could certainly start your own collection, or business, if you chose to."

Gilles shook his head. "I have no desire to do that. I don't like the role of 'boss'. I can make decisions, but I draw the line at total responsibility. Do you understand what I mean?"

"I suppose," John replied. "That's likely why I never went into private practice. I enjoy working with other staff, not running a company."

"Not like Rebecca Richards. She's the queen of organizational skills. She'd be a real knockout in politics, wouldn't she?"

"Don't suggest it to her," John said with a laugh. "Or she might hand me the company."

Cari covered her mouth while she yawned. "Okay, guys, it's been nice to visit with you, but I think I'm about to fall asleep. Take a hike."

John and Gilles looked at each other. "Rather bossy, isn't she?" John asked.

"True," Gilles responded. "But somehow her beauty helps to make up for it."

"Oh, good grief!" she sputtered. "Save the comments, you two. Go and bug Tammy. She must be feeling better after sleeping in."

"Good idea," Gilles replied. "And she's not quite so bossy either."

"Oh, by the way, Cari," John added. "I decided that we should change your nickname. *La Femme Courageuse* was no longer appropriate."

"Well, let's hear it, Mon Ami," she retorted.

"*La Femme Dangereuse.* Don't you think so, Gilles?"

"True. She drives like a demon, and attracts danger wherever she goes. Good choice, John."

"Oh, get out of here!" Then she smirked. "Before I clobber one of you with my cane."

Chapter 42

Cari went to visit with Louise and Tammy the next day, after they came to pick her up. Frau Mueller insisted on sending along several fresh pastries, and Tammy didn't have the heart to tell her that just the smell of them increased her nausea. "You two can eat them," she whispered to the others.

"Have you decided what to do with your belongings?" Cari asked Louise. "I mean, there's only so much you can bring on the plane. And what about the house?"

"The house is only rented, so that won't be a problem. The owner should have no trouble finding new tenants." She had checked Cari over carefully, and advised against a massage until some of the bruises had healed. "As for the furniture, I can sell it. That just leaves my clothes to pack." She gestured with her hands. "You can see for yourself that I haven't accumulated a lot through the years."

"Except for books," Tammy remarked. "Are you going to ship those later?"

"I suppose so. Why don't you help me sort through them?"

"Sure. Maybe it'll keep my mind off my stomach."

"Still that bad, eh?" Cari asked.

"Yeah. It makes it kind of hard to appreciate Louise's cooking talents."

"'This too shall pass'," Cari said. "That phrase has been all too relevant to my life in the past couple of years."

"Hey, I've got an idea," Tammy said. "Why don't the three of us start our own club? We could call it the TTSP Club—this too shall pass. I think we can all relate, don't you?"

Louise smiled at the suggestion. "I'm in favor, Tammy. But will we let anyone else join?"

"No. At least not for a while."

"And what will we do, as club members?" Cari asked.

"Well, as soon as I can handle food again, we can go out for dessert once a month."

"Sounds good to me. It would have to be chocolate, of course."

"And washed down with strong coffee," offered Louise. "Shall we write up an agreement?"

"That's not essential," Tammy insisted. "*We'll* know what we're doing. And why. Let's plan on next month. How about the second Monday night of each month?"

"Sure," Cari replied. "We shouldn't run into many holidays like that." She clasped Tammy's shoulder. "Great planning, Kid. Now, let's start sorting through these books while Louise takes care of her clients."

Just then someone knocked at the door. Cari immediately tensed. "Make sure you check through the window first."

"Don't worry, Cari," Louise chided. "Besides, I already know who it is." She went to open the door, and Cari heard a baby crying.

"So, is this the half-way house for hospital rejects?" Trish asked as she sauntered into the living room. She looked from Cari to Tammy, a fierce frown on her face. "Louise is the only *unscathed* person in the room." Then she grinned. "Except maybe for

Katrina, here." She gave her crying daughter a quick kiss. "And she'll be fine as soon as I feed her." She sat down on the sofa next to Tammy. "Then who wants to babysit while Louise gets me back into shape?"

"Oh, could I?" Tammy whispered. "She's the most beautiful baby I've ever seen."

"Of course," Trish replied. "With Hans for a father, how can she be anything else?"

"You're not exactly *ugly*, Trish," Cari said.

Trish just made a face and lifted the bottom of her sweatshirt. "Pardon me, ladies, but it's Katrina's lunch time." She soon had her brand new daughter contentedly nursing, and she relaxed her shoulders. She glanced over at Cari. "So, did the police tell you about the car, yet?"

Cari shook her head. "What do you mean?"

"Well, it seems that the gas tank was punctured. Maybe they were hoping that you'd get in and try to drive off. Just starting the engine could have provided enough sparks to torch it. They figure the guys must have waited around for awhile, and when nothing happened, they decided to 'help' the situation."

"Hence, the cigarette?" Cari asked.

Trish nodded. "Yup. A hundred thousand dollar car, poof!"

Cari felt her cheeks flush. "I'm really sorry, Trish. Will your insurance cover it?"

"Of course! You think I'm worried about replacing a *car*, when I nearly lost a *friend*?" She shifted Katrina from one breast to the other. "Besides, I highly doubt that I would have driven it much anymore. Life will revolve around four door models from now on, I suspect." She smiled when Louise brought her a bottle of water. "Thanks. I'm still getting used to drinking enough now. It seems like I'm always thirsty."

"Trish, you barely look like you've had a baby in the past couple of days. How could you possibly lose the weight so fast?" Louise asked.

Trish shrugged. "High metabolism? Excess water? Beats me, but I'm not complaining." She looked at Cari again. "So, Hans tells me that a certain young police officer made it his *duty* to see you home the other night."

Cari blushed again. "Yes, he did. Good thing, too. I passed out just inside the front door. I don't usually take Demerol and then go someplace after. I'm used to sleeping it off. It was *not* a pleasant experience." Then she smiled. "But he was kind of cute."

"Good grief!" Tammy groaned. "Can we take you *anywhere*, Cari? You always have guys falling all over you."

Cari winked at her. "I could always send some in your direction, Kid, but they're always too old for you."

"I'll find my own, thanks," Tammy insisted. She suddenly went white. "Excuse me!" she muttered, just before dashing out of the room.

Trish frowned as she looked after her.

"Antibiotics," Louise remarked. "She's already lost several pounds since last week."

"That doesn't sound too great. Is she okay otherwise?"

"Getting there," Cari answered. "She's not in pain now. That's an improvement."

"And she's finally getting some sleep," Louise added.

A still pale Tammy came back a few minutes later, just in time to take Katrina from Trish. "She shouldn't give you any trouble for a while. She'll likely just sleep."

"We'll manage," Cari assured her. "Go and relax. Don't forget, Louise is flying back with us."

Trish scowled at her. "I may never forgive you for that, Cari."

"Sure you will. Hans and Katrina will keep you too busy to remember."

Cari was sound asleep when John came to pick her up. Louise invited him to stay for supper and he agreed. "I already told Frau Mueller that we wouldn't be there tonight."

"Okay."

"Has she been sleeping for very long?"

"Not really. Maybe half an hour. Why?"

"She's been having nightmares, but she doesn't seem to remember them when she wakes up."

"Is she still taking pain medication?"

"Not that I know of. I think it's likely just related to what happened to her. Whatever the reason, she's been tired and edgy for the past two days. I'm glad she's resting."

"She'll be fine, John."

"That's what everyone keeps telling me. But in the eleven months that I've known her, she's been in the hospital twice, and that doesn't include the other night." He shook his head. "Is it any wonder that I worry about her?"

"Not when you're in love with her," Louise said, a slight smile on her lips.

John didn't answer her. He simply went to the window and looked out.

"It's no secret, you know."

He turned to face her. "You've known us for just over a week, and it's that obvious?"

"Yes. To anyone who watches the two of you together."

John made sure that Cari got up to her room safely. Then he stood in the doorway a moment longer. "Just call me if you need anything."

Cari smiled. "Thanks, but I'll be okay. Goodnight, John."

"Goodnight."

John stared into the darkness as he listened to Cari calling out in her sleep. *Don't. Stop. Please don't hurt me.* Over and over. She finally grew quiet, but he couldn't get to sleep himself. *Something more is upsetting her than what happened two days ago. Just what is it that's disturbing her? What is she dreaming about?* He put his hands behind his head. *I wonder if she'll ever trust me enough to tell me.*

Cari sat up in bed and tried to steady her breathing. *I'm okay. I was just dreaming. Nobody is going to hurt me. Not Mark. Not Kyle Richards. Not Jerry Neilson. Not those two thugs. I'm safe. And I need to sleep.* She rubbed her face with trembling hands. *I want to go home, but I don't want to run and hide. Please help me, God. I need rest. I'm tired. Please help me to deal with the memories. Please help me to sleep.*

Chapter 43

"So, Gilles, what's the itinerary this time round?" Cari asked as they all sat around Louise's living room.

"Well, we leave here on Monday morning, by plane." He grinned at her. "We won't try to find out how you'd like the mountains on the way back. Then we stop in Paris again, but we'll spend the night at the *Ritz*. You may not get the chance again for a while. We'll stay there until Wednesday morning, and then take the Concorde to New York."

"Really?" Cari asked. "Anxious to unload us are you?" she teased.

"Not at all. Then we spend the night with Tammy's grandparents. At least you ladies will. John and I can stay in a hotel for the night."

"Grandma won't let you," Tammy asserted. "She'll make room."

"Very well. We'll all squeeze into the Jacobs' home for the night. Then back to LA on Thursday evening. How does that sound?"

"Great," Tammy replied. "Except for that time change things again. Man, I got so mixed up on the way over. Now it's going to be in reverse." She shook her head. "I won't remember what time it is from Monday to Thursday."

"Then Gilles and I will keep track for you," John assured her, placing an arm around her shoulder. "You'll do fine."

"So," Cari interrupted, "Why the Ritz? Your grandparents certainly have enough room for all of us, and it would spare you the expense."

John coughed slightly, and Gilles laughed. "That's the least of my worries, Cari. I'm paying for this now, not my father. Don't worry about it. Just have a good time."

Tammy furrowed her brows for a moment. "This sounds like we may need to do some shopping, Cari. What do you think?"

"Good plan. We did our sightseeing last time. This time we hit some high fashion shops."

Louise laughed. "And what, pray tell, will you be shopping *for*?"

"Oh, just something classy enough to wear at a hotel like that," Tammy replied.

"Oh," Cari said. "I need to call Mike and Julie and ask them to get a bed for my spare room. Any preference, Louise?"

Louise just shrugged. "I figure I'll be as bad as Tammy. I haven't been further than Zurich in fourteen years. I'll just be glad to *have* a bed to sleep in."

"Okay. Julie can pick it out then. She has great taste." She turned to Gilles. "Sorry to interrupt again, Boss."

"No problem."

They all talked for another hour, making sure that everyone was clear on the details. John was taking care of the tickets. Tammy would phone her grandparents. Gilles had already reserved suites at the Ritz. Louise was still arranging to sell her furniture. And Cari needed to return the borrowed cane to the hospital, and get herself a new one.

"I know just where to look, Cari," John told her. "There's a shop not far from here, where they make walking sticks, canes, umbrellas. All handcrafted. I'm sure you'll find something you like."

"Thanks. I sure don't want to go home without one." Her shin was healing, but the bruise was huge, and still very colorful.

"We'll go after breakfast, then."

"Oh, you were right, John. This is beautiful work." Cari admired several different canes, finding it hard to narrow the choice.

"How about this one?" John asked, holding out a darkened pine model, with mountain goat for a handle. "You'd certainly never forget where it came from."

"That's true. Let me check it for size." She took it from him, and set it on the floor. "Perfect. Just like it was made for me." She looked up at him and smiled. "I'll take it."

The man at the counter was pleased by Cari's choice. "My best work, Fraulein. I enjoyed working on this one. I hope it will be useful to you."

"I'm sure it will. How much is it?"

The man named a price, but before Cari could even reach for her purse, John had a credit card on the counter. "I'll take care of it," he said. "Consider it a 'get well' present."

Cari wasn't about to argue in front of a stranger, so she simply smiled. "Thanks." She left the store soon after, glad to have such a beautiful piece of work to maintain her balance. "You didn't have to do that, John."

"I know. But I *wanted* to."

They all had supper at Frau Mueller's on Sunday evening. She cried at the thought of them leaving. She hugged Tammy and told her to say hello to Rick for her. She also admonished her to put on some weight once she got back home. Tammy promised to try. She remarked to John that he'd been much too busy on his 'vacation' this year, and that he should do better next time. And she wanted Cari to keep in touch. She simply kissed Louise on each cheek and told her to take care of herself.

Cari slept little that night. Her mind was too full of thoughts, and memories from the trip. *I came dating Gilles, but now that's already over. John asked me if I love him and I never answered. Gilles was beaten up. Tammy had surgery. I got stitches. John is fine.* She smiled to herself. *Good thing somebody stayed out of trouble. I was sick on the train, but I loved the drive to Chur. We've stayed in buildings, and have eaten in restaurants, that are hundreds of years old. It's been a very full trip. Not to mention meeting Louise, and landing myself a roommate. And possibly a 'mate' for Rick. I wonder how that's going to turn out.*

She rolled over and looked at the moonlight coming through the window. *Thank You for taking care of us, Lord. I know that things could have turned out so differently. For all of us. I still don't know what's going to happen when we get home. And there's a lot of flying to do before then. Please keep us all safe. Help Tammy not to be so nauseated. Help Gilles to know what to say to his mother when he gets home. Please help me to make Louise feel welcome in the apartment.*

Cari laughed softly. *I'm sorry, Lord. Here I am telling You how to do everything. What I should be doing is trusting You. I already know that You'll watch over us. Thank You.*

"This is a neat plane," Tammy said as they buckled into the Piper Chieftain. "Sure is different from a 727, isn't it?"

"Very," Gilles acknowledged. "I decided to charter a flight to Paris. You can see a lot more from a small aircraft. There's a big difference between a few thousand feet, and thirty-five. I hope you like it."

Cari was leaning against the window, already groggy from the Gravol. "I'll likely still miss the scenery, Gilles. I'm falling asleep." She looked over and smiled at him. "But thanks for trying."

"You're welcome."

To her surprise, Cari stayed awake for the entire flight, and she was grateful that she did. She took dozens of photos as they flew across the country, and on towards Paris. "I can't believe how beautiful it is. Such a contrast to LA. I think I'm going to miss it."

"Me too," Tammy answered from behind her. "What about you, Louise?"

"I don't know yet. I guess I'm kind of caught between the two. It's been so long since I left the States, Tammy. Switzerland has been home for a long time. I didn't come here as a tourist. And I'm not leaving as one, either."

"Yeah, I guess so. But that doesn't mean it won't turn out to be a great decision."

"That's what I'm hoping."

John slipped into the seat next to Cari. "Do you need to change rolls of film yet?"

Cari shook her head. "Not yet. But sometime before we get to Paris. Enjoying yourself?" She knew that he'd been reading most of the time.

"I am now," he replied. "How are you feeling?"

"Not too bad." She shrugged. "But I'll probably make a rather *stiff* entrance at the Ritz." She grinned at him. "Do you think I'll look distinguished enough with my new cane?"

"You always look good," he murmured close to her ear. "I'd be proud to be seen with you anywhere." He reached for her hand, and held it for several minutes. "You don't need to feel self-conscious in front of me."

"Thank you," she breathed, very conscious of his body next to hers. And the warmth of his strong hand. "I'll try to remember that."

"Hey, break it up, you two," Tammy said from over the seat. "I'm still functioning in my role as official chaperone. Go back to your seat, Mon Ami."

John stood up and looked down at Tammy. "Yes, Ma Petite." He went back to his seat, buckled himself in, and picked up the book he'd been reading.

Louise began to laugh so hard that Tammy nudged her. "What's so funny?"

When Louise could finally talk, she said, "Tammy, it's lucky for your dad and me that we never had you along when *we* were alone. We'd have been in *serious* trouble with you."

"Maybe," Tammy replied. "But probably not."

"Hey, no fair, Kid!" Cari protested. "Why the special dispensation for Rick and Louise?"

"Because they've both been married before. I figure I could cut them a little slack."

"Huh!" was John's outraged response. "I happen to have seen the windshield fog up when Louise dropped him off, Ma Petite. And he did *not* get out of the car right away."

Tammy was silent for a moment, but Louise had begun to giggle again. Finally, she replied, "Well, my mom and dad used to do that sometimes. I'd watch from my bedroom window. I guess my dad hasn't lost his touch, after all." She seemed to consider the matter settled.

"He certainly hasn't," Louise whispered, but they all heard her.

"Whoa, a limo this time?" Tammy asked when they had retrieved their luggage at the airport.

"Yes," Gilles replied. "It's red carpet treatment all the way, or at least for most of it." They were soon ensconced inside the plush automobile, snacking from the mini fridge. They were all thirsty after their flight. "And I've rented it for our full time here, so we can come and go in style."

Tammy took a sip from a frosty bottle of Evian. "You know something, guys? We don't have a name for Louise. We'll have to think of something on the way to the hotel."

"True," John said. "Any ideas?"

"What are you talking about?" Louise wondered aloud. "What names?"

"I," Tammy stated with a hint of arrogance, "am *Ma Petite.* John is *Mon Ami.* Gilles is *L'homme d'Art.* And Cari is dubbed, *La Femme Dangereuse.* Alias, *La Femme Courageuse.*"

"There must be a story behind *that* change," Louise remarked.

"How about *La Bijou*?" suggested Gilles. "For those amethyst eyes."

"No, it reminds me of the theatre," Cari countered. "How about something to do with her hands, since she's a masseuse?" She looked from Gilles to John. "Help me out, guys, my French is distinctly limited."

"*La Femme Competent*?" John offered.

"Competent?" Cari asked.

"Proficient."

"Well, that's true, and in more than just massage."

"Yeah, she's a great cook too," Tammy acknowledged. "I think it fits. What d'you say, Louise?"

"I like it." She smiled at Cari. "Though yours sounds much more exciting."

"Okay, that makes it official. Louise is now, at least for the rest of this trip, La Femme Competent." Tammy shook her hand. "Welcome aboard, Louise."

"Thanks."

Chapter 44

"Oh, boy!" Cari whispered. She'd seen the Ritz on television, and in pictures, but it was entirely different up close. "This is unbelievable, Gilles." She looked down at her clothing, suddenly very conscious of her linen pants, and silk blouse.

"You look fine, Cari," he remarked. "You have no one to impress, do you? It's the *hotel* that impresses people."

"Personally," John said with a smile, "I think all three of you look wonderful."

"Yeah, right!" Tammy scoffed. "I look like I'm anorexic. I can hardly wait to buy a new pair of jeans."

"Not until after we register, and go eat," Gilles insisted. "Let's go dazzle a few locals, ladies."

Actually, they did garner a lot of attention. Tammy looked even more delicate than usual, and still a bit pale. Louise had her gorgeous eyes, and a beautiful crinkle cotton suit on. She could have passed for a visiting model, rather than a recently widowed masseuse. And Cari had her handcrafted cane, setting her somewhat apart. The valets almost jumped to assist her, making pleasant comments in French, which left Louise grinning at her.

"What are they saying?" Cari demanded.

"Oh, just the usual. 'Can we help you, mademoiselle? May we get your luggage? Would you like to go directly to your room?' At least that's what they're saying *to* you. What they're saying to *each other* is even more interesting."

"Louise!" Cari tripped on a step while her head was turned. Sure enough, two young men, and an older one, came to her assistance. She suddenly had a gentle, though firm, hand on each elbow. The third man asked her if she was all right, in somewhat stilted English. "Yes, I'm fine, thank you. *Merci.*" He held the door open for her, bowing slightly as she passed.

Cari was literally *ushered* into the lobby, not sure if she felt pampered or pestered. Gilles said something to the men, and they led her to a comfortable chair. She smiled, though it was somewhat forced. Then she grabbed hold of Louise's hand and pulled her over. "So, help me out! What is going on?"

Louise sat down on the chair next to her. Tammy remained with John, once more looking and acting like his daughter. It was probably a good way to keep comments to a minimum in regard to her.

"Nothing much is happening, Cari," Louise replied, her tone gentle. "They just find you very beautiful, and they wonder why you need the cane." She grinned then. "And they also wondered if you'll be staying with Gilles or John while you're here."

The color drained from Cari's face and she bit her lip. "This is worse than going back to Gilles' grandparents, Louise."

"Well, you have to admit, we do make an intriguing little group. A handsome man of about forty, with a teenage girl hanging onto his arm. Another man, about thirty, who seems to be in charge of it all. And then the two of us. What are people supposed to think?"

"They're not!" Cari hissed. "They're just supposed to show us to our rooms, and carry the luggage."

"Come on, Cari, have you never sat around and watched people? I've always liked doing that, especially in a place like this. You never know who might walk in here." Her expression sobered. "Besides, I think Gilles chose this hotel because of all the security. Likewise, the limousine. He wants us to have a good time, but a safe one. Try not to spoil it for him."

"I'm sorry. I guess I just don't like all the attention. I never have." Then she looked around. A subtle smile graced her lips. "But speaking of security, I'd like to have a look at their system. It seems pretty state of the art to me. I wonder if Gilles could arrange that for me."

"Likely. Men as wealthy as he is can *arrange* a lot of things. Why don't you ask him during lunch?"

"I just might do that."

Just then, Gilles returned to them, along with John and Tammy. Another uniformed gentleman was with them.

"Cari, Louise, I'd like you to meet Monsieur Dargis. He's the concierge for our suites. He'd like to show them to us, to make sure that everything is acceptable."

Cari cocked an eyebrow at that. "Acceptable? What could possibly be a problem here?"

Monsieur Dargis seemed to like her response. He reached for her hand. "May I have the honor of escorting you, mademoiselle?"

"Certainly," Cari replied, getting to her feet. She tucked her left hand beneath his elbow.

"Right this way, please."

Cari stood inside the room and looked around. "I can't believe this," she breathed. "I have never seen anything so beautiful."

"Over this way is the adjoining room, mademoiselle, for your friends. This is the dressing area. Each bedroom has its own bath." Monsieur Dargis went on to explain many of the features of the suite, including the balcony area. He also drew her attention to the basket of fruit, plate of cheeses, bottle of wine, and assortment of bon bons. "If you need *anything* at all, mademoiselle, please just ask."

Cari had no doubt that he meant it. What amazed her was that she actually thought of something. "Well, actually, Monsieur Dargis, I would really appreciate a map of the immediate area, and a listing of some of the best dress shops." She smiled as he made careful note on a discreet pad of paper from his jacket. "And I don't drink wine, so would it be possible to have a bottle of cider instead? Either sparkling grape or apple would be fine."

He nodded. "Anything else?"

"Well, yes. I know you have a pool here."

"Yes, mademoiselle."

"Could you write down for me where I could purchase a swim suit? I'm afraid that I didn't think to bring one along."

"Certainly." He then looked to Louise and Tammy, who both seemed stunned by their new surroundings.

"I'm fine," Tammy managed to say.

"I would really appreciate a small box of truffles from *La Maison du Chocolat.* Perhaps 250 grams," Louise said. She sounded for all the world as though she were used to this sort of arrangement. Cari suddenly remembered that she very well might have been, once. She had grown up in a wealthy home in Boston. "And it would be nice if you could have the cider brought in a bucket of ice, please." She smiled warmly and switched to French. "*Je sais que tes services va être bien compensé, Monsieur Dargis.*"

"*Merci, Madame St. Denis. C'est va être un vrai plaisir.*" He bowed before addressing Gilles and John. "*Et vous, messieurs? Quelque chose?*"

John shook his head. "*No, merci. Rien pour le moment.*"

Gilles rubbed his chin, seemingly deep in thought. Then he snapped his fingers. "*Pas ici, Monsieur. Mais dans ma chambre, s'il vous plait."* He smiled at the women. "Would you like to eat in the dining room for lunch, or just order room service?"

"Room service," Tammy replied. "I've become totally sold on it." She gestured to the sitting area. "And there is certainly enough room for all of us."

"Sounds good to me," Cari remarked. "Louise?"

"Fine." Then she winked. "The sooner we eat, the sooner we can shop."

Gilles laughed. "As you wish, ladies. Anything in particular?"

"Rich, French, and creamy," Tammy said. "I have a lot of lost ground to make up for."

Monsieur Dargis bowed once more before leaving the room with Gilles and John. Louise watched them go.

"I wonder what Gilles is being so secretive about. It's not like he's arranging *personal* entertainment, or anything. What's he up to?"

"I have no idea," Cari replied. "But, if he wants us to, we'll eventually find out." She reached for a small cluster of grapes and popped one into her mouth. "Oh, these are perfect." She ate the rest of what she was holding. "Well, I suppose that we should freshen up before lunch, girls." She set her cane on the bed and limped to the bathroom without it. She gritted her teeth as she ran warm water into the marble sink. *My leg is killing me. How am I going to get through the rest of the day?* She washed her face, and then used some of the lotion that was available in the ample amenities basket. *I think I could really get to like this kind of lifestyle. At least from time to time.*

Lunch arrived just before John and Gilles did. Three waiters spread a tablecloth, napkins, china and silver, and crystal. Then they started to remove the silver covers from the various dishes.

Tammy's eyes grew huge.

"Goodness sake! Gilles, what is all of this?"

"I assure you, Ma Petite, it's all French, rich, or creamy." Veal with cream sauce, a pureed vegetable soup, French bread, still warm, with a dish of butter. Crepes, stuffed with cheese, and covered with a white wine sauce, and a tray with several types of pastries. "If this doesn't help you gain weight, nothing will."

"I'm stuffed," Tammy declared just before setting aside her napkin. "Now, let's go work off this meal by doing some shopping. Where do we go first?"

"To check your wallet," Cari replied. "How much do you have left of what your dad sent with you?"

"Most of it. I got sick, remember? And it's in Traveller's Checks, so I shouldn't have any trouble exchanging them, should I?"

"You can do that here in the hotel," Gilles told her. "I'll go with you." He looked down at his watch. "Why don't we meet downstairs in twenty minutes, by the front desk?"

"Fine," Cari answered with a smile. "I'm looking forward to riding in that limo again. Nothing like being in the lap of luxury."

Gilles patted her shoulder. "It can be nice, Cari. It can also be a very lonely place."

Chapter 45

"Can you believe these prices?" Cari asked Louise as they browsed through another designer shop.

"Yes, as a matter of fact, I can." She wistfully fingered a satin blouse. "I'd forgotten for a long time. I guess life was quite simple after I left Boston. But I've always liked beautiful clothes. My mother used to shop in New York several times a year. Some of these names are sold there, too."

"I'm the opposite, I guess. Off the rack of a department store. Hand me downs from friends." Cari smiled then. "Except for last year's Christmas party. I spent a small fortune on a formal gown, and everything to go with it. I'll admit I felt a bit like Cinderella that night."

"Oh? And who was your prince charming?"

Cari looked away, and felt color rush to her cheeks. "John. You should have seen the tux he wore. It was amazing."

"I'm not surprised. He always looks great, even in casual clothes."

"Yeah, that's what I've always thought."

"See anything you like, ladies?" Gilles asked as approached.

"Of course," Cari replied with a slight laugh. "Who wouldn't. But actually choosing something, and paying for it—now that's a different story."

"Not today."

"What do you mean?" Louise wondered.

"I've already spoken with the woman over at the sales counter. I told her that I'm paying for each of you to choose a dress. So, now that the question of money is settled, do you see something you're just dying to take with you?"

"Well, as a matter of fact . . ." Cari murmured. She immediately went back over to a selection of silk shirtdresses. She found one in the color of cocoa, with pearlized buttons down the length of it, and a soft belt for the waist. A sales clerk came over to show her to a dressing room. She admired her reflection in the full length mirror. *Perfect, absolutely perfect.* Until she noticed her battered shin. She furrowed her brows. *Well, I'll just have to get some new stockings, and shoes, and a purse.*

Cari exited the dressing room, and handed the dress to the attendant, asking her to wrap it for her. The young woman smiled and took it over to the counter area. Cari waltzed over to Gilles, in a manner of speaking, and grinned at him.

"So, you're bent on spoiling us, are you? The hotel, the limo, now shopping. Why?"

"Do I need a reason? I have more money than I'll likely ever spend, Cari. I'd like to share more of it with friends. Besides, what beautiful woman doesn't enjoy buying a new dress? And," he added, his tone softening, "I think all three of you deserve something special to remember this trip, especially after what you've gone through."

"Well, whatever your reasons, Gilles, thank you. Now, excuse me while I find all the things I need to go with the dress."

Louise chose a matching skirt and short blazer of lavender crushed suede. Like Cari, she found herself a purse and shoes to go with it. Tammy decided that she couldn't leave without a sapphire blue, long-sleeved, velvet sheath dress. She informed them that she was going to wear it with her hair up, if she could find the right clips or combs to do so.

Once the dresses were purchased, wrapped, and on their way over to the hotel suite, John informed them that they still needed to go to *Hermes* so he could buy each of them a scarf.

"My way of saying thanks for making this such a memorable *vacation*."

"Boy, I think we're on a roll today," Tammy exclaimed. "Let's go."

Choosing scarves didn't prove to be as much of a challenge as the dresses. This time the ladies just had them wrapped and carried them back to the waiting limousine. That's when they finally noticed that John and Gilles had been doing some shopping themselves. John had purchased a new suit, and several dress shirts, and two more silk ties. Gilles had found a sports jacket and some loafers.

Back at the hotel, Cari, Louise and Tammy all found another surprise waiting for them.

"Flowers," Tammy whispered. "Nobody has ever given me flowers before. Wow." She gently fingered the arrangement of red roses, baby's breath, and white carnations. Then she picked up the card.

"Ma Petite;

This is to let you know that we think you are a very special girl. You endured your suffering with courage and humor. Now we'd like to spoil you a little.

L'homme d'Art and Mon Ami"

Cari's assortment was altogether different. Violets, lily of the valley, and asters.

"La Femme Dangereuse;

A woman of your diverse talents and abilities deserves the very best that life has to offer. At least for the moment, let us give it to you.

LHA and MA"

Louise had a vast bouquet of gladioli, in a rainbow of colors, placed in a crystal vase, and loosely bound by a violet colored ribbon.

"La Femme Competent;

Though we may not have known you long, your character has shone through many times. Please accept these as a token of our friendship.

L'homme d'Art and Mon Ami"

There was also a stunning wicker basket on the table where they'd eaten lunch. It was full of bath products, massage oils, shampoos and perfumes. Another note was with it. Cari read it aloud.

" *'Dear ladies,*

We could think of no better way for the three of you to truly pamper yourselves, except perhaps to send you to a spa. Enjoy your afternoon, and we will eagerly await your company at dinner tonight. We'll come for you at 7:30. Please wear your new dresses, and we'll be more than happy to escort you to the hotel restaurant.

Gilles and John'"

"These guys are blowing a bundle on us," Tammy said. "Doesn't it make you feel like royalty?"

"Kind of," Cari replied, placing the note with the basket, and opening a bottle of perfume. "Mmmm, I think I just found one that I like. But first, I'm going to soak in that glorious tub in my bathroom."

"Don't you want to try out this massage oil?" Louise asked. "I know you're sore after so much walking and standing today."

"And sitting on the plane," Tammy added. "Why don't I get ready while Louise gives you a massage? Then the two of you can have the bathrooms all to yourselves."

"Sounds good to me," Cari replied. "Now that we've finally stopped *doing* anything, I'm exhausted. A massage sounds heavenly, Louise." She gestured to the basket. "Take your pick; I think there are four or five in there." She picked up a small sack of bath salts. "I'll save these for after."

By 7:30, all three were ready. Cari wore her scarf neatly knotted around her neck. Tammy had hers like a sash, crossing her right shoulder, and tied at her waist. Louise had hers like a headband, complimenting her outfit beautifully. Each smelled faintly of bath oils, salts, and powders, and ultra feminine perfumes. They looked, and felt, gorgeous.

The men knocked at the door. "May we come in?" Gilles called.

Louise went to open the door. "By all means. How could we possibly refuse the request from those who have treated us so well?" She held the door while they entered.

John's gaze swept over each of them. "Well, Gilles, I'd say it was worth every franc. What about you?"

"Absolutely. We'll be the envy of every man in the *Espadon* tonight. Shall we go?" He offered his arm to Louise, while John escorted both Cari and Tammy. "The City of Lights has met its match."

They lingered over dinner for two hours before Cari pleaded fatigue, and excused herself from the table. Tammy and Louise still seemed to be enjoying themselves.

"I'll escort you, Cari," John said as he got to his feet. "At least a dozen men have been eyeing you all evening. I'm not about to let you wander off alone." He smiled, but he sounded deadly serious.

"Fine. Thank you." Cari rubbed her forehead for a few seconds. "You should have stopped me after the second coffee." She looked at the others as John took her arm. "Goodnight. See you in the morning."

"Goodnight, Cari," Louise answered. "Have a good sleep. Tomorrow we can just relax."

"Sure," Tammy echoed. "I like the sound of that, too. But first, I think I need to sample one more of these petit fours."

Gilles got to his feet and bowed slightly. "Goodnight. Rest well."

By the time they reached the elevator, John had his arm around Cari's shoulders. They held hands down the corridor to the suite. Once she had the door unlocked, John turned her to face him. He gently cupped her face in his hands.

"Whatever perfume you're wearing, it's been driving me crazy all through dinner. I hope you wear it again—often."

Cari smiled, though fatigue was taking hold of every muscle in her body. "Glad you like it."

John caressed her cheeks with his thumbs. "Have a great sleep, Cari. I'm looking forward to relaxing with you tomorrow." His blue eyes were sparkling. "I love you," he whispered.

When his lips met hers, Cari was suddenly wide awake. She leaned her cane against the door and put her arms around his neck. *What is it about this city? It turns me into a complete idiot.* After several moments, she pulled away from him, though he still held her face. "Why do we keep *doing* that?" she whispered.

John smiled as he raised his eyebrows. "It seems rather obvious to me. We find each other irresistible." His hands dropped to her waist and he pressed his cheek against hers. "And it's *not* just the perfume either." He kissed her again, still gentle, but more insistent than before.

"Thought so," Tammy said from the hallway. "Can't leave you two alone for five minutes!"

John released Cari and passed her cane to her as Tammy and Louise approached them. Cari turned and opened the door, stepping into the suite, her cheeks crimson.

"Goodnight, John," she rasped.

"Goodnight." He turned to look down at Tammy, who was just beside him. "You have the tenacity of a blood hound, Ma Petite."

"I know," she replied, her arms crossed over her chest. "And I'm sure you'll be thrilled to dump me back at home in LA. But we aren't there yet. So, you'd better behave. Goodnight." She sauntered into the suite, leaving John and Louise in the hallway.

"I don't envy you," John said.

"Oh? What do you mean?"

"You and Rick will have to watch your step around her. She has this *knack* for showing up at very awkward times."

"So I see." She smiled and patted his arm. "You'll survive, John. And you'll be able to tell your grandchildren about how a teenager broke up your romantic evening in Paris."

"Too bad she's still too young for her *own* boyfriend. Then maybe she'd leave the *rest of us* alone."

"Oh, I wouldn't count on it."

John smiled. "Neither would I. And I'm not sure I'd really want it any other way. Goodnight, Louise."

"Goodnight."

Chapter 46

Cari sat up in bed, her arms around her left knee, and tried to put her emotions into perspective. It wasn't working. *Gilles is sure that I love John. So is Tammy. John has asked me that. Now he tells me that he loves me. What am I supposed to do? Should I quit my job? Should I just go into business for myself? And, even if I did all that, would John back off? Not likely.* She leaned back against the pillows and stared up at the lace canopy. *If only he were a Christian, none of this would even be an issue. I could tell him how I feel.* She bit her lip. *But for the time being, I don't dare.*

Cari frowned in the semidarkness. *Loving John is really not the problem, is it? It's not knowing what to do about it. And even if he were saved, would I be ready to risk a serious relationship with a guy again? It's been almost two years since Mark, but is that long enough?* She clutched the linen duvet with trembling fingers. *Would John betray my trust too? And what about my scars? Mark didn't think I was 'worth the effort' before them—what about now?*

Cari moaned softly. *Maybe it would be easier to just become an old maid. I could stop worrying about guys altogether.* Tears spilled down her cheeks. *Who am I trying to kid? I'm already lonely. I don't want to spend the rest of my life that way, no matter how much money I could earn. And I want to have kids. Am I asking too much, God? Do You have something better in mind for me, and I just can't seem to see it?*

There was a soft rapping on the bedroom door. Cari started to get up to answer it, but her right leg hurt too much.

"Who is it?" she asked, her voice somewhat muffled by her tears.

"It's Louise. May I come in?"

"Sure. It's not locked." Cari wiped at her cheeks, but she knew that Louise would be able to tell that she had been crying anyway. She reached over to turn on the lamp next to the bed.

Louise entered the room wrapped in a soft robe, and came over to sit on the bed. "I couldn't sleep either, and I knew you were still awake. Want to order some hot cocoa, and sit and talk?"

"No," Cari replied, her shoulders tense. "I-I mean, I don't like hot cocoa."

"Okay, I didn't realize that. How about some chamomile tea? It usually relaxes Tammy. Or, there's always the old standby—warm milk."

"I'm not sure that I need either one," Cari said. "But go ahead if you want something."

Louise shrugged. "Mostly, I'd like to talk. How about you?"

"Fine. Anything in particular on your mind?" Cari smiled. "Or, maybe, a certain *person*?"

"Well, I'll admit I've given Rick a lot of thought since he flew home. But he's not the only reason I can't sleep."

"Oh? What else?"

Louise repositioned herself, and sat cross legged on the ample bed. "Actually, I've been wondering what it'll be like for you to have someone sharing your apartment. I know you're sure it won't be a problem, but, well, what if it is? It's not as though I have a lot of money to throw around these days. What if the State of California isn't interested in licensing me to practise? Will I end up being a *tourist* for a few months, and then fly back to St. Moritz, where I'd be assured of a job? I'm beginning to wonder if I've made one of the biggest mistakes of my life."

"What about Rick? And Tammy? Surely you don't think of either of them as *mistakes*?"

"No, of course not. But that's part of the problem. They're both so eager for me to move there. Maybe I should have waited until I'd had the time to apply for several positions first." She clasped her hands together. "I normally don't rush into *anything*, Cari. Certainly not so many things at once."

Cari smiled at that. "Sometimes, Louise, God doesn't give us a lot of options. It's downright terrifying to simply *trust* Him, especially for all of the things that you've mentioned. You're talking to someone who has lived in the same apartment for years, gone to the same church, associated with the same friends, maintained the same career. Then, all of a sudden, presto! New friends, new career, new car. And more travelling than I've ever done before in my life. It's had its scary moments, but most of the changes have been very positive."

"What about your personal life? Are you still resistant to change that?"

Cari sighed. "That's a lot harder than all the other things. At this point, I honestly don't know what to do. Feelings certainly aren't a reliable gauge. That's likely why I've been praying so much on this trip."

"Your *feelings* looked pretty clear earlier this evening," Louise teased. "So did John's."

"That's what I mean! If I allowed myself to make decisions based on feelings alone, I'd probably be married to John by now. But, emotions aside, I know that would be a mistake."

"Because he's not a Christian, right? That's what Tammy told me is the main stumbling block."

"Yes. It has been from the beginning."

"And you're willing to wait and see if that changes?"

"I don't know! That's how I ended up dating Gilles—albeit briefly. He asked me almost the same thing." She crossed her arms over her chest. "And I still ended up with John, time and again."

"Well, you've given Tammy something to do," Louise said with a laugh.

"Oh, sure! Did she tell you about some of the lectures she's given us?"

"Yes, she did." Louise propped her chin with her left hand. "She's got amazing insight for a teenager, doesn't she?"

"Exceedingly. Who needs a psychologist when there's Tammy around?"

"She's hurting more than she lets on, though."

"What do you mean?"

"Well, not physically. At least I don't think so. But the thought of never being able to have children is always in the back of her mind. Couldn't you see it on her face when she held Trish's little girl? She's only fourteen now. What about when she's sixteen, or eighteen, or twenty? What if she shies away from guys later on, just because of her fears? I'd hate to see that happen."

"So would I," Cari responded. "I'd like to see her go through college, get married, and have a few kids. It's such a lovely picture, isn't it? But it's a bit like someone tossed something on the canvas, making the paint run in a few places. It's still pretty, but not quite what it was originally."

They sat in silence for several moments. "Are you sure you're not describing us as well, Cari? I'm so afraid of making another mistake, that I'm almost ready to book myself on the next flight back to St. Moritz. And you're afraid to let a man close to you, because of what your fiancé did." She smiled and leaned forward, reaching for Cari's hand. "I think maybe Tammy had a stroke of genius when she started the TTSP Club. It'll be interesting to see what happens for each of us."

"Yeah, it could be at that," Cari replied, giving Louise's fingers a gentle squeeze. Then she yawned. "For the moment, I think we should try to get some sleep."

"But I've got the munchies," Tammy called from the doorway. "How about room service, ladies? It isn't even midnight yet, and I just had a nap. Let's get a snack."

Cari reached beside her for a cushion and tossed it at Tammy. "How can you even *think* about food after the huge dinner we had, Kid?"

Tammy made a face and tossed the cushion back. She missed and hit Louise. "Sorry. Actually, I'm more thirsty than hungry. But I want something hot, not a pop from the mini-bar."

"Oh, all right," Cari said, easing herself to the side of the mattress. "Go check the menu while I get dressed. I'm certainly not going to answer the door in my pjs."

Louise laughed. "Cari, in a hotel like this, the staff are trained not to ask any questions. The waiter wouldn't likely bat an eye."

"Tough," Cari replied. "I'm getting dressed anyway."

"Suit yourself," Tammy said. "I'm going to go and decide what I want."

At precisely midnight, Cari answered the door, and a waiter came in with a small cart, laden with a silver tea service, and beautiful china cups and saucers. A single, red rose was in a bud vase. And there was a small plate of wafers to go with the tea. After everything was laid out on the table, Cari thanked the young man, and gave him a tip. Just as she was about to close the door, the little cart got stuck for a second, and bumped against her right shin. Cari immediately grabbed for the doorframe, not having her cane to support her.

The waiter saw what had happened. "Oh, je m'excuse, mademoiselle."

"It's all right," Cari murmured, knowing she was lying. She leaned her head against the doorframe, trying to ignore the pain coursing through her lower leg. *Deadly accurate, sir. You nailed it right on.* Fatigue and pain got the best of her though, and she closed her eyes.

"Mademoiselle, ta jambe! Your leg, it's bleeding." The waiter seemed to be more distraught than Cari. He pulled the offending cart into the hallway, and knelt down in front of Cari. He clamped his hand over the spot where the blood was seeping through her woollen pant leg.

"Louise," Cari called, her eyes still closed. "Louise?"

The bedroom door opened. "Yes?" She came closer. "Cari, what happened?"

"C'est ma faut," the waiter explained. "J'ai fait blesser sa jambe."

"Et, maintenant, sa coule?"

"Oui. C'était pas fort, Madame." He moved his hand aside for Louise to have a look. Then he caught Cari just as she slid down. "Je pense qu'elle a besoin d'un medicin, Madame."

"I'll be okay," Cari still insisted.

"Shut up, Cari," Louise ordered. "Amène elle dans la chambre à coucher, s'il vous plait." She patted Cari's cheek. "Stay awake. I'm going to call for a doctor."

"No." Cari opened her eyes and glared at Louise. Almost. Then the waiter deftly picked her up off the floor, and she saw her pant leg. "Oh. Maybe you'd better."

The waiter soon had her on the bed, a pillow propped beneath her leg, and his hand applying firm pressure again.

Cari looked up at him and frowned. "You don't have to stay."

He suddenly smiled. "Oui, mademoiselle. The doctor is my

brother. He would be very angry with me if I did not do my duty."

"Why?" she wanted to know.

"Because I am studying medicine also. I work here to pay for school."

"You're getting your hands and your uniform all dirty."

"C'est rien." He looked down at her leg. "May I examine it more closely, mademoiselle?"

"Oh, go ahead," Cari muttered. "I just had the stitches removed a couple of days ago. I think the gash is probably open again, at least a little."

Louise came into the room with a stack of linen napkins. "Here, use these," she told the waiter. She moved the pant leg out of the way and sighed. "And just when it was starting to heal."

"C'est pas vraiment serieuse, Madame. Peut être mon frère va juste regarder." He took the napkins and held them against the gash. "The bruising is very bad, mademoiselle. Did you fall?"

"No," Cari answered, her tone crisp. "I was kicked." She watched his expression darken. "Now you can tell all the hotel gossips about it."

There was a knock on the door of the suite, and Tammy, still clad in pjs, ushered in a doctor. He commenced a rapid interchange with the waiter, his brother, in French, but Cari figured she knew what they were saying. He finally turned to look down at her.

"So, another misadventure, mademoiselle," he said.

"Yes," Cari replied. "I've had plenty of them so far." She remained silent while he examined the injury. "Well? Do I need stitches again?"

"No, that won't be necessary. Just some antiseptic and a bandage."

Cari thought of her cut foot in Mexico, and furrowed her brows. "Last time a doctor in a foreign country told me that, I wound up in two hospitals before I got home."

The man smiled at her. "I assure you, that won't happen this time. Oh, you'll be sore. And I suggest you stay off your feet tomorrow, if possible. Otherwise, you seem fine." He soon had her leg cleaned up, and a thick bandage wrapped around it. "Voila, mademoiselle. How do you feel?"

"Better, thank you," Cari managed to reply. Then she forced a smile. "But I never got to have my tea."

The waiter looked down at her. "Mademoiselle, I will personally go and bring you a fresh pot. Would you like anything else?"

"No, thank you." Then she grinned. "Actually, yes. I'd like an *opera*, please. I've seen them before, but I've never tried one. Are they as good as they look?"

The waiter smiled, obviously amused. "Better," he replied. "And it will be my gift, for having hurt you."

"It was just an accident," Cari protested. "Besides, our friend is paying for all of this." She gestured to the room. "I don't think he'll care about an extra pastry."

"Perhaps not," he conceded. "But *I* care. I will be as quick as possible, but I'm afraid that I'll have to change clothes first."

"Fine. We're not in a hurry to get to bed anyway. Are we, ladies?"

Chapter 47

True to his word, the waiter, whose name was Jean-Luc, came back with a fresh pot of tea. He also had a small plate, with a large opera on it, for Cari. He flicked open a napkin for her lap, passed her the plate, and a small silver fork.

"Would you like your tea now, mademoiselle?" he asked.

"Yes, please," she replied, just before taking a forkful of the pastry. "Ooo, this is wonderful."

Jean-Luc poured the tea for each of the ladies, flavored it as they desired, and served it.

"Are you in much pain, mademoiselle?" he asked Cari when she had finished.

"No. I'll be just fine. Thank you for asking." She shifted against the plush pillows. "Will you be working again tomorrow? I mean, later today."

"Oui."

"Could we arrange to have you take care of our room service calls?"

Jean-Luc flashed her a gorgeous smile. "Mademoiselle, most anything can be arranged here."

"For a price," Louise added knowingly. "When will you be back on duty?"

"From midi, noon, until midnight."

Cari furrowed her brows. "Are you still supposed to be working, right now, I mean?"

"No. I was finished my shift earlier," he replied. "But I did not want to send someone else to disturb you." He bowed from the waist. "It's been a pleasure to serve you."

"Thank you," Cari answered with a smile. "You know, Jean-Luc, I think you'll make a fine doctor. You have a sense of dedication, and a wonderful bedside manner. I appreciate both."

"Merci, mademoiselle. Is there anything else I can do for any of you?"

"No thank you," they chorused.

"Very well, I will just gather the tray and leave you to your rest. Bon nuit."

Once he was gone, Tammy sighed dramatically. "Isn't he a doll? I'm not sure which I like better, his eyes or his smile."

"Tammy, you'll likely never see him again after tomorrow," Cari reminded her.

"I know, but I still think he's a doll."

"And I think we'd all better get some sleep," Louise said. "It's 2:00 a.m. Good thing we don't have anything planned for the rest of the day. I just may stay in bed until lunch time."

"Not likely," Cari retorted. "You'll probably get up for breakfast, and then go work out, or have a swim." She frowned. "Great, I buy a new bathing suit, and now I cut my leg again. I suppose I could always sit on the edge of the pool and just dangle my left leg in the water."

"Or you could sit around and watch everybody else," Tammy suggested. "You may see some very famous people around here."

"I don't want to people watch until I've had at least eight hours of sleep," Cari insisted. "Goodnight, you two. See you later."

Louise did, in fact, rise early and go to the pool. She met Gilles and John there. She informed them that she and Tammy and Cari were planning to eat in their suite all day, but invited them to come for dinner.

"Unless Cari has something else in mind," she added. "She was still asleep when I came down here." She'd already done several laps in the pool, so she sat and towel dried her dark hair.

"I need to go over and see my grandparents for lunch," Gilles remarked. "But I'll be back in time for dinner. I assume it won't require formal dress?"

"No, I don't think so," Louise replied, setting down the towel and picking up her hairbrush. "Casual should be just fine."

"You've missed this lifestyle, haven't you?" John asked.

"More than I realized," Louise admitted. She set down the brush. "You know, you get so used to a certain way of life. In my case, it was a beautiful home, a chauffeur, household staff, the best private schools, the finest clothes."

"Then you met Pierre St. Denis," Gilles remarked.

Louise nodded. "Yes. And I walked away from it all. We got married by a justice of the peace, flew to St.Moritz, and rented a flat for a few years. Then the house." She gave a slight shrug. "I finished my education, and worked from home." She took a sip of orange juice from her glass on the table. "I always tried to tell myself that wealth wasn't really important. But, that doesn't mean that I never *missed* it."

Gilles reached for his cup of espresso. "My life has been much like yours, Louise. I've never wanted for a thing. But the older I get, the more I realize that *money* isn't what gives a sense of security or completeness. It was never meant to. It's a tool to be used." He grinned as he sipped the bitter coffee. "I think that's one of the reasons I'm enjoying this trip back so much. Seeing the pleasure it's been bringing to you, and Cari and Tammy."

"You're not saying that you'd enjoy being poor, are you?" John asked.

Gilles laughed. "No, of course not." His expression sobered. "I grew up in Mexico City, John. Don't think I'm unfamiliar with the suffering of the poor. My parents, my mother especially, have always supported orphanages, hospitals, and mission works throughout the city. What I'm saying is that I don't ever want to hold so tightly to my possessions, that I lose sight of those around me. But, there is far more pleasure in *giving* than there is in just going over bank balances, and stock portfolios."

"I suppose," John conceded. "My employer might agree with you on that. She and her husband are very wealthy. Yet, they are extremely generous to their employees, and not just senior staff."

"And that produces loyal employees, doesn't it?" Gilles asked. "When people are treated well, they tend to put more effort into their work."

"Some of us didn't grow up with wealth, Gilles," John continued. "And we grow to like it quite well."

"I'm not surprised. I know that Cari is doing very well financially now, but she still clings to the same values that she had while a police officer."

"True. I was referring to myself, though. I grew up in San Diego. My father was a marine mechanic until he retired. My mother never worked outside the home. I was an only child, and we always had a roof over our head, and food on the table, but no extras. I never resented that, it was just the ways things were."

"But you studied at Harvard, didn't you?" Gilles asked.

"Yes. I won an athletic scholarship to college, and then an academic one for Harvard. I also worked as a waiter, or did landscaping, or gave tennis lessons to rich kids. My parents still live in the same house in San Diego. It's smaller than the beach house I own in Malibu, but they won't move. I did give them a new vehicle a few years ago." He smiled at the memory. "And that was a chore in itself. They both went through the depression and war years, and to them a *gift* can sometimes seem like *charity*."

"But they're proud of you, aren't they?" Louise asked.

"Yes," John replied. "My mother kept every clipping about any accomplishment of mine. They don't begrudge me what I've earned along the way. They know that I worked and studied hard to get it. It's just that they're content with their own life the way it is."

"Ah, contentment," Gilles said. "One of the most important things that we can ever strive for in life. Your parents are blessed indeed." He got up from the table, effectively ending the conversation. "Now, would you care for another match of handball?"

Cari slept until 10:00, but she was in no hurry to get up. She read in bed for another hour before bothering to get dressed. Then she left her room, cane in hand, and went into the sitting area. Tammy was lounging on a sofa, munching on grapes.

"So, Kid, what shall we order for lunch? I'm getting awfully hungry."

Tammy finished chewing before giving an answer. "I don't know. Maybe we could just have something American this time. Like burgers and fries. I think I've maxed out on Swiss and French cuisine for the moment. How about you?"

"Sounds fine. And maybe some Caesar salad too. Let's check

the menu. Is Louise here?"

"She went down for a swim, but that was a couple of hours ago. She should be back soon."

Just then the door opened, and Louise walked in. "Hi! Did you sleep well?"

Cari assumed that Louise must be asking her, so she replied, "Just great. Now I'm starved. We've decided on burgers, fries and salad."

"And milkshakes," Tammy added.

"Mmmm, sounds very appealing," Louise replied. "Oh, I saw John and Gilles down in the health club. I invited them to join us for dinner tonight, but it'll just be casual this time. I told them we'll be eating in our suite."

"Okay," Cari said. "That saves us the bother of tracking them down. I wonder what they'll be doing all day."

"Well, they were playing handball right now. I don't know about later." Louise grinned at Cari. "But I'd be very surprised if John stayed away from you *all* day."

Cari felt her cheeks flush. Then she remembered John saying that he was looking forward to relaxing with her. She shrugged. "Well, we're not going anywhere, so he'll know where to look, won't he?"

"Are you going to tell him about your leg?" Tammy asked. "He'll likely figure out that something happened. Your limp is a lot worse again."

Cari bit her lip. "I don't want to make a big deal out of it, but you're probably right. I guess I'll just tell him right off the bat. That way he won't be able to complain, will he?"

Tammy giggled as she sat up on the sofa. "Not unless he's here when Jean-Luc brings the food."

"What is that supposed to mean?" Cari demanded.

"Cari, you think John won't notice *another* young guy acting concerned for your welfare, and catering, literally, to your needs? Especially one so handsome? Get real."

"Tammy, sometimes you drive me nuts," Cari sighed.

Chapter 48

John knocked on the door of the ladies' suite at 2:00 p.m. It was Tammy who answered it.

"Hi, John. We thought you might show up this afternoon. We've been working on the puzzle that my dad brought while I was sick. Want to help?" She stepped aside so he could enter the room.

"Why not? I'm usually pretty good at puzzles." He saw that Louise was seated at the table, and so was Cari, but her right leg was propped up on another chair. "What—"

"I accidentally got bumped in the same spot last night, by the room service cart," Cari answered without even looking up at him. She placed a piece along the border of the puzzle. "It's all taken care of, and I'm staying off of it today. No big deal."

John joined them at the table. "When, last night? I thought you were tired."

Tammy laughed. "And you thought that would stop us from getting the munchies at midnight? Boy, Mon Ami, you have a lot to learn."

John managed a smile as he surveyed the hundreds of puzzle pieces on the table. "How big is this?" he asked.

"One thousand pieces," Tammy replied. "I seldom bother with smaller ones." She handed him the box lid. "And this is what it should look like when it's done."

John examined the lid. It looked like an Amazon waterfall, surrounded by lush vegetation. "You like a challenge, do you?"

"Sure," Tammy replied, fitting in another piece. "And puzzles keep my hands and my brain busy."

"But they don't slow down her tongue much," Cari teased.

"You're a fine one to talk, Cari," Tammy retorted. "There's never a moment of peace when you and Dad play *Scrabble*."

"True," Cari conceded. "But that's only because Rick is so stubborn, and hates to lose."

"Hah!" Tammy scoffed. "You may not be a poor sport, Cari, but you're a merciless winner."

"Can we just get back to the puzzle, please?" Cari asked. "We want to get it done this afternoon."

"Ambitious goal," John remarked, finally matching two pieces in front of him. "Considering we don't even have the border completed."

At four, they all decided it was time for a snack, and John called to order some pastries and coffee. When Jean-Luc brought the food, John immediately noticed the way that he looked at Cari. It was obvious that the waiter was more than just 'solicitous'. John spoke with him in French, and very quickly ascertained that Jean-Luc was the waiter who had bumped into Cari the night before, and that Cari had specifically requested him to serve their suite. John wasn't thrilled, though he had to admit that the service was impeccable. He was relieved when the young man left, until Tammy informed him that he'd be back at dinner.

"Um, Louise," Cari muttered, "I think I've been sitting like this for too long. I'm getting a cramp in my leg." She began to rub behind her knee.

"Then you should likely put it down for a while," Louise replied.

"But first let me help you." Louise turned her chair to face Cari's and began to work the muscles in her calf. "You're not kidding. Your leg is taut."

Cari gripped the edge of the table and closed her eyes. John watched her clench her jaw. He kept watching until he saw her face relax.

"Thanks, Louise," Cari stated with obvious relief. "I don't know what I did before I had you at my beck and call."

Louise eased Cari's foot to the floor. "Probably suffered in silence," she replied with a smile. "How's that?"

"Much better, thanks." Cari passed her hands over her face. "I think I'll take a break, guys. You'll manage without me, at least temporarily." She reached for her cane and got to her feet, grimacing when she evened her weight between both feet. "I think I'll go check out some of the shops in the hotel. I didn't do that yesterday." She limped across the room, towards her sleeping area.

"I thought you're supposed to stay off your feet," John reminded her.

"I have been, up until now. And I will be again afterwards. For the moment, I'm going to get a bit of exercise." She went into the bedroom and returned with her small purse slung over her shoulder.

"Mind if I join you?" John asked, not sure how she'd respond.

Cari considered for a moment. "I think I'd rather go by myself, John. I haven't spent much time alone this whole trip. A bit of solitude might be nice." She smiled at him. "Besides, Tammy and Louise still need your help with the puzzle." She made her way to the door. "I should be back in about an hour. See you later."

Tammy and Louise didn't even reply, both deeply engrossed in the puzzle. It was more than half done, and becoming easier. John turned back to the task at hand, a keen sense of rejection eating at him.

Cari browsed through several shops, selecting postcards, souvenir spoons, and a set of linen napkins. She still wanted to purchase something for Rebecca Richards. She asked one of the sales clerks for some ideas. When she mentioned that Rebecca had a large collection of figurines, he smiled, assuring her he knew just what to choose. He led her to a glass enclosed case, filled with porcelain figures, dishes, etc. Cari looked over each one, and finally selected a figurine that reminded her of her employer. She asked to have it gift wrapped, and sent to Rebecca's home, knowing that would be easier than trying to fit it into her luggage.

"Anything else, mademoiselle?" the clerk asked, obviously pleased with her generous purchase.

Cari tapped a finger against her lips for a moment. Then she smiled. "Yes. I'd like those leather driving gloves, right there in the display case. I think they're the right size for my friend." When she had them in her hands she smiled broadly. "Oh, they're very well made, aren't they? I'll take them. Wrapped, please."

"Would you like this to be sent somewhere, mademoiselle?"

"Just here in the hotel. To Mr. John Maxwell's room, please."

"Certainly." The clerk carefully wrote down the information. Then he tallied the items and Cari offered him her credit card.

"Thank you for your help," Cari said as she picked up her purchases from the counter.

"My pleasure, mademoiselle." He bowed, much as Jean-Luc had done.

Just as Cari was crossing the lobby, an idea occurred to her, and she decided to act on it before changing her mind. She went over to the reception area, and requested to see the manager. The clerk immediately asked if there was a problem with something.

"Oh, no," Cari assured him. "Everything is just fine. I'd only like to ask him a few questions."

"Just a moment, please."

Cari waited patiently, watching more and more people, some well known, enter the lobby, and check into the hotel.

"May I be of assistance, mademoiselle?" a man asked from beside her.

Cari turned and looked up at him. He was more than six feet tall, and had distinguished looking silver gray hair. She smiled. "I was wondering if you could do me a favor."

There was a slight lift to his left eyebrow, making him appear even more aristocratic. "What kind of *favor* might that be?"

"Would it be possible to see some of your security system?"

"I beg your pardon, mademoiselle, but why would you inquire about such a thing?"

"I'm in charge of the security department of a large law firm, in Los Angeles, California. And, I'm always curious about how other businesses handle things such as surveillance." She shrugged. "I like to stay informed about any new equipment that might make my staff more efficient."

"Well, it's not normally done, mademoiselle," he replied.

Cari decided to use any leverage she had. "I'm also a private investigator, currently in the employ of Gilles Rodriquez. I'm sure he could put you at ease about my ability to keep matters of security to myself."

Once more the raised eyebrow. "Monsieur Rodriquez? He's a very distinguished guest. I've known his grandfather for many years. His father is a well known art collector."

"Yes, the very same. That's why I was hired."

He looked her over carefully, and rubbed his chin for good measure. "Very well, mademoiselle. I will show you some of our security measures. Follow me, please."

"What is taking her so long?" John asked. "It's six-thirty already."

"She likes shopping, Mon Ami," Tammy replied. "And she said she wanted some time alone. I don't think you need to send out a search party." Tammy stood and admired the completed puzzle. "Too bad we'll have to take this apart, after all that work."

"I'm sure you'll have other chances to put it together," Louise said. "For now, why don't you go and call your Dad?"

"Good idea, except that I'm planning to call him from Grandma and Grandpa's tomorrow anyway. I think I'll just go and read for a bit." She headed off in the direction of the bedroom she was sharing with Louise.

John was still pacing the room. He stopped when Louise laughed.

"You worry far too much, John. You'll really have to lighten up. You'll also have to stop being jealous every time another man notices Cari. She's a beautiful woman. She can't help but be noticed. But even you can see that she neither *invites* the attention, nor *returns* it."

John raked his fingers through his hair. "I know. I suppose that's part of what makes her so charming." He turned to face her. "Was Pierre ever jealous of you?"

Louise looked down at the floor. "No. He knew he had my heart, so he didn't care how other men looked at me. If anything, he was flattered by the attention. He had won the prize. Besides, his gambling kept him preoccupied much of the time."

John slowly shook his head. "You deserved better, Louise. I sincerely hope that you find happiness in the rest of your life."

She smiled. "Thank you, John. Isn't that what you wish for yourself, too?"

He didn't answer. He simply sat down on the sofa, and waited for Cari to return.

Chapter 49

"Oh, Sunshine, you're so thin!" Marion Jacobs exclaimed when Tammy was secure in her arms. "Are you feeling better, at least? Your father called us to let us know when you were in the hospital."

"I'm fine, Grandma," Tammy insisted as she stepped free of the embrace. Then she grinned. "And there's somebody I really want you to meet. Louise, this is my grandma, Marion Jacobs. Grandma, this is Louise St. Denis."

Marion gave Louise a quick hug, as was her way of greeting most guests. "Nice to meet you. I hope you'll be comfortable tonight. I'm afraid we've got all three of you girls in together."

"We'll be fine, Mrs. Jacobs," Louise replied with a warm smile. "We're getting quite used to each other's company."

Marion frowned when she noticed Cari's limp. "Something happened to your leg, didn't it?"

Cari sighed. "I'm sure Tammy will be glad to tell you all about it, Marion." She gave her a hug. "It's nice to be back. And don't worry too much about her. She's been eating almost non-stop since we left St. Moritz."

After a brief nap, Cari, Tammy and Louise all helped to prepare supper.

"Truth to tell," Cari said as she peeled some carrots, "it'll be nice to eat food that isn't loaded with cream. It's amazing that we don't all have clogged arteries by now."

"Oh, you enjoyed every mouthful," Tammy retorted. "Especially the sachertorte and opera."

"I didn't say that I didn't enjoy it, Kid. I'm just glad to get back to what I'm used to."

"What about you, Louise?" Marion asked. "Are you anxious to try shellfish from the east coast? Or maybe some New England clam chowder?"

"Mmm, that does sound good," Louise replied. "With a nice thick slice of homemade bread." Louise paused while slicing potatoes. "You know what I miss? Maple syrup from Vermont. I used to love it as a kid."

"My dad makes great pancakes," Tammy remarked. "He's not too hot with much else, but pancakes he does well." She set the salad bowl on the counter. "But we'd have to track down some *real* syrup, though. We usually just get the off the shelf kind."

"I think I have some right now," Marion answered. "Let me check." She went to the fridge and looked on the door. "Yes. Here it is." She held up a half full bottle. "How be we all have pancakes and syrup for breakfast tomorrow?"

"Sounds great to me, Grandma."

On the flight to LA, Tammy sat between John and Gilles. Cari and Louise were across the aisle. Half way there, Louise turned to Cari.

"I'd like to try to contact my family, Cari. Once I'm settled. All I have to go on is my old address and phone number, and the name of my dad's business. Will that be enough?"

Cari stared at her for a moment. "It might be. But it's been fourteen years, Louise. Are you sure you really want to do this?"

Louise looked down at her clasped hands. "It's more than *wanting* to. I think I *need* to. Besides, Pierre is dead. Maybe it's time for me to find them again. I've changed a lot in all these years. Maybe they have too. My sister would be almost twenty five by now. I'd like to know what she's doing. She could be married and have kids." She shrugged. "I'd rather know the truth than to just guess for the rest of my life."

"Okay. Give me a chance to get over the jet lag from this trip before I tackle anything else." She smiled. "But I can start making some inquiries in a week or so."

"Thank you."

"In the meantime, make me some lists of any information that might help me. Names of friends, business associates, the school your sister was going to back then, clubs your parents belonged to. The more you can think of, the better chance I'll have." She reached over the armrest and patted Louise's hand. "And if I find them at all, *then* you can decide if you really want to contact them."

"I hate time changes," Tammy grumbled. "It's evening in LA, but I'm ready for bed." She grabbed her carryon bag and stepped into the aisle. "Well, guys, let's go through Customs. This could take a while."

It did. Between gifts, and souvenirs, and Louise's antique canvas, it did take a long time to clear Customs. By then, Cari was as tired as Tammy, and her leg was bugging her.

"I can hardly wait to get home and go to bed," she told Louise. "And knowing Julie, the place will be spotless, and the fridge stocked with groceries." She smiled. "She's the next best thing to having a mom."

Once in the luggage claim area, the small group was descended upon by Rick, Ricky, Jeremy Hastings, Mike and Julie Patterson, and Christa. It took five minutes just to get through all the hugs and introductions. Rick managed to whisper a quick greeting to Louise.

"It's great to see you again. I'll call tomorrow."

Mike and Julie were taking Cari and Louise to the apartment. John was taking a cab home. And Christa offered to give Gilles a ride to his hotel. He accepted politely.

"Thank you, senorita." He picked up his suitcase and garment bag. "And to return the favor, perhaps I could treat you to supper?"

Christa's cheeks flushed with mounting color. "I'd like that, Senor Rodriquez."

"Gilles, please."

"All right. Gilles."

Jeremy Hastings grabbed Tammy's luggage as he looked at her. "Man, Tam, you must have really been sick. You look like a scarecrow."

Tammy turned, hands on extra slim hips, and glared at him. "Shut up, Jer. It's not like I had a choice, you know."

"Hey, sorry. I didn't mean to insult you. Really. I-uh, I guess I was pretty worried about you, when your Dad had to fly over there and everything."

Tammy rubbed her forehead. "Sorry I got mad. I'm just tired."

Ricky put his arm around her shoulders. "Hey, Sis, you'll get back to normal eventually. Don't sweat it." He paused, bringing her to a stop as well. "You know, I never thought I'd admit it, but it just hasn't been the same without you around the house. Glad you're back."

"Thanks, Ricky."

"Well, here we are," Cari said as she unlocked the door to her apartment and stepped inside. "C'mon in, Louise. Make yourself at home." She tossed her suitcase on the couch, and slipped off her shoes. "I've had enough planes to last me a while. I think I'm almost looking forward to LA traffic jams again."

"I doubt that," Mike replied as he closed the door behind them. "We're staying for supper, by the way. Julie has it cooking, since she knew you'd be too worn out to do it yourself."

Cari grinned as she looked at Louise. "See? I told you. Let's check out the spare room."

"It's lovely," Louise said as she took in the twin shaker style bed, a matching dresser, a night stand, and a small desk. She set down her luggage. "It looks great." She turned to Julie. "Thank you. You even chose my favorite color for the bedspread and curtains." They were lavender. "I feel spoiled."

"Good," Julie replied, giving her a motherly pat on the arm. "I love decorating. Actually, it's what I work at, part time."

"So, how are things at the LAPD?" Cari asked Mike. "Still keeping busy?"

"As always." He crossed his arms over his chest. "But I'm anxious to hear *all* about this trip of yours. Judging from what Rick said, it didn't exactly come off without a hitch."

Cari shook her head. "No, we had more than our share of those, Mike. But, how be we talk during supper? Right now I'd like to look through my mail."

"You also have several messages on your answering machine," Julie said. "Maybe you should check those first."

"Good idea. Excuse me. And Louise, help yourself to

whatever you need."

"That was a great meal, Julie," Cari stated. "Thanks so much for all you've done."

"Thank you for the linen napkins. I've never seen anything so beautiful. I can hardly wait to use them."

Cari and Louise yawned at the same time, making Julie laugh.

"Okay, girls, off to bed with you. Mike and I can clean up before we leave."

"Sorry, Julie," Cari said. Then she yawned again. "I give up. I've been looking forward to sleeping in my own bed for days anyhow. Why fight exhaustion?" She got up from the table. "Goodnight." She gave both of them hugs. "Goodnight, Louise."

"Goodnight." Louise also got up from the table. "I'm not used to travelling anymore." She smiled. "Thank you for supper, and for everything else."

"We hope that you'll soon feel at home here in LA," Julie replied.

"I think I already do." She stood there for a moment, a wistful expression on her face. "You know, I think as soon as I decided to let go of Switzerland, and all that was familiar, I think God started to fill my heart with new things." She smiled again, tears forming in her eyes. "Including new friends. Goodnight."

Once she left the room, Mike and Julie looked at each other.

"Rick doesn't stand a chance," Mike said. "She has amazing eyes, doesn't she?"

"Yes. Now you know why he's mentioned her so often since he got back. How long do you think they'll last?"

"Christmas?" Mike guessed.

Julie shook her head, a grin enhancing the sparkle in her eyes. "Thanksgiving."

"What about Cari and John Maxwell?"

Julie frowned. "I can't tell. Though it's plain that something happened while they were gone. We'll just have to wait and see."

Mike got up from the table and grabbed a couple of plates. "And then there's Christa. Do you really think she'll get anywhere with Gilles Rodriquez?"

"With Cari out of the picture? Maybe." Julie smiled. "Why? Don't you want a millionaire for a son-in-law?"

"I'm just not sure that I want any guy that *charming* in my house too often." He kissed her cheek. "I have my own interests to consider, you know."

"Thanks for supper, Gilles." Christa withdrew her keys from her purse. "It was nice."

"Yes, it was," he replied with a smile. "But I think that had more to do with the company than the food. Thank you for the ride, Christa."

"Will you—" Christa looked away before finishing her sentence, embarrassed.

"Will I what?" Gilles prodded, his tone gentle.

"Will you be moving to LA?" she managed to say. "Eventually, I mean." The keys were hurting the palm of her tightly clenched hand.

"Quite possibly. Does your interest mean I'd be welcome to visit again?"

"Well, sure," she stammered. "I mean, I—I think that would be really nice." *And I also think I'm making a complete fool of myself.*

"That's nice to know." He picked up the bill, glanced at it, and signed his name and room number. "But I have things to take care of back at home first. Not all of them pleasant, I'm afraid. But I'll keep in touch. John Maxwell is taking care of some legal matters for me. And I'll be interested in how Tammy's health improves." Then he grinned again. "And to see how long before Rick Benson and Louise St. Denis get married."

Cari lay in her own bed for the first time in a month, feeling strangely content. *It's been interesting, Lord. And challenging, and terrifying. Romantic and scenic. Fun and fattening. Thank you for bringing us back safely. Please be with Louise, and help her to adjust to all the changes. And please help me when I look for her family. Fourteen years is a long time. They could be anywhere by now. Or they might all still be living in the same house. She's already been through so much, Lord. Please keep your hand on her. It's never easy to let go of what we're used to. Thank You for being with us every step of the way.*

ALSO BY SHERRY MARTIN-LEGAULT

PAINFUL REMINDERS

Painful reminders: we all have to live with them, but Cari's have already cost her a relationship, a career and her health. Now that she's getting her life back together, a stalker is planning to move in for the kill.

Learn more at:
www.outskirtspress.com/painfulreminders

LaVergne, TN USA
22 July 2010
190374LV00002B/5/P

9 781432 760571